PRAISE FOR THE INSPECTOR DAVID GRAHAM MYSTERY SERIES

"The characters feel like old friends."

"Inspector Graham is my favorite."

"I'm in love with him and his colleagues."

"A terrific mystery."

"This newest is like seeing old friends again and catching up on the latest news."

"These books certainly have the potential to become a PBS series with the likeable character of Inspector Graham and his fellow officers."

"Delightful writing that keeps moving, never a dull moment."

"I know I have a winner of a book when I toss and turn at night worrying about how the characters are doing."

"Love it and love the author."

"Refreshingly unique and so well written."

"Solid proof that a book can rely on good storytelling and good writing without needing blood or sex."

"This series just gets better and better."

"DI Graham is wonderful and his old school way of doing things, charming."

"Great character development."
"Kept me entertained all day."
"I didn't want the story to end."
"Please write more!"

THE INSPECTOR GRAHAM MYSTERIES

ALSO BY ALISON GOLDEN

The Case of the Screaming Beauty

The Case of the Hidden Flame

The Case of the Fallen Hero

The Case of the Broken Doll

The Case of the Missing Letter

The Case of the Pretty Lady

The Case of the Forsaken Child

COLLECTIONS

Books 1-4

The Case of the Screaming Beauty

The Case of the Hidden Flame

The Case of the Fallen Hero

The Case of the Broken Doll

Books 5-7

The Case of the Missing Letter

The Case of the Pretty Lady

The Case of the Forsaken Child

THE INSPECTOR GRAHAM MYSTERIES

BOOKS 1-4

ALISON GOLDEN

GRACE DAGNALL

Cover Illustration: Richard Eijkenbroek

Published by Mesa Verde Publishing
P.O. Box 1002
San Carlos, CA 94070

Edited by
Marjorie Kramer

There is more treasure in books than in all the pirate's loot on treasure island.
Walt Disney

To get free books, updates about new releases, promotions, and other Insider exclusives, please sign up for Alison's mailing list at:

https://www.alisongolden.com/graham

USA Today Bestselling Author

THE CASE OF THE
SCREAMING
BEAUTY

ALISON GOLDEN Grace Dagnall

THE CASE OF THE SCREAMING BEAUTY

BOOK ONE

Published by Mesa Verde Publishing
P.O. Box 1002
San Carlos, CA 94070

Edited by
Marjorie Kramer

NOTE FROM THE AUTHOR

The events in this prequel take place a short while before *The Case of the Hidden Flame*, the next book in the Inspector David Graham series of cozy mysteries. It is set in the beautiful countryside of Southern England.

The Case of the Screaming Beauty is a classic prequel to the other books in the series, all of which are complete mysteries. They can be read and enjoyed in any order. I've made sure not to include any spoilers for those of you who are new to the characters. Any existing fans of Inspector Graham's investigations will still find plenty of fresh action and mystery, as well as a little background detail on some of the major players in the Inspector Graham universe. All in all, there is something for everyone.

I had an absolute blast creating this book—I hope you have a blast reading it too.

Alison Golden

CHAPTER ONE

A MELIA SWANSBOURNE STRAIGHTENED up, wincing slightly, and admired the freshly-weeded flower bed with an almost professional pride. It was, she mused, as though she were fighting a continuous, low-level war against insidious intruders whose intentions were not only to take root and flourish, but whose impact on the impeccably arranged beds and rockeries of her garden was as unwelcome as a hurricane. Amelia was ruthless and precise, going about her work with a methodical focus that reminded her of those "gardening monks" she'd once seen in a documentary. Perhaps, she chuckled, moving onto the next flower bed, weeding would be her path to enlightenment.

As she knelt on her cushioned, flower-patterned pad and began the familiar rhythm once more, she let her mind go where it wanted. How many other women in their early sixties, she wondered, were carrying out this basic, time-honored task at this very moment? She pictured those quiet English gardens being lovingly tended on this very temperate Sunday morning, silently wishing her fellow gardeners a peaceful and productive couple of hours. It must have been true, though, that she faced a larger and more demanding test than most. The gardens of the *Lavender Inn* were spread over an impressive and endlessly challenging four and a half acres.

Guests loved walking in the gardens. They had become a major attraction for many of the city folk who retreated from London to this country idyll. Among the visitors were those all-important ones who checked in under false names, and then, after their visit was over, went back to their computers to write online reviews, the power of which could make or break a bed-and-breakfast like the *Lavender*. The gardens appeared often in comments on those review websites, so Amelia knew her work was an investment, however time-consuming it could be. Keeping the gardens in check—not only weeded but watered, constantly improved, pruned, fed, and composted—would have been a full-time job for any experienced gardener, but Amelia handled virtually all of the guesthouse's horticultural needs on her own. She preferred it this way, but it did take its toll. Not least on her aging knees.

The gardens had proved such a draw and the satisfaction of their splendid appearance was so great that Amelia had long ago judged her efforts to be very much worthwhile. Besides, it was a fitting, ongoing tribute to her late Uncle Terry, who had bequeathed Amelia and her husband this remarkable Tudor building and its gardens. The sudden inheritance had come as quite a shock. Cliff, in particular, was worried that he was entirely unready to be the co-host of a popular and high-end B&B. However, Terry had no children and had been as much a father to Amelia as had her own. It made her proud and happy to believe that the place was being run well and that the gardens had become the envy of the village of Chiddlinghurst, and, judging by those reviews, beyond.

A bed of roses formed the easterly flank of the main quadrangle, within which Amelia had spent much of the morning. They were looking particularly lovely; three crimson and scarlet varieties found their natural partners in the lily-white species which bloomed opposite on the western side. By the house itself, an imposing Tudor mansion with all its old, dark, wood beams still intact, there were smaller beds and a rockery on either side of a spacious patio with white, cast-iron lawn furniture. Further over, against the western wing of the inn, was a bed of which Amelia was particularly proud: deep-green ferns and low-light flowering plants, their lush colors providing a quick dose of restful ease among the brighter hues around them. Amelia took a moment to let the greens sink into her mind, soothing and promising in equal measure. She indulged in a deep, nourishing breath and began truly to relax and enjoy her morning in the garden. Which was why the piercing scream that burst from the open window of the room just above the bed of ferns turned Amelia's blood as cold as ice.

Dropping her trowel and shedding her heavy work gloves, Amelia dashed across the immaculate lawn of the quadrangle and up the four stone steps that led to the patio. Peering through the conservatory doors, she could see nothing out of place. She was quickly through and into the dining room and then the lobby. She took the stairs as fast as her ailing knees would allow, and within seconds of hearing the scream, she was knocking at the door of a guest room.

"Mrs. Travis? Can you hear me? Is everything alright?" Amelia panted, her mind already racing ahead to the horrors that might accompany some kind of tragedy at this popular house.

"Mrs. Travis?" she repeated, raising her hand to knock once more.

The door opened and Norah Travis was smiling placidly. "Hello, Amelia. Whatever is the matter?"

"You're alright!" Amelia observed with a great sigh of relief. "Good heavens above, I feared something awful had happened."

"I'm sure I don't know what you mean," Norah assured her. "It's been a pretty quiet Sunday morning, so far."

There was nothing about Norah which might raise any kind of alarm. As usual, there wasn't a blond hair out of place, and her bright blue eyes were gleaming. If anything, Amelia decided, she looked even younger than her twenty-seven years.

"I could have sworn," Amelia told her, gradually regaining her breath, "that I heard a scream from the window there," she pointed, "while I was outside in the garden. Clear as day."

"Oh, I've nothing to scream about, Amelia," Norah replied. "Could it have been someone else? I don't think I heard anything."

Cliff won't let me hear the end of this. He'll say I'm losing my marbles, that I've finally gone loopy. And who's to say he's wrong? "It must have been, my dear. I'm so sorry to have disturbed you."

Amelia bid Norah a good morning and returned downstairs, distracted by the chilling memory of the sound, as well as its mysterious origin. She could have sworn on a stack of Bibles....

CHAPTER TWO

A ROUND ELEVEN O'CLOCK, Cliff Swansbourne returned along the gravel path to the front entrance of the *Lavender* in his battered but supremely reliable Land Rover Defender. A Sunday morning ritual as old as their tenure at the inn, Cliff's forays to the farmers' market in nearby Dorking were legend, both for his chipper, sunny banter with the stall-holders, and for the bewildering array of local produce with which he returned. Cliff was not, his wife had often observed, a planner. The dinner menu seemed to compose itself, in his head, during the course of an hour's purposeful striding around the market, and he always managed to return with ingredients for something sumptuous and appealing that would arrive on the dinner table a few hours hence. From the distinctive fragrance wafting from the back of the Landy, Amelia suspected fish.

"Did you know," Cliff began, handing a brimming tote bag of supplies to his wife, "that salmon can fly?"

Amelia gave him a quizzical look. *Which of us, just*

remind me, is going bloody loopy? "You don't say," she replied noncommittally.

"The bloke said this salmon had flown down from a Scottish loch first thing this morning. Freshest fish you've ever seen," he promised. "I got a damn great forest of dill, too. We've still got those cedar planks, haven't we, dear?"

Amelia carted four large bags of groceries into the kitchen and set them down on their sturdy, traditional wooden table. "They're in the pantry somewhere, I think," she said. "Look, this is going to sound a bit silly, but..."

"You?" Cliff mocked. "Silly? Never in a million years..."

"Just hold your tongue for half a second, you impossible man," she said, bringing him to a halt in the middle of the kitchen and hugging him. "Thanks for going shopping. The salmon is going to be wonderful. I know it."

"Certain as Christmas," Cliff replied. "Now, what's going to sound a bit silly?"

Amelia shook off her reservations and put it plainly. "Have you ever, while I've been out..."

"Never," Cliff replied, his back straightening defiantly. "And you can't prove that I have. I was nowhere near the scene of the event." He paused. "Whatever the event was," he added, less certainly. "Not guilty, I'm saying."

"Will you shut up and listen?" Amelia demanded, punching him on the shoulder as she had done many times during moments of frustration over the thirty years they had been married. "Have you ever heard Norah Travis, or any of our other guests, scream?"

Cliff raised an eyebrow.

Classic Cliff. He won't take this seriously until I make him.

"Scream, you say?"

"I did."

"What kind of scream?"

"Does it matter, you daft bugger? A scream, you know, an explosion of sound caused by pain or anxiety or..." She stopped. Cliff would need no encouragement, she felt quite sure.

"Or... nookie?" he said, wiggling a raised eyebrow.

"Calm your ardor, Romeo. It wasn't that kind of scream," Amelia told him.

"Ah," he replied, a little deflated. "Well, no, if I'm honest, I haven't heard such an ejaculation."

"Cliff, for the love of God..."

"Not once, seriously. Why?"

"Well, I was out in the garden, and I could have sworn there was this sudden, piercing scream from Norah's room. You know, over on the west corner."

"I know the one, darling. I work here too if you remember. But why would she be screaming on a Sunday morning? Realized she'd woken up too late for church? Doesn't seem the type."

Amelia shrugged. "Hardly. And that's just the thing. I ran to her room to make sure she was alright..."

"Ran?" Cliff said. The eyebrow returned skyward. "You *ran* somewhere?"

"I mean, yes," Amelia replied, sensitive to these jabs about her age and her increasingly perfidious knees. "I'm no Olympic sprinter or anything, but I got there in record time. And Norah denied having made or heard any such sound."

They sat around the kitchen table, the overflowing

bags of produce temporarily forgotten. "Tricky," Cliff observed. "Very mysterious."

"So what do you think?" Amelia asked, stumped.

"I think," he said, taking her hand fondly across the table, "that it's time we called the men in the white coats."

Amelia stood and lambasted him, just as he'd hoped. "Now listen here, you rotten little sod! I'm not the one losing it. I've never claimed, for instance, that salmon can fly! And what about that time you went into town to get the newspaper in your underpants?"

Cliff defended himself. "It was half-past five in the morning, there wasn't a soul to be seen, and I was trying to save time," he explained. "All about efficiency."

"Codswallop."

"Suit yourself," Cliff remarked, standing to begin finding homes for the groceries, "but I'm not the one imagining screams out of thin air."

Amelia shook her head. "I didn't imagine it, Cliff. It's not like I was smelling toast while having a stroke. I'm of sound mind," she said, wagging a finger at his skeptical smirk, "and I know what I heard."

"Darling," Cliff began, "there are a number of things a lady might do, by herself, in the privacy of her room, on a lazy Sunday morning, which might make her scream. And once confronted with the evidence that she had been overheard," he added, "what makes you so sure that Norah Travis would be comfortable sharing such intimacies with her landlady? She's been here a grand total of two nights. It's not as though you're sisters."

"True," Amelia had to concede. "But, as I say, it wasn't that kind of scream."

"Everyone's different. It's the twenty-first century, my sweet. People get their jollies in all manner of ways. We mustn't judge, especially paying guests, and we mustn't harass people who are simply enjoying some alone time."

Amelia bent over and aggressively shoved a sack of potatoes under the bottom shelf of the pantry. "Impossible man," she said again before wrenching open the door that led to the gardens and stomping away.

CHAPTER THREE

THE SALMON WAS no disappointment. Grilled to perfection and carpeted with flavorful dill, it was preferred to their standard alternative Sunday evening offering of Beef Bourguignon. Vegetarian lasagna also remained untouched in the fridge. Once Cliff and Amelia had cleared away the tables and loaded the dishwasher, they poured themselves their customary glass of dry white wine and sat around the kitchen table once more. These routines gave their lives a pleasing structure, but also provided a vital time to stop, talk, and exchange news of the day. With so much hurrying around and their reservation book pleasingly full, this was a quiet oasis of time which both cherished.

"Did you notice that Norah Travis entirely demolished her salmon?" Cliff said, sipping his wine. "Damn near ate the bones it came on."

"Well done, chef," Amelia said, raising a glass in salute.

"Didn't hear her scream once," Cliff noted.

"Oh, for heaven's sake. I told you what I heard. And you can believe whatever you want."

Cliff chuckled easily and reached over to a side table for their reservations book. "I believe, oh co-proprietor of mine, that the *Lavender Inn* is just about fully booked, from September through the New Year. And," he added, flicking forward a good number of pages, "in decent shape beyond then. I don't know how we've managed it."

"Bloody hard work," Amelia told him. "My knees have paid for that garden with their very lives. And you're doing wonders with the kitchen and all the supplies. Not to mention keeping Doris on the straight and narrow."

Like a good matron on a hospital ward, a good housekeeper was critical to their success. Doris Tisbury was second to none. "She needs no help from me," Cliff demurred. "I'd trust her with everything from a double-booking to a Jihadist insurgency."

"Let's hope it doesn't come to that. I've just got the garden looking splendid," Amelia replied, deadpan.

"You have indeed, my sweet," Cliff said, acknowledging her comment with a salute of his wine glass. "What I'm saying is, you know, with business being so good, we might revisit the idea of, you know..."

"'Sodding off to Mexico'?" Amelia quoted. "Isn't that how you put it? Seriously, that old plan again?"

"It's not old, but it's certainly a plan. And a good one," Cliff said, topping off both their glasses. "Think about it. White sandy beaches," he said, his gestures becoming expansive, "hammocks slung between two palm trees... Tell me you don't daydream about it. Because I most certainly do."

Amelia couldn't resist. "When you're not

daydreaming about what might make the delectable Norah Travis scream."

"A man is permitted his fantasies," Cliff replied. "But I'm serious, darling. We've worked bloody hard, as you so rightly observed, and there's going to be plenty of money coming in, especially once the rates go up for the festive season. I mean, you've seen the bookings..."

"I've seen them, and they're fantastic," Amelia replied, leaving the important and inevitable 'but' unsaid.

"Not now," Cliff concluded. "You've said that before. More than once." His disappointment was real, and he refused to hide it. Forty years of work as a structural engineer, then an assessor, then a trainer and mentor to the young 'uns.... He was ready to put aside ownership of the *Lavender* and get on with his master plan for retirement by lying on warm, dry sand, dipping his toes in the Pacific, and having someone bring him martinis on the hour. But month by month, he could feel it slipping away.

"We need more time, and we need more money," Amelia told him, ever the practical one of the pair. "Even if we sold up tomorrow, how long do you really think the money would last?"

"Depends if you let me blow the whole lot on coke and strippers," Cliff joked.

She took his hand. "Darling," she began, still deadpan, as was their way, "I know it's your life's dream to snort Bolivian marching powder off some pretty girl's unmentionables, but I need you here, with me, on planet Earth. Just for a couple more years."

Cliff was deflated, despite his fooling around. "Well, bugger."

"I'm sorry. Soon, I promise. All the strippers in Tijuana."

Cliff finished his wine and gave his wife a smile laden with subtle meanings. "I love you and I trust you. We're a team, and this is where I belong. Just don't promise paradise and then deliver another four years of fishing the pin-bones out of salmon and chopping up mountains of dill. I couldn't take it."

They finished their wine and Amelia headed to bed. Cliff sat in the kitchen for longer than he would have chosen, picturing the simple, relaxed life he had worked so hard for. *She's right, again. As always. Why did she have to be so damned pragmatic?*

It was Amelia who had steered him away from those expensive and alluring mid-life distractions, twenty years ago: the sports car, not unexpected but certainly expensive; the mad, medically inadvisable plan to hike from Lands' End to John O'Groats *and back again*; and his simmering, exotic pipe-dream of a beach retirement in Mexico.

The arguments had been fierce, but once he understood that she loved him and wanted to help, he realized that he had floated a little adrift as he hit forty-five. They needed a solid plan, not a high-end fancy pair of wheels worth four years of his old salary. It was then that a peaceable calm returned to the Swansbourne household. Amelia had stood by him as he'd shrugged off the "bloody nonsense," as he'd taken to calling it and risen to the top of his profession. She would stand by him now, he felt sure.

Remarkable woman, he reflected as he turned out the lights and headed upstairs. For a second, a noise from outside pierced his consciousness but he shook his head and turned back to his musings. *Wouldn't trade her in. Not for anything. Not even for a luxury yacht full of strippers.*

CHAPTER FOUR

DORIS TISBURY WHEELED her cart, piled high with towels and sheets, along the second-floor hallway of the *Lavender*, humming a tune which had been stuck in her head all morning. Was it Tchaikovsky? Or from an opera? She couldn't remember, but it was a jaunty, upbeat tune that fit her mood. There was cleaning to be done. Each time Doris closed the door on a room she knew now to be immaculate, there was a tiny jolt of satisfaction. The world was as it should be, everything was in its place. Doris made emphatically sure of it.

Approaching sixty and with the sturdy forearms of an artisan baker, Doris was originally a "Yorkshire lass" and currently a no-nonsense housekeeper. She had infinite patience for the tedious chores with which she was tasked but absolutely none whatsoever with people who "mucked about," as she put it. Her children and grand-children knew this expression far too well. The penalties for "mucking about" were the forfeiture of dessert, or pocket money, or—horror of horrors—additional household chores. Doris was no brute, but rather a disciplinarian. She believed that quality and rigor and getting things done without fuss or delay was what was required for an upstanding life. She brought a forthright thoroughness to the *Lavender*, and the inn thrived, in good measure, due to her firm dedication to duty.

Most of the *Lavender's* guests were early risers. They might wish to travel to one of the attractions close by or in London or enjoy one of Cliff's massive, traditional, cooked breakfasts. Some took in the gardens with an early morning stroll. On the odd occasion this might not be the case, however. Doris would knock, wait a polite interval, enter the room, and find the guest either still asleep, or doing something they'd rather Doris had not seen. She'd have dared to boast that, during her years at the *Lavender* and at other hotels previously, she had been exposed to just about every sordid human pastime, whether it was happening right in front of her, or through the casual discarding of incriminating evidence. Nothing could shock Doris, she would claim. Not even that business last year with the Maltese businessman and his suitcase full of...well, let's not think on that.

Norah Travis' door was next. Doris knocked her accustomed three times, calling through, "Housekeeping!" in as bright a tone as she could manage and knocked again. She counted to five, as she always did—just to lessen the frequency of those awkward encounters—and then used her master key to open the door.

Doris peered into the room. The bed had not been slept in, there was no doubt about it. Even if Norah had, for some reason, chosen to make it herself, there's no way she'd have matched the precise, geometrical perfection that Doris brought to her work. There was certainly no sign of the young lady.

Doris patrolled the room, emptying the trash can and giving the dresser a little squirt of furniture polish. The room smelled slightly musty, so Doris opened both of the windows to air the place out. Then she stepped toward the bathroom, anticipating the usual towels on the floor. Instead, she was shocked to look down and see the soles of a pair of shoes. As Doris pushed the door further open, she saw that the shoes were attached to Norah Travis and that the woman was sprawled on the bathroom floor, immobile.

"Ms. Travis?" Doris breathed. "Oh, goodness, I'll get help, dear..." But as she turned, she saw that Norah's once-pretty face and long blond hair were thickly coated with blood that was staining her blue blouse and that the skin of her exposed neck and shoulders was an unearthly, alabaster white.

CHAPTER FIVE

C LIFF LOOKED UP from tossing a giant bowl of salad as Doris rushed into the kitchen. He knew at once that something terrible had happened.

"It's Norah Travis," Doris managed to say, hands to her mouth, but then the grim news stuck in her throat and wouldn't come out.

"Doris?" Cliff said, dropping the salad tongs and walking across the kitchen to his dumbstruck house-keeper. "Doris, what's happened? Is something wrong?" The awful truth was etched on Doris' face so clearly that Cliff needn't have asked.

"She's dead, Mr. Swansbourne," Doris said, finding her voice at last. "In the bathroom. On the floor."

"Jesus." Cliff was away, taking the stairs two at a time. When he arrived at the door of Norah's en-suite, one glance told him everything. The attractive blond was beyond all help and had been for some hours. A guest of the *Lavender* dead. Cliff gasped, recoiling from the sight, and seized the wooden doorframe for support. "Oh, no."

Amelia had gone to the local nursery, one of her favorite places, for seedlings. There was no telling when she would be back. The weight of the responsibility that bore down on Cliff as he stared at Norah's body frightened him.

"Cliff? What's wrong?" Cliff looked up to see a familiar face. It was Tim Lloyd, a guest so regular he was almost a family friend. "Oh, God, is it Norah?" Tim asked, brazenly stepping past Cliff into the bathroom to survey the tragedy for himself. "Christ, Cliff...Have you called anyone?"

"Just... Just now found her," Cliff said, his heart racing worryingly. "Doris found her first. Amelia's in the village." Cliff made himself look down. "Norah, she's... I mean, there's no hope, is there?"

"Call 999," Tim told him, taking charge. "I'll stay here with... the body." Tim was fresh from the shower after his morning walk in the garden. He pushed black hair out of his eyes as he leaned over Norah.

"Alright. Don't let anyone else in. I'll be right back." Cliff gathered his resolve and headed downstairs to the lobby phone.

Tim could hear the call going through, Cliff's somber relaying of the events, his sadness as he told the dispatcher that CPR would be of absolutely no use at this stage. The body at his feet was Tim's first, and he found himself remembering how he'd always assumed it would be a grandparent or old neighbor, not a lovely blond woman in her twenties. Downstairs, Cliff was quiet for a moment before Tim heard him confirm the address and some other details that Tim didn't catch. Perhaps Cliff was responding to instructions about not moving the body or keeping people away until the police arrived.

"It's done, Tim. They're on their way," Cliff told him as he returned to the doorway of Norah's room. "You haven't touched anything, have you? I wouldn't want your fingerprints all over this."

"Oh, no," Tim replied. "But I want to help in any way I can. This is such a... a terrible tragedy," he said, eyes downcast.

Cliff kept his distance, staying by the bathroom doorway, while Tim stood over the body, not two feet from Norah. "I think it's better if we leave this one to the professionals, don't you?" Cliff advised the younger man. "They're sure to want to interview you and our other guests." The specter of negative publicity gave Cliff an unpleasant shudder but he pushed it away, remonstrating silently with himself as he remembered that a young life had been snuffed out.

"I feel a little responsible," Tim was saying. He stared at the body again in a way that at least to Cliff in those anxious moments seemed rather odd.

"Guilt is a natural response to something like this," Cliff cautioned, shaking his head. "You had nothing to do with it, I'm sure."

"But I recommended that she stay here, you see. Norah needed a place to go. A safe place," Tim said. His eyes were fixed on the dead woman, almost as though in hope of sudden reanimation.

Cliff took a step closer to Tim. "Are you saying she was in some kind of trouble? In London?" he asked. Norah had mentioned that, like Tim, she was from the nation's capital.

Tim pursed his lips. "There was a divorce. Very messy. And the husband's not a nice character at all. He threatened her, followed her around. Norah needed a quiet place to collect her thoughts, figure out what to do next. I thought the *Lavender* was perfect for her. It's just," he said, welling up, "so sad that it ended this way. Do you think it was an accident? That she slipped and fell?"

Cliff watched Tim leaning over Norah's body, inspecting the terrible impact at the back of Norah's skull. "There's no way to say until the professionals get here, is there? Look, I'm going to wait in the lobby and bring them up. Please," Cliff said sincerely, "don't touch anything. I don't think you should even be in here."

But Tim was still staring at the awful wound, his eyes flitting from the basin to the bathtub, figuring out how Norah might have met her end. Tim Lloyd, investigative journalist, Cliff remembered as he descended the stairs in a strange, unpleasant fog. Tireless seeker of the truth, then. Or maybe just a juicy story.

CHAPTER SIX

C LIFF OPENED THE front door and looked up at a tall, burly police sergeant. "Thank you for coming so quickly," Cliff said. "This is just dreadful."

Sergeant Harris removed his uniform cap and stepped inside. "I'm sure it's been a difficult morning," he said in a low baritone. "But we'll take care of it. We've got one of our very best on the way here. Happens to live in Chiddlinghurst, as a matter of fact."

Cliff showed Harris upstairs, but even before they reached the room, there was another knock at the front door. Cliff returned downstairs and opened the door. "Good morning, Mr. Swansbourne." Cliff looked up at the man standing on the doorstep. "Detective Inspector Graham."

After peering briefly at the badge which Graham held up for his inspection, Cliff said, "Yes, of course," and invited him in. The DI was in his thirties, in a grey suit, and was already scrutinizing the establishment with the air of one very much accustomed to doing so.

Graham was silent for a moment as he took in details, his eyes moving quickly among the paintings by the stairs, the ornaments on the side tables, the Persian rug on the floor. The DI seemed to be absorbing the scene as though he'd be called upon later to describe its every feature.

Graham reached the top of the stairs and confirmed the basic details with Cliff. "Our housekeeper, Doris Tisbury, found her at about 9:45 this morning," Cliff reported.

"And has anyone else been in the room since then?" Graham asked, notebook open.

"Only myself and Tim Lloyd, a guest," Cliff replied. Although he felt sure that Tim had acted inappropriately, Cliff knew it was important to tell the police every detail.

DI Graham reached Norah's room and continued his careful visual survey of everything in the vicinity. Cliff watched him, finding something of the savant in the way Graham drank in the colors and shapes around him. The detective turned to look into the bathroom, noticing the same pair of shoes on the victim's feet that Doris had first seen. Beside them was Tim Lloyd, kneeling by the body, as if in the middle of carrying out his own examination.

"Sir, stand up, please!" Graham said at once. Tim paused where he was for a moment, and Graham was about to repeat the order when Tim rose, rather nonchalantly, Cliff felt, given the circumstances.

"I'd say she's been dead for about twelve hours," Tim opined, rubbing his chin.

Graham took a firm grasp of Tim's arm and led him from the bathroom. "You are Mr. Lloyd?" Graham asked.

"I am."

"You understand that this is a potential crime scene?"

Graham said, his rising color the only indication that he was holding onto his temper with some effort.

"I've assisted in police investigations as part of my work. In New York," Tim explained. "As a journalist."

"A journalist. But not a medical investigator. Or a coroner. Or a police officer," Graham said mildly. He stared intently at Lloyd.

"No," Tim admitted.

"Or, indeed, as anyone remotely linked to the professional business of solving crimes."

Despite his appearance, Graham's anger was still only barely under control. If there was one thing Graham couldn't abide, it was nosy people contaminating crime scenes with their unschooled amateurism, however well-intentioned. Six months before, with less restraint than he was currently showing, Graham had flown completely off the handle, yelling into the face of a terrified volunteer who'd had the misfortune of finding the body of a missing bank teller in the woods during a massive search. Graham had initially thanked the man for his efforts—the woman had been partially buried in a remote copse and was difficult to see—but once Graham learned that the volunteer had moved strands of the woman's hair from her eyes upon finding her, he'd virtually exploded. With all the popular CSI-type shows on TV, Graham had thundered to Sergeant Harris later, you'd have thought people might have learned to keep their bloody hands to themselves.

"Return to your room, Mr. Lloyd. And stay there. Do you understand?" Tim understood and was gone in moments. After watching him leave, Graham turned to Cliff. "Mr. Swansbourne? Tell me everything you know about the deceased. Was she a regular guest?"

Cliff related what he knew and was feeling woozy

enough to consider sitting on the edge of the bed, but he quickly rethought the notion in light of DI Graham's rigorous crime scene attitude. "It was her first time staying with us. A friend of Tim Lloyd, as it happens. He said something about her being recently divorced and her husband being a nasty character."

Graham's pen filled two pages of his notebook with what seemed to be Egyptian hieroglyphs but were actually a finely honed set of abbreviations combined with old-fashioned shorthand. Graham was more than a trifle behind the times in some ways, but his note-taking was far more efficient, he felt certain than typing anything into one of those tablets for which he felt considerable disdain. "Alright, then." Graham closed his notebook. "Thank you, sir. You did everything right." Cliff's reply was to give the DI a lopsided smile. "I'm going to call our pathologist, a top man, and we'll see if Mr. Lloyd's crime-fighting enthusiasm has left any trace of what might actually have killed this poor woman."

CHAPTER SEVEN

G ILBERT HATFIELD—BERT to his friends— struggled simultaneously with London's Monday morning traffic and the knowledge that shedding light on whatever had befallen Norah Travis would almost certainly mean his having to miss the afternoon game. Life as a Charlton Athletic fan was tough enough without being stuck in a morgue while your team kicked off their first home game of the season.

As he gradually left the busy city streets behind, entering the far more pleasing landscape of the rural county of Surrey, the pathologist who was heading reluctantly into his sixties, negotiated the tight lanes with special care. After narrowly missing a fellow motorist who wasn't paying enough attention, he turned right, then left, then straight on at a crossroads before rolling down a gently sloping street into the almost too picturesque Chiddlinghurst. It reminded Bert of those preserved villages from the nineteenth century that were transplanted brick by brick to create a museum celebrating times past. High-end cars in driveways and the range of satellite dishes mounted as discreetly as possible on the sides of centuries-old dwellings were the only signs of encroaching modernity.

The *Lavender Inn*, for its part, could very well have been plucked from the past, its shining white paintwork, and deep black beams a pleasing contrast. And the gardens...even a person lacking green-thumbs like Bert was apt to be staggered. The planning and hundreds of hours of hard work that had gone into them were instantly obvious. It was an unfortunate fact that a guest had either chosen or been obliged to come to the end of their lives while overlooking the gardens' formal splendor.

Apparently overwhelmed—or perhaps simply under-staffed—on this busy Monday morning, the local ambulance service arrived only minutes before the pathologist. Bert found them glum and feeling a little pointless as the crews sometimes did when there was so obviously nothing to be done. Mostly in these circumstances, the paramedics kept the firefighters company or talked things over with the police. This case was an exception. Everyone stood silently. DI Graham was on his own. Bert knew from experience that the police officer was waiting for him and preparing to note down as much medical data as Bert was prepared to give him.

"Still refusing to join the twenty-first century then, Detective Inspector?" Bert asked, poking fun at Graham's notebook.

Graham was in no mood to have his idiosyncrasies pointed out and gave as good as he got. "Still scraping around at the bottom of the league table?" Graham shot back, his mischievous grin proving that the DI wasn't *all* business.

Bert thumped his chest with a stern fist. "Charlton 'til

I die, DI Graham, as you well know. It's just a run of bad form. They'll be back in the premiership in no time."

Graham scoffed. "Codswallop. We've got more hope of solving this one by dinner time."

At that moment Cliff Swansbourne walked up and Graham's professional center returned. He introduced the still slightly ashen innkeeper. "I want you to meet Dr. Bert Hatfield. One of the best pathologists in the business. He'll make his initial inspection of the body and the scene. We will make arrangements to move the body after that. Sergeant Harris will take photos and we'll both be conducting interviews," Graham explained to Cliff, "but then we'll be out of your hair. Another forensic crew will be along this afternoon to clean up. Standard procedure." Cliff left them to it, thankful to return to the kitchen and the routine of preparing dinner. Whether anyone would feel up to eating it was another question entirely.

Half an hour later, there was a rap at the kitchen door. "The medics are all done here, Mr. Swansbourne," Sergeant Harris said. Cliff followed him outside to where DI Graham and Bert Hatfield stood chatting. The ambulance crew slammed the back doors to their vehicle.

Cliff offered his thanks to Dr. Hatfield as the ambulance drove away. It had only been an hour since Doris had found Norah's body. Amelia had missed the entire incident. Perhaps it was better that way. With no cell phone, she had been out of reach. Cliff shuddered as he imagined the effect of a death—possibly a murder, at that—would have on her.

Bert spoke briefly with Cliff, offering condolences for the morning's tragic events and returned to his old BMW. The pathologist followed the ambulance down the winding country lanes. The area around Chiddlinghurst was an unashamedly rural part of the country, undisturbed by the spate of house-building on "greenfield" sites that had blighted the verdant areas surrounding London. Tall hedgerows flanked the lanes. Smart, green signposts gave distances to the half-mile, indicating places so tiny and hermetic that few non-locals would ever have cause to visit. The local hospital at Carrowgate was twelve miles away and just large enough to be suitable for the postmortem.

Once he got to the morgue, Bert's first tasks, as ever, were to establish the time and cause of death. With no other marks on her body except the scars from a childhood appendectomy, the blunt-force trauma to the back of Norah's skull was the leading, perhaps obvious contender for the cause of her death. Bert drew blood for toxicology screens and requested a full workup of the lab results, which would show whether Norah was pregnant, taking drugs, drunk, or poisoned.

Dr. Hatfield generally operated under guidelines that discouraged the shaving of the victim's head, but in Norah's case, it proved necessary. The impact wound was just to the right of the base of her skull, a rectangular indentation. There was another mark on her left temple; Bert suspected that she'd hit the bathtub on the way down. Using his phone, the pathologist checked his own photos of the crime scene and began to piece together the violence that had deprived the world of the lovely Norah Travis.

Computing the time of death was straightforward. Coagulation and other factors showed that at least twelve hours had passed; Norah's death had occurred late on Sunday night. Bert returned to the wound and examined it closely. There was a marking—parallel horizontal lines.

He leaned closer and searched his memory for similar patterns. It took a moment or two, but before long he was comparing the breadth and height of the wound to those of a very familiar object. Bert looked up some example dimensions online and within moments, he could say with certainty how Norah Travis had been killed, his interest in the fortunes of his beloved Charlton Athletic briefly forgotten.

CHAPTER EIGHT

SERGEANT HARRIS WAS an experienced, dedicated officer. He had long since developed an immunity to the strange, tragic fragments of life left behind when someone dies violently. But in this case, there was an unavoidable sadness. Norah Travis had been young and beautiful. If she had been murdered it was probably over nothing of any real consequence. Harris finished taking the last photos of the crime scene, and just as he was packing away his camera, Doris Tisbury appeared in the doorway. "You asked to see me, Sergeant?" she said. She was all business, with a touch of defiance in her tone from the outset.

"Yes, thanks," Harris said, far more mildly. He'd gotten further in investigations using charm and wit than he ever had with threats and intimidation. "I'm sorry you had to be the one to find Ms. Travis this morning," Harris continued. "It's never an easy thing, but you did everything right."

Doris accepted the praise gracefully. "But all the prudence in the world won't bring her back, will it?"

Harris took one more look at the spattered floor and took his leave, beckoning for Doris to follow. They went to the room next door and took seats in the armchairs by the window. Harris brought out his tablet. "Can you tell me exactly what happened when you found Norah?" he began.

Doris relayed the events as clearly as she could. How she saw Norah's feet, worryingly still and lifeless, and then her entire prostrate body. How she quickly realized that Norah had been dead for some time. "Several hours," Doris estimated with a sad frown. "I'd say she probably lay there all night. No one to help her."

Recognizing the need to push on, Harris asked, "Did you touch or remove anything from the crime scene?"

"Of course not," Doris answered at once. "I know better than that. Watch endless police dramas on TV, I do. You know, CSI and all those. Love a good mystery, me."

Harris tapped the tablet. "As do I, Mrs. Tisbury."

"Besides, I don't meddle where I needn't. My back wouldn't tolerate it," Doris said, reaching for an obviously troubled spot at the base of her spine.

Harris nodded compassionately. "Only one more question, and it's just routine," he said, his usual pacifying preface for what was about to be an awkward inquiry. "Where were you between dusk yesterday and dawn this morning?"

Doris inflated slightly. "Me?"

"Just routine, like I say," Harris assured her.

"I was at home," she almost snapped. "With my husband and two of our grandchildren. We played Trivial Pursuit. Then I watched some telly with Dennis and went to bed."

"Thank you, Mrs. Tisbury. I didn't mean to intrude. I'll let you get back to your work, now."

Doris brightened quickly. "Not at all, Sergeant. You've got a job to do."

Harris stood and escorted Doris to the door. "Would you do something for me? Let Mr. Lloyd know that I'd be grateful for a minute of his time."

If Doris was a plain-spoken, straight-talking interviewee, then Tim Lloyd was as slippery as an eel. Harris found his answers evasive and short, the signs of someone with a secret. Harris thought Lloyd looked like a lawyer, maybe, or a schoolteacher, slightly pale, with that foppish black hair swinging around his eyes as his head turned. He struck Harris as nervous, maybe even just a touch guilty.

"So, when did you first meet Mrs. Travis?"

Tim blew out his cheeks. "Would you mind if we call her Norah?" he asked. His hands were fidgety, as though he were aching for a cigarette.

"When did you first meet Norah, Mr Lloyd?" Sergeant Harris repeated.

"Why do you need to know that?" In reply, Harris raised his eyebrows a tad. "We worked in the same building near Marble Arch," Tim said.

"And...? Harris prompted again.

"We got coffee from the same machine sometimes and struck up a kind of friendship."

"And how close did you become?" Harris asked. He might have put it more delicately, but he had tired of Tim's evasiveness.

"I don't know that has anything to do with..."

"Please, Mr. Lloyd," Harris said, for the third time that interview. "Just answer the question, would you?"

"We'd had coffee a few times, outside of the office," Tim explained. "But that's all."

"And you recommended that she stayed here," Harris prompted.

"Yes. The *Lavender* is my home away from home. I like to get away from the stresses of city living and my job. My parents brought me here first when I was seven, you know. Lots of memories. Besides, Amelia and Cliff are just brilliant."

"I'm sure," Harris said. "And where were you yesterday evening?"

"I had dinner with the others. The salmon was delicious. Then I went to bed."

"Were you alone, sir?"

"I don't see how that is any business of yours."

Harris sighed. "Just answer the question, sir."

Tim sniffed. "Yes, yes I was, if you must know."

"Thank you. That's all I need for now, sir. You can go."

"Look, I'm as determined as you are to find out who did this," Tim blurted. "I've worked on criminal cases before."

Harris towered over Tim. For a strange second, Tim wondered if Harris' uniform might burst open to unleash a Hulk-like, bear-monster within, but the sergeant simply glared at him. "I believe DI Graham has already given you direction on that matter."

Tim gulped slightly. "He has."

"Leave well alone," Harris said, just for a little reinforcement. Then, he was once more the helpful bobby with a solemn duty. "Thank you for your time, sir. We'll be in touch if we need you further," he said, tapping the cell phone in his breast pocket.

Harris caught up with DI Graham at the reception desk. The DI was on the phone.

"Thanks, Bert. Good work." Graham ended the call and turned to Harris. "Well, Sergeant, the postmortem is over, and the results are in. Now, who had "golf club" as their answer for the murder weapon?"

"Not me," Harris admitted, rather surprised. "Doesn't really belong in a bathroom."

Graham shrugged. "That's the thing about murder, isn't it? They never quite happen as one would prefer. For the most part, they're crimes of passion, committed suddenly and with little planning."

"Indeed, sir," Harris told him. "All we need now is to *find* the blessed thing."

CHAPTER NINE

"I'VE INTERVIEWED THE housekeeper, the one who found the body, and the other guest, Tim Lloyd. That leaves the owners. There was·no one else here last night." Harris turned the guest register around to show his boss. "Just the two guest rooms were occupied, Lloyd's and the victim's. A group of seniors checked out the day before yesterday, something to do with a bowling competition."

Graham's eyebrow rose in curiosity. "Bowling? With the lanes and strikes and what have you?"

Harris saw the funny side but kept his laughter in check. It wouldn't do for Graham to believe he was being made fun of. "Crown green bowls, sir. With the little white one and the..."

"The jack," Graham told him. Harris gave him a quizzical look. "Just pulling your leg, Sergeant. My grandparents played. Got pretty good, too."

Harris checked his tablet, which seemed as indispensable to him as a pen and notepad might have been to an officer from two generations earlier. Or even one,

Graham reflected. It was easy to appear a dinosaur these days if you hadn't handed over the running of your life—and the basic duties of your profession—to a couple of gadgets. As he'd explained to a young officer the other day, Graham was more "old school." The younger man had simply shrugged and returned to his phone.

"Shall we interview them together? Mr. and Mrs. Swansbourne," Harris asked.

"Let's do 'Mr.' first," Graham told him. "He was in the house when the body was found, right?"

"Right, sir."

Under their questioning, Cliff confirmed his earlier version of events and added some details including how he'd warned Tim to keep away from the body. "I also think I may have heard something as I lay in bed last night."

"From which direction did the noise come, Mr. Swansbourne?" Graham inquired.

Cliff shrugged, "I couldn't really say. Outside? Or perhaps from across the lawns, from the other side of the building where the guest rooms are. This place is quiet at the moment and noise carries. It wasn't shouting or anything untoward." Cliff blushed now. "It could even have been animals. I can't be specific. I was falling asleep. Oh, I wish I could be more helpful, Inspector," Cliff said.

Amelia was much more emphatic.

"A scream?" Graham wanted her to confirm.

"Clear as day," Amelia promised him. "From Norah's room, or close thereabouts. But I could have *sworn*," she said, fist in her palm for emphasis, "that it came right from her room."

"What kind of scream?" Harris asked.

Puzzled for a second, Amelia said, "An uncontrolled shout."

"Could it have been 'Help'?" Harris asked.

"No, I don't think so. More like, 'Aha!' Like a discovery or a surprise of some kind," she continued.

"A good surprise or a nasty one?" Graham asked.

"Hard to say," Amelia replied. "It's difficult to think of it as a happy sound, now that she's..."

Harris had learned to quickly recognize when his interviewees needed a little re-direction. "You were out in the garden, you say, when you heard the scream?"

"Yes," Amelia said. "Sunday morning's a big gardening time for me. Not that you'd be able to tell, today." She cast a rueful glance at a cluster of wayward leaves, though Harris thought the gardens damned near perfect.

"I went to her room to check if she was alright, but she opened the door as right as rain. I went away with egg on my face, none the wiser. I can't really help you any more than that."

"Alright, Mr. and Mrs. Swansbourne, thank you for your time." The police officers finished their notes and stood to take their leave.

"The gardens look spectacular," Graham told Amelia. "A real achievement."

"Thank you, but I didn't win in any of the categories at the Horticultural Society last year," Amelia remembered bitterly. She struggled to accept compliments at the best of times. And with the cloud of a murder investigation swirling around her, now wasn't the best of times at all.

Graham waved away the concern. "Those things are always fixed. It's a racket. Decades of domination by organized crime syndicates," he added with a wink. "It's like a mobster's ball."

The two police officers enjoyed watching Amelia laugh herself silly for half a minute, all of them grateful for the welcome respite from the heaviness of their situation.

After Amelia composed herself she said, "Do you really think Norah was murdered?" Violence was an incongruity entirely unwelcome in the quiet, restrained world of the *Lavender Inn*.

"I'd say so," Graham replied. "I know it's not what you want to hear, but everything's pointing that way at the moment." Shaking her head at the callous interruption to their quiet lives, and the definitive end to another's, Amelia left the two men to their work. But something bothered Graham. "It makes me nervous," he told Harris, "when there isn't even the whiff of a suspect. Tends to mean that there's a juicy back story I haven't heard yet."

Harris saw his cue. "Should I invite Mr. Lloyd to join us again, sir?"

CHAPTER TEN

B ACK IN THE guest room neighboring Norah's own, Tim Lloyd was becoming even less co-operative now that he had two officers to contend with. "Her husband wasn't a nice guy," Tim was explaining. "He wasn't good for her."

Graham let Harris do most of the talking. Harris' natural gruffness and gravity gave the questions an edge, and his tone was one that warned Tim that lying was inadvisable. "So why did Norah marry him?" Harris asked.

Tim shrugged theatrically. "There's no logic to some women, Sergeant."

"Hang on," Graham interjected. "Your earlier statement makes Norah sound like someone you occasionally had coffee with. Who knows, maybe a quick taxi back to your place to play hooky for an afternoon. And now," Graham continued, raising a silencing hand against Tim's objections, "you're an expert on her marriage, its trials and tribulations. It sounds like you were acting as some kind of amateur marriage guidance counselor."

"I never said I was an expert. She just told me a lot about her situation, and I saw her need to get away from it all. So I recommended this place." He stopped, eyes down. "And now she's dead."

Harris gave Tim a moment before asking his next question. "What can you tell us about her husband?"

Tim took a deep breath and seemed to space out for a few seconds, glancing out of the window. Then, he spoke with sincerity. "Nasty piece of work, like I said. She should have divorced him years ago. Should never have married him in the *first* place, she sometimes said."

"Go on," Harris said, typing continuously.

"He was never happy with anything she did. Always wanted her to change her appearance, her hair, you know, always looking for the next model to upgrade to. And he's a *nobody*," Tim said, the frustration giving his voice a serrated edge, "a layabout, a benefits cheat. A con artist, and not even a very good one."

"Sounds a real charmer," Graham commented, wryly. *Also sounds like the pot calling the kettle black. After all, the towering Adonis that is Tim Lloyd is hardly catch of the day, either. Especially considering Norah's looks. She could have had any man in the world....*

"He's *scum*," Tim Lloyd told them with surprising vehemence. "I'd bet my goddamned *house* that he did this."

"Steady on there, Mr. Lloyd," Harris said. "This will go more easily if everyone remains calm." Another standard pacification line, straight from the manual, but it nearly always worked.

Graham pushed slightly away from the doorframe against which he had been leaning. "Do you play golf, Mr. Lloyd?" he asked.

"Golf?"

"Yes, sir. You know, little white ball, St. Andrews, the Ryder Cup, nineteenth hole...."

"Of course I play golf," Tim snapped. "Just about everyone who stays here does. We're right next to a great golf course. What of it?"

"Your clubs. Where are they?" Graham persisted.

"In the clubhouse," Tim told him. "Why do you ask?"

"Merely routine," Graham replied. "And a final question, Mr. Lloyd, if you don't mind. Can you account for your whereabouts on Sunday evening?"

Tim gave them both a sheepish look, and then said, "I already told your man here. I was in my own room, across the hall."

"Not with Norah, then?" Graham wanted to confirm.

Tim gave a timid shake of his head. "I was... How shall I say?" Tim said. "In the dog house. Said a couple of stupid things. All my own fault. I slept on my own, at Norah's request."

Graham jotted down his usual detailed notes and made to leave. "I see. So you confirm that you were in a relationship with the victim?"

"Well, of a sort. Not a very stable or established one, obviously." Tim looked up. "But I was trying. I'm not a cad. Norah was a very...free. And I *didn't* kill her."

"Got it. Thank you for your time, Mr. Lloyd. Sergeant, shall we?"

The two policemen walked out together, Harris closing the door behind them. It was nearly 4 p.m. and neither man had found time for lunch amid the interviews, photos, speculation, and conjecture they'd spent their day dealing with. Harris got his phone out and got directions to a pub in a neighboring village where DI

Graham was less likely to be recognized, where they could mull things over in peace. Fifteen minutes later, they found the *Fox and Fable* to be just about perfect and not at all busy. Over a quiet drink and a bowl of Mary-Anne's famous hand-cut homemade fries, the two officers weighed the case so far. They found it very thin.

"We'll have to wait until Bert tells us more about the cause of death," Graham told his colleague. "But I can tell that you're keen to pursue the jealous husband."

"I am," Harris agreed, chewing a fry, "but don't crazy ex-husbands normally beat up the new boyfriend as well?"

Graham was nodding. "He shows up, finds them together, perhaps even *in flagrante*, and then boots him out before smacking his ex-wife on the head with a golf club. Simple."

"What? Lloyd doesn't stay and defend her?" Harris argued.

"Nope, how about he turns tail and clears off, leaving the defenseless Norah to the jealous rage of the incensed husband," Graham said, continuing the thread.

"And Lloyd doesn't report the murder or call an ambulance? He just hangs out at the B&B until poor Mrs. Tisbury finds Norah the next morning?"

Graham sighed. "It's a bit thin, isn't it?"

Harris nodded. "It's a bugger. And then, for Lord knows what reason, Lloyd tramples all over the crime scene like he's some kind of amateur Sherlock-bloody-Holmes," Harris added. "Contaminating the evidence."

"Bert will be able to tell us if anything is amiss," Graham said. "He's a thorough man. I'm suspicious of Lloyd, too. Norah could have rejected him and in a fit of rage, he might have bashed her over the head Remember how Mr. Swansbourne thought he heard noises from over in their direction?"

Harris finished his pint. "Well, first things first. We need to talk to the husband."

"Yes," Graham said, finishing his own drink. "But I don't think for a second that he'll be pleased to see us."

Harris felt his phone vibrate. "Oh, lovely jubbly," he said. "Background check on the aforementioned Mr. James Arthur Travis of picturesque Peckham in south London." Harris summarized the report for the DI. "Two convictions for driving offenses, license currently suspended owing to a second conviction for driving while intoxicated." Harris tutted like his grandmother used to. "Three arrests and two cautions for fighting in the neighborhood, one charge of assault on a police officer, later dropped. Served three months for affray and breach of the peace, but the other cases didn't go to court."

"Lovely fella," Graham said brightly. "I'll take him home next weekend to meet my mother."

Harris continued reading. "Currently address is blah-blah, phone number, you know the drill... Ah, what's this?" Harris said, tilting the phone slightly. "'Suspected involvement in the Hatton Garden jewelry heist,'" he read, eyebrows raised, "'either as an advisor or accomplice to some degree. No charges brought.' What a scintillating and varied career the young man has had. Wife stated as Norah Taylor, twenty-seven, 'estranged.'"

"They need to update that last bit," Graham added sadly. "Fancy a trip into foggy London town tomorrow, Sergeant?"

CHAPTER ELEVEN

"**I** SUPPOSE YOU'D better come in." The house was an identical copy of all those around it, neat but just a little box-like, with a climbing frame in the front garden and a crumbling, forgotten hosepipe propped up against the wall. The place could have used a lick of paint and looked rather forlorn under London's typically cloudy, mid-morning sky. However, Graham was careful not to judge Nikki Watkins during one of the worst weeks of her life.

"I'd like to begin," Graham said delicately as they took seats on two sofas in a living room that smelled of cigarette smoke, "by expressing our condolences, Ms. Watkins. Your sister's passing is a tragedy, and I want you to know that we're putting everything we have into finding out what happened."

Nikki was perhaps thirty, but cigarettes and cheap gin were unkindly taking their toll on her skin. She said nothing but lit a Chapman's with a big, heavy butane lighter and sat cross-legged on the couch opposite the two officers.

"We interviewed everyone at the inn, and we will be speaking with Mr. Travis this afternoon," Harris added.

Nikki gave a strange, dismissive snort and took a massive pull on her cigarette before tipping her head back and blowing a cloud of grey smoke into the smoggy air. "That bastard," she croaked. "Good-for-nothing sack of..."

"You're referring to Mr. Travis?" Sergeant Harris checked as he typed.

"Wriggled his way out of three jail sentences. Cheats on his taxes, on his benefits, the bloody lot. But no, Norah never saw that side of him, did she? Always defending him, at least when they first got together. She was always spouting some head-in-the-clouds crap about him 'having a dream,' and 'harboring ambitions.'" Nikki tutted from within her cloud of smoke. "As if that man could find his own arse with both hands, map, and a compass," she snorted. "He's a lazy, no-good little..."

Graham could have finished the rest himself. He'd interviewed hundreds of people as part of his investigations—perhaps over a thousand, by now—and there was always that one character in the tale who had never endeared himself to the others, the one who was the object of derision, the perpetual disappointment, the one who'd let himself down or kept the wrong company. Most often a young man, he was the one who everyone always assumed would "never amount to anything."

"Ms. Watkins, could you shed some light on their relationship? Norah seems to have stayed with him far longer than many would have." Graham was doing his delicate best, but there was no subtle way of asking what many must have wondered. *How did a total loser like Travis snag a blond bombshell like Norah?*

"They married young. Too young," Nikki told them.

"She wanted away from our parents, bless them, and Travis promised that he was on the up-and-up, that they'd be vacationing on the French Riviera, or shopping in New York. And she swallowed it!" Nikki exclaimed, still amazed that her sister could have been quite so gullible. "After two years of marital 'bliss,' she finally woke up and smelled the coffee. Finally, Norah recognized what we all knew—that he was just a sham. No prospects, no education. Just a career criminal, waiting for his big break."

Harris typed quickly, while Graham made shorter, hieroglyphic notes in his notepad.

"But he couldn't even get criming right," Nikki commented bitterly. "'He was always getting caught or was a suspect and had to lie low. Any number of times," she recalled. "Chronic underachiever, even when he was on the wrong side of the law."

Graham made another note and then said, "Actually, Ms. Watkins, we prefer our criminals incompetent and bumbling. Makes them a lot easier to catch," he smiled.

"Well, he got caught alright, but nothing stuck. Eventually, Norah saw the writing on the wall and decided against spending three or four years visiting that useless nobody in jail, trying to keep it together on the outside while he relaxed in some daycare for the unforgivably stupid, and she walked. Not before time, neither."

Harris raised an eyebrow to the DI, who returned his glance. "What we're really trying to decide," Graham explained, "is whether Mr. Travis should be considered a suspect."

Nikki knocked ash down her black t-shirt in a fit of throaty laughter. "Suspect?" she wheezed. "He's got to be a suspect! Who the hell else would have done something like this?"

"We're having the same suspicions that you are, Ms. Watkins, but until we can prove it beyond a reasonable doubt, Mr. Travis remains a person of interest in this case," Graham explained, "but not yet a *suspect.*"

Nikki almost spat her next words. "Think whatever you want. Do your interviews, get your lab boffins on it, analyze his DNA and his fingerprints, and what have you. But I *know,* right now, sitting here, that he lost control. He couldn't handle her leaving him. Failure in business, in school, in crime, and now in his marriage, too."

"What made her finally leave?" Harris asked.

Nikki was reluctant now. "Couldn't say," she shrugged, suddenly appearing reluctant to trash talk her ex-brother-in-law.

"I think you can, Ms. Watkins," Graham said with as much gentle encouragement as he could, "and even if you don't think it's relevant, or you aren't certain it's true, it might help us."

Nikki reached for a cigarette before realizing she already had one smoldering between her yellowed fingers. She inhaled the last quarter-inch of tobacco with the enthusiasm of one enjoying a pleasure unlikely ever to be repeated, then let the smoke escape in a slightly gray cloud of noxious fumes. She reached for her next cigarette before she'd stubbed the previous one out.

"She was seeing a man. A nice man," she said mildly. "Worked near her office in Marble Arch, I think he did."

His fingers traveling at speed across the screen of his tablet, Harris asked, "Was his name, Tim?"

"Yeah." Nikki paused. She tilted her head slightly. "He's not caught up in this, is he?"

"What can you tell us about him?" Graham asked.

"I only met him once. Seemed nice. Certainly a darn

sight better than that worthless ex-husband of hers," Nikki said venomously. "Norah talked about going on vacation with him. Just as a friend, she said."

"Did her ex know about Norah's friendship with Tim?"

Nikki stubbed out her second cigarette without taking a drag and put the ashtray aside. "No, I don't reckon he knew. But, you know what? Travis was clueless about her. Just assumed that he was the center of her world, just like he was the center of his own. I think he might actually have been stupid enough to believe that Norah would come back to him, even after everything." Nikki shook her head incredulously. "I mean, he broke their wedding vows before their first anniversary. Saw other women, hit her... She had bruises one night, not three months after marrying. I told her to call the police, but would she?"

Harris fielded this one. "Did she ever report him? We always encourage victims of domestic violence to come forward, Ms. Watkins."

Another derisive snort. "And what the bleedin' hell do you reckon old Jimmy would have made of *that*?" she demanded. "Her life wouldn't have been worth living!"

Graham followed the thread a little further. "Do you think Norah wanted to come to the police, and perhaps her husband threatened her?"

Nikki leaned against the back of the sofa. "I couldn't say. They fought like cats and dogs, but they were man and wife, you know what I mean? She had a weird loyalty towards him. She used to say, 'When you're married you love together, you fight together, and if the time comes, you go down together.'"

Her words reminded Harris of something a marriage

counselor had once said during the first separation from his wife, Judith: "A marriage takes two. One won't do."

"I don't think she would have ever grassed on him," Nikki continued. "Nah, I reckon he lost it one night and went down to see her. Her having a separate life wouldn't have sat well with him. Things probably got out of hand." Nikki's face turned mulish and she crossed her arms. "You must find him, bring him down."

As the two men left, Nikki looked pale and upset. She had that look in her eye which Harris and Graham had both seen too often. It was the pain of loss, sudden, irreversible, and impossibly hard to bear, one which would go on hurting and nagging and gnawing for years.

In Graham's experience, the only thing that even *began* to assuage that kind of pain was seeing the person responsible for it in the dock and subsequently convicted and sentenced. The perpetrator doomed to years of incarcerated misery offered a form of karmic wiping of the slate and only then could the person lost be grieved over. Understanding this gave Graham an edge, an oddly emotional resolve, a steely determination. He would find that closure for Nikki. For her and for himself, he'd find the killer, whoever it was.

CHAPTER TWELVE

"£2 25,000" HARRIS COUNTERED.

"Give over," Graham said. "You can't ask more than £210,000 for that."

"Alright, what about this one?" Harris pointed to another brick home as they drove slowly down the street. They were looking for number eighty-eight.

Graham evaluated the house, as they often did on streets like this. "Needs new guttering, yard isn't all that great. Say, £205,000?"

Harris played his part in their ongoing joust about London's outrageous property prices. "Two *hundred*," he let the gigantic sum sink in, "and five *thousand* pounds?"

"I'd say," Graham said.

"For *that*? We're not in sodding Kensington, you know," Harris reminded him.

"It's not falling down or anything. £205,000 sounds reasonable."

"Jesus, but this one really *is* falling down," Harris muttered as they pulled up outside number eighty-eight.

"Drags down the whole neighborhood. What would you pay?"

Graham made a face. "£160,000 or so, but you'd be buying it for the land and starting again."

"I think we can take it that Mr. Travis is not a man given to spontaneous bouts of home improvement," Harris concluded. Then he grinned at his boss. "See, I'll make detective any day now."

James Travis had made his home in what was by far the less pleasant half of a semidetached dwelling, perhaps two miles from his sister-in-law's address and uncomfortably close to one of the main rail lines that brought commuters in from the south. The front yard was a scramble of limp, tangled grass, and detritus—a discarded child's bicycle with only one wheel, well-chewed dog bones, and a blue and red garden gnome which looked as though it was someone's favorite air rifle target. Graham knocked on the door where the green paint had flaked away.

"Good afternoon," Graham said as the door swung open. "Would you be Mr. Travis?"

Standing in the doorway was a shirtless, skinny man of around thirty-five. He had short blond hair and an unimpressed, sneering expression. "Eh?"

"I'm Detective Inspector Graham, sir. This is Sergeant Harris. We'd like to ask you a few questions."

"What about?" Travis asked defiantly.

Your ex-wife, who died violently not two days ago, you pig-ignorant troglodyte. "We're investigating the death of Norah Travis, sir. You spoke with one of my London-based colleagues this morning. I was at the crime scene in Chiddlinghurst yesterday," Graham said.

"And what?" Travis demanded. "You think I went

down there and murdered her?"

Graham cleared his throat. "Could we speak inside please, Mr. Travis?"

"Why?"

The defiant tone, Travis's slovenly appearance, and the lamentable state of the place were all useful data points for Graham. On their own, they might not implicate James Travis in the murder of his ex-wife but they offered clues to the character of the man. Anyone with a nose, a sense of social justice, or an enthusiasm for human compassion would have found Jimmy repugnant. He was like a lobotomized skinhead on poppers. But Graham had learned long ago that everyone has a rich inner life, an invisible counterpart to the aspect of themselves they showed to the public. Although he may appear one way now, James Travis was almost certainly more complicated than his bony, vaguely anarchistic exterior might suggest. To uncover whether that interior was laudable was Graham's mission.

"This isn't a conversation you want to have on your doorstep, sir, what with all the neighbors seeing. May we?" It wasn't a true question and Harris all but barged past Travis into the house. Like Nikki's, it smelled of cigarettes and also burned toast with an aesthetic appeal that was but a single notch above a crack den in Graham's view.

"When did you last see your ex-wife, Mr. Travis?" Graham asked once they were all seated around the kitchen table. Sitting in the living room would have necessitated two hours of assiduous cleaning.

"Can't remember," Travis answered. "It's been ages. Got no idea where she's been sleeping or anything."

Harris tried something. "We are sorry for your loss,

Mr. Travis. This is a tragedy."

"Eh?" Travis had still not located a shirt nor offered the officers anything to drink." Tragedy? Yeah, sure, mate. Call it whatever you want. But for me, she was a pain in the arse when we married, and she's been a pain in the arse ever since," he whined.

The two policemen exchanged a glance. "Can you account for your whereabouts on Sunday night, sir?" Harris asked.

"Hackney. With a bunch of my friends. Got the last bus back at about three in the mornin'," Travis told them.

Graham asked next, "Do you play golf, by any chance?"

A skeptical look jarred Travis' face. "Do I do *what*?"

For the second time since the investigation began, Graham prepared to explain the basics of a globally popular sport. "Golf, you know, with the clubs and the ball."

"No, Detective chief whatever-your-name-is, I don't play bloody golf. That's for posh geezers, innit? Do I look like I'm bloody posh?"

Graham let Harris ask the rest of the basic interview questions while he poked around the house. He found nothing to interest him. Travis appeared to be on the inside exactly who he said he was on the outside—a scruffy layabout with low-level criminal tendencies. When they returned to their car, Graham gave Harris directions back to Chiddlinghurst and explained his theory.

"We'll get the Hackney lot to check out Jimmy's alibis, but I'll tell you right now that I don't think he killed Norah."

Harris glanced over at his boss. "Really?"

"Bet you a hundred quid. Oh, he was glad to be rid of her," Graham noted, "but nothing about him, however unpleasant and cave-dwelling he might appear, shouted 'murderer' to me. And I've met more than my share. He's not resourceful enough to negotiate his way to the Home Counties of his own volition, murder someone in an unfamiliar place, set up an alibi, and put on that performance of innocence. He's way too limited."

"So, there's something else going on here besides the jealous husband and the ex-wife with the new boyfriend," Harris observed.

"Could it have been Tim Lloyd?" Graham wondered to himself. "And, if so, why?" he said next, staring out at the traffic. Rain began to fall, light but persistent.

"Or, to ask it another way, sir, why would Tim kill her and then hang around the hotel for the next twelve hours so the local constabulary could interview him as part of a murder investigation? What advantage was there to staying, once the deed was done?" Harris changed lanes to pass a bus full of teenagers, some of whom entertained themselves during their journey by giving the officers a two-fingered salute.

"To maintain the impression of innocence," Graham said, ignoring the unruly teens, "We always imagine that the killer strikes and then flees the scene. But more often than you'd think, the murderer stays around, gathers information, and tries to blend in. Some criminals get a kick out of watching the enormous amount of fuss their crimes generate. It's why they often revisit the scene of the crime."

Harris thought it over. "Do you see Tim Lloyd as the type to kill someone and then be cool enough to stick around?"

"I don't. But I also don't love the theory which implies that the murderer walked in off the street, clubbed Norah over the head, and then vanished. I mean, there are such things as contract killings, but they're exceptionally rare and seem implausible in this instance."

Harris nodded. "And I don't see Mr. Travis stumping up a couple of grand for someone to bump off his wife."

"Not even for a minute," Graham agreed. His phone rang. "It's Bert. You know where to turn, right? Junction eleven." Harris nodded and Graham took the call. "Hello Bert, what's the good news?" Graham listened for a minute, thanked the pathologist, and hung up. "He's identified our murder weapon."

"Wait, what? We already know it was a golf club!" Harris asked, confused.

"No, sorry, I mean Bert knows what *kind* of golf club it was."

"Ah," Harris said.

"It was a driver." DI Graham made another note in his book. "Big, powerful. Ideal for knocking down a defenseless woman and taking her out."

"Could it have been wielded by another woman?" Harris said.

"Who, Amelia? What possible motive could she have?"

"Or Doris?" the sergeant tried next. "Decides she's fed up with people leaving their dirty towels on the floor," he said, affecting Doris' Northern accent.

"Be serious, Sergeant," Graham said mildly. "Besides, Doris has a gold-plated alibi."

"Well, bugger," Harris said, deflated.

"Indeed," Graham agreed.

CHAPTER THIRTEEN

USK WAS SETTLING on the village of Chiddlinghurst when the two officers arrived back. They made straight for the *Lavender*, parking the police car in the gravel driveway at the front. Graham always felt a little self-conscious about showing up in such a highly visible police vehicle, but his own unmarked Audi was in London. He justified his misgivings on the basis that it was reasonable to think that the public gained security and confidence from seeing the badge of the constabulary, especially just after a gruesome and unexpected murder right in their midst.

Cliff Swansbourne greeted them at the door. "Welcome back, travelers. Did you find answers in London?"

Graham shed his suit jacket and loosened his tie. "Somewhat, Mr. Swansbourne. Could we bother you for a cup of tea?"

"Of course," Cliff replied, but then seemed to beckon slightly for the two men to follow him. "Got a couple of details I wanted to pass on," he whispered. "Things that might help your investigation, you know?"

They retreated into the kitchen, which seemed a little overly cautious to Graham, seeing as the inn was virtually empty. "You've already been very helpful, Mr. Swansbourne," Graham was saying. "It can't have been easy..."

"Tim Lloyd," Cliff said without further preparation. "I had a word with him earlier today, while you were in town." Cliff tossed a tea bag into a remarkably ancient teapot and followed it with boiling water. "Amelia was there too, but she's visiting her sister tonight. Every Tuesday evening, without fail. Murder investigation or none."

"Nothing more important than family," Sergeant Harris contributed, then winced slightly.

Graham took the offered mug of tea. "What did Mr. Lloyd have to say? Please be precise. I'm sure I don't have to remind you," he said, reaching for his notebook, "of the seriousness of this matter. You must relay everything he said, word for word if you can."

Cliff was nodding. "It's just that... Well, we've known Tim since the first week we took over the place. He loves it here. Home away from home, all of that. He's never caused any trouble, except maybe just occasionally being a little too familiar. I mean, we're hoteliers, not his family, though he's been very kind and a very regular guest. Amelia indulges him, you see," Cliff explained, turning to Harris. "She's got a soft spot for him. In fact, she told me not to pass any of this on, but I just have to..."

With a flat palm extended, Graham said gently, "Take your time, sir. These things are always easier if you take a couple of deep breaths first."

Cliff followed his advice. Graham and Harris could easily see that this unwelcome case had brought with it more stress and distraction than Swansbourne was ready to cope with. Not only had there been a death in their inn, but a *bone fide* murder. An accident or a heart attack would have been one thing, but this meant that someone had stolen into their quiet, rural establishment and beaten a woman to *death* with a golf club. It would have been hard on anyone, but Graham had the sense that Cliff Swansbourne, for all his maturity and experience, might not be built from the sternest stuff.

"I went to speak to him," Cliff confided. "I was upset with him for his behavior yesterday morning. You know, hanging around the crime scene like that, poking his nose in. I thought you were going to tear him to bits when you found him with the body, Detective. Would have served him right, too."

"Simply trying to maintain the integrity of the scene," Graham explained.

"Well, I told him I didn't think he should have been there, nosing around. And do you know what he said? He told me, as God is my witness that he and Norah were very close. 'Closer than any of you think,' he told me. They were planning to head off to the Caribbean together in a couple of days, for heaven's sake! Hadn't told anyone! We thought Norah was staying at least through the end of the week."

Harris was typing, Graham was writing, and Cliff seemed more unburdened with each passing moment. This information had clearly weighed on him.

"Well, as you know," Graham clarified, "he told us that they were on friendly terms, the occasional coffee, perhaps something more intimate. But going on holiday together—that's a new piece of information."

"I mean," Cliff said, "I'd always assumed he was trustworthy but he lied about how close they were, and for no good reason that I can see. Can we trust him, even now?" Cliff asked them.

"Mr. Swansbourne," Graham began, "we'll speak with Mr. Lloyd again in the light of this new information."

"But why not just tell us everything?" Cliff wondered aloud. "Who cares if he was in love with Norah, or about to jet off somewhere with her? She's divorced, he's single. It's the twenty-first century," he marveled. "We've got men marrying men and women marrying women, bless them all. It's a much more tolerant society than the one I grew up in. Why would Tim lie about a straightforward relationship? What can he be hiding?"

"You're making some good points, sir," Graham told Cliff. "We'll be speaking with Mr. Lloyd some more, rest assured."

"I just want to be as useful as possible," Cliff explained. "You know, the faster this is resolved, the faster we can put the whole nasty episode behind us. It's made us both re-think whether," Cliff said, his eyes welling slightly as he glanced around the kitchen, "we really, truly want to be here."

Harris contributed his two cents. "Anyone would understand that, sir," he said, handing back his empty tea mug, "but it would be a great shame if a cowardly act like this ended up changing the direction you're taking. I mean, your reviews are all five-star, and the gardens look incredible..."

"Amelia's doing, I assure you," Cliff said. "She could run this place with one hand tied behind her back. Put her and Doris Tisbury together and literally, anything becomes possible."

Silently, broodingly, DI Graham let a thought percolate up into his consciousness and, for the first time, receive genuine and careful thought: *Capable of anything... Including murder?*

He put the thought aside for the moment, along with a raft of other theories. "With our interviews complete," Graham said, "barring one more little chat with Mr. Lloyd, we'd like to move onto the forensic stage."

Cliff frowned. This sounded immediately like more disruption, more police presence, more pathologists and scientists busying themselves in his well-kept hallways. "I thought Norah's body was over at the morgue, you know, for the examination."

"It is," Graham confirmed. "But we've got a strong lead on a murder weapon."

Cliff brightened. "Oh? That's good news. And so *quickly*." He marveled again at the pace of change. "Guess you're just as good as those detectives on TV."

I'm a darn sight better than that fictional shower of incompetence. And I'm still getting warmed up. Graham let the remark pass. "Do you have any golf clubs on the premises?"

"Yes, of course. A number of our regular guests leave their sets here in-between visits. They prefer that to carting them back and forth, you know."

"We'll be needing access to every single one, if you don't mind," Graham informed Cliff.

After another long frown and a surprised shake of the head, Cliff said, "But there are over a *dozen* of our guests' golf bags in the shed. You need to search through all of them?"

"In actual fact," Graham told him, "we'll only be examining the drivers in detail, and the rest more superficially. But there's a strong chance that the murder weapon is among them."

"Well, of course. Whatever you need."

"We'll make a start first thing," Graham promised him. "The local Scenes of Crime lads are very efficient. They'll be here for the morning, I imagine, but by lunchtime, we should be out of your hair."

Cliff saw the two men to their car and then returned to the kitchen table. *Perhaps it really is time to pack this in. Sell the murder story as some salacious piece of gossip to a glossy magazine, get a handsome check, and retire for good. Sun, sand, and margaritas.* Right then, at the end of a long and horrid day, it sounded as good as it ever had.

CHAPTER FOURTEEN

C HRIS STEVENS WAS the Scenes of Crime
Officer on duty, an energetic and thoroughly
professional man with a thin, black mustache
and almost famously nerdy glasses. Universally respected
for his work but not celebrated for his sense of humor,
Stevens was in a bullish, problem-solving mood as he
strode down the hallway of the *Lavender*. He began sizing
up the murder scene within moments of his arrival, just
after eight on this promisingly sunny Wednesday
morning.

"There's always contamination of some kind," he
explained to the small crowd which gathered outside the
room—the Swansbournes, DI Graham, and Sergeant
Harris.

Amelia was watching these events with interest, but if
she were honest, she would have rather that the bunch of
them finished their work and disappeared. She liked DI
Graham well enough, and the burly sergeant was nice
and very professional; if there *had* to be a murder investi-

gation at the *Lavender*, this cast of characters was as discreet and helpful as she could have hoped for. But their uniforms and medical bags, the paraphernalia of police work and evidence gathering... these things didn't *belong* here. They were an unwelcome reminder that mere yards from where she and Cliff slept, something utterly terrible had happened.

The next to arrive was a curious but frustrated Doris Tisbury, whose sole hope for the day was to finally clean the murdered woman's room. Something about the incompleteness of her task genuinely bothered Doris, as though the murder scene were a missing piece from her personal jigsaw, and only her prompt and thorough attention would bring her mind some rest. Her son, a schoolteacher and certainly no medical expert, had "diagnosed" Doris with "OCD" or some such, and it drove her batty to hear him carry on about "reward circuits" and "habituated compulsions" that she knew nothing about, but which were clearly directed at her. Back in the day, Doris informed her son testily, neatness was considered a virtue, not frowned upon as something requiring treatment by a psychiatrist or worse. Not for the first time, she considered that she'd been born in the wrong century.

"Mr. Lloyd isn't up yet, I don't think," Cliff told Stevens as the bespectacled forensic scientist located his swabs and a camera. "But he was the only one, besides Doris, who was in here before the police arrived."

Cliff and Amelia kept their distance as Stevens began taking a swab from the floor by the bathtub. "I'll need a DNA sample from him and from Doris. Hopefully, our killer left some small fragment of himself behind."

"Or herself," Amelia added.

Stevens straightened up and slotted the swab away in its plastic tube. "You know how many murders there are by golf club every year in the UK?" he asked.

Amelia bristled. She wasn't sure she liked this officious young man with his know-it-all air. "I'm sure you'll enlighten me."

"Somewhere around none," the SOCO told her. "It's an extremely uncommon murder method. I can only think of two, historically, and they were all *ages* ago. Men committed both of them. In fact, the vast majority of murders ultimately prove to have a male perpetrator," he added. "Particularly those involving clubs, bats, sticks, or other methods of beating a victim to death."

Cliff attempted to lighten the atmosphere. "I don't know, Mr. Stevens. In the hands of our Doris, I'm sure a golf club could lay waste to nations."

Doris loved this kind of banter and gave as good as she got. "Not me," she said, picking up fresh towels from her cart and heading down the hallway. "I'm a lover, not a fighter."

Cliff cracked up laughing as the big-framed Doris marched off to her daily chores. It was the first time he could remember laughing—or even *smiling*—since Doris had first delivered the terrible news.

"Well," Amelia said, close to a fit of the giggles herself and grateful for a little light relief from the heaviness that had blanketed their days since Norah's body had been found. "There's an image to conjure with."

"I'd rather not," Cliff managed through his laughter.

Stevens ignored the entire exchange and silently wished for some time alone. There were always curious onlookers, and Stevens didn't mind in principle, but they invariably found cause to contribute some theory or other which was apt to knock Stevens off his stride. He was a scientist, not an investigator, and he simply wanted to collect evidence before feeding it into DI Graham's investigative process. Besides, it was to be a busy morning, even once he'd finished with this blood-stained bathroom floor.

Around thirty minutes later, Cliff showed Stevens to the shed and opened the door. There was that reassuring, slightly musty odor of leather and metal emanating from the interior as the door creaked open. Cliff had been offering guests inexpensive, secure golf club storage since he and Amelia had taken over the *Lavender*. It made economic sense. The only costs were a new lock and a motion-detector system for the back garden. There was one problem, however. A family of foxes who lived in the countryside beyond the village visited regularly. They would set off all the security lights as they trotted brazenly through at night. On occasion, guests complained bitterly to Amelia and Cliff about being woken by a blast of bright light invading their bedrooms in the middle of the night. Cliff's response was to produce his phone and show a video of the cheeky culprits and their kits gamboling across the lawn. The guests would inevitably pipe down, charmed at the sight. And so, thanks to the storage shed, Cliff made some easy money that allowed him a quality of wine a notch above that he would have drunk otherwise. Easy money was one of Cliff's favorite things.

Cliff was about to pull bags full of clubs out onto the grass for Stevens' inspection before the SOCO let him know, a tad too brusquely for Cliff's own tastes, that he'd need to inspect each club in situ.

"We mustn't compromise the scene, sir. We must protect it. Even if the murder weapon isn't here, if the killer touched a bag, for example, we might get a partial print off the leather." Cliff backed off to watch the thirty-something Stevens do his work. "My first task is to search for what *isn't* there," he said. "If the murderer took their weapon from this shed and abandoned it elsewhere, there'll be a driver missing."

A few minutes later, careful tallying of the clubs showed Stevens that not a single golf bag lacked a driver. "All present and correct," he muttered.

"So now what?" Cliff asked.

Without answering, Stevens pulled out his forensics kit. It surprised Cliff to see that the SOCO carried his equipment in a backpack as though he were a college student. Cliff had been expecting some kind of futuristic tool bag. In his imagination, it glowed blue neon and jetted out steam when it was opened. Stevens didn't even carry one of those natty, black leather bags, like a country doctor from the 1950s. In Cliff's view, a backpack was prosaic by comparison. "Now," Stevens told him, "I meticulously swab every golf club, starting with the drivers, to see if there are any bloodstains."

"And if there are?" Cliff wanted to know.

Stevens enjoyed appearing an expert in front of laymen but did not possess the insight to realize that by doing so he encouraged their questions, questions he didn't appreciate. Stevens could be

chippy at the best of times, curmudgeonly at worst, but he kept his resentment at Cliff's interruption from his expression. A sigh and a slightly curt tone were the only indications of his predilection not to suffer fools easily.

"Then we'll probably have found the murder weapon. Unless the denizens of the local golf courses are given to smearing blood on their clubs as part of some gruesome and ancient hazing ritual," he said. It was the closest thing to a joke Stevens had uttered since he'd arrived, a record which would stand all day.

CHAPTER FIFTEEN

"WELL THEN, I'LL leave you to it." Cliff started to leave, a nice cup of tea and a bacon sandwich firmly on his mind, when an old man appeared next to the shed.

"Morning, there, Clifford!" the man said, his overly loud tone hinting at his deafness. Bob Sykes was one of those men who had been very old for a very long time. If Cliff were pressed, he'd have guessed Sykes was pushing ninety, but the man himself claimed to have long since forgotten. "Old age," he was fond of saying, "always comes at a bad time." Despite his vintage, Sykes was a groundskeeper at the nearby golf course.

"Morning, Mr. Sykes," Cliff responded. There wasn't a person in Chiddlinghurst who would dream of referring to Mr. Sykes by his first name. Cliff handled the introductions between Sykes and Stevens.

"Now what's this I hear," Sykes asked, his voice a reedy tenor, "about a pretty lady coming to grief in one of your bathrooms?"

"I'm afraid we've had a murder, Mr. Sykes," Stevens

explained. "We're investigating exactly what happened, and we're getting closer every hour."

Sykes leaned on a weather-beaten golf club. "Well, I heard about it, and it's a rotten thing to happen, ain't that right, Clifford?"

"Damned tragedy," Cliff told him.

"I says to the wife," Sykes related, "I says, 'A murder at the *Lavender*? Never in a million years. There's scarce ever trouble with the Swansbournes,' I told her."

The stress of the past few days and the inevitable damage to the *Lavender*'s reputation showed momentarily on Cliff's lined face. "Well, it's poor Norah I feel sorry for," he said finally. "We'll muddle along alright, but she's. . ."

"In a far better place," Sykes said, curling a bony finger toward the sky. "Mark my words, Clifford. Far better and more beautiful than any place we've ever seen with these mortal eyes."

Stevens raised his head from his work. "I'd like to believe that."

"Are you getting spiritual in your advanced years Mr. Sykes?" Cliff asked.

The old man cackled. "Wait 'til you're as old as I am," he told Cliff. "Spend a moment staring mortality and eternity in the face and then tell me there's no splendor or comfort to be found in a vision of the celestial city. There's power in that message, young 'uns, I tell you."

"Or perhaps," Cliff said, "you're squaring things with the Divine before you shuffle off to meet him."

Another cackle. Sykes sounded like an ancient witch when he laughed. "It certainly wouldn't do," the old man said, "for me to get all the way to the Pearly Gates and find my name's not on the list." He leaned once more on the golf club and only then looked down at it with a spark of realization in his eyes. "Well, I'll be a monkey's uncle. I was nothing more than a hair's breadth from forgetting what I came over to say!"

"What's that, Mr. Sykes?" Cliff asked. His bacon sandwich daydream had receded alarmingly, and he was keen to get it back on track.

"I found this driver in the bunker on the fourteenth," he said, lifting the club on which he'd been leaning. "Wondered if one of your guests had forgotten it. Funny place to have a driver out, wouldn't you say? The middle of the fairway, with bunkers all around?"

Cliff wisely decided not to touch the driver but motioned to Stevens, who took it between gloved thumbs and forefingers as though it were a holy relic. "Where precisely was this found, Mr. Sykes?" Stevens said, excitement in his voice.

"Half-buried, it was," Sykes reported. "Like someone tried to hide it there, and either did a rotten job or someone else dug it up part of the way. I found it sticking out of the bunker, like a bit of old shrapnel on a beach."

"And when did you make this discovery?" Stevens asked, already preparing to swab the metal where the club would meet the ball. *Or the back of Norah Travis' head.*

"Not an hour ago," Sykes replied. "My first thought was that somebody had forgotten it, but then I thought of you. I got myself wondering if one of you policemen might like to have a look at it. There was word going around the pub last night that the young woman was hit over the head with a golf club. That was the rumor, anyway, unless my old hearing let me down again. Of all the sorry ways to meet your maker...."

"No, you're quite right," Stevens said. "We're confident the murder weapon was a driver."

"Well," Sykes said, "I'm relieved not to be entirely losing my marbles."

Stevens gave Cliff a meaningful glance and then reached for his cell phone. "DI Graham?" he confirmed. "Chris Stevens, SOCO... Yes, I'm in the shed in the back garden." He glanced at Sykes who grimaced comically, enjoying the moment. "I've got a local resident here, groundskeeper at the golf club. And the thing is, sir, I'm pretty sure he's brought me the weapon that was used to murder Norah Travis."

CHAPTER SIXTEEN

LOUISE HOVERED NERVOUSLY by the doorway to the crime lab as if afraid of being accused of trespass. Or, as her boss sometimes called it, "lurking." She was always hesitant to disturb Bert Hatfield when he was in one of his "beautiful mind" moods. The largest whiteboard she had found in the office supply catalog covered one wall of the lab and Bert had spent the first hour of this Thursday morning scribbling on it with zest and purpose.

"Er, sir?" Louise tried, tapping tentatively at the door frame.

Bert didn't miss a beat, his marker squeaking noisily on the board. "Louise, my dear, if I've told you once, I've told you a thousand times. My colleagues call me Bert," he explained, still writing, "and you're my colleague."

"Yes, sir."

There was another animated squeak. "Oh, for pity's sake," he said with a reassuring smile. "With what can I help you, oh timid shrew?"

Lurking—yes, that was the word—immediately behind Louise was an even more reluctant figure, a teenager in a smart grey and black school uniform.

"Bloody hell," Bert exclaimed, finally capping the pen and slotting it onto the board's metal rail and peering at the schoolgirl. "Do they still make you wear those ghastly things?"

Louise found her voice once more. "This is Fiona. From St. Aidan's." The silence betrayed Bert's having entirely forgotten about this long-planned work experience visit. "It was in your calendar," Louise added.

"Bugger," the pathologist muttered. "Quite alright, quite alright. Come on in, Fiona. Sorry about all that." He ushered her into the room and politely dismissed Louise who returned to her front desk duties. "You've arrived on a rather auspicious day, as it happens."

"Really?" the fifteen-year-old asked. She had bright blue eyes and a quiet curiosity which Bert found both pleasant and rather admirable, particularly given that his lab dealt almost exclusively with the lamentable and gruesome.

"You'll have heard about the murder over in Chiddlinghurst?" he asked, leading Fiona around two tables stacked high with books and papers toward his desk in the corner. In truth, there could have laid almost anything under the tremendous weight of documentation Bert had accrued and "stored." It gave the lab the feel of a much loved but slightly shabby library whose main topic was death: manners of bringing it about, and the people guilty of having done so.

"Norah Travis," Fiona replied crisply. "Very sad. Only twenty-seven, wasn't she?"

"Well done for reading the news," Bert told her. "I didn't think young people bothered with it."

Fiona was not, as Bert would find during a memorable morning, a typical fifteen-year-old. She had bent over backward to be assigned this rather special position, writing letters and using her father's modest influence as a human resources manager for a local pharmaceutical company. To be a pathologist had been her dream since childhood, and she had little interest in any other career. Hers was no morbid fascination with death, however. She was passionate about the *process*, the hard science of sleuthing one's way from complete confusion to stand-up-in-court certainty. She wanted to catch bad people, of course, and bring closure to families, but her focus had always been on *how* a murderer was brought to justice. "It just revs me up," she had explained to a slightly perplexed career counselor at her school. "I can't explain it."

"I read the news all the time," Fiona reported honestly. "Are you working on evidence connected to her case?" A flash of excitement accompanied Fiona's question. *I might help solve a murder! On my first day!*

"I am," Bert reported. "We've had a couple of strokes of luck, but we're not there yet."

He opened three different files on the computer and allowed Fiona to read them. She did so quickly, perched on a black stool by Bert's desk, taking notes on a spiral-bound pad. Then Bert had a thought.

"You've signed all the non-disclosure stuff, right?" Fiona nodded. "Good. Because you really can't discuss any of this with anyone. Not until we've taken the case to court. Alright with you?"

"You can trust me," Fiona said. Bert believed her at

once. There were some people you just knew wouldn't let you down.

Once Fiona had finished reading and taking her notes, Bert filled her in on the rest.

"Thankfully, we're blessed with a gifted SOCO. You know what one of those is, don't you?"

"Scenes of Crime Officer," Fiona replied.

"Good girl. Now, our man Stevens is very thorough, really one of the best. With his help," Bert said, reaching across to an object wrapped in plastic, "and a lucky break, something has fallen into our laps. Care to identify it?"

Fiona took the golf club in her hands as though being handed a piece of the original Cross. "I don't play golf, so I don't know what type. But it seems heavy," she said, weighing the thick-handled club in her hands.

"It's a driver," Bert said. "Heaviest of the lot. If someone raised this and brought it down," he said, mimicking the motion, "or swung from the side, they'd cause a serious injury, wouldn't you say?"

Fiona tried swinging the club in an imitation of the murderous impact. "Fractures, for sure," she said.

"Now," Bert said, taking back the club. "We've got a theory that Norah Travis was hit, very hard just the once, by a golf club. See here," he said, returning to the computer screen and bringing up images from the post-mortem. "Notice this pattern of crossed lines? They're different in every manufacturer, of course."

"And this pattern," Fiona said, almost touching the screen, "matches the club the SOCO found?"

She was brimming with an excitement kept under control only by the severity of the case and the gravity of her surroundings. Before this moment, Fiona would never have dared believe that she'd be allowed even to *see* this lab, never mind examine the evidence under scrutiny. She was on cloud nine.

"It does. Within tolerances. But there's a way we can make sure, and that's how I was going to spend my morning," Bert said, giving her an almost conspiratorial grin. "Care to join me?"

CHAPTER SEVENTEEN

DETECTIVE INSPECTOR GRAHAM sat rather gloomily in the dining room of the *Lavender* bed-and-breakfast at just after 9 a.m. on this promisingly bright Thursday. He was not, by his own admission, at his best in the morning. His doctor had warned Graham about this, though he had provided no concrete method of setting aside the feelings of fatigue, ennui, and dissatisfaction he generally felt in the hours between waking and mid-morning. They assailed him with a regularity and severity that created a debilitating vicious cycle. He had a depressing sense that he would be unable to achieve anything; that this new day, and his hard work, would come to naught.

The thought that plagued him popped into his head unbidden and repeatedly during these lulls: that he was a charlatan, a failure. The dark whirling of those thoughts had conspired to drive him to the edge more than once. He knew, intellectually, that giving in to his demons would only take him over that edge. He cursed happenstance for shaping the *Lavender's* dining room in such a way that the well-stocked bar was easily visible. *Not now*, his better self said yet again. *Not now and not ever*.

Instead, he drank tea. The depressed mind, he'd come to understand, has less ammunition with which to flatten its victim when provided with constant novelty. Silencing the demons had seemed impossible until they'd shown themselves usefully appeased by regular and various infusions of caffeine. Graham would never have believed it, and his doctor was surprised enough to write up his case in a minor journal, but tea—perhaps the neurochemical opposite of alcohol—was saving David Graham's life.

Amelia had been helpful enough, after Graham's initial request, to serve him a rotating assortment from the six teas they had in the kitchen. On this sunny Thursday morning, David was trying to lift his gloom with a jasmine tea from Anhui province in China. It was rather complex, he found to his satisfaction. If its taste had had a color, this tea would have been lilac or rosy-pink, gentle on the senses but certain of its own virtues. Within moments of inhaling its vapors, and only a minute after finishing his first cup, DI Graham's view of the world was quickly changing. He welcomed the sunshine not as a chronometer of his regular morning depression, but as a warming, healing light which would ensure a good day. Synapses fired anew. He felt as though an MRI of his awakening mind would show a riot of yellows and reds as energy filled those parts of his mind kept dormant and shadowed by his sadness.

After the second cup, to his great relief, the blues were banished. He turned to his notebooks with a fresh alertness and began interrogating for the third or fourth time, everything he knew about this frustrating case. The pieces he'd found simply would not fall into place. He had found no one who had had a motive *and* the opportunity to murder Norah Travis. He turned all the facts over in his mind. Perhaps he'd been thinking about the case all wrong. As the effects of the tea took hold, and his mind raced in that way that he loved, like a greyhound finally given its druthers to chase an elusive rabbit down the track, he stopped and re-read a note he'd made on Monday, during his initial interviews.

A note that he hadn't followed up. *Come on, Dave, you're slipping. You're better than this.*

"Is Mr. Swansbourne in this morning?" he asked Amelia as she brought a fresh pot of the Anhui jasmine.

"Yes, I think he's just finishing shaving. Would you like to see him?"

Cliff, when he appeared, was looking a little better, not as drawn and stressed as he had in the days prior. "Beautiful morning, isn't it?" he said as he took a seat opposite Graham.

The now cheery, almost giddily contented part of Graham's mind obliged him to agree, but there were far more serious topics at hand than the sunshine, however welcome it was. "Cliff, I've got to ask you about something you said back on Monday."

Amelia chipped in from the kitchen. "Good luck with that, Detective Inspector. Our Cliff could tell you what he had for breakfast in 1976 but he's like Swiss cheese on anything more recent."

Her husband scowled good-naturedly, and then asked Graham, "What was it I said?"

"You told me," Graham replied, referring to his notes, "that you'd heard voices coming from the direction of the guest's rooms on Sunday evening. I'd like to know more about what you heard."

Cliff gave a funny, bashful smile and rolled his eyes. "Well, you know...I wasn't sure. I don't want to cast aspersions. And it seemed so...irrelevant."

Graham said nothing but readied his pen and notebook.

His discomfort very obvious, Cliff muttered, "It's hard to know what to say. You know..."

Graham exuded patience, but inwardly his investigative self burned to hurry the truth from Cliff, even at the risk of being rude. "Let's say that I don't," he said.

"They were...well, you know. Tim and Norah." Cliff fidgeted under the table like a seven-year-old called into the headmaster's office.

The DI held his temper by a narrow margin. "Go on."

"It was...love, I think," Cliff murmured. "The sounds of love."

Amelia returned to the doorway between the kitchen and dining room, her hands on her hips. "For heaven's sake, Clifford. It's not the sodding 1950s anymore. He means they were *at it*, DI Graham." Cliff winced. "Having some nookie," she continued. "Bonking for Britain, most likely."

"Amelia Swansbourne!" Cliff gasped.

His wife was unmoved. "Well, what should we call it, you impossible man?" she demanded. "Marital relations?"

DI Graham held a hand up in mute appeal. "I get the picture, believe me."

Cliff turned to Graham. "Look, I could have been wrong. The wildlife around here can get pretty noisy, too. It's hard to distinguish what's what at times."

"Did you hear this also, Mrs. Swansbourne?" Graham asked.

She shook her head. "No, my husband enjoyed that all on his own."

Acutely uncomfortable, Cliff reddened, his shoulders hunched. "That's what I think I heard," he said simply. "Hope it helps."

"It might," DI Graham observed. "You'd be surprised how many big cases are broken open by the tiniest detail. Thanks, Mr. Swansbourne. Please, continue what you were doing. I'm sure you're a busy man."

With a hotel emptied by fallout from the murder, bookings being canceled left and right after a painful social media reaction, and Doris efficiently cleaning the mostly empty hotel, Cliff found himself with little to do. He headed for his Land Rover Defender while Graham pored over his notes.

'The sounds of love', he wrote. *Interesting, but hardly conclusive and if true, not the story Mr. Lloyd offered. I'm still missing something.* The thought nagged at him, like a confounded blister, for the next hour.

CHAPTER EIGHTEEN

FIONA OBSERVED DR. Hatfield with rapt attention as he went about what was, for him, a relatively routine task, but which produced a flurry of notes and questions from the young student.

"I thought these were incredibly expensive?" she asked, as they both stood over a square, black machine that looked like a laser printer but with four top compartments, each with its own thick, gray lid.

"Oh, they are," Bert told her. "Thermal cyclers are about £200,000 a pop," he said, closing the lids and pressing a sequence of buttons on the panel at its front. "But a friend at the Met owed me a favor after I broke open a case for them last year, and he was good enough to let us have one of these beauties on loan."

Fiona searched her memory for a second. "The Angela Forrest murder?" she gasped. "That was *you?*"

Bert gave her a proud smile. "I don't want to sound like I'm boasting, but that was the smallest sample of DNA ever to be successfully used to prosecute a murderer. I didn't think we'd pull it off."

The whole country had spent days in shock after the discovery of thirteen-year-old Angela's body in a churchyard near Folkestone. She had been exceptionally bright, a gifted athlete and artist abducted after hockey practice by a "man with a white van." The hunt for her killer had found vocal and useful support from the national newspapers, particularly the oft-criticized "gutter press" of tabloids and glossy weekly magazines who had called for her killer's prompt execution from the outset.

Thankfully, the death penalty wasn't available but there was a tremendous satisfaction when the judge handed down the stiffest penalty he could: life in prison without the possibility of parole. Keith Marshall, a name now added to the list of Britain's most hated child-murderers, would never walk free. Bert Hatfield's exemplary work was central to Crown's evidence.

"I remember something about a new technique," Fiona said. "Using tiny amounts of DNA but copying them."

Bert was impressed. "You're on the right lines. You see our sample, there?"

Fiona nodded. They had already swabbed the golf club. "Well, there isn't all that much of it, is there? We're talking about tiny, broken fragments of DNA. Not enough, on its own, for us even to tell if the material belonged to a man or a woman."

"So..." Fiona said, thoroughly engaged as ever.

"So, we need to copy that tiny fragment as many times as we can, and from the results, we can produce an incomplete but useful DNA profile."

Thinking the process through, Fiona asked, "But how will we know it's Norah's?"

Bert reached over to his desk and brought out a test

tube with a sample swab inside. "From the postmortem. If we can match what we find from the golf club with the sample I took from Norah..."

"We'll know this was the golf club that killed her!" Fiona exclaimed excitedly.

"There you go. Now, this will take a moment so let's grab a coffee while it's doing its thing."

"Thing?" Fiona asked, peering at the device.

"It's going to repeatedly heat and cool the sample— hence the name 'thermal cycler'—in the presence of an agent that will help to create new strands of genetic material," Bert explained.

"Agent?" Fiona asked, her notebook ready.

"Actually, an extract from a type of bacteria that just happens to be terrific at helping DNA strands copy themselves. But let's not get too technical." Bert led Fiona from the room, and although the teenager would have loved to get a lot more technical, she followed him along toward the reception area where the customary 10:30 a.m. pot of coffee was being readied.

"Louise, you're an angel," Bert told her, reaching for the steaming pot.

Louise was putting down her phone. "Oh, I know," she quipped. "Sir, would you call DI Graham? He's got a question for you."

"Bert?"

"Good morning. How's sunny Chiddlinghurst?" Hatfield asked Graham.

"Bloody frustrating," the DI admitted. "But I've got a question. The kind I can't believe I haven't asked before."

Graham's tone was a little worrying. He seemed genuinely angry with himself, though Bert knew him as a mild-mannered sort of chap. "Go ahead," Bert told him, glancing over at Fiona. "I've got some special help today, so we're ready for whatever the world of crime can throw at us." Fiona grinned over the rim of her coffee cup.

Graham got straight to the point. "Was there any evidence that Norah was sexually active on the night she was murdered?"

"No, I don't think so."

"Are you sure?" Graham pressed, his tone impatient.

Take it easy, old chap. There's no need to get snippy.

Bert again looked over at Fiona and held up a finger in a polite request for her patience before taking this delicate conversation back to the lab. "Let me check the records again, David, but I really don't remember anything." Bert reached his desk and opened a file on his computer. "Well, it's hard to say with a hundred percent certainty, but there were none of the classic signs."

"How do you mean?" Graham demanded.

Hatfield took a couple of breaths. The DI sounded genuinely rattled, as though he was holding Bert responsible for slowing his investigation. *I can't manufacture evidence, you know.* "We did all the usual tests," he said, paraphrasing two pages of the report, "and found no evidence of sexual contact immediately before, or in the days before her death."

Graham was silent for a moment. "But that doesn't mean it didn't happen, right?"

"I can't be absolutely sure. You know...Well, we're both men of the world, right, Detective Inspector? There's more than one way to skin a cat, and all that, but there was no *sign* of sexual contact."

Graham tersely thanked the pathologist and hung up. Bert spent a long moment with a puzzled, worried expression on his face, and then nudged open the lab door and gave his work experience student an artificial but convincing smile.

"Fiona? The PCR machine is calling."

CHAPTER NINETEEN

S ERGEANT HARRIS ARRIVED to find the DI alone, brooding over his notes. Graham was sipping tea as though it were the elixir of life. "Morning, sir."

"Ah, Harris. Have a seat, would you?" Graham was building a picture of what might have happened in the hours before Norah's sad departure from this earth. His progress energized him.

"Look, this is a bit of a funny one, but I want to brainstorm something with you. In confidence," he emphasized.

"Fire away, sir," Harris said. He wore his summer uniform, the sleeves of his white shirt rolled up, his cap set on the table, his black tie neatly in place.

"Bear with me here, Sergeant, but...what might, all other things being equal, make a grown woman scream at 11 o'clock on a Sunday morning?"

Harris' eyebrows formed a puzzled furrow, then rose in an unmistakably amused inquiry.

"Yes, before you ask, I want you to skip the obvious. I

know Tim Lloyd was here at the *Lavender*, but I can't prove they were together."

"Well, if she wasn't yelling out in pain, that leaves a fairly short list of possibilities," Harris observed.

"Short, but I want it anyway," Graham said. "Have a go."

"Right," Harris said, considering the matter. "Well, she might have been injured, as I say. Got to consider it."

"Bert found nothing on the body that suggested an injury," Graham replied. "Well, except for the bloody great thwack on the back of her head from a golf club."

"Yeah, let's not forget about that," Harris said. "Remember, Mrs. Swansbourne thought it might have been a shout of surprise. You know, a shock, or something."

Graham pondered this. "A spider, maybe? You know how some people are."

"What about a cockroach?" Harris offered.

The DI tutted disapprovingly. "I wouldn't let Mrs. Tisbury hear you talking like that."

Harris grinned. "Well, was there anything scary on TV?"

"On a Sunday morning?" Graham reminded him.

"Or she read something on her phone. Got a surprising text. Who knows?"

Harris meant no harm by this flippant comment, but it summed up the lamentable state of their investigation so concisely that Graham felt a sudden welling up of anger. To Harris' surprise, Graham's notebook hit the desk with a thud of frustration. "Not us, and that's the bloody problem."

It didn't take the experienced eye of a psychologist for Harris to recognize that his boss was taking something rather more than a strictly professional interest in this case. It had become something *personal*, a battle of wits, one which Graham couldn't bear to lose. Such intense, emotional involvement was never a good sign for a professional police officer. Cases were to be puzzled out, solved through guile and perseverance, not seen as some intense, personal battle with the perpetrator or other, less definable demon.

"Begging your pardon, sir, but..."

"What?" Graham snapped.

"Are you alright?" Harris asked with very genuine concern.

Graham stopped short of another angry growl and sighed heavily. "Not really, Sergeant. I'll be honest."

Harris spoke with great care. He knew Graham only through their work. There'd been the occasional chat in the pub, but even then, they discussed only cases.

"If you need to talk to someone, sir... I've been on the force a long time. And I know what it can do to a man, this kind of work. The stress, the odd hours." He paused to make sure that he wasn't about to overstep an important boundary. "And, if things at home are difficult, sir... well, that doesn't help."

For a long moment, Graham stared at the starched, white cloth that lay across the dining room table. Then he poured himself yet another cup of Anhui.

Harris watched him with real sympathy. It had been five months, and yet it was clearly still too soon to bring up the shocking tragedy that was so plainly weighing on the senior police officer. This case was Graham's first on "active duty" since it had happened. He had spent most of the intervening months alone, on compassionate leave, the time spent in either a silent, empty house, or in his office reviewing case files. On the nights he'd felt unable to return home, he'd slept fitfully on a cot in his office. His wife, Isabelle, had retreated even further—to her parent's home in the wilds of North Wales. Their disappointing, depressing, terse phone conversations were little comfort.

Returning to lead an investigation had been a breakthrough for Graham, but after four days without an arrest, he was struggling to maintain his professional detachment. His unresolved grief was threatening the fragile emotional equilibrium he had strived so hard to create. And he knew it.

Graham finished his cup of tea and stood smartly. "You know what really helps?" he asked.

"Sir?" Harris said, standing too.

Graham slid the notebook back in his pocket. "Catching murderers. Let's nail this bastard, Harris." He made toward the door of the *Lavender*. "Come on, chop, chop. We've got work to do."

Fiona's eyes glittered enthusiastically with the thrill of discovery. "We have a match," Bert Hatfield announced. "Isn't technology wonderful?"

Scrutinizing the on-screen results, Fiona asked, "How certain is it? I mean, there are plenty of blond women of her age walking around."

"Not that many," Bert advised, "who were recently struck in the back of a head with a golf driver."

"Admittedly," Fiona said sheepishly.

"The chances of a mistake are around a billion to one. So, if it's not Norah, it might be one of, say, six or seven other people on the *whole planet*."

"So, what now?"

"Now, I tell the harassed DI Graham that we definitively have the murder weapon. The trouble is," Bert said, sighing, "that we've got not even a smidge of a fingerprint. Which tells us something."

Sensing another invitation to brainstorm possibilities, Fiona asked, "Does sand wipe away fingerprints?"

"Not particularly," Bert answered. "But murderers often do."

"So, the driver was deliberately wiped clean, and then buried in a sand trap on the golf course."

"Yup," Bert confirmed. "But by whom?" He raised a forefinger to make his point.

The pair sat for a moment in thoughtful silence. Bert hated dead ends. They always made him feel as though he'd omitted to take the right approach. *Just use better tools, ask better questions, Bert.*

"What else have we got?" he said. Bert returned to his desk and pulled up the list Louise had made of Norah's personal effects. "Worth another glance, I'd say," he said, mostly to himself.

Although both he and Stevens had pored over Norah's clothing, her small, bright red suitcase, and toiletries from the bathroom, he couldn't see any harm in doing so again. Hatfield showed Fiona the list, and together they methodically located and inspected each item. "Hair clip, plastic, green," he read out loud. "Woman's blouse, white, blood-stained. Hairbrush, black plastic, with fibers." Nothing seemed even remotely amiss.

"Do you see anything unusual?" Fiona asked.

"No," Bert responded. "Neither did Stevens the first time we went through this process." Dr. Hatfield had gotten used to Fiona's questions, but he was a little tetchy. While he was known for his patience, even Bert became frustrated when an apparent wealth of evidence refused to yield anything of value.

Fiona lifted a plastic evidence bag to the light. It contained a piece of paper. Bert read from his list. "Lottery ticket, Saturday's draw." There were three other objects—chewing gum, a bottle of painkillers that Bert had already thoroughly tested, and a tape measure. "And that's all, folks," he said. "The life and times of Norah Travis, deceased."

"Not a lot here," Fiona sighed.

"I need another coffee," Bert said. "Come on, we'll bother Louise for a moment or two."

"Bothering Louise" was a long-established and enjoyable tradition for Bert, and Louise was good enough to humor him. Between phone calls, answering email inquiries from police officers and medical staff, as well as taking care of the endless filing and copying, Bert brightened his assistant's day with a series of terrible, old jokes. He had a legendary store of utter howlers and was in the middle of the one about the guy with the van full of penguins when Fiona, who hadn't been paying too much attention to him, exploded.

"Sir?!" she almost shrieked. "Dr. Hatfield?!" she gasped, clutching her phone.

"What on earth's the matter, child?" Bert asked, the rest of the joke abandoned.

"The numbers...The lottery ticket," she stuttered.

"What about it?" he said, turning her phone so that he could see. And then, as he realized the implications, he turned to his assistant. "Louise, get DI Graham on the phone," he said. "He won't believe this."

CHAPTER TWENTY

A FTER YET ANOTHER inspection of the crime scene, a slightly purposeless wander around the hotel to "soak up the atmosphere," and more long sessions of staring at his notes while drinking Anhui jasmine, Graham could put off the inevitable no longer. His earlier optimism had dimmed once more, and though he remained determined, he simply couldn't see a way forward in the case.

Hatfield had confirmed that they'd found the murder weapon, but the lack of fingerprints, or an obvious owner, was almost unbearably disappointing. To make matters worse, the conflicting evidence over Norah's romantic life made little sense. Something, or someone, had lied to him. Either Tim Lloyd was making up the story about being "in the doghouse" on the night Norah was killed and the postmortem evidence wasn't revealing what truly happened, or Cliff was mistaken or.... Graham's thoughts whirled. It was maddening.

At around five, Graham reached his home, a quaint cottage that dated to the turn of the 1900s. So reluctant was he to be there that he'd stopped at a junction and turned the other way, before forcing himself to double-back and park in his driveway for the first time in ten days. The garden needed a tidy. Leaves dotted the little front lawn. He took a deep breath as he turned his car engine off. It would be awful, but he knew he needed to do this.

The silence after opening the front door still hollowed him out as he entered. It was so glaring, so incongruous in a house where there had been such light and life and noise. The kitchen was squared away. Someone must have done that, but Graham couldn't for the life of him remember who. Earlier, instead of the clean, shiny coun-tertops that now presented themselves, he would come home to find cheese crackers scattered across the surface, crumbs often scrunched underfoot. Small, brightly colored, partitioned plates were stacked in the corner. Alongside them were matching cups, adorned with the latest cartoon princess whose signature tune was sung so often that it had driven him into the long, back garden many times. Oh, how he longed to hear that song now.

Life would be forever divided in two, "before" and "after." Before, Isabelle had hated housework, and Graham had found himself too busy to help as much as he'd wanted. Their home had been cluttered but lively, full of energy, laughter, and endless activities. When she wasn't working at the hospice, Isabelle spent all her time with their daughter. She had shepherded Katie through life, encouraging her bright curiosity, her willingness to try new things, her quirky sense of humor. By the age of five, Katie was already comfortable eating any vegetable she was offered—to the envious surprise of her classmates' parents—and was making up little jokes that were just about beginning to make sense.

He should have been there more, Graham knew. A young child needs attention and love and guidance, not an exhausted father with so many other things on his mind. He'd hated the necessity of "outsourcing" some of the responsibilities of raising a child, as Isabelle had called it, and they had struggled to afford a nanny, but there was nothing for it. They needed the help. Cora had genuinely loved Katie without indulging her, and they had trusted her implicitly. The crash wasn't Cora's fault. It was just one of those things.

Graham burned with anger at the memory. Without realizing it, he'd climbed the stairs in a slow trance and found himself at Katie's bedroom door. Her toys were still on the floor, where she'd left them. He hadn't stepped in there since the night of the accident, when from the doorway he'd watched his wife, eerily silent with grief, slowly curl up in the tiny bed that still held the fragrance of their little girl.

The evidence from the closed-circuit cameras was conclusive. A delivery van ran a red light at twenty miles per hour over the limit. The collision was inevitable. The back-left of the car took all the force of the impact.

Graham sat on the floor of Katie's bedroom and leaned against the side of her bed, knees tucked under his chin. His eyes closed as his forehead touched the softness of her girly pink blanket, memories of reading her bedtime stories dancing in his mind. The wave hit then. It tumbled over him at first, then violently engulfed him, sucking him down, his anguish annihilating his consciousness. Graham knew only complete obedience to the tyranny of sorrow would transport him through the dark, desolate tunnel that lay before him. He'd resisted until now, but he had grown weaker. Now, he was ready. Finally, the tears came as he surrendered like a sacrifice at the altar of heartbreak, his defenses finally breached. It was time to embark on grief's journey.

At six-foot-three and with the build of a rugby prop forward, Harris wasn't known for his athleticism. Nevertheless, the big man covered the ground with surprising speed. His orders were simple: keep trying DI Graham, get to the *Lavender*, and don't let anyone leave.

"Sir?" he panted. "Thank God. I've been trying you for..."

"What's the problem, Sergeant?" Graham asked. His voice seemed quiet and hollow, his manner so very different from the zealous determination he'd shown earlier.

"Sir, I don't know how we overlooked it, but, well, Norah won the lottery on Saturday night."

Graham had spent half an hour sitting in his car. He had been entirely unsure of where to go, but certain that he couldn't be in his house for another second. Then, impulsively, he'd headed in the direction of Wales, and Isabelle. He hadn't thought things through. She hadn't answered her phone, and with each mile, he knew it to be a fool's errand. "Really?" he managed into his phone, immediately looking for a place to turn around.

"Nearly six *million* pounds, sir."

The DI sat bolt upright in his seat. "*Jesus*, Sarge."

"That's about right, I'd say. She was the only winner

last week." Harris had double-checked the numbers and then had two colleagues do the same, just to be sure.

"And she must have known about it by the time she was murdered," Graham offered.

"I'd go further than that, sir," Harris said. "I'd say it goes some way to explaining our mysterious Sunday morning scream."

"Bloody hell. You're at the *Lavender*?"

"Yes, sir. Just arrived."

"Brilliant. Don't let anyone leave." Graham attached the magnetic blue light to his car's roof and began to bully his way through the evening traffic.

"Already on it, sir," Harris replied, grinning as he heard passion return to his boss's voice as the DI cursed at his fellow motorists. "See you soon."

CHAPTER TWENTY-ONE

G RAHAM'S MIND WAS split animatedly between the evidence and the traffic. He ran through his thoughts again, as though delivering an oft-recited poem. In his mind, he tracked each suspect from a starting point on Sunday, all the way through to the moment of the murder, and after. As he did so, new thoughts began to crystalize. It was as though he'd downed a pot of energizing tea, but this was simply his investigative mind at work, driven by the frustrations of the case, the urgent need to take *control* of something, and the raw excitement of doing so at ninety miles an hour with his blue lights blazing.

Even if he were wrong, even if he'd make a fool of himself in the attempt, he would gather the whole bunch of them together at the *Lavender* and have it out. Put everything in the open. Show them that he had the measure of this case, that he could still "pull a Dave Graham" when the moment called for it.

Graham's car was very fortunate to arrive at the *Lavender* without serious damage. Flashing blue lights or no, he'd taken extraordinary risks while crossing junctions against the signal and jinking around slower cars which, on this occasion, meant everyone else on the road. After thirty-five minutes' hectic thought and speeding, Graham swerved into the hotel's beautifully kept driveway, sending a cloud of gravel spinning into Amelia's perfect flower beds.

"Sergeant Harris?" Graham called as he burst through the door.

"Present and correct, sir," the big sergeant replied, appearing from the dining room. He leaned in closer. "I don't know how much like the ending of a 1940s murder mystery you wanted this to be, but everyone's here. They're around the dining room table. Figured it was best, sir."

Graham peered through the doorway to see an anxious-looking Cliff and Amelia, Tim Lloyd, Doris Tisbury, and even old Sykes, sitting in perplexed silence. As Graham entered, his mind racing as though he'd just finished his third pot of tea, Cliff stood.

"DI Graham, I'm hoping there's a special reason for this," the *Lavender's* proprietor said. "We've tried our best to be helpful, but with the police coming and going like this, it will be very hard to rebuild our business."

Graham nodded with understanding. "Have a seat, Mr. Swansbourne. All shall be revealed."

Cliff was hardly satisfied. In the days since the tragedy, Amelia had noticed that her husband was becoming withdrawn and very concerned about their future. His long-cherished Mexico plan, seemingly coming closer, day-by-patient-day, was now seriously in question. How could they plan for a relaxed retirement when the world was getting to know their establishment as a "murder hotel?" Amelia had tried her best to see the bright side. They could theme the *Lavender* around the murder, she'd suggested half-seriously, bring in the morbidly curious at five-star rates.

"Have you found him?" Tim Lloyd asked next. "The murderer?"

Graham fixed him with a steady stare. "I may have, Mr. Lloyd. I ask you all for some patience while we bring this sad chapter to a close. I believe," he said, addressing the whole, rather unsettled group, "that we now have sufficient evidence to make an arrest. As you might know, what happens after that is down to our colleagues at the Crown Prosecution Service. They'll decide if we've got enough to secure a conviction. But I'm increasingly confident," Graham told them, then added, after meeting the gaze of each of them, "that we have." The atmosphere was tense.

Harris pondered as Graham paced, checking his notebooks one last time. *Bet we've got the bugger where we want him, and he's in this room. Or, someone here knows who did it.* The prospect of finding their killer electrified Harris. He was also dying to see Graham in action, back to his best, juggling evidence like the accomplished master he was. *Go get 'em, boss.*

CHAPTER TWENTY-TWO

"METHOD," GRAHAM BEGAN, the only person in the room on his feet, "motive," he added, checking the famed triumvirate off on his fingers, "and opportunity. We've been searching, Sergeant Harris and I, for a very particular combination of these three elusive elements." Harris sat near the door to prevent any ill-advised attempts at an escape from this anxious situation. It was about to become acutely uncomfortable for at least one of the participants. "Norah was young, beautiful," Graham said, and then added, "and, let's not deny it, *desirable.*" Harris watched the room's reactions, trying to read the flickers of eyelids, folding and unfolding limbs, tilts of the head.

"She had recently divorced and was in a fragile state after escaping a difficult and sometimes traumatic relationship." Graham turned to Tim, whose expression was dark and concerned. "As Mr. Lloyd well knows."

Tim misread this comment as an accusation of some sort. "I had nothing to do with..."

"Hold that thought, for the moment, if you would, sir," Graham told him. "I'm afraid I'm obliged by habit to do what my former sergeant used to call my 'speechy thing.' I think a lot better out loud. If you'll indulge me." It wasn't a request, but Lloyd nodded his assent, anyway.

"She was in a new relationship, apparently a happy, if casual one," Graham said, bringing another unwarranted nod from Lloyd. "She was planning a vacation, and to everyone we've spoken to who knew her, she seemed at her happiest in years."

He referred quickly to his notebook, more to ensure that he hadn't forgotten anything than to remind him what would come next. The evidence had already laid itself out in his mind with almost all of the connections firmly in place. It remained only to present his findings to those involved, judge their responses, listen to their defense, and name the killer.

"Mr. Sykes," Graham said, his voice raised to ensure the old man would hear. "Would you tell us all, once more, how you came across the driver you handed to my colleague, Mr. Stevens?"

Sykes started as though waking from a brief but deep sleep. "Eh?" he asked. "Oh, yes...in the bunker, it was, on the fairway. Bloody strange, I said to myself, to leave a perfectly good golf club under a foot of sand."

"And how did you come to see it, buried as it was?" Graham asked him.

"Well," Sykes said, thinking back. "I suppose it was jutting out of the sand just a bit. You know, enough for me to see there was something there."

Graham took a step toward the ancient groundskeeper who wore a green polo shirt from the nearby club. "Are you in the habit of patrolling the fairways, searching for buried murder weapons?"

"Beg pardon?" Sykes said. In these last few years, as his deafness took a greater hold, this pair of words was perhaps his most common response. Cliff patiently repeated the question for him.

"I walk the course, as I'm required to," Sykes replied defensively. "What of it?"

Harris saw that Graham had decided to address the least likely suspect first. He wondered why but knew better than to question DI Graham's methods. "You wouldn't be the first person," Graham informed him, "to present important evidence to the police in order to deflect suspicion."

Sykes listened intently, his head cocked to one side. He chewed on Graham's comment for a moment. Then he said, "You know, I'm flattered, young man."

The DI had hardly expected this. "Flattered, Mr. Sykes?"

The old man chuckled to himself. "I've been strolling around God's great earth since there were posters of Lord Kitchener on walls of London pubs demanding that we do our duty and fight the Germans in Flanders," he recalled. "I've taken lives, I don't mind admitting it. But that was in Korea when I was even younger than you are now. I couldn't hit a golf ball even twenty yards these days. No," he chuckled again, "my fighting days are long past."

To Harris and the others, it seemed that Graham had gotten off on the wrong foot, making a frivolous accusation against a man who couldn't possibly have been involved in Norah's murder.

"Quite so," Graham said. "Forgive me, Mr. Sykes."

A wave of his ancient, leathery hand and another cackle of mirth let Graham know where he stood.

"I hope," Tim Lloyd officiously opined, "that you've brought something more concrete than *that*."

Harris scowled at the man, but Graham answered the question with grace. "Just getting warmed up, Mr. Lloyd. Perhaps," he said, "you might explain why you were banished to your room on the night Norah was murdered."

Tim almost stood, but the looming, guardian presence of Harris stopped him short. "Why?" Tim gasped. "Why should I do that?"

"To defend yourself. Come now, Mr. Lloyd. We're all adults here. Norah and yourself were involved in a physical relationship," Graham said, deliberately choosing a delicate phrasing. "Expectations would suggest that you and Norah were together on the night she was murdered but you insist that Norah turfed you out on that Sunday evening and you slept in your own room alone. Very odd, wouldn't you say?"

Tim folded his arms. "She was angry with me," he explained. "I said some stupid things. I regretted them, and I apologized, but she told me her ex-husband made her feel second-best and she wouldn't stand for feeling that way again."

"Mrs. Tisbury," Graham said. "You are our only source on these matters. Did Tim sleep in his room on Sunday night?"

Doris sat immobile, like a fleshy, imperturbable battle cruiser at anchor. "He did," she answered. "But Norah did not."

"You're certain?" Graham asked.

"Detective Inspector," she began in a tone which would brook not the least argument, "I've been making hotel beds since before your parents were courting. I'd know in an instant if they'd been slept in. Hers was just as I'd left it that morning."

CHAPTER TWENTY-THREE

G RAHAM LET THE room chew this over.

"Six," he finally said into the silence. "Nineteen. Twenty-two. Twenty-nine. Does this have a familiar ring to it?"

Sykes piped up. "That'll be the lottery, that will," he told them. "You need two more numbers."

"I do Mr. Sykes. Thirty-three and thirty-five. I'm sure there was a bonus ball too, but Norah didn't need it." He turned his head to look at Tim. "Did she, Mr. Lloyd?"

Scarlet-faced and looking as guilty as sin, Tim replied, "That's right."

"She was planning to celebrate the win, was she not?" Graham asked him. "Perhaps seeing if Cliff had a bottle of champagne behind the bar. Probably by engaging in activities designed to culminate in emitting the 'sounds of love', even." Graham looked pointedly at Cliff before turning back to Tim. "But you screwed it up, didn't you?"

Lloyd gave every impression of wanting to vanish into a hole in the floor. "It wasn't my greatest moment."

"Tell us what happened," Graham demanded. He

was visibly angry with Lloyd, as much for his deceit as for his careless mistreatment of Norah at her time of greatest joy.

"I put pressure on her," he said. "I've been wanting to start my own company. Investigative Reporters for Hire," he said. "I'd even picked out a logo I liked."

"Oh, for heaven's sake," Amelia scoffed.

"I needed money upfront, and all I said was...well, when Norah told me about the lottery win, I suggested that she could back the company, give me a solid start."

Graham pinched the bridge of his nose. "So, within moments of your being told of Norah's good fortune, you decided to bully her into getting your new company started."

"Like I said, not my best moment," Lloyd admitted.

"Why did you not mention Ms. Travis had won the lottery?"

"I should have. I thought it might implicate me. I thought it best to just stay right out of it. I'm sorry." Tim Lloyd had the expression of a bloodhound, morose and sheepish.

"You're a hapless twerp, Tim," Graham told him. "Nice enough, but bloody hapless."

Harris was surprised, but then Graham set up the finale Harris and the others had been waiting for. "But not a murderer."

Amelia turned to Graham and begged, "So, *who* on earth did it?"

"There's another piece of evidence which we have to consider," Graham told them. He was enjoying this role, both the meticulous combing-through of the evidence and the showmanship such a group interrogation demanded. "I received evidence from a reliable source that Tim and

Norah were anything *but* falling out on Sunday evening. Isn't that so, Mr. Swansbourne?"

Cliff gave an uncertain glance, first at his wife, and then at Harris. "Well, I was only reporting what I thought I heard."

"Naturally, sir, that's all any of us can do. But, wouldn't you say, that the 'sounds of love' you claimed to hear from the direction of the guest's rooms across the lawns are, not to put too fine a point on it, rather *distinctive?*"

He squirmed in his seat. "I'd say so."

"Not the kind of thing you're likely to misconstrue."

Cliff pursed his lips. "I really don't know what you're driving at."

Graham stopped. "Driving," he said. "Driving, yes. An interesting choice of word."

Cliff looked appealingly at Amelia. For the first time, Harris saw something genuinely of note in the wealth of body language around the table. *He's reaching out to her. He wants her help. He fears what Graham might say next.*

"I think you do know what I'm *driving* at, sir. Do you deny that you visited Norah in her room on Sunday afternoon or early evening?"

Harris was surprised yet again. This was entirely new. Was Graham just guessing now or playing a more subtle game?

"I don't remember," Cliff began.

"Did she, at any point, share with you the news that had been such a profound shock that very morning, that she'd cried out in gleeful surprise?"

Amelia's head snapped around. "I *knew* it! I *knew* I wasn't losing my marbles!"

Graham took a deep breath. "Here is someone who

needed money even more desperately than Tim. Someone friendly and respected enough to feel that he might simply be given a chunk of Norah's winnings for being a *nice chap*. Someone whom the police would never suspect."

CHAPTER TWENTY-FOUR

STILL CONFUSED, AMELIA turned to her husband. "Cliff, what's he talking about..." she began, but the truth dawned with a shuddering, horrid certainty. "Oh, my God." She grasped his hand as he stared mutely at the tablecloth. "Cliff, tell him he's wrong. There's no way..."

"Amelia..." Cliff whispered.

"I *won't* believe it! That lovely young woman. You *couldn't* have, Cliff..." Tears smeared Amelia's eye makeup. Around the table, as the truth became clear, stunned expressions turned to ones of uncomprehending horror as the group realized that this man whom they liked and respected could be capable of such a thing.

"I'm sorry..." Cliff managed, his voice tight. "It was slipping away from me. My dream, my plans for retirement." Amelia's hands were at her mouth as though suppressing a scream. "You said it too many times, Amelia. 'Next year,' or 'in a while.' And I've worked like a bloody slave for this place, years of day-in, day-out grind. I couldn't cope with it anymore, love."

"But..." Amelia stuttered, "*murder*, Cliff? Over something as meaningless as *money*?"

"Not money, escape. I needed her to share it with me," Cliff explained, almost *sotto voce*. "Just enough to get us loose from this place, get settled over there."

"Over *where*?" Sykes demanded. "What was so damned important you had to put everyone through all of *this*?"

Amelia said it for him. "Mexico. Retirement in the sunshine. It's what he's always wanted. And now..." she said before she stopped and dissolved into tears.

Clifford Swansbourne, his years now heavy upon him, stood with such aching slowness that Sergeant Harris felt no need to restrain him. There was not the least spark of escape or violence in the man. "I've done the most terrible thing," he confessed. "I saw what was happening to my life, to our dream. We deserve a little comfort later in life, and that's all I wanted. But I went about it as though I'm an evil man. But I'm not. I'm *really* not."

Amelia said nothing, despite Cliff's imploring eyes.

"I bumped into Norah in the hallway on that Sunday. She was going down to the garden to read, and she was just so happy, so jolly. I asked how she was doing, and she told me, whispered it, that she'd had this lottery win. Said she was keeping it a secret but she couldn't help but tell someone. She didn't say how much, but I knew it was more than a tenner, you know." A ghost of a smile played on Cliff's lips but nobody laughed.

"And then?" Graham prompted, writing continuously.

"Well, I congratulated her, as anyone would," Cliff said. "She went to read in the garden and I went back to the kitchen, but the thought wouldn't leave me. Just five percent, maybe, of her winnings would have set us up. Enough to invest in one of those high-interest accounts. We could have lived off the interest while someone else worried about this place and we enjoyed ourselves."

Sykes was glaring at him as though Cliff were the worst imaginable evil. "The devil's work," was all he muttered.

Cliff pressed on. They could all see his need to unburden himself, however painful it was. Amelia sat pale and dumbstruck in her seat. "Later, instead of heading to bed, I went to Norah's room. I saw Tim coming out and hid down the corridor until he'd gone. I never heard any 'sounds of love.' Foxes, more like. Anyhow, I walked up to Norah's door and she invited me in. She seemed a bit red-faced so I guessed something had happened with Tim. I—I somehow found the words to ask her about the money. I can't say she was receptive, I was virtually a stranger to her. I told her about working all those years, unable really to save much, but she just stared at me." He wiped his eyes with his sleeve. "Then she said something terrible."

Harris prompted him. "Go on, sir."

"She said, 'It's men like you, the takers, the scroungers, who make me sick.' That's what she said. She waved the ticket in front of me, taunting me."

None of the others needed to be told how Cliff felt, but he explained anyway. "Right then, I saw Mexico slipping away, receding over the horizon. I knew I'd never get there. I knew I'd die under a cloudy sky in some nursing home, and I just couldn't..."

"Oh, Cliff," Amelia moaned finally. She said nothing more.

"I keep a spare driver around for chasing animals—cats, foxes—out of the garden," Cliff explained. "I couldn't sleep, you know, mulling things over. Worrying about the future. And thinking to myself how other people always," he said, his fists bunching, "*always* get the luck."

Graham was nodding slowly. "You were angry with her. Angry at what she said, the injustice of it, and at her good fortune."

"I left but I couldn't shake her words from my mind. I still don't know how that driver got in my hands, and I can't remember walking back to her room." Cliff was shaking now. "I don't know why she opened the door again at that late hour. But..." He began to sob, the memory of his terrible crime overwhelming him. "I lost control," he explained through his tears. "Never in my life have I done anything like it. Not once before." Tears streamed down his lined face, and they knew that he was finished.

Graham had one more question he wanted answered. "Mr. Swansbourne, once it was over, why didn't you take the ticket as your own? You weren't to know that she'd told Mr. Lloyd about her win. She said she was planning to keep it a secret."

Cliff said nothing, his eyes downcast. But Amelia knew the answer. "I'd never have believed it, Detective Inspector," she explained. "Cliff had a problem, a long time ago, with gambling. He made me a promise then, and he's never broken it. Not in thirty years. If he'd presented that lottery ticket as his own, it wouldn't have been credible. I'd have known in an instant something was up."

"Like he'd just murdered someone?" Tim Lloyd said bitterly. "Just goes to show, we never really know each other." Harris glared at him, and Lloyd fell silent.

"You were planning a sunny retirement, Mr. Swansbourne. But now," Graham said, completing the thought, "you will spend your last years behind bars."

Graham found Sergeant Harris at his shoulder. "Sir," Harris said to his boss, "would you mind?" Graham nodded and moved to allow Harris to clasp Cliff's arm. There was no resistance, not now. Cuffing the murderer's hands behind his back, Harris saw no reason to delay. "See you in the car, sir. Mrs. Swansbourne, it might be best," he said, leading Cliff to the door, "to call a lawyer."

Graham stood and tried to enjoy the moment as Harris guided Cliff to the car and put him in the back seat. There was a satisfaction; the sort of closure one might feel upon paying off a mortgage or completing a dissertation. But there was no surge of excitement, no urge to celebrate the victory. Content though he was to have gotten his man, Graham felt, in the final analysis, just too bloody sad.

EPILOGUE

CLIFF SWANSBOURNE WAS sentenced to fifteen years for the manslaughter of Norah Travis. He will be well over seventy before being considered for parole. He suffers from depression and during her monthly visits, his wife Amelia encourages him to tutor younger inmates in the prison's kitchens.

Amelia continues to run the *Lavender* with the help of Doris Tisbury. The gardens look a little less perfect and Amelia has advertised for a local chef to help in the kitchen so that she can attend to them more often. Amelia has no desire to retire and claims that she will work at the bed-and-breakfast "until I drop." Tim Lloyd never returned to the *Lavender Inn*.

Jimmy Travis was eventually arrested and sentenced to two years for drug dealing. He served six months and was monitored via an ankle bracelet on his release. He has not re-offended, but his parole officer has warned him to expect an ASBO (Anti-Social Behavior Order) if he doesn't mend his ways.

Shortly after Cliff Swansbourne's sentencing, Nikki Watkins found herself pregnant. She gave up smoking and when she gave birth to a healthy daughter named her Norah.

Detective Inspector Graham was offered and accepted a position he applied for on Jersey. Jersey is a Channel Island located just off the coast of Northern France in the English Channel. When queried by Sergeant Harris about the wisdom of moving to a sleepy, isolated community, Graham's response was to demur, saying, "I have the feeling that it's going to be just perfect." The offer came at just the right moment for the Detective Inspector. He received the job offer on the same day as his wife, Isabelle filed for divorce.

Sergeant Harris was sorry to see DI Graham leave the Met, but wished him well. Harris was reassigned to the Fraud Squad. He misses the action of CID but credits the regular hours with helping save his marriage to Judith.

Fiona did extremely well in her school exams, receiving top marks in all her subjects especially biology, chemistry, and mathematics. She is now at sixth form college. Her ambition is to attend university to study medicine. To that end, she spends her summers interning at various hospital pathology labs in London and the surrounding area.

Inspired by her sharp mind and ambition, Dr. Bert Hatfield kept in touch with Fiona and acted as her mentor. He continues to regale his assistant with questionable jokes and drink too much coffee. Revealing the secrets of the deceased holds as much appeal to him as it ever did.

AN INSPECTOR DAVID GRAHAM MYSTERY

USA Today Bestselling Author

THE CASE OF THE HIDDEN FLAME

ALISON GOLDEN Grace Dagnall

THE CASE OF THE HIDDEN FLAME

BOOK TWO

Published by Mesa Verde Publishing
P.O. Box 1002
San Carlos, CA 94070

Edited by
Marjorie Kramer

CHAPTER ONE

CONSTABLE JIM ROACH made sure that he wasn't being watched and then took a long moment to assess his appearance in the mirror. He knew that he would have only one chance to make a first impression, and he was determined to single himself out as a man of both neatness and integrity; someone who could be entrusted with the most challenging, perhaps even the most *dangerous* investigations. The new boss could well be his long-awaited passport to promotion. Roach might—the thought made his breath catch in his throat—*even* get to see a dead body for the first time. That was worth ensuring that his tie was straight, his uniform was spotless, his jacket buttons gleamed, and his hair was neatly in place.

There. Perfect. Roach grinned conspiratorially at the face in the mirror and returned to the tiny police station's reception desk, where he busied himself with unusual energy. "Shipshape and Bristol fashion," he muttered as he straightened the lobby chairs and then belatedly flipped over the calendar of fetching Jersey postcards from August to September. Behind the desk, there was a smattering of filing waiting for him, put off for weeks but accomplished in about six minutes once he put his mind to it. He slid a deck of cards into a desk drawer. "No solitaire this shift, Constable Roach," he admonished himself. "The new boss wouldn't like it."

He heard familiar footsteps strolling into the reception area from the small hallway beyond, where the "new boss" would have his office. There followed an even more familiar voice, its Cockney accent robustly unchanged despite six years on Jersey.

"Bloody hell, Jim." The man stopped and stared. "Are we trying to win a contest or something?"

"What's that, mate?" Roach asked from behind the flip-top reception desk.

"I've never seen the place so tidy," the burly police officer exclaimed. "Expecting company, are we?"

Barry "Bazza" Barnwell loved nothing more than needling his younger colleague, especially when Roach let slip his desire to get ahead in the Constabulary. Barnwell was older than Roach but he was as content as could be to remain what he called a "beat cop," while Roach had dreams of a sergeant's stripes and then much more. Scotland Yard. CID. Chasing down terrorists and drug runners and murderers. *That* was where the action was. Gorey Constabulary, pleasantly unchallenging as Barnwell found it, was merely a stepping stone for Constable Roach.

"It never hurts to put your best foot forward," Roach said, continuing to tidy stacks of paper behind the desk.

"What are you thinking, eh?" Barnwell asked, leaning on the desk. "Once Mister High And Mighty arrives, he'll second you to the bloody SAS or something? 'Our man in Tangiers' within a month, is it?'"

"Bazza," Roach replied wearily, polishing the much-abused desktop with a yellow duster. "You may be happy on this little island, but I've got aspirations."

"Have you, by God?" Barnwell chuckled. "Well, I'd see a doctor about that if I were you. Sounds painful. Not to mention a likely danger to yourself and others."

Roach ignored him, but there was little else to occupy them during this quiet, summer morning. Besides, Barnwell was having too much fun.

"I'm not sure you're cut out for armed police or the riot squad, you know," Barnwell chattered. "Chap like you? What is it now, a whole *five* arrests... And three of those were for tax evasion?"

This got Roach's goat. "There was that plonker on the beach who was trying to do things to that girl. Remember that, eh? Saved her *honor*, I did."

Barnwell laughed at the memory. "Oh yeah, first-rate police work, that was. She was only *there* because he'd already paid her fifty quid, you wazzack. And he was only *trying*," Barnwell added, "because he'd had a skin-full at the Lamb and Flag and could barely even...."

Saved by the phone. It was an old-fashioned ring—Roach had insisted—not one of those annoying, half-hearted tones that went *beep-beep* but a proper telephone *jangle*.

"Gorey Police, Constable Roach speaking," he said, ignoring Barnwell's descent toward the reception floor in a fit of his own giggles. "Yes, sir," Roach said crisply. "Understood, sir. We look forward to meeting you then, sir." He replaced the receiver.

"You forgot the 'three bags full, *sir*,'" Barnwell offered.

"Get yourself together, mate," Roach announced purposefully. "Our new overlord approaches."

"Who?" Barnwell asked, straightening his tie and biting off the remnants of his laughter.

"The new DI, you unmentionable so-and-so. And if you show me up, so help me...."

Roach became a whirlwind once more, carefully adjusting the time on the big wall clock, one which looked as though it had done a century's steady labor in a train station waiting room. Then, to Barnwell's endless amusement, Roach watered the plants, including the incongruous but pleasingly bushy shrub in the corner, before trundling through to the back offices.

The hallway led to the DI's new office. It had been hastily refurbished as soon as they had got word of the new appointment. Roach already knew it to be "shipshape." There was also a second office occupied by Sergeant Janice Harding. Janice was their immediate superior but given the regular antics of the two constables, she often felt more like a nanny or a middle school dinner lady.

"Sarge, he's on his way from the airport in a cab," Roach announced.

"I heard the phone five minutes ago, Roach," Sergeant Harding complained, standing suddenly. "What took you so long to tell me?"

Normally immune to any kind of fluster, it was both unique and amusing to see Janice sent into such a tizzy over this new arrival. Roach suspected that her interest was less in the possibility of career advancement and more in the new DI's reputation as a good-looking, old-fashioned charmer. There hadn't been a lot of luck with the men lately, Janice would concede, a point of particular concern given Jersey's limited supply of eligible bachelors. And, with Harding rapidly approaching her 'Big Three-Oh,' it was high time for that to change.

Janice brushed down her skirt and ignoring Roach's looming presence in her doorway, tidied her hair in the mirror.

"Well, Roach? Is the reception area looking..."

"Shipshape and Bristol fashion," Constable Roach reported proudly. "And his office is just how he asked for it."

"And what about Constable Barnwell?" she asked. Janice leaned close and whispered, "He hasn't been drinking, has he?"

"Not that I can tell," Jim whispered back.

"Good. We could all do without dealing with that nonsense, today of all days."

She shooed Roach out of the way and carried out her own inspection of their small police station. Roach shrugged as Janice found a number of things to improve— she straightened the framed map of Jersey on the main wall and the two portraits of previous police chiefs—and then he went to find Barnwell who was in the station's back room where they stored equipment and other items not required on a day-to-day basis.

"Remember what I said," Roach called out with all seriousness. "Professionalism and respect, you hear?"

"Loud and clear, Roachie," Barnwell quipped, hanging spare uniforms up in a neat line. "I'll make sure there's no getting off on the wrong foot."

Roach eyed him uncertainly. "You really want to be in here when he arrives? Or behind your desk where you belong?"

"I'll be wherever I happen to be, matey," was Barnwell's uncompromising reply.

CHAPTER TWO

AS LUCK WOULD have it, Roach was answering a phone call from a member of the public when the new Detective Inspector walked in. It was a relief for Roach not to have to *look* busy as he noted down the details of a stolen bicycle lifted during the night from a back garden shed a few miles away.

DI Graham carried a black suitcase in each hand and wore a smart, dark gray suit. Sergeant Harding was waiting for him. "Detective Inspector Graham, I'm so pleased to meet you and to welcome you to Gorey," she smiled. "I hope your flight was smooth and uneventful?"

Graham set down the suitcases with a sigh of relief and smiled back, extending his hand. "Very smooth, thank you, Sergeant."

"Oh, you can call me Janice," she said, twice as flirtatiously as she had planned and three times more than Graham would have preferred.

"And this must be Constable Roach?" he asked,

approaching the desk with his hand out, just as the tall, red-headed man was finishing his call.

"Pleasure to meet you, sir," Roach said, just as he'd practiced. He nearly curtsied but stopped himself just in time.

"Anything interesting?" Graham said, glancing at the phone.

"Stolen bike, out near the golf course. Not unusual for this time of year. I'll head over there in a moment and take a statement," Roach said. He was pleased with how he sounded. Professional, on top of things.

The station's only other permanent appointment appeared. Harding introduced him. Roach watched the new boss's demeanor as he took in the burly six-foot frame of Constable Barnwell with a curious interest. Was he looking for signs of drink? Roach wondered if that particular piece of intelligence had filtered up to London or not. If so, what did the top brass know about *him*? Was Graham here to ensure that a potential high-flyer was given every chance to prove himself? A golden future offered itself to Roach in those heady moments. Then it was back to earth.

"I'll take that statement," Janice told him rather curtly. "I can do it once I've dropped off DI Graham at the *White House Inn*."

There would be, Roach saw at once, absolutely no discussion on this point. Fifteen minutes alone in a car with their new arrival was apparently well worth the tedious grunt work of noting down this routine complaint.

"Very good, Sarge," Roach replied. "You'll enjoy the *White House Inn*, Detective Inspector. Nice place." He thought on for a second. "Roomy."

"I'm sure I will," David Graham told him, refusing a polite offer of help with his suitcases. He slid them into the trunk of the station's sole blue-and-white police car and, still fawning over him like an adolescent, Janice drove him along the coastal road toward his accommodation.

"You've arrived at just the *best* part of the year," Harding enthused. "The tourists can be a nightmare, but there never seems to be more than we can cope with," she said. "It will make a big change from London."

Graham was soaking up the scenery; the small, neat houses by the road, the farms with walking, fluffy clouds that must have been sheep, the pleasant mix of sultry summer warmth and upbeat, fun-loving energy that Jersey had become famous for. As they approached the cliffs on which the *White House Inn* perched, the green fields gave way to a sparkling blue ocean and the marina beyond that were festooned with pleasure craft of all sizes.

"Beautiful," Graham said. "Not a lot like London, you're right there, Sergeant Harding."

Tourists gathered in little knots, eating ice cream, deciding where to have a late lunch, sometimes popping into one of the local shops for supplies.

"The *White House Inn* is up there," Harding pointed. It was an imposing, solid building, aptly named. Its paintwork shone brilliantly in the early afternoon sunshine. It reminded Graham of a rural French chateau, uprooted and then plonked on this towering cliff, providing perhaps the most spectacular and restful views on the island.

"A little B&B would have done the trick, you know," Graham admitted.

"Oh, nonsense," Harding said, waving him away. "We

wanted you to feel welcome here. I'd be happy to help find you somewhere more permanent, but I'm sure you'll be comfortable at the *White House Inn* for the time being. Their tearoom has the best cakes on Jersey and..."

"There's a tearoom?" Graham interrupted, his curiosity instantly piqued.

"They have all those 'frou-frou' types of teas if you like that kind of thing." Harding chuckled. "Why?"

"Oh, nothing," Graham replied, biting down his enthusiasm. "Just good to know," he added with a slight smile.

The lobby boded well, high-ceilinged and tastefully decorated with flowered wallpaper, statues, and a venerable grandfather clock which thundered out the two o'clock chime just as he was checking in.

"Ah yes, Detective Inspector Graham," the clerk said, finding him quickly on the reception desk's tablet. "I've put you in one of our nicest rooms overlooking the marina."

"Splendid," Graham said. "Is the hotel busy at the moment?"

His black hair swept back by copious gel, the clerk reminded Graham of an extra from a pulp novel set during the Roaring Twenties. All that was missing was the pencil mustache and a quick blast of the Charleston.

"Almost full, I'm glad to say. Mostly long-termers," he said, and then explained further when he saw Graham's quizzical expression. "Retirees, sir, people who prefer to live more active independent lifestyles than those to be had living in one of the retirement homes here on the island. There's plenty to do," he said, handing Graham a brochure from behind the desk. "Sailing, swimming, windsurfing, fishing.... Enough to keep anyone out of trouble." The man winked.

"Trouble?" Graham said, quickly.

"Just my little joke, sir. Here's hoping you'll have a quiet stay on Jersey. We're an unspectacular bunch, I'm glad to say. Not too many gangsters here," he added, risking another "little joke."

"Splendid," Graham replied again as he scanned the brochure. "I'll unpack and then maybe try a pot of one of your famous teas."

"Best on the island, sir," the clerk said proudly, handing Graham his key. "I do hope you enjoy your stay." The man tapped his tablet a few times and scuttled over to welcome a trio of tired-looking Germans who were sweating profusely with the weight of three truly gigantic suitcases.

A well-traveled and rather sophisticated man despite his rustic Yorkshire roots, Graham was not easily impressed by hotel rooms, having seen many. However, his room at the *White House Inn* was large with a comfortable bed and wonderfully appointed. It boasted views of the ocean, the marina, and Gorey beach that were breathtaking. Graham opened the windows wide and took three long, deep breaths of cleansing sea air.

"Entirely adequate," he mused to himself before heading down to the tea room in the hopes of a delicate Assam or Darjeeling. "Yes, indeed. This will do nicely."

CHAPTER THREE

NEARLY ONE HUNDRED feet below, a tall figure of purposeful—one might say *military*—bearing was striding down the beach on his afternoon walk. Colonel Graves, a man whose retention of his army title was not simply an affectation but also a statement of his values, brought down his tall cane into the sand with a mechanical precision that in its very rhythm pleased him greatly. It was important to maintain one's routines, he'd always felt. Especially during retirement, when one was apt, in the absence of care and discipline, to become addled and flabby, two things which were anathema to the seventy-year-old ex-officer.

In an open-collared, eggshell-blue shirt, and pressed khaki shorts, Colonel Graves was every inch the self-exiled retiree, enjoying the sunshine and spending his hard-earned savings. For him, a life of service had left little time for family or even courting. There had been women, of course, but none who had wanted to stick by the kind of chap who would jet off to war every few years, returning each time a little more cynical, a little less certain of his belief in the fundamental goodness of humanity, each time somehow *older* than before. He had survived the Argentine fighter bombers strafing his ship in the Falklands, the best efforts of Saddam Hussein's Republican Guard, and six months among the Taliban of Helmand before something in him had simply said *stop*. And so, to Jersey, where he busied himself keeping in shape, visiting the old German fortifications from World War II, and keeping an eye out for Miss Right.

Or, he chuckled—hang it all, we only live once—*Mrs.* Right.

It was his attentiveness, which let not a detail pass by, which brought him a discovery both heartbreaking and, even for a military man, unbearably gruesome.

Just where the beach met the sea wall the sand swelled up into a mini dune, perhaps four feet high, studded with tufts of grass and a discarded soda bottle, Graves noted with distaste. But then there was something else, and it attracted his eye because it absolutely *did not belong*.

It was a dainty, pale, human hand.

"Well, what in the blazes...?" he muttered darkly.

His first thought, given the location, was that this might be someone washed onto the beach from the ocean. An unfortunate migrant perhaps, dead from drowning or exposure and deposited here at high tide. This would hardly be his first encounter with a corpse, but a quiet beach on this idyllic little island was the last place he'd expect to see one. He frowned and slowly approached the slight rise of the dune, peering at the hand as if it might transform into something innocuous, and this strange moment might then be discarded as no more than a reason to visit the eye doctor.

Colonel Graves kneeled by the dune and carefully smoothed away a little of the sand that covered what was the almost translucent skin of an inanimate forearm. On closer inspection, the Colonel knew at once that this was no washed-up asylum seeker. Nor was this some prank, kids burying their mother in the sand and then forgetting about her as ice cream and soda beckoned.

There was a silver bracelet, rather expensive, which shone brightly now in the sun. And it was instantly familiar.

"Oh, no," Graves shuddered. "Oh, good *heavens*, no..."

"Gorey Constabulary, Constable Barnwell speaking." Barnwell's bright and cheerful manner contrasted markedly with the tone of this caller, only the third of the day. It was the sound of a man still struggling to bring his emotions under control despite decades of practice.

"Yes, I'm...erm...This is Colonel George Graves, and I'm calling from the beach, just opposite the pier and about ten yards west of the stone stairs that lead down from the *White House Inn*," the caller said. Barnwell, struck by the Colonel's precision, began making notes at once. "Yes, sir?"

Graves took a breath. "There's...Well, a *body* here."

Barnwell's eyebrows shot up. He gesticulated toward the office where Roach was filling out a report. "*Get in here!*" he mouthed.

"I see, sir," Barnwell said into the phone, bringing his

most professional and sober tone. "Have you checked for signs of life?"

"Yes, and I'm afraid there are none," Graves said soberly. "No pulse. And...Well, I believe I may *know* her, you see."

Barnwell's bushy black eyebrows were aloft once again. Just for a second, Barnwell felt that he might be about to hear a man confess to murder. His heart raced.

"Are you able to identify the deceased, sir?"

Graves cleared his throat and bit back the urge to unleash some of the emotions he was feeling. It wasn't *fair*. They'd met only a few months earlier, just after Graves arrived on Jersey.

"I believe it's Dr. Sylvia Norquist. She's a resident at the *White House Inn*. I have..." he began, fighting back his first tears in many years, "I have no idea how she came to be here."

No confession, then, Barnwell noted. His shoulders slumped.

"Well, sir. You've done the right thing. And I'm sorry for your trouble. As it happens," he said, one hand aloft and circling in his continuing efforts to alert Constable Roach's, "our new Detective Inspector has just checked into the *White House Inn*. I'll let him know what's happened and ask him to join you immediately."

"Do I need to do anything?" Graves wanted to know. "Call her family?"

"Let's wait until there's a formal identification. Would you stay where you are for the moment? Detective Inspector Graham will be with you shortly."

"Of course," Graves said. He squatted uncomfortably by the dune, part of him needing to hold the small, ash-white hand, another repelled by it, and yet another stunned at the continued, harsh *unreasonableness* of the world.

"Oh, my darling," he whispered, a single tear finally rolling down his face. "My darling girl. Whatever happened?"

CHAPTER FOUR

DI DAVID GRAHAM found Graves sitting on the sand a little away from the site of the body. The elderly man looked shattered, ashen, old beyond his years.

"Colonel Graves?"

Graves stood and extended a hand, more by habit than any impulse to be friendly. "At your service."

"I'm truly sorry, sir. I understand that you knew her?" It was always troublesome, Graham found, to select the most appropriate words in these situations. Referring to the deceased in the past tense tended to reinforce the unrelenting reality of the loss, but discussing the victim in the present seemed strange, uncomprehending, a form of denial.

"Quite well. We were..." It took all the military man's training to keep his composure. "I was going to ask her to marry me, you see." Colonel Graves' gaze became distant, his jaw muscles tensing rhythmically as he began to contend with the pain of his grief, with the lost promise of happiness so brutally snatched from him.

Graham brought out his notebook and began making notes. "And when did you last see Dr. Norquist, sir?"

Graves thought for a moment. "We had dinner two nights ago at a restaurant by the marina. She was in excellent spirits, full of life," he said, with significant pain. "We are both residents at the *White House Inn*," he explained further.

"But you hadn't proposed yet?" Graham asked as sensitively as he could.

"No," Graves said, shaking his head sadly. "Should have taken my chance, eh, Detective Inspector?" Graves felt the need to sit down again, his legs unsteady, his balance betraying him. "Oh, *God*, the poor girl..."

Graham brought out his phone, turning away from Graves to mask his words amid the sounds of waves.

"Barnwell? Yes, I'm here with Colonel Graves. I need an ambulance—discreetly, Barnwell, let's not make a fuss if we can help it...and the pathologist.....Good man. Quick as you can. And send Harding to secure a room at the *White House Inn*. Sylvia Norquist."

Graham took a moment to spell the name. He turned to see Graves staring inconsolably along the sandy beach then spoke into the phone once again.

"That's it for now, Barnwell."

Two volunteer Community Support Officers in their reflective yellow tunics kept back a small crowd as Dr. Marcus Tomlinson and his assistant delicately brushed sufficient sand from the body to carry out their initial investigation. Tomlinson was a forty-year veteran of such scenes. A pathologist since shortly after qualifying as a doctor, he was thorough and perceptive. Little escaped him. He took Graham to the shoreline so they could speak without being overheard.

"The time of death will be difficult to determine. The sand, sea, and salty air all combine to mess with the state of the body." Tomlinson was apologetic.

"Can you give me a clue?"

"My best guess is sometime in the last eighteen hours. I can't be more accurate than that, I'm afraid."

"Hmm." Graham was surprised. "So she could have ended up here in the middle of the night, or she may have keeled over at midday on a busy beach?" he said, thinking out loud. "And anything in between."

"Admittedly," Tomlinson added, "she was felled on one of its quietest stretches." They both glanced around and noted the secluded nature of the spot, beneath the steps but away from the broader, more popular stretch of sand. "I'll know more once we complete toxicology screens and the autopsy," Tomlinson told Graham, "but for the moment we can't rule out foul play."

"Oh?" Graham said. The complexity of this case ballooned before his eyes.

"She's in her sixties, and according to the Colonel, in robust health apart from needing a double hip replacement. Although you hear the uninitiated say it often enough," Tomlinson warned, "people generally don't simply keel over and die unexpectedly. After four decades in this business, I've become a firm believer in cause and effect. Plus, she was buried. It's windy today but not so much that it would have whipped up sand to that extent."

"So you think," Graham asked, his voice deliberately low despite the waves crashing a few feet away, "she was murdered?"

Tomlinson shrugged. "Like I say, no way of knowing until the postmortem is in." The pathologist shrugged and closed his notebook. Like Graham, he was a paper-and-pen man. "Standing here, right now, I'd bet fifty guineas and dinner at the *Bangkok Palace* that Dr. Norquist met her end neither by her own hand nor by natural causes."

DI Graham cursed colorfully under his breath. "You know I've only been here five minutes?" he mused aloud.

"And we haven't had a murder here since the Newall Brothers axed their parents for their inheritance money, back when you were in college," the older man replied. He gave Graham a comradely pat on the back. "Well, DI Graham, welcome to the Bailiwick of Jersey."

CHAPTER FIVE

RS. MARJORIE TAYLOR, the matronly owner of the *White House Inn*, was caught between moments of great anxiety, genuine grief, and her wish to be as useful to the police as possible. She couldn't believe that a refined, gracious lady like Sylvia Norquist—a respected oncologist and a pillar of their close-knit community—could have been taken from them so suddenly. So *terribly*. Why, she had eaten lunch just a couple of hours ago! But being the good citizen and innkeeper that she was, Mrs. Taylor worked to find a balance between helping the police and carrying out much-needed rumor control, lest her guests suddenly checked out *en masse* in a fit of panic and ruin her summer season.

"We'll aim to cause as little disruption as possible," DI Graham informed her during a short meeting in her office just off the hotel's lobby. "But it's important that no one except the police enter her room. We can do without 'Police Caution' tape everywhere," he assured her, "but we must be thorough."

"I appreciate your discretion," Marjorie said. "This is just so...*awful.*"

It was the same word everyone seemed to use on first learning the sad news. "Too *awful,*" one said. "Simply *awful,*" commented another. The only person who had said no such thing was Constable Roach, who saw not just a silver lining to this cloud, but also a cloud that was laden with gold. Career-making gold, at that. He could barely believe his luck. He was involved in a *murder* investigation.

Sylvia's was a corner room on the third floor which meant, to Marjorie Taylor's relief, that the police could gather evidence without disturbing the rest of the hotel. Still, the sight of blue uniforms caused some flutters, and the spreading news brought a tense, worried atmosphere to the place. Marjorie told the tearoom staff to waive everyone's checks for the rest of the day and the bar staff to do the same in the evening. It was the least she could do, she told herself.

Dr. Norquist's room was neat almost to the point of obsession.

"No signs of a struggle," concluded Constable Roach almost as soon as he entered the room.

Sergeant Harding elbowed aside him. DI Graham followed her.

"Thanks, Sherlock," she whispered with heavy sarcasm. "Once you're finished here, you can get back to finding Jack the Ripper. For the moment, just watch the stairs like I told you to. And keep Mrs. Taylor company. She's a bit jittery with all that's going on."

"Yes, ma'am. No one's to come up without your say-so," Roach replied crisply, hiding his hurt feelings at her tone. Referring to his boss as "ma'am" was for Graham's

benefit. She was "Janice" or "Sarge" customarily and for a few moments, Roach harbored some ill-will toward her. *When I release my tell-all book in a few years and become a crime-fighting media celebrity, you'll rue the day.*
...

"So Dr. Norquist was here at lunchtime," Graham said, looking about the room.

"Would seem like it, sir," Harding responded.

"And she ordered the fish," observed Graham. "Mostly uneaten, too." Atop the room's oak dresser was a gleaming, silver tray with a single plate, a small vase with a bright daisy, and silverware. Graham sniffed the food. "Chili, ginger, sea bass...no sign that the fish was off," he concluded.

Harding squeezed her hands into latex gloves and poked at the fish using Sylvia's fork, "If the fish had been rotten enough to poison her, wouldn't it have been obvious as she was eating it?"

"Yes, we can rule that out," Graham told her, writing the details in his notebook. "Mrs. Taylor?" he called out. "Do you know who brought Dr. Norquist's lunch today?"

Mrs. Taylor appeared around the corner of the doorway, the intensely curious Constable Roach hovered behind her.

"That would have been Marcella," she replied. "Lovely girl." Mrs. Taylor turned to Harding. "From Lisbon. She sets the tray outside the door and knocks. That's always been our policy."

"So she wouldn't have gone into the room. Would she have heard anything through the door?" Graham asked.

"We are not in the habit," Marjorie replied a little testily, "of listening at our guests' doors, Detective Inspector. Sylvia had a male friend, and one never knows what one might overhear. My guests are very private people. You know, I could think all day and all next year, and I still couldn't think of a single soul who might want to hurt that dear lady."

Graham finished his notes and slid his notebook back into his jacket pocket. "Well, I suspect *someone* did, Mrs. Taylor," Graham said soberly. "And I'm afraid," he added with a frown, "that they're right under our noses."

CHAPTER SIX

S ITTING RESOLUTELY UPRIGHT, staring out to sea from his table by the window, Colonel Graves ignored the pot of tea laid out for him by the concerned and sympathetic staff of the *White House Inn*. As Graham approached, Graves made to stand, but the detective waved him to stay in his seat.

"At ease, Colonel," Graham said but regretted the quip. This wasn't the moment for levity. Graham could see the Colonel had gathered himself a little since their encounter on the beach, but both men knew that Graves would carry the emotional weight of his terrible discovery for the rest of his life.

"Have you found anything new, Detective Inspector?" Graves asked. He still looked ashen and careworn, but his straight back and clipped diction gave him a stoical air, like that of a man forced to deal with the worst kind of news but doing so with grace and determination.

One of the tearoom's more experienced waitresses, the aforementioned Marcella from Portugal approached with her notepad, and Graham couldn't help ordering a pot of Fujian jasmine.

"Nothing concrete," he admitted to Graves. "At this stage, it's more a case of eliminating lines of inquiry. We know that Sylvia was not poisoned by her lunch, but that's about all so far."

"Poison?" Graves spoke the word in a hushed, stunned tone. "So this was deliberate?"

Treading carefully, Graham said, "We mustn't jump to conclusions, certainly not as early as this." Marcella returned with the tea tray, and Graham poured his tea with an almost ritualistic fluency of movement. "I'm waiting to hear back from the pathologist. I'm sorry," he said, meeting the older man's gaze. "This must be just awful."

Colonel Graves sighed. "Did you serve, Detective Inspector? I've seen things so dreadful I've sworn never to speak of them to anyone. Colonel Graves leaned forward, steepling his hands on the tabletop. "Things happen to your friends, to your enemies, that humans should never do to one another. But," he said, straightening his back once more, "that's war. One does what is necessary. But Sylvia was not at war, Detective Inspector. She never hurt a soul. It is *that* which bothers me the most."

Graham noted the word—*bothers*. It wasn't what the Colonel meant, but it suited a man trained in the art of self-control, well-practiced in keeping hidden that which should not become public. Graham felt a genuine sympathy for him, which was why he resented the necessity of eliminating Graves from the inquiry.

"Colonel, I'm sorry to ask this, but..."

"Where was I at lunchtime today?" Graves finished for him.

"As I say, I'm sorry…"

"You're following procedure, Detective Inspector. I'd have been surprised if you hadn't asked me. Not a little disappointed, too."

"Really?" Graham asked, lifting the teacup sufficiently to enjoy the floral waft of jasmine floating off his tea.

"Sylvia was to be my wife," Graves said solemnly. "At least, if she had accepted my proposal she would have become so. And I expected her to, you know." He was nostalgic once again. "I'm not the finest catch in the ocean, I'm sure of that, but we would have been *happy* together. That's all any of us wants, isn't it?"

Graham felt reassured by this more philosophical side to the Colonel but was aware that Graves had yet to answer his question. "So, at lunchtime?" he said. "Just for my notes."

"I was on the phone to my real estate broker in London for about an hour, all told. Bloody tedious stuff but it had to be done. I'm trying to make a few quid over in the States with quick house renovations in desirable areas. Buy them, do them up, sell them on, you know. Here," he said, handing Graham his cell phone. "You can check the call history. No warrant required," he added.

"That won't be necessary," Graham said, privately resolved that he was not in the company of a killer. There had been a flash of concern just after Graves had admitted being of a mind to propose to Sylvia. The Colonel would hardly have been the first man to react badly to a refusal, but there was nothing in his behavior to suggest that he was anything other than sadly and unfortunately bereaved.

"She wanted to come on my afternoon strolls," Graves

continued. "I always head down the beach for a mile or two after lunch. But Sylvia suffered terribly with her hips."

Graham was writing once more. "Was it very serious?" he asked.

"Serious enough that she could barely have gone down the steps to the beach unaided," he said. "Stairs were tremendously painful for her. Without the elevator, she'd have been restricted to the ground floor of this place," he explained, looking around the *White House Inn's* tearoom.

At once, Graham began wondering how Sylvia Norquist had managed the stairs down to the beach. *Had she been in the company of someone? Perhaps a murderer? And why would she submit to going on such a painful walk?* Graham made another note and then slid the notebook home inside his jacket.

"Well, Colonel, if you think of anything which might help us, please do get in touch." Graham finished his cup and rose, extending his hand.

Graves did the same, his grip firm despite slightly unsteady legs. "I will." He leaned close. "You'll let me know, won't you? If you find who did this?"

"Of course," Graham said. "You'll be the first to know," he lied.

CHAPTER SEVEN

THE *WHITE HOUSE Inn's* lobby was mercifully clear of concerned guests, leaving Mrs. Taylor to continue telling Sergeant Harding and Constable Barnwell every last detail she could think of regarding her guests and their relationships with Sylvia Norquist. The police officers were developing a picture of a quiet but personable lady who was both respected and admired. Some of the guests had reported seeing Sylvia and Colonel Graves dining together some evenings, or taking a leisurely afternoon tea in the hotel. The couple was thought to be adorable.

Mrs. Taylor put it as only she could. "Two lonely people, providing comfort and company for each other in their later years. It was enough to warm the heart."

Alongside the tales of a blossoming romance, though, were the very beginnings of what Detective Inspector Graham knew might become *leads*. He desperately needed information that might bring this case out of what was the least welcome type for a detective; one where the victim was found alone, there was little forensic evidence, no witnesses, and no immediate suspects or motives. Graham just *hated* those, but he turned the emotion into a determination to gather more evidence, interview more people, and pester the lab until they came up with something more concrete than Tomlinson's educated guesswork.

"Tell me about the Pilkingtons," he said, reading the name from Sergeant Harding's list of those to be interviewed. "It says here that they knew Dr. Norquist."

"Oh yes," Mrs. Taylor said at once. She was proving to be quite the store of gossip, which made her an ideal source of information in a case like this. "They've been friends for a long time. I could be wrong," she said cautiously, "but I believe Mr. Pilkington was under Dr. Norquist for a time."

Barnwell's artless, barely constrained guffaw caused a rapid re-phrasing from Mrs. Taylor. "I mean, he was her *patient*," she clarified, red-faced. "Cancer, I think." She swatted Barnwell's uniformed arm in chuckling rebuke.

Graham paid the bawdy comedy no mind and pressed on. "I'd like to speak with them both. Are they here at the moment?"

Janice and Graham left Barnwell in the lobby and Mrs. Taylor directed them to the Pilkington's room. Janice knocked on the door. A couple opened it. They were in their early sixties. Mrs. Pilkington was made up, her brunette hair set and sprayed.

"Mr. and Mrs. Pilkington, I'm sorry to disturb you, but I'm sure you've heard..." The couple waved DI Graham and Sergeant Harding into the room. They took a corner armchair and the desk's leather-bound seat. Graham could see at once that the Pilkingtons were an affluent, sophisticated couple. Their room was as neat as Sylvia's had been, but their belongings spoke of money; a handmade pashmina scarf, a Gucci purse, and Mr. Pilkington stood in an immaculate Savile Row suit.

The gaunt, long-faced Pilkington said nothing, content to let his wife do the talking. "Sylvia was our doctor, back in London." Mrs. Pilkington offered. She sat on the edge of the bed, her Gucci bag clasped tightly as though one of these recent arrivals might make off with it. "She cured Nigel's cancer. Amazing doctor," she gushed, as one might describe a new hairdresser whom you simply *had* to try.

"Were you aware," Harding asked, "that she was here on Jersey? You know, before you arrived?"

Anne Pilkington shook her head. "Such a coincidence bumping into her here."

But then it was Nigel's voice they heard, low and sad. "I knew. Dr. Norquist is the reason I encouraged Anne to move here for the summer. I've been seeing her, you see."

Mrs. Pilkington twisted suddenly to face her husband. "Nigel? Why didn't you...I mean...How could you...?"

Entirely unwilling to bear witness to an impromptu domestic hissy-fit, Graham interrupted. "When, Mr. Pilkington?"

"The first time was about six weeks ago," he said, a little more confident now, as though the presence of police officers might protect him from his wife's sudden and growing anger. "I met her in the village," he smiled thinly, before catching Anne's furious expression and wilting slightly.

"And you spent some time together?" Sergeant Harding asked delicately. It relieved Graham to hear that her tone carried no insinuation, but this did nothing to calm Mrs. Pilkington, whose assumptions of her husband's infidelity were as plain as the lettering on her Gucci bag.

"We caught up, as old friends do," he explained, his face innocent. Graham wondered why his wife had rushed to assumptions and anger and concluded that, as in most long marriages, there were undercurrents that others could never know. Secrets that might never see the light of day, lest the delicate house of cards came crashing down. "I saw her on...what would it be," he searched his memory, "the end of last week. We had coffee in the village."

"You said you were going to the *post office* to send a card to Margaret after her dog died!" Anne Pilkington exclaimed in a furious roar. Graham judged her reaction commensurate with her husband having confessed to killing the dog during a deranged Satanic ritual, rather than anything as benign as having coffee with his old doctor. "Why?" she demanded, tears starting to fall.

As the couple confronted each other in stony, accusatory silence, Sergeant Harding caught Graham's eye and mouthed, *"What the heck?"*

Graham shrugged with genuine confusion. *These older couples*, he mused to himself. His parents were the same. Forty-one years of marriage and they could still get each other riled up over the simplest thing.

But this exchange between the long-married couple threatened to derail their interview and might limit how much they learned about Sylvia's comings and goings. Graham stepped in.

"Mrs. Pilkington, we're trying to build a picture of Sylvia's habits and relationships. At the moment, her only romance seems to have been with Colonel Graves, and they were close to becoming engaged." He hoped this news might assuage Anne Pilkington's coursing anger.

"Seems to have been?" she demanded, almost shrieking at the detective.

"Anne, listen," Nigel said in the plaintive tone of a man entirely disinterested in a protracted argument with his hysterical wife. "I needed her advice. It's...well, I should have told you months ago, but..."

Anne's expression changed as quickly as a cloud covers the sun. "Nigel? What is it, darling? *Tell* me."

Nigel glanced awkwardly at the two officers, and Graham was halfway to standing before Nigel spoke again. "The cancer. It's back. And it's bad."

Jesus. Graham watched the two embrace and console one another for an awkward minute before it was clear they would learn nothing more until the couple gathered themselves.

"We'll be going," Harding breathed. "Thank you for your time, and...we're sorry for your troubles. Both of you."

Graham nodded in comradely approval, and they took their leave, closing the door very quietly behind them. "Conclusions, Sergeant Harding?" Graham asked as they headed down the hallway toward the stairs.

"Don't marry a crazy, suspicious person," she said.

"Very droll. Do you think Mrs. Pilkington was genuine? I mean," he said, stopping at the top of the stairs, "was she learning of the renewed acquaintance between Sylvia and her husband for the first time?"

Harding shrugged. "It sounded pretty convincing to me, sir. If that was acting, it deserved an Oscar. Why do you ask?"

Graham's notebook was out once more. "Because if she had suspicions about an affair between the two, she might have murdered Sylvia to bring an end to it."

"But that means that if what he says is true, and he was only meeting her for advice, she murdered Dr. Norquist for nothing."

"Yes."

"Blimey," Janice said, staring down the stairway as she processed this information.

While she did so, Graham made a string of notes in his distinctive, cursive handwriting, a legacy of strict schooling, and a passion for neatness. His pen only stopped when they spotted Marcella down the hallway.

CHAPTER EIGHT

"**W**OULD YOU TELL me whose room this is?" Graham asked Marcella as she stopped beside a door to a guest's room. The diminutive woman, as young as twenty, Graham guessed, picked up a lunch tray set in front of the door.

"Alice," she said at first, but then corrected herself. "Miss Swift." Marcella was visibly uncomfortable. "I bring her lunch every day," she said, her Portuguese accent drawing out the vowel sound until the word was closer to 'launch'. "Is a problem?"

"No, no," Graham assured her. "Carry on as normal, please."

Marcella seemed grateful to be excused but more due to the challenges of communicating with the police than any nefarious involvement in the day's events. Graham knocked on the door with three swift taps.

"Marcella?" came a voice from inside.

"No, it's Jersey Police, Miss Swift. May we have a word?" Sergeant Harding called out.

"The police?" Alice said, blinking, as she opened the

door. Then her tone softened, and her face fell. "Oh, I suppose you're here about that poor woman?"

"Yes, I'm afraid so," Graham told her.

"Terrible thing. Come in," Alice said, beckoning the pair inside. Graham saw that her room was rather more austere than the Pilkington's. *Though the same could be said of Harrods.* A wooden contraption dominated the room. He took a moment to identify what it was.

"You're a weaver," Graham finally said, admiring Alice's work. "How wonderful. Is it a hobby or your profession?"

Alice returned to the wooden stool by her loom but turned to face the two officers. "A little of both, I'd say," Alice replied. Approaching forty, she was far from unattractive but there was something stand-offish about her character which made him slightly suspicious. "I'm planning on opening my own shop in London," she added.

"Wonderful!" Graham said again. Inwardly, he wondered at the economic sense of such a venture, but when someone is driven by a will to accomplish something, they often find a way. Or learn an expensive lesson.

"Have you found out anything more about Sylv—, I mean, the victim?" This question was to Sergeant Harding. Janice had stepped back to allow Graham to question Ms. Swift. The sergeant had noticed that one of the advantages of his natural charm and authoritative manner was that female witnesses were more forthcoming.

"Well, the investigation has just begun," Harding told her. "We're only getting started."

Alice brushed hair out of her eyes and regarded Graham again. "Surely you can't believe that one of the guests did this?" she said.

Something clicked in Graham's mind. "Did *what*?" he asked.

"I mean..." Alice began. "She was only in her sixties, wasn't she? That's no age, these days. Unlikely to have been natural causes, though you never know, people do drop-dead sometimes for no good reason."

Graham was glancing around the room, taking in the spools of material, the neatly lined-up pots of dye and paint on the mantle, the smaller threads carefully wrapped around templates the size of business cards and stored in a basket, ordered by hue.

He thought back to Tomlinson's comment on the beach. "In fact, unexpected deaths from natural causes hardly ever happen," he said, almost to himself. Alice watched him become distant for a few moments. Then, Graham remembered the lunch tray.

"Can I ask what you've eaten today, Miss Swift?"

Taken aback and squinting at the detective, Alice answered, "Well, I hardly think that has anything to do with it."

"Answer the question if you wouldn't mind, Miss Swift." Harding's gentle nudge was sufficient.

"Coconut chicken and rice," Alice said. "The chef has been adding some light, Asian-themed lunches to the menu. It was very nice. Not too spicy."

Even before she'd finished her description of the meal, Graham was focusing on the tapestry which was in a half-completed state on Alice's loom. The bright azure blue of the ocean caught his eye first, then two sailboats, racing neck and neck, their sails billowing. On the shore beyond, onlookers waved cheerily under a sky dotted with wispy clouds.

"This is terrific," he said.

Alice shone with pride. "It's a wedding gift for the son of a friend. He's marrying a landlubber from Sevenoaks but swears he'll make a sailor of her."

"Very imaginative," Graham continued appreciatively, drawing a raised eyebrow from Harding. Utilizing one's charm to encourage a reluctant witness was one thing, but this was far closer to simple flirting. She felt a stab of jealousy. Alice was smart and creative, probably well-traveled too, and what man would fail to be impressed by those gorgeous, carefree curls, and the way her flowing, hippy-dippy dress stretched tight across her chest like a canvas on a frame, or indeed, the threads on her loom.

"Sergeant, I think we're done here," Graham told her. "Thank you for your time, Miss Swift."

The artist stood and shook Graham's hand, settling for a cute wave to Sergeant Harding. Janice faked a smile and tried to set aside her grumpy thoughts. *Try working for a living, sweetheart. Sewing pretty pictures of boats is hardly that. A shop in London...? Give me a break.*

Outside, Graham caught Janice's downcast expression. "A suspect?" he asked.

It wasn't what Harding had expected. "Why should she be?" They descended the stairs together. "She barely seemed to know Sylvia, and I can't see a motive there. Unless Sylvia insulted one of her stitch-pictures."

"Tapestries," Graham corrected her. "And she's got genuine talent."

"A pair of them, by all accounts," Harding grumbled, *sotto voce.*

CHAPTER NINE

A DAPPER, CHEERFUL Dr. Tomlinson strode into the police station's reception area, slid a manila folder onto the desk in front of Constable Barnwell, and tapped it twice with his finger. "Tell your new boss," the elderly pathologist said proudly, "that he owes me dinner at the *Bangkok Palace*."

The toxicology screen had been returned in record time, partly at DI Graham's urging but mostly because Tomlinson was genuinely curious to know the truth. Murders were not exactly a dime a dozen on Jersey. In his time as pathologist here, he'd dealt with only five, and that record went back to the early 1980s. There had been suicides, of course, some of which had initially raised suspicions of foul play, but the evidence had quickly confirmed otherwise. In most cases, Tomlinson was forced to submit the sad, dreary ruling that another ambitious stockbroker had bitten off more than he could chew and ended his days in the harbor or a luxury apartment in the company of a bottle of scotch and some pills. It was a lot more CSI-Jersey than CSI-*New* Jersey, all in all.

"Okay, then. Let's have it." Graham waved Tomlinson to a seat in his office, and the older man closed the door. The DI had returned to the station from the *White House Inn* to review what they'd discovered so far. He was enjoying the day's second pot of tea, its invigorating and slightly floral scents lending a welcome elegance to his bare and unimpressive office.

"Asphyxia," Tomlinson enunciated. "It's the only thing I'm certain of at the moment."

Graham turned the report to face him and scanned its conclusions. "Before she was buried in the sand, or after?"

"Before," Tomlinson confirmed. "No sign of sand in her airways. You'd have expected that," he explained, "if she were alive, even if she were unconscious when buried."

Unlike most police officers or even members of the public, Graham knew that asphyxia was a *mode* of dying, not a *cause*. "So, what killed her?"

Tomlinson retrieved the report and took a seat, wincing as his old knees bent. "Well, it's relatively simple. It's all in the weight of the *lungs*, you see."

"Lungs?" Graham asked, reaching for his notebook.

"Heavy lungs show that the victim's heart went on beating for a time—perhaps as long as twenty minutes—after respiration ceased."

This was news to Graham. "That long?"

"Surprising isn't it, how determinedly the human spirit clings to life, even when all hope is gone and brain functions are damned near ceased? But, Sylvia's lungs were no heavier than yours or mine."

Graham put two and two together. "So, her heart stopped at about the same time that she stopped breathing."

"Or even before," Tomlinson added.

"But why?"

"That's where you have me," the pathologist confessed. "Right now, I don't have a reason. Something caused her heart to stop, but otherwise, it was perfectly healthy."

"So what do you think happened?" Graham asked, curious to learn if the older, more experienced man had a theory.

"My view hasn't changed from when I saw her on the beach. I'd bet my last penny and all the others that Sylvia Norquist's death was no natural event. Like I said then, people rarely just keel over. Besides, if she quietly died of natural causes in her hotel room, who in God's name would find the body and then drag it down some stairs to bury it in the sand?"

"So, it's murder," Graham breathed. "You're certain?"

"As Christmas. Dinner is on you, Detective Inspector."

Graham nodded. He wasn't sure if Tomlinson's findings were good news or bad. Part of him had been willing Sylvia Norquist's untimely demise to be the result of an odd manifestation of natural causes. That a murderer was lurking in the *White House Inn* was unsettling, especially given the paucity of apparent motives. At least, so far.

"What's your best guess for cause of death?" he asked, deliberately pressing Tomlinson.

"A poison," the pathologist said at once. "Something which causes the body to shut down, the heart and respiration to stop. But I can't be sure. Could we ask the local doctors if they've prescribed anything which might cause an overdose? The kind of thing which wouldn't show up on a toxicology screen?"

"It's a long shot," Graham countered. "Most of that stuff is tied up in patient confidentiality. It could be weeks before we get a warrant to search any doctor's records, even if we could identify the prescribing physician. And there must be dozens, even somewhere as small as Jersey."

"There are twenty-nine," Tomlinson replied crisply. "I know most of them. I could put the word around, you know, see if anything comes up."

"Like what?" Graham asked, returning the folder.

"Oh, you know, a 'special request' by a patient who presents themselves in the doctor's office without the appropriate symptoms, or one who seems to be faking it. They don't just hand out potentially fatal doses of prescription medication like candy, you know." Tomlinson returned the folder to his leather medic's satchel and crossed his legs.

"So, I'm assuming there was nothing untoward in Sylvia's lunch?" Graham asked.

"That fish," Tomlinson confirmed with a flourish, "had not even a passing acquaintance with toxic substances. The food at the *White House Inn* isn't exactly *cordon bleu,* but it needn't be *cordoned off,* either." Both men allowed themselves a quick chuckle at this dark humor.

"Now, what about her hip pain?" Graham asked.

Tomlinson frowned now. "Severe. Very painful. One look at her hip joints told me there's no way she would voluntarily have navigated a long, stone staircase unless there was George Clooney at the other end. And even then it would have been a monumental struggle."

"Was she on painkillers?"

"Nothing out of the ordinary," Tomlinson answered. "And certainly nothing in amounts that would kill her."

Graham changed tack. "What about the time of death? Were you able to narrow it down?"

"Sorry, old chap. The answer to that little mystery set sail with the tide. There were just too many confounding variables."

Graham sighed and thought aloud. "A woman poisoned by something she eats or drinks, doesn't report it or ask for help, and ends up down on the beach despite being half-crippled, where she's half-buried in the sand."

"It's a bugger, isn't it?" Tomlinson offered, standing to leave.

"Yes," Graham answered, distracted. "It most certainly is."

CHAPTER TEN

MRS. TAYLOR WAS at pains to point out just how desperately she wanted to help. "But if my paying customers see policemen sniffing around in the kitchen," she said with a worried frown, "they'll head straight for the restaurants in town and never eat here again. It's a *full third* of my income each year, that restaurant," she explained.

"Believe me, Mrs. Taylor," Graham told her, "we'll be as discreet as we can. Just being thorough, you know."

They were escorted to the kitchens as though being secreted to the den of a reclusive cult. Mrs. Taylor even stopped at each turn to check the hallway ahead and at one point, remarked that the "coast was clear." Sergeant Harding found the entire thing highly amusing but hid her giggles behind her uniform sleeve. Her new boss didn't seem to be a man for comedic trifles, nor was she keen to appear girlish and insensitive. Quite the reverse, in fact.

"I'll have the staff come back here to be interviewed," Mrs. Taylor announced as they reached the cool, dry storeroom behind the kitchens. "There are serving hatches that give out onto the dining room from the kitchen, but in here you won't be seen."

Graham recognized from the outset that he would have to indulge Mrs. Taylor's rather paranoid fixation on the delicate sensibilities of her guests. He would admit that seeing uniformed officers snooping around a kitchen was hardly a resounding advertisement for the *White House Inn's* culinary fare, but they were just doing their jobs.

Marcella was working in her late-afternoon role as a waitress and general kitchen helper, alongside five other staff members. Three were long-term employees, the others were seasonal. One had worked at the *White House Inn* for six summers in a row. "I like the island, and I like Mrs. Taylor," the young sous-chef told them. "How can you beat sunshine, low taxes, and have great beaches just down the steps?"

"How, indeed," Graham commented. "Do you keep records of the guests' breakfast orders, by any chance?"

"Oh, yeah," the chef replied. "We have to, in case there's a billing screw-up." He quickly found Sylvia's order and read it out as if ordering his staff to prepare it once more. "Muesli, the small fruit platter, toast and marmalade, a boiled egg, tea, and orange juice." He looked up once more. "We squeeze it ourselves, each morning. Absolutely magic."

Graham wrote everything down, as usual, the others waiting patiently while he inscribed the details. "And her lunch? Did you prepare that yourself?"

The sous-chef checked his order slips again, leafing through them. "She's in room 211, right?" He searched on. "Yeah, here she is. Erm...I was doing the vegetable quiche, actually. Her order would have gone to Santi, the other lunch chef. Good guy. His braised beef is the bomb." Then the young man noticed something else. "Hmm. This might be important."

Harding tilted her head to read the handwriting on the slip. "A glass of Chardonnay?" she asked. She turned the slip to show Graham, whose mind was quickly racing, aware that alcohol was as common a vector for poison as any other.

He looked the chef squarely in the eye. "Who exactly was responsible for the bar at lunchtime?"

Marcella was trembling within a minute of sitting down in the storeroom. "Please understand," Harding was telling her, "you've done nothing wrong. We just need to know about the wine you served to Sylvia Norquist. Tell us everything you can remember."

The slender Portuguese girl traced the events in her mind. "I received the order by phone and wrote everything down. I'm sorry for my handwriting," she said with a shy smile. "Then I told bar I wanted Chardonnay."

"Did they pour it straight away?" Graham asked, his pen hovering over the surface of the notepad in anticipation.

"I can't remember..." Marcella said at first. "There's always so much things happen. Is so busy and crazy during lunch."

"Take your time, and think back carefully," Sergeant Harding advised her.

Marcella's eyes went misty as she tried to replay every detail. "It was waiting on bar top, as normal," she said

after a moment. "I put it on tray with food, and I think...
yes, I walked upstairs because elevator busy."

Graham walked her through those few moments like
a hypnotist. "You walked to Sylvia's door...Did you knock
as normal?"

"Yes, of course," she said, hearing the sound in her
mind. "She maybe on phone. She said leave tray outside."

Sergeant Harding felt for the first time, the human
nature of this loss. A vivacious woman, well-liked and
romantically involved, taken from the world in a blink.
"And then?" she asked Marcella.

"I left tray and went on to next delivery. Little later,
maybe...hour or two?" she asked, "there was talk to
kitchen staff from Mrs. Taylor. She say we not deliver
anything else to 2 1 1 and stay away. I worry," she recalled.
"Mrs. Taylor never say anything like this before."

"And that's when you knew something was wrong?"
Graham asked her.

"Poor woman," Marcella sniffed. "I so sorry for her."

Sergeant Harding was as keen as her boss to keep the
interview on track. "What about the wine glass, Marcella?
What happened to that?"

The girl blinked a few times. "Glass?"

"Yes. It wasn't in the room," Graham told her. "No
sign of it."

"But...I deliver glass of wine with lunch tray,"
Marcella insisted. "Was not there?"

Both officers knew that no glass had been found, but
Graham felt the need to be absolutely sure. He couldn't
risk such a vital piece of evidence being overlooked. "Sergeant, would you ask the forensics team to make a special
effort to look for that glass?"

Harding left quietly, and Graham finished up the

interview on his own, hoping that being one-on-one with Marcella would neither scare her nor cause her to hide anything. "I need to know just one more thing. Who else had wine with lunch today?"

Marcella brightened. "Oh, is easy. I check bar receipts. They need to bill guest, so they always right." She left and returned thirty seconds later with a stack of slips similar to the restaurant orders the chef had so usefully kept. "Only one!" she reported, handing the slip to Graham.

"Thank you, Marcella. This really is very helpful." Graham took down a note: *Glass of wine, lunchtime. Room 219. Alice Swift.*

CHAPTER ELEVEN

"**N**O SIGN OF it, sir," Harding reported to her boss as he stood in the lobby of the *White House Inn*. "The team leader says they've turned the place upside down. No wine glass."

"*Damn*," Graham breathed. "We need to find it. This is a real long shot now," he said, glancing at his watch, "but we've got to try." They headed to the kitchens and found the staff busily preparing for dinner. "Marcella?"

The Portuguese woman's face fell and brightened only slightly when she saw Sergeant Harding's warm smile. "Is more problems? I told you everything about everything..."

"Please," Graham said. "You're not in any trouble."

"It's about the wine glass, Marcella," Harding said. "The one you brought to Sylvia Norquist's room. Do you remember what happened to it?"

Marcella shrugged apologetically and motioned to the big double sink in the corner of the kitchen. "Is cleaned. Everything is cleaned every day before dinner. No mess for guests to see," she said, her hands sweeping away an imaginary table of dirty dishes. "Chef insists about it."

"But the lunch tray was still in the room."

"Then glass will be there." Marcella shrugged her shoulders.

Harding sent her back to work while Graham took a moment to swear colorfully under his breath.

"No break there, boss. Sorry," she said, half a second from putting a reassuring hand on his shoulder but wisely thinking better of it.

"No poison in the food," Graham said, partly to her and partly to himself. "No glass from the room to confirm that was the source. And no witnesses."

Sergeant Harding tried to lift his mood. "You know what Sherlock Holmes would call this kind of case?"

Graham cracked half of a smile, despite himself. "A 'three pipe problem'?" he tried.

"Maybe four. But we'll get to the bottom of it, sir. Don't you worry about that."

Graham took out his notebook and flicked through it, as though the meticulous recording of events might somehow transform into new data, an alternative theory, a lead of some sort—*any* sort.

"I need a cup of tea, Sergeant Harding. Will you join me?"

Despite her initial hopes of seizing her chance to get to know Graham a little better, Harding soon found that this was to be a very quiet, thoughtful cup of tea indeed. Graham barely spoke, and then almost entirely to himself. She was there as a sounding board; her hopes of learning more about this surprisingly sophisticated man dashed almost as soon as they sat down.

"Dead. On the beach. Couldn't have walked there."

Graham took a sip of his tea, and an eyebrow raised in... what was it, recognition? Surprise? It was hard for Janice to say, not knowing him very well. DI Graham put the cup down carefully, almost soundlessly, and continued. "Hip replacement. Couldn't have managed the steps...Hmm."

His notepad was out again. Harding watched Graham read and flick through his notes as she sipped her tea. It seemed best to say nothing and let him think.

"Sort of engaged to the Colonel. Strong chap. Military through and through, but genuinely upset. Wouldn't you say, Janice?"

It surprised Sergeant Harding both to be included in this monologue and to hear Graham call her by her first name. He seemed in another world, caught up in details of murder and suspicion, leads and evidence, people and their potential motives. "I think we can stick with your original thought," she replied, "and rule out the Colonel. A man like him doesn't show his emotions, but you saw enough and I think we can conclude that his grief was real."

"Not a lot of murderers," Graham continued in the same faraway tone, "report the body to the police. Not many at all. They tend to let someone else do that. No, he's in the clear."

More notes, more tea, and more thoughts. "Pilkingtons. She was upset. Furious with him."

"I'm a Dutchman if I understood her reaction," Harding offered.

"Hmm. Dutchman." Graham was away in a cloudy world of investigative thought.

"Sir?" Sergeant Harding asked, willing this strange monologue to at least *begin* to make sense.

"They had nothing against her, Harding. She cured the man's cancer, for heaven's sake. A bit of suspicion is one thing, but...do you remember the look on Mrs. Pilkington's face? She had no idea her husband knew Dr. Norquist was on the island or that it was anything but a coincidence that found them in the same location."

"Again," Harding told him, "that was a genuine reaction. I'm no mind reader, but..."

"No, you're right. They were both telling the truth." The DI's thoughts meandered silently for a long moment. "Alice. Barely knew her, right?"

"Who, Sylvia?" Harding asked, trying to keep up.

"Headed to London. Sits in her room all day. But had some wine."

"Drinking with lunch, eh?" Harding joked. "Typical creative type."

Graham ignored her, but not unkindly. He was fully occupied, bringing in every detail for this grand synthesis of all they had learned so far. "Where in the seven hells," he said more strongly, "is the wine glass from Sylvia's room? The tray was still there. We *saw* the tray, Sergeant." Graham finally looked straight at her. "There was no glass. None."

Harding nodded. "I remember."

"Damn," Graham said again. "Too many unknowns here. Too many. Except one."

"What's that, Detective Inspector?" she asked, hoping the additional formality might bring him out of his reverie.

"That we're officially in a murder inquiry. And," he added with a quirky smile, "I'm not even jolly well unpacked yet. Whoever said that Jersey was some quiet little island?"

Harding drove him back to the station, glancing over at her new boss with growing respect and something more, an admiration which came from watching a fine mind at work. By the time they arrived, she was fizzing with excitement.

CHAPTER TWELVE

T HE TWO CONSTABLES faced each other across the reception desk. They each gesticulated, checking off points on their fingers, holding up palms to ask for silence, but their clamorous discussion only became audible to observers when Graham and Harding opened the main door to the station.

"All I'm saying is..." Barnwell began.

"If you'll let me finish..." Roach interrupted.

"You're not giving me a chance to make my..."

"Gentlemen," Graham said in a stentorian tone. "Have I wandered, by chance, into the back room of a local pub, or am I, as it truly seems, actually in a...what's it called again, Sergeant...a *police station?*"

"Sorry, sir," the two men said together, eyes downcast like truanting schoolboys.

"But don't let me stop you. I just trust that, should a member of the public need either of you, this discussion would be put on hold." Barnwell gave the reception desk's phone a guilty glance. "May I ask what's got you both quite so riled up?"

There was a moment of silence while the two men figured out who would speak. "It's this case, sir, at the *White House Inn*," Barnwell said. "We've been mulling it over a bit, that's all."

"Mulling?" Graham replied. "Mulling, you say? Well, I love a good mull." He pulled up a chair in the reception area and sat as though about to watch an engaging documentary. "Mull away, Constables."

Barnwell began. "So, here's what I've been thinking, sir. We know she took some kind of poison, right?" Graham let Barnwell continue despite his assumption. "She decides to do away with herself and thinks in the middle of doing it, 'Well, I'm about to shuffle off this mortal coil, I may as well have a nice view of the ocean while I'm getting ready to meet my maker'. See?"

"So, it's suicide, you're saying," Graham clarified.

"Yes, sir. She wanders down in a haze of depression and sadness and what-not, and then dies on the beach." He dusted off his hands as though having solved the case at a stroke.

"Constable Roach?" Graham asked. "Do you concur with your colleague?"

Roach cleared his throat. "Begging your pardon sir, but that's bollocks."

Barnwell spun round to confront the younger officer. Graham cut him off. "Hang on, Barnwell. Let's hear it," he said, motioning to Roach. "But be a good chap and mind your language in front of your superior." He nodded to Janice.

"Sorry, Sarge," Roach said genuinely. "Here's what I'd like to know. How's a lady who's virtually crippled supposed to walk down those steps, eh? Imagine your Nana trying to do that! She'd bloody well croak on the way down before she even got to the beach. I don't care what kind of painkillers she was on."

"Interesting point, Constable," Graham said.

"And she can't have killed herself. She was buried in the sand!" Roach added. "Who in their right mind walks along a beach, finds a dead body, and then thinks, 'Hey, I know, I'll bury this poor woman in the sand so that the scene is well and truly contaminated and the police won't have the first clue as to what happened'? Doesn't make any sense, Bazza, think about it."

"The tide!" Barnwell maintained. "The tide comes in and washes the sand over her."

Graham stood and straightened his tie. "I think I'm going to agree with Constable Roach's assessment of your theory, Barnwell."

"Huh?" Barnwell said.

"The part about it being bollocks," Roach told him in a loud whisper behind his hand.

"It's incomplete," Graham said charitably. "But that doesn't mean you should stop thinking about it. Include this in your mulling, though: *time*. These events took place and belong to a point in the pasts of everyone involved. Begin at the time of death and replay the movie backward; who was where, doing what, and why?"

Slightly stunned but thoughtful, the two constables watched Graham and Harding leave the reception area. Janice sported an amused smirk as she accompanied the DI to his office and closed the door.

"I wasn't joking around with them," Graham told her as they sat down in the office. "Well, not entirely."

Harding looked at her watch. She was thinking about

getting home. "They both need a firm hand, from time to time."

"They're fine officers, I'm sure," Graham said. "But investigative policing is an art. Speculating doesn't get you anywhere. It's all about the evidence." He stopped short. "I'm sorry, you know that full well. And I'm sure you want to get home rather than listen to me blathering on."

Harding willed herself into silence, though there was much she could say. About how glad she was that this cultured, interesting, competent, charming man had arrived in their midst. About how she felt he would shake up local policing and bring some real professionalism to their rather provincial world.

"I'll be heading home, then. It's been quite a day, hasn't it, sir?" She gave him a friendly smile.

"As first days go, Sergeant, it's been one for the books."

CHAPTER THIRTEEN

THE NEXT MORNING, Barnwell had only just set up the reception desk for the day when the phone rang.

"Gorey Constabulary, Constable Barnwell speaking."

"Ah, good morning. It's DI Graham."

"Morning, boss," Barnwell said brightly. "You're up early."

Graham ignored the remark. This was, Barnwell found, a trait of the DI's. He was all business, no chit-chat. No time to shoot the breeze when there was a murderer on the loose. "Let's meet in the lobby of the *White House Inn* as soon as you can get here, Barnwell. Leave the desk to Roach. I've got an assignment for you."

As he replaced the receiver, Barnwell couldn't help but think, with an enjoyable jolt of *Schadenfreude*, just how jealous Roach would be. Perhaps Graham's arrival was *his* passport to promotion and security. A couple of decent performances on the job, and he might even be made Sergeant once Janice moved on. It was a heady thought.

Barnwell found Graham hard at work in the lobby, despite the early hour. "It's true what they say about birds and worms, Constable Barnwell," Graham assured his colleague. "People's memories tend to be at their freshest after a good night's sleep and a strong cup of tea. That initial boost of sugar and caffeine can do wonders for recall," he said, toasting Barnwell with a fine china cup. It brimmed with a hard-to-find Japanese tea, redolent with the scents of a misty meadow. "It's amazing what details we'll hear today that were unavailable to us just a few hours ago."

Mrs. Taylor emerged from her office, looking fresh from the shower. "No cancelations last night, I'm happy to say!" she reported, bustling around and then heading into the dining room to check on preparations for breakfast. Barnwell followed Graham, who was peppering the *White House Inn's* proprietor with questions, toward the smells of breakfast—bacon, eggs, and sausage. His stomach growled plaintively. He'd planned to grab his usual, leisurely mid-morning bacon sandwich at the St. George Café near the station, but with Graham's diligent attitude to the morning hours, there wouldn't be time.

Shortly, Barnwell's daydream of a plate piled high with a cooked breakfast was disturbed by the demands of his profession. "Barnwell, I want you to investigate the Pilkingtons, Alice Swift, and the Colonel until you're certain that you know every detail of what they did yesterday between the hours of ten and two." Barnwell's shoulders swept back, and his spine straightened like that of a parading soldier. "Leave nothing to chance. No detail is too small, no finding irrelevant until proved so. I need to know how well they all knew each other, and especially, for how *long*. You with me?"

"Yes, sir," Barnwell snapped out. "I'll get right on that."

"Well," Graham said, checking his watch. "Maybe let them get out of bed first. It's not even seven."

"Will do, sir," Barnwell said, slightly less martially. "What about Constable Roach?"

"I've got something else in mind for him. Just stick to those four people like glue, and write down *everything*," Graham told him. Then there was a cheeky grin. "You can, can't you?"

"Sir?"

"*Write*, Barnwell."

"Yes, sir," the constable replied, entirely without irony.

"I'm pulling your leg, man." Stony silence was Barnwell's response. Graham shrugged off the urge to sigh at the man's plodding, unimaginative sincerity. *It takes all sorts to make the police force. And this kind of assignment should sort the police from the sort-of police.* "Off you go, then. Remember, every detail written down. See you about lunchtime." He gave Barnwell a comradely chuck on the shoulder. "Come and get me if you discover something momentous."

Graham spent a few more minutes striding through the hotel alongside the perpetual whirlwind of morning energy that was Mrs. Taylor. She wasn't meaning to be unhelpful, she explained, she was just trying to run a busy hotel in the summer. Graham ascertained that she'd told him every last useful thing, expressed his gratitude once more and retreated to the lobby.

Sergeant Harding had arrived and was already in

the *White House Inn's* back office, checking their list of interviewees. "You know, there's one guest we haven't spoken to at all yet. This guy," she said, tapping the list. "Likes to set up his meal reservations in advance," she said, proud of this modest piece of sleuthing.

Graham thought for a moment. "Set up an interview, Sergeant. Let's see what he has to say for himself."

CHAPTER FOURTEEN

LATER THAT MORNING, Graham found Carlos Alves sitting in a deck chair on the garden terrace of the *White House Inn* over-looking a calm sea which sparkled in the mid-morning sunshine. Cigar smoke wafted on the breeze. Alves had thick, black hair that made its own decisions. He wore a white, cotton summer shirt and Chinos. As Alves rose to shake Graham's hand, the Detective Inspector judged him to be a little over fifty, but in good shape, and with surprisingly rough hands.

"I take it that you sail," Graham said after they exchanged the pleasantries.

Carlos glanced down at his hands and smiled. "Perhaps it doesn't take a detective to know this, eh? I have a motor-sailer, thirty-four feet, harbored at Cowes during the winter. I like to sail between the islands in the summer. Normally, I stay on Guernsey or Sark. I like the quiet there."

For a mainlander like Graham, even one who spent his childhood in the remote countryside of the Yorkshire dales, the idea of spending extended time somewhere *smaller* than Jersey was close to unimaginable. Sark was barely bigger than the village in which he had grown up. "Beautiful islands," he said neutrally.

"Maybe you are surprised," Alves guessed. "Why don't I go down to the Greek Islands or the Pacific, no?"

Graham shrugged slightly. "We all tend to end up wherever makes us happiest."

A change came over Carlos' face, and it became stern and businesslike. "You are here," he said in his most serious tone yet, "about the death of Dr. Norquist, yes?"

"That's correct," Graham said. "We're interviewing everyone at the hotel, and..."

"I'm glad she's dead," Carlos said. He looked away at the ocean, then back at Graham, as if challenging him to make an accusation.

"I'm sorry, Mr. Alves?" Graham asked, shocked. The case seemed to crack wide open.

"She was a terrible woman." Alves raised a finger as if in warning. "And a *dangerously* incompetent doctor."

Graham wrote down every word, wishing for once that he had some recording technology to capture this moment of confession. "I'm listening," was all he said.

Carlos sighed. "But I did not kill her."

Graham's body seemed to sag under him. "But you knew her well?"

"Well enough," Alves explained, taking a long sequence of puffs on his cigar, as though the nicotine hit might steel him for this emotionally fraught discussion. "She was the doctor of my son. His name was Juan-Carlos."

Graham didn't need a detective's training to discern what had happened. "I'm sorry, Mr. Alves." Graham waited, discerning that it would better to speak less and listen more.

"He was sixteen years old. Can you imagine that, Inspector?" Carlos asked, his face etched with pain now. "He was healthy, happy. Full of life. He played soccer for his school. Was chasing girls all the time," he said with a nostalgic smile. "Then he says he finds problems in walking. His legs won't do as they're told," he explained. "Then his vision becomes strange, seeing two of everything. At dinnertimes," Carlos went on, "he can't swallow, almost choking on his food."

"It sounds terrible," Graham said consolingly.

"Our family doctor, he didn't really know. But there were tests, and tests and *more* tests," Carlos said, reducing a year of worry, heartache, and despair to a few words, "and they find a tumor. Here," he said, fingers at the very back of his neck, where the spine meets the skull.

"A brain stem tumor?" Graham asked gently.

"Is treatable, but is difficult," Carlos continued. "You need *real professional,*" he said, fist in his palm, every syllable clear. "The *best.*"

"And so you met Dr. Norquist."

Carlos nodded and then lifted his cigar to his mouth again but stopped short. He gave Graham a rueful, slightly ashamed look, and placed the cigar back in its ashtray, forgotten. "My wife, Gloria, she has a friend whose baby girl had the cancer...Oh, Inspector, the most terrible kind. Of the *eye,*" he said, pained at the memory. "Two years old. But Dr. Norquist was assigned to the little girl, and she *survived!*"

"Medical science is remarkable," Graham commented.

"Ah, no," Carlos said, hands aloft. "This was not just

science according to my Gloria. No, no," he said, shaking his head in wonder. "This was *God*. Gloria was as certain of this as we are certain that we're on Jersey. She was *convinced* that the sacred spirit came down and saved that little girl. The spirit, working through Dr. Norquist. Do you understand?"

With his parents' relaxed attitude to church-going, particularly as their children grew older and found other ways to spend their Sunday mornings, Graham had never been a devoted man of faith, but he respected the sincerity of those who were. "I think so, sir."

"Gloria insisted on having Sylvia Norquist as our son's doctor. And if you ever met my wife, you would know that when she *insists* on something, it's *must* happen, you know?" He chuckled. "No matter that Dr. Norquist wasn't a specialist in brain cancers. No, it would be God guiding her hands, and he would deliver our son from this devil-cancer. You see?"

Mostly, Graham could see how a family was torn apart by grief and by the tragic results of a poor decision. He could also see that his initial hopes of hearing a confession were being dashed. If anyone he'd so far met possessed a comprehensible reason to want Sylvia Norquist dead, it was this man. However, this did not sound even a little like the confession of a murderer.

"Dr. Norquist studied and practiced and got advice from everyone," Carlos explained. "She made it her life for *months* to attack this complex cancer. It was like a battle, like she was fighting for her own life, you know?"

"But, despite her efforts, the treatment failed?" Graham asked with all the sensitivity he could find.

"She should have refused to treat him. She didn't know what she was doing."

Carlos stood and made for the ocean, but after a few steps, he stopped and turned. "You know, I understand boats. And shipping, freight, that kind of business. But with my son's diagnosis, I would become an *expert* on the human brain stem. I could give you a lecture right now," he assured Graham, "like a professional, on every aspect. Yet, despite my diligence, and Dr. Norquist's efforts, the treatment didn't work. My son died."

"A most dreadful tragedy."

"And it *could* have happened to any patient, treated by any doctor, but it happened to *my* son, treated by *her*." The pain, Graham could plainly see, was undimmed by the passing of time, and seemingly not even a little assuaged by the death of Dr. Norquist.

"Mr. Alves," Graham began, "I'm sure you realize how this might seem to an investigator."

"I'm a grieving father, Detective Inspector," Carlos said. "Not a fool."

"Then...I must ask if you know anything that might help with our inquiries?"

Carlos reclaimed his cigar, shaking his head. "I was on Guernsey yesterday, Detective Inspector. I sailed back overnight. It's my favorite time to sail, in the cool and the dark. Nobody else around." Alves puffed on his cigar. "There are harbormaster's records on both sides," he assured Graham.

"I have no reason to suspect you're being dishonest with me, sir, but I have to admit you have a strong motive."

"If I had killed Dr. Norquist," Carlos said, cigar aloft in an expansive gesture, "maybe a jury would not send me to jail in the circumstances. But imagine if they *did*. I'm fifty-three years old. I would be an old man when I got out if I ever did. I could not sacrifice my remaining years, all the time I have left with my Gloria who is already without her son, just to punish this woman. I could *not*."

Graham filled another page with cursive. Carlos used the silence to say something that stilled Graham's hand.

"I shouldn't say this," Carlos said, tapping off the cigar ash, "but I wish to express my thanks to whoever is responsible for this crime. Truly. I ask God's forgiveness for this, but it is how I feel." He stopped, puffed once more. "Are you a father?"

For barely a second, Graham paused in his writing, his eyes clouding over. He shook his head, "No."

"Hold them close," Carlos said, his eyes glistening. "You never know how long you will have them." With that, he turned back toward the ocean, his cigar lodged between his lips now, puffing intently as he watched the sailboats rounding the headland at the tip of the beach.

"Thank you for your time." Graham stood and headed straight back inside, filling his notebook quickly, before the memories faded.

CHAPTER FIFTEEN

G RAHAM DRANK HIS tea with a mechanical, heedless air as he sat alone in the *White House Inn's* tearoom. It was fairly quiet. It would be half an hour before the lunch crowd arrived. For a change, rather than bringing together the facts in an orderly, determined way, Graham was letting his thoughts come as they may. The tea helped, as it always did. Perhaps the sea air, also. Sometimes, he found it was best to to keep quiet and allow a well-trained mind to do its work.

"Constable Roach?" he called over.

The young officer was standing discreetly in the lobby, almost hidden by a giant coat stand. "Morning, sir."

"I need you to do something for me." Moments later, Roach was on his way down to the harbormaster's office, searching for news of an arrival early this morning. Graham believed that he knew true grief and a genuine story when he experienced them, but he'd never be able to look his colleagues in the eye if Carlos Alves turned out to be the murderer and all Graham had done was sat with the man for a sympathetic chat.

Janice appeared. They had routed calls to Jersey police headquarters in St. Helier while they focused on the investigation.

"Sergeant Harding, do you have a phone that can play videos?" Graham said.

"Of course, sir." Harding nearly told him that all phones could do that nowadays but decided against it. Instead, she proudly showed him her phone, one of the latest models. It had cost well over a week's salary and worked like a charm. Graham explained what he wanted, and they sat together to review the results.

"You see, we've been going about this all wrong," Graham told her. "We'd assumed that the journey from here," he said, tracing a path on the table in front of him with his finger, "down to the beach would have been awkward and painful for Sylvia."

"I'm sure it would," Harding agreed.

"But what if..." he said, turning the phone from portrait to landscape to give them a wider view. "What if it were *impossible?*"

The video Graham had had Harding pull up showed part of the trials of a new drug. In the video, a woman of an age similar to Sylvia Norquist's, perhaps a little older, was struggling to walk. Sweating, pale, and in immense pain, she could barely take three steps together on level ground. She grasped a handrail as though she would drown without it. "Sergeant," he said with a smirk, "I don't know how often you find yourself saying this, but..."

"Constable Roach was right," Janice conceded. "There's no way on God's green earth that Sylvia Norquist could have walked down those steps. No way at all." Harding raced to put two and two together. "Are you suggesting that she was *carried?*"

"In broad daylight, at lunchtime, on a beach at the tail end of summer." Graham grimaced. "That, believe it or not, is our best theory."

Harding thought for a second, then shut down the phone and looked square at her boss. "If I may quote the distinguished philosopher, Jim Roach, sir...I think that's bollocks."

Constable Barnwell checked in throughout the day. He was a little like a child sent off to find the toothpaste aisle in the supermarket, proud to be given such a responsibility but uncertain whether his parents would still be there when he got back. Although unused to being invested with such trust, the constable was proving himself a surprisingly tenacious investigator. Graham was pleased to see him write reams of notes.

His more responsible colleague, Constable Roach, had also done his best for the new boss. Carlos Alves had, in fact, traveled back from Guernsey that very morning, and the details of his stay on Jersey's sister island and his smart sailboat all checked out. Graham could not rule the bereaved father out of the investigation entirely as he would have preferred, however. The history between Alves and Dr. Norquist was far too compelling for that, but Graham could at the very least put aside suspicion of any direct involvement in the killing. As Graham pondered over yet another pot of fine tea later that afternoon, he considered that Alves was neither the kind of man nor was he carrying the kind of grudge that suggested poisoning as the preferred method of murder. He could well imagine a calculating, incensed Alves beating Sylvia to death or strangling her as he watched the last light leave her eyes, but he couldn't contemplate Alves *poisoning* her. It lacked the intimacy of violence Graham would have expected Alves to crave.

No. Something else was going on, and they were still some way from what any investigator worth their salt would call "a lead." Graham finished this tea feeling energized, quick of mind, and light of foot. He called Dr. Tomlinson.

"Do call me Marcus, old chap. I have a feeling we'll be spending a great deal of time together, and I don't hold with needless formality," Dr. Tomlinson told him.

"Marcus it is, although I'm sorry to disturb you so late in the day. Do you have plans for dinner?" Graham wondered.

"Thought you'd never ask."

Two hours later, in a quiet corner of the *Bangkok Palace*, the two men were served crisp Thai lagers and an appetizer of sticky rice and *jaew bong*. Fearless of spicy food, Graham found to his delight that the innocuous-looking sauce was laced with pungent shallots and searing chilies. It tasted ferocious and to Graham's mind, delicious.

Tomlinson was far more wary. He dipped each ball of rice only fleetingly into the sauce's midst. "Christ alive," he muttered. "I might be too old for this kind of thing. How about a nice, uneventful coconut curry?" he asked the waiter. Graham ordered a dish marked with three chilies on the menu and the waiter gave him a knowing smile as if both impressed at Graham's audacity and slightly fearful for his continued wellbeing.

"So, I suppose we're all rather curious," Tomlinson began. "What brings an accomplished Detective Inspector like yourself…"

"To a quiet, provincial backwater like this?" Graham smiled.

"Well, something like that. Gorey Constabulary is hardly a hotbed of ambition. The previous DI was in his position for sixteen years and showed absolutely no interest in ascending the ladder of investigative prowess," Tomlinson explained. "He fit right in."

"But surely," Graham countered, "Jersey is full of aspirational young people? Didn't I read that the economy is booming?"

"The *banking* sector, yes! The *police* sector, not so much." The waiter set the steaming, aromatic coconut curry before the doctor who inhaled the vapors with relish. "With so little to challenge them, beyond the odd missing person, the local force has been resting on its laurels pretty much continuously since the Newall murders. Even the cases involving corrupt bankers get sent over the water to the financial crime boffins who work on the mainland."

"Resting on their laurels, you say. I guess that includes Roach and Barnwell?" Graham asked as his seafood curry arrived. Its deep, glossy red color gave ample warning of the raging fires within.

"They're good lads," Tomlinson chuckled. "I was a little nervous about having them work on a murder investigation like this but with your leadership, I'm sure they'll do you proud. Just don't count on miraculous flashes of insight from either of them."

"I won't," Graham said, trying his curry. It was excellent and supremely hot.

CHAPTER SIXTEEN

"**S**O BEYOND JOINING a booming economy, what brought you down here?" Tomlinson asked again. It was a persistence born not of an impolite, gossipy impulse, but a genuine curiosity. Graham was so unlike his predecessor, far better trained and much more polished and assured that his presence seemed strange without further explanation. In fact, Tomlinson had considered that Graham was sent to Jersey specifically *because* Sylvia Norquist's murder was anticipated by someone in the London hierarchy. Tomlinson penned thrillers in his free time and occasionally applied flights of fancy to real-life situations that better served as fictional plots.

"The job came up," Graham said simply, "and I applied."

"But why?" Tomlinson pressed.

"Change of scenery, I suppose. A fresh challenge."

Tomlinson set down his spoon and dabbed his mouth with his napkin. "Challenge?"

"Sure."

"Dear chap, your main challenge, this highly unusual murder aside, will be to keep yourself busy! Do you know that Roach plays solitaire on the reception desk for about three hours of each shift? And that Barnwell..." He paused. "I shouldn't tell tales out of school."

"He drinks," Graham said. "There's a look in his eye. I recognize it all too well." Something in Graham's tone, a firm undercurrent, told Tomlinson both that Graham knew what he was talking about, and that his experiences may well have been first hand. Wisely, the doctor did not press further. A change of subject was in order.

"Is there a Mrs. Graham?" he asked with a raised eyebrow.

"There was," Graham told him, and Tomlinson immediately regretted his question. It did not take much digging, it seemed, to reveal the complexities of this unfamiliar man. Not that Tomlinson didn't accept Graham's reasoning for transferring to this rural idyll. It just made more sense if there were deeper reasons. Perhaps, he wondered, Graham was pushed as much as pulled toward an obscure assignment like this one. But if so, why not Scotland or a quiet Sussex village?

"I'm sorry," Tomlinson said openly. "None of my business."

"We were heading in different directions," Graham said next. "We had very different priorities."

"Well, whatever your priorities *aren't*, I'd say that you've already shown yourself to be an assiduous and competent detective," Tomlinson said, raising a glass in salute to the new Detective Inspector.

"Too kind, Marcus." Graham paused. "I guess that means you can call me David."

"I will, if I may. The previous DI went by 'Buster,' but I hardly think that fits you."

Graham took a moment to laugh it out. The more he learned about his predecessor, the more he seemed the typically comical, buffoonish, rural stereotype. Seriously overweight according to Harding. Lax with his personal hygiene according to Barnwell, who himself didn't smell as though he'd just stepped off the set of a deodorant commercial.

"Sounds like quite a character. A big pair of shoes to fill," Graham said diplomatically.

Both men laughed now, the ice thoroughly broken. Tomlinson was glad to see the younger man enjoying himself and the indelicate questions about his past forgotten.

But it didn't take Graham long to get back to business. "I'm afraid we have to talk about this blessed case," Graham said, handing Tomlinson another beer.

"Fire away, David. I'm as puzzled as you are if I'm plain."

"What's really bothering me at the moment," Graham explained, "except for who might have killed her, is the *timing*."

Tomlinson stirred the remaining third of his curry with his spoon. "Hmm?" he asked.

"Dr. Norquist's body was found a couple of hours after lunch." Graham paused, his mouth full of lightly-spiced chicken. "So we assumed that the poison was delivered with lunch. Poor Marcella seems to have been the unwitting accessory."

"That's as far as I'd got, too," Tomlinson confirmed.

"But you pinned her death to within an eighteen-hour period. So, what if," Graham asked, pointing his chopsticks at Tomlinson, "we got it completely wrong. What if she was murdered the previous *night* and carried down the stairs to the beach?"

Tomlinson washed down his curry with a long pull on his beer before answering. "Buried in the dark, when nobody was about?" he conjectured. "Makes more sense than the murderer lugging a dead or dying Sylvia down those steps in broad daylight."

"And what about the poison?" Graham pressed.

"Yes, I was coming to that. I reviewed some old textbooks, and you know, there aren't a lot of poisons that leave so few signs for the postmortem. The classics," he said, ticking them off on his fingers, "are strychnine, cyanide, and arsenic. They all leave telltale signs of their role."

Graham made a wheeling motion with his chopsticks as he braved the nuclear firestorm that was his red seafood curry.

"Strychnine, for example, causes convulsions that leaves the body locked in an arched position. Cyanide famously leaves a scent of bitter almonds," he added. "But our Sylvia seems to have died from something that pretty quickly stopped her heart and her breathing leaving no evidence behind."

"So, what are you thinking?" Graham asked, drawing cool air across his scorched tongue.

"Don't have a clue, old chap. Give me another day to check with some colleagues in the business and to continue the postmortem."

The returning waiter heard the term and blanched slightly. "Is everything to your satisfaction, gentlemen?" he asked warily.

"Only one thing," Graham asked, now visibly sweating. "Next time I come in," he said, pausing again to bring cool air into his mouth, "could you make mine a little hotter?"

CHAPTER SEVENTEEN

SERGEANT JANICE HARDING hovered uncertainly at the big double doors. Despite the authority of her rank and uniform, it was hard to shake the feeling that she was trespassing. The hallway was brightly lit but exceedingly quiet, not only because of the early hour but also because not one of the "patients" in this part of the hospital would ever make a single sound again.

"Isn't this a little...unorthodox?" she had asked DI Graham as he had confidently swept down the hallway toward the morgue. Barnwell and Roach followed behind, Roach looking positively exhilarated.

"We're police officers, Sergeant," he reminded her. "Police work has dull moments and exciting parts. And inevitably things like this."

Graham pushed open the doors and found Dr. Tomlinson, clipboard in hand, standing by a mortuary table. He wore a face mask and motioned for all four of his visitors to don them before continuing. Barnwell needed some assistance with his but got there eventually.

Before them was a sight that elicited different reactions from each officer.

"I'd like to introduce Dr. Sylvia Norquist," Tomlinson said with a singularly inappropriate flourish and brought back a white sheet to reveal the corpse that lay underneath. Harding's hand flew to her mouth. Barnwell stared as though in the audience at a freak show. Roach's eyes narrowed studiously. For him, this was a learning opportunity, and not one that was likely to come around often.

"Asphyxia, lady, and gentlemen. A dangerous constriction of the supply of oxygen to the brain causing unconsciousness and death. The chief cause of Dr. Norquist's demise."

"But," Graham said, continuing, "asphyxia doesn't *explain* her death. It merely gives us the reason she expired. Every asphyxia has a cause. Not to sound like we're in medical school or anything, but could you name some?" Graham asked the trio of police officers.

Roach raised a hand before Graham gave him a look. "Strangulation," he offered.

"That's one," Tomlinson agreed.

"Smothering?" Harding tried.

"That's another," Graham replied.

"Depressurization? Like, on a plane?" Barnwell said next.

"Sure. Other things are likely to kill you just as quickly way up there, but okay," Tomlinson allowed. "However, there are no signs of smothering, no paleness to the skin around the nose and mouth. No ligature markings," he said, his pencil at the body's neck to illustrate his point, "which might indicate strangulation. And she wasn't on a plane when she died. So..."

"What else causes asphyxia," Roach thought aloud, "but doesn't leave any trace?"

"Here come two big words that I want you to get used to," Tomlinson said. "Tachycardic arrhythmia." He paused. "Anyone want to try making sense of that?"

Graham chuckled. "From medical school to a linguistics class in one swift leap. Why do we do *cardio* exercise?"

"To get our hearts racing," Harding offered, remembering her fitness instructor's commands during aerobics class.

"Excellent. And what might an 'arrhythmia' be?" Graham asked.

"Like a rhythm?" Roach tried.

"Yes, but in this case," Tomlinson said, his hand aloft in a light fist, "a *lack* of rhythm." He pumped his fist in a steady pulsing movement before pausing, restarting, and stopping again. "Something made her heart beat so abnormally that it fatally compromised her ability to breathe."

Barnwell was fixated on Tomlinson's pulsing fist. "So, she went and had a heart attack and asphyxiated, *at the same time?*"

"Well, one resulted from the other, but you've got the idea, young man," Tomlinson told him. "So...what could make a healthy human heart behave like this?"

All three stared down at the spotless, white floor tiles in thought.

"Electricity?" Harding said first.

"There would be characteristic burning under her skin if that were the case," Tomlinson said.

"No stab wounds or sign that anything hit her?" Roach said.

"Not even a little bit. No signs of a struggle in her room, either," Graham said.

Then Barnwell lit up. "*Poison.* You suspected that all along, didn't 'cha?"

Graham clapped the constable on the shoulder and gave Tomlinson a wink. "Marcus, would you be good enough to introduce these fine officers to the murder weapon in this case?"

They could not have been more keyed up if Sherlock Holmes were walking them through his deductions. "*Aconitum variegatum*," Tomlinson announced, bringing from behind the table a small bunch of delicate, purple-blue flowers. "Of the order *Ranunculales*, but of course you knew that," he grinned.

"A *plant* did this to her?" Harding gasped.

"Not just any plant," Tomlinson told them, passing each a stalk topped with a group of the flowers. "You can see how it gets one of its colloquial names, *Monkshood*."

Even at first glance, they could. A tall, drooping, purple cover and pairs of petals on either side protected the center of each flower. "They're rather pretty," Harding said. "Almost like something my grandmother would have in her garden."

"Oh, I agree," Tomlinson said. "But like most attractive plants, the bright color is there as a warning. These flowers," he said, taking the stalks back carefully as though removing unlit sparklers from lighter-toting teenagers, "are bloody deadly. Mash up a big handful of these stalks and petals, dissolve the results in alcohol, and you have something called *tincture of aconite,* otherwise known as *Wolfsbane.*"

"Sounds like something out of Harry Potter, doesn't

it?" Graham quipped. "But it's real, and it's not nice at all."

"Slip even a *teaspoon* of this into someone's drink," Tomlinson told them, "and your victim would be as dead as a doornail inside four hours, six hours tops. But it doesn't show up on a toxicology screen and leaves behind neither a telltale smell nor color."

Harding, Roach, and Barnwell were now hanging on Tomlinson's every word, their eyes eager.

"But, you see, I noticed there was a tiny amount of foam around Dr. Norquist's mouth. Few things make us *literally* 'foam at the mouth.'"

"I suppose not," Harding said, eyeing the corpse warily.

"And I could tell from the way the sand clung to Dr. Norquist's body that she'd been sweating before her death. Then, we found her stomach to be entirely empty. That's normally a result of having vomited recently and heavily. If someone has been poisoned," Tomlinson told them, "this is the best thing for them."

"Aren't you supposed to...whatcha call it," Barnwell was saying, "*induce* vomiting?"

"You are, to expel the stomach contents," Dr. Tomlinson agreed. "And she did, but not fast enough, unfortunately.

"Wow," Roach breathed.

"Indeed, Constable. It's not something," Tomlinson said with a note of pride, "that your garden-variety pathologist would have spotted. But after some investigative work and discussions with my colleagues, I have learned that the foam, the sweating, the lack of a signature all indicate poisoning by the aforementioned *aconitum* or *Wolfsbane*. And once it reaches the heart, it will stop it dead."

CHAPTER EIGHTEEN

GRAHAM TOOK OVER. "Once her heart failed, so did Sylvia's breathing. Asphyxia ensued. Can you believe that growing and owning the plants, even the tincture, is perfectly legal?"

"It's been used for centuries in Chinese traditional medicine," Tomlinson added. "And aromatherapy. Quite safe on the skin, but damned near always fatal if you're dosing someone's drink with it."

Barnwell clicked his fingers. "The Chardonnay."

Roach stared at his colleague as though he'd stolen his girlfriend, but Graham was impressed. "The Chardonnay and the glass it was in are the most promising pieces of evidence, but there's no bloody sign of them."

Tomlinson covered Dr. Norquist's body. "Not yet, anyway. Fingers crossed, eh?" He thanked the team and ushered them out. "Keep in touch, David. We're getting close, I can feel it."

The four officers talked the matter through all the way back to the station and then in an animated, focused huddle in DI Graham's small office. Graham was eager to know what Barnwell had learned during the previous day's sleuthing. "I saw you striding around that hotel with a purposeful air, Constable. What did you discover?"

Barnwell flipped through his notebook. "It's pretty much as we expected, sir. The Pilkingtons, well...They're a funny pair. Very argumentative at the moment. She's furious with him for hiding the return of his cancer and for spending time with Dr. Norquist without her knowledge."

"How did you find that out?" Roach wanted to know.

"Easy. You just stand behind a potted fern," Barnwell explained like it was the most obvious thing in the world. "You look like you're doing nothing except guarding the lobby, and you keep your ears open. People will say all sorts in front of a stationary copper. It's like you're not even there."

"Any sign that Mrs. Pilkington might have hurt Sylvia?" Graham asked though he was pretty certain of the answer.

"No, sir. The way I see it, if she'd killed Dr. Norquist would she still be giving her husband daily bollockings for having had coffee with her?" Graham nodded.

"Good point," Harding observed. "What else?"

"There's that South American bloke, Carlos Alves," Barnwell reported. "He was down at the marina for a while, but he spent almost the whole time on the terrace, just staring out to sea."

"He's got a lot on his mind," Graham informed them.

"Such as?" Roach asked, irritated to be playing second fiddle to the likes of Barnwell. "Guilt, maybe?"

"His son died," Graham said.

"On the victim's watch," Barnwell reminded them. "I checked and there was a question of negligence, of her not being up to the job. It was in the papers. There was an internal investigation at the hospital, but they decided against suspending her or taking it further. His wife," Barnwell said, then whistled, "sounds like *quite* the character. I wouldn't want to get on the wrong side of her. They're an odd couple, right enough."

"Grief," Graham commented quietly, "does terrible things to a person."

Only Harding spotted the distant, despondent look on his face, but she said nothing.

"Doesn't that make him our prime suspect, sir?" Barnwell asked. "There's certainly motive, wouldn't you say?"

"I would, but I interviewed him in detail, and saw no reason to suspect that he's here to do anything but sail his boat and stare at the sea. He's grieving, not vengeful. Not actively, anyway."

Roach joined Barnwell's protests. "Seriously, sir, I think we should consider him." The others nodded. "Didn't you say that he's glad she died?"

"He said that. But he didn't kill her," Graham replied. "Leave him for now. What about the others?"

"Alice Swift keeps to herself. She was in her room for almost the whole day. Came down for morning tea but had lunch and dinner brought to her room by Marcella," Barnwell said.

"She's working on a tapestry," Graham explained. "A talented woman."

Harding frowned but quickly regained her composure. "No indication that she's mourning or troubled by Dr. Norquist's death. It's not clear that she even knew her. We can probably just rule her out."

"Who did she have tea with?" Graham asked.

"Er... Colonel Graves," Barnwell said, consulting his notes.

The conversation stopped. "Wait, they *know* each other?" Harding asked.

Barnwell checked his notes again. "They talked about money, that was all I could gather. It was hard to hear," he reported. "There were other people around and they were leaning in close, you know."

"Money?" Roach wondered aloud. "What's the Colonel doing now he's retired from the army?"

"Real estate investments, across the pond," Graham told him. "Maybe Alice and he are in business together. She seemed wealthy enough, right, Sergeant?"

"Wealthy enough to open a weaving business in a ritzy, expensive part of London," she remarked. "Didn't seem like she was short of a penny."

"What about Sylvia?" Graham said. "She wasn't exactly poor, either."

"I mean," Harding said next, "anyone who's staying at the *White House Inn* has a good chunk of cash under their mattress, that's for certain. What does Mrs. Taylor charge her long-termers, maybe £70 a night?"

"About that. Or maybe a little more," Graham confirmed.

"Here's a theory," Barnwell began. "The Colonel is in financial trouble, right? Housing market over in the States takes a dip or whatever. He asks Dr. Norquist for a loan, and she says no."

"Go on," Graham said, a little skeptical already.

"So he puts pressure on her to show him that she loves him, that she trusts him, by giving him money. But it all falls apart between them because she won't fork over the cash. He's short on the mortgages or whatever, so his properties are at risk of being foreclosed on."

It was a more thorough theory than Graham had expected, but it wasn't without weaknesses. "And so..."

"So, he poisons her. End of story."

Barnwell sat back, a look of pride settling across his face.

"Well, that was anti-climactic," Harding grumbled.

"Got a better suggestion?" Barnwell shot back.

"Take it easy, Constable," Graham told him, but kept his tone light. The man was trying his best, he could see. "We've already satisfied ourselves that Colonel Graves is genuinely grieving."

Barnwell shrugged. "Can't you grieve for someone's death even if you're responsible for it?"

"That's pushing it a bit," Roach argued. "I mean, the bloke was properly upset. You heard his voice on the phone, right when he found her. You said he sounded devastated."

"And," Harding said, finger aloft, "we already know how frequently the murderer calls in the body. Right, sir?"

"Right, Sergeant," Graham agreed. "It's not 'never,' but it's pretty rare."

"Bugger," Barnwell cursed. "Thought I was onto something, didn't I?"

Graham gave him a consoling look. "Keep doing what you're doing, Constable. We'll crack it, I promise."

Barnwell wasn't ready to give up just yet. "Couldn't we talk to him, one more time?" he asked. "I mean, it's just the way he and Miss Swift were sitting together in the tearoom, leaning close, keeping their voices down. It just...I don't know, it just seemed *odd*."

Roach couldn't resist. "Well, you'd know *odd* when you saw it."

Barnwell ignored him. "Sir? How about it?"

Graham was on his feet. "We'll crack this case by being thorough. Let's do it."

"Righto," Barnwell said, giving Roach a provocative look before following his boss out to the car.

"You drive," Graham ordered. "I'll call him."

CHAPTER NINETEEN

B ARNWELL DROVE WITH deliberate care and attention, partly to impress Graham but also because of the number of tourists who appeared to be woefully unfamiliar with Jersey's driving code. They were milling around and slowing everyone down. *As usual.*

"I wouldn't have thought of that, boss," he said.

"Hmm?" Graham replied. He'd been writing in his notebook.

"Inviting the Colonel to dinner. It's a nice touch, given what he's been through this week."

Graham clicked his pen closed and slotted his notebook away. It had become the most fluid of actions, achieved almost without thought like changing gear or shaving. "It's not purely charity, Constable. People tend to say more when they believe they are not under suspicion. As far as the Colonel is concerned, we're just confirming background details."

The *White House Inn* was busy, but Mrs. Taylor found Detective Inspector Graham and Colonel Graves the quietest table available. They found themselves sitting on the terrace overlooking the English Channel. Carlos Alves was there. He was smoking a cigar. He nodded gravely at the two men and carried on with his evening vigil, scanning the waves as though the happiness so brutally stolen from him might somehow emerge from the deep.

"I'll take a dry sherry," Graves told Marcella. "And for you?" The Colonel looked at DI Graham.

"Oh, just water. Thanks, Marcella." Marcella glided away.

The men regarded each other. "I want to begin by thanking you," Graham said. "Your assistance has been invaluable in this investigation."

Colonel Graves was surprised. "I only did what anyone would do. I'm also hoping that there might be some kind of closure for me in finding whoever did this to Sylvia."

"Well, we're getting closer all the time," Graham assured him. "Look, I'm sorry if this is indelicate, but..."

"Please," Graves said, his palms open.

"It's about your real estate investments. You mentioned them briefly when we last spoke. Can you say a little more about your portfolio?"

Marcella returned with their drinks. Graves took a sip of his sherry. He smiled. "Looking to invest, Detective Inspector?"

"On *my* salary?" Graham snorted. "Hardly."

"Well, I can tell you how it works," Colonel Graves said, setting down his glass on the pristine white tablecloth.

"You don't mind if I take notes? Just routine," Graham assured the Colonel.

"Not a bit. But no stealing my investment ideas! I worked bloody hard for that money." Their starters arrived. Marcella was gone in a second.

"So are you one of several investors?"

"That's right," Graves said, stabbing a shred of romaine lettuce with his fork. "We form a syndicate. We all pitch in, get the place bought and fixed up, generate some interest among the right crowd, and sell it. The agent gets a cut, and after all the taxes and what-not, the rest is divided between the members. The amount we receive is more than we put in, at least that's the theory. It's a gamble though. You're never quite sure if it will work out."

"And how many of you are there?" Graham asked. His carrot and ginger soup was rather tasty.

"Seven, this time around. I've got a deal going on in Tampa at the moment. We're looking to clear probably..." He calculated in his head. "About $30,000 each, maybe a little more."

"And once it's done?"

"Then we go again. I'm a serial investor. I never have more than one deal going at a time. I only deal in cash, you see. I'd never borrow to front a property deal."

"Why not?" Graham asked. "Most people do."

Graves chuckled. "Not me, old chap. Too wise," he said, tapping his nose. "If I borrowed beyond my means and everything went belly up, I'd owe some blood-sucking bank a sodding fortune with nothing to sell except the shirt off my back. When I started, I put my all into this, I did. But I am not rich and each time I hold a little back, preferring to keep it in the bank. My reserve steadily grows with each new deal. Slow and steady, that's me."

"Why take the risk at all?" Graham asked.

"All I wanted," Graves said, his face falling, "was to do a few good deals over there, cash in once I'd made a modest sum, and marry Sylvia. I thought we'd get ourselves a nice little cottage somewhere," he said, glancing out into the bay. "I just wanted to live out our lives together quietly. I was almost there." Sadness permeated him now, and Graham felt for the man. A life of service and sacrifice, and now no one to share what was left.

"I'm sorry, Colonel. It's dreadful, what's happened." Graham felt like saying more, even reaching to take Graves' arm or shoulder, but it seemed inappropriate.

Colonel Graves took a deep breath. "We all go on, you know. Life doesn't stop because you have a bit of rotten luck."

Graham's eyebrows shot up of their own accord. Something about the Colonel's tone told him the older man didn't just mean Sylvia's passing. "Rotten luck, Colonel?"

"Yes, the Tampa deal. Well, not rotten luck exactly. The buggers got a step ahead of themselves. Nobody consulted me, of course. Must think I'm bloody made of money." The Colonel's anger was genuine, and coming so soon after grief and sadness, it was a shock to Graham.

"Do you mind if I ask about it?" Graham deliberately pushed his notebook away a few inches, as if reassuring the Colonel that they were speaking off the record.

"There was another apartment in the same building. My investor friends saw this as easy money. We were already marketing to the right clients, already canvassing the right neighborhoods. May as well get two sales for our efforts, right? So they quickly chucked in another $75,000 each to buy the second apartment. I mean, can you imagine?"

"A little rich for your blood?" Graham guessed.

"Too bloody right! They never even asked me before they committed. And then they turned around and threatened not to work with me anymore if I didn't join in. In danger of losing my place in the syndicate, I was. Getting turfed out because I lacked the...Well, you know what I mean."

"I think I do. Very presumptuous of them."

"Oh, they've been doing this kind of thing for years, the bloody *sharks*. Thinning down the ranks until there's only three or four of them left to share the best leads, the best deals. They court potential investors, persuade them to join, treat them nicely, then squeeze them out when they don't show sufficient fortitude, the willingness to front *serious* cash. It's a cutthroat business, Detective Inspector. Unless you're bringing millions to the table, they treat you like an amateur."

"So, where do you stand?" Graham asked.

"Up a certain navigable waterway without a certain instrument," the Colonel grimaced. "Until..." His eyes gained a curiously faraway look. "I probably shouldn't mention this, but I know I can speak in confidence."

Graham pushed his notebook another few inches away. "My lips are sealed."

Leaning in close, the Colonel delivered the news in a conspiratorial whisper. "Alice loaned me the money. All of it. Fronted me for the second apartment, helped me keep myself in the game. I showed those buggers who they're dealing with!"

"Alice Swift?"

"The very same. Remarkable woman. Sees the best in people."

"I'm sure," Graham replied. Inwardly, he was a blur of thought. He had so many questions, each more difficult to pose than the last. "And, if it's not too indelicate a question, what was the nature of your repayment agreement?"

"Oh, all fair and above board," he said. "I even started paying her back a little last month—profit from the proceeds of a small sale up in the Florida Panhandle that wrapped just before I took on the Tampa deal. Only my third effort and not a bad one," he said, rubbing his hands slightly. "But nothing on the scale of these Tampa properties," he said as if in awe of the risks he'd agreed to take.

Although badly distracted by this new complexity to their case, Graham kept up appearances for the remainder of dinner. Just after nine, Graham left Graves to enjoy an after-dinner Scotch. "I might catch up with that fellow, Alves," the Colonel told him as Graham took his leave. "Not much of a talker, but when he does...*fascinating* chap. Been *everywhere*."

Graham bid the Colonel goodnight and went to his room. He decided to sleep on the new information Colonel Graves had given him. He'd rise early, and call his team together for a morning meeting.

Later, as Graham tried to drop off to sleep, he let his thoughts meander. He hoped to settle on something other than the unhappy demise of Sylvia Norquist but he was kept awake past midnight by the persistent thought that this case, frustrating and elusive by turns, was finally ready to break wide open. Something told him that tomorrow would be the day.

CHAPTER TWENTY

I NITIALLY, GRAHAM THOUGHT
that bringing in a whiteboard on an easel might help
them brainstorm more efficiently. Seeing it now,
covered in scrawled notes, scratched-out, half-deleted
ideas, and a couple of hare-brained diagrams, he was
beginning to wonder. They had been 'bringing together
the investigative strands,' as he'd originally put it, but
which in reality proved closer to arguing like cats and
dogs, for three hours. He was ready for a break.

"Okay, take ten, boys and girls," he said, relieved to be
shooing them out of his office for a few minutes. "We'll all
feel better after a breath of fresh air and a cuppa."

The two constables argued all the way to the front
door where they berated each other for the duration of
Barnwell's cigarette. Back in his office, Graham gave
Sergeant Harding a tired smile and shook his head.

"Feel as though we're getting anywhere?" he asked.

Harding took one look at the board, grabbed the
eraser, and cleaned the entire thing. Then she began
writing in large, clear letters.

"We've got Sylvia." Janice wrote the name on the board. "Late of this parish. Known to all the suspects," she said. "This fits with the very high probability that the victim knew the murderer."

"Near certainty," Graham confirmed.

"There's the exotic and charismatic Mr. Carlos Alves. Visitor from South America," she said, writing his name on the board with a dotted line to Sylvia. "Father of a teenaged boy who died while under her care."

"Bloody tragic," Graham added.

"But *not present* during the period leading up to the murder. We have confirmation of that," she said.

"From none other than the investigative powerhouse that is Constable Roach," Graham quipped.

"Marvelous. His terrifying wife is nowhere to be seen, and we have no reason to believe she's on Jersey, so the people with the most obvious motive can be ruled out."

"99%," Graham confirmed. He was never happy with "always" or "absolutely." There had already been too many exceptions and rarities during his career.

"Then we have the Pilkingtons," she said, adding their names to the board, "known to Sylvia through her work. Nigel was the recipient of successful cancer treatment, though in his unfortunate case the 'Big-C' appears to have returned."

"Much to the shock of Mrs. Pilkington," Graham added.

"And she was just as shocked that her husband had seen Sylvia without her knowledge. And angry. Are we putting that down to...well, them just being a funny couple?"

"You tell me, Sergeant. How likely is it, all things

considered, that an oncologist becomes involved with a very sick patient?"

"It must happen, but I can't think it's too frequent."

"And, not to be rude about the man, but you saw Nigel. Not exactly male-model material. Am I right?"

"You are," Harding confirmed. "I mean, it wasn't as though the years were weighing heavily on Sylvia. She could have done so much better."

"Hard to say," Graham said. "I've only ever seen her buried in sand, or laid out on a mortuary slab, dead as a dodo."

Harding continued writing. "So, whatever is going on between the much-troubled Pilkingtons, we can't pin a murder on them."

"Very difficult to do at present," Graham agreed. "They only have reasons to be grateful to her. And mad at each other, but that's not the point."

The board was filling with names, lines, and notes, but at least it was a more orderly depiction of the case than their previous attempt. "Okay, so we're assuming Alves didn't pay off an assassin?" Harding posited.

Graham was shaking his head. "I really can't imagine him murdering Sylvia in any other way than with his own two hands. Revenge killings are brutal. This was a quick bit of poisoning. Doesn't fit."

Sergeant Harding agreed. "And even if he had paid to have her poisoned, would her killer use a method like *Wolfsbane*?"

"Unlikely. Too indirect, open to error. Besides in the circumstances and if they chose poisoning, I would think they'd favor something that would draw out the process, not kill her in the course of an unpleasant afternoon."

Standing back from the board, Harding said, "So, we're looking for someone else entirely."

"Yes," Graham said. He stood and began pacing around the tiny office. "Think about this," he was saying. "Would the murderer stay around on Jersey after doing the deed?"

"If I'd just done someone in, I'd take myself as far away as possible," Harding told him, brushing chalk off her hands.

Graham tried the opposite approach, just to play Devil's Advocate. "But the murderer might have stayed in town to deflect suspicion. As if to say, 'Look, I'm still here! I've got nothing to hide!'"

"But in that case," Harding countered, "we'd have something on them, some connection or motive or... *something*."

CHAPTER TWENTY-ONE

G RAHAM TOOK THE chalk. "Next. Colonel Graves."

"Our erstwhile paramour and real estate mogul." Harding laughed gently.

"Now, now, Sergeant," Graham said, admonishment in his tone. "He's hurting, and he's the real deal."

"You told me," Harding countered, "that no one can be ruled out entirely."

"But how does he benefit from killing the woman he's about to propose to? If he'd hoped to gain access to her wealth, he would have done better to marry her first." Graham stared out of the small window. "It's possible he killed her in a fit of temper after she would give him neither her hand nor her money, but she was just a sweet, retired doctor. There's nothing to suggest she'd turn him down and he was crazy about her. I sensed nothing malevolent about them at all, not in my dealings with Colonel Graves nor from the reports of them by others."

"That's true. Half the hotel knew about the two of them. And Mrs. Taylor, of course."

Graham stopped short. "Can we rule her out, too?"

"Oh God, yes," Harding said at once. "Murders might boost a hotel's reputation if a celebrity is involved and a few decades go by, but all she's done since we arrived is remind us how important the summer is to her business."

"Exactly. It does her no good to have a bunch of police officers running around."

Harding thought on. "I mean, there's no way she's in a weird love triangle with Sylvia and the Colonel is there?"

DI Graham couldn't help a quick, indulgent laugh. "Wow, Sergeant, that's imaginative. I mean, we've got no reason to suspect it, but I like your ingenuity."

Barnwell reappeared at the door. "Oi, what the bloody hell happened to my diagram?" he demanded. "I *had* something there."

"What you *had*," Harding informed him, "was fit for a kindergarten art class. This," she announced, "is much better."

Arms folded, Barnwell took his seat and let the two continue to brainstorm. Roach slid in next to him. He turned over yet another page of his legal pad, ready to keep track of his thoughts as he had throughout the investigation.

"What about Alice?" Harding prompted.

"She loaned Graves money," Graham told them. "It might not be in any way relevant, but I just want to put it out there."

"Was that for his property investments?" Roach asked.

Graham explained about the syndicate Graves had been putting money into, the way he was being pressured by the investment group. "He's already started paying it back," he added.

Barnwell chortled obscenely. "Paying it back *how*, exactly?"

Harding gave him yet another exasperated look, hands on her hips. "What are you talking about?"

"I mean, you saw her. That Alice, she's totty she is," Barnwell said, narrowly preventing himself from clarifying his point with a lewd gesture. "Is it so impossible to believe?"

"That Colonel Graves was cheating on his beloved Sylvia? Or that Alice Swift, with all of her..." Harding could barely believe she was stooping so low, "*assets*, would be interested in a seventy-year-old ex-soldier with the stiffest..."

"Steady on," Barnwell interrupted.

"*Upper lip*," Harding enunciated, "you've ever seen." She rolled her eyes at Graham. *How can I work with these buffoons?*

"Let's put a pin in that one," Graham said diplomatically. "Does Alice have any motive to harm Sylvia?" Three pairs of shoulders rose slightly, then dropped back down. "Thanks, team. Excellent police work," the DI said with heavy sarcasm.

"If there isn't anything to find," Barnwell objected, "we won't find it, will we?"

"Okay, you're right," Graham allowed. "So, who are we left with?"

"There's suicide. We haven't gone back over that," Barnwell insisted.

"Because it's bollocks," Roach countered.

"So sure?" Graham asked.

Roach was adamant. "She was happy, in love, living on the beautiful island of Jersey in summer with plenty of money. What *possible reason*..."

"I don't want to give this idea more credence than I should," Graham said cautiously, "but just because someone *seems* happy doesn't mean they *are*."

"Look at Marilyn Monroe," Harding offered.

"I often do," Barnwell replied.

"Moving on," Graham decided. "If none of the hotel staff are suspects, and we can rule out everyone we've interviewed, then..."

"We're kind of nowhere," Roach said despondently.

Graham stood. "I'm going for a walk. If a bolt of investigative lightning strikes you in the next half-hour, call me."

It was a warm, sunny lunchtime outside, one of the hottest days of the year so far. Graham left his jacket behind and rolled up his sleeves. It might even, he wondered to himself, be an opportunity to replace his pasty Londoner look with something a little more exotic. Not to mention *attractive*.

He walked west, on autopilot almost, toward the ocean. The cliff tops gave spectacular views of the other Channel Islands beyond and then the coast of France, especially on a day as clear as this. He reached the top after twenty minutes meandering stroll and sat down on the grass. Quite a few years earlier, he'd been invited to a meditation retreat in Scotland that had scenery a little like this; green meadows, sparse tiny villages with twisting roads disappearing into the next valley, and breathtaking views of the serene, sparkling Atlantic. He'd spent a long weekend simply breathing in and out. It hadn't *really* been his thing if he were honest. By the third day, he was bored beyond belief, but the invitation had come from a particularly alluring brunette named Isla, and he could hardly refuse, especially when she'd asked so nicely....

With no warning whatsoever, a light bulb went off in his head. It illuminated areas of his mind, details of his memory that had languished in darkness. New connections were made, even as he sat there, stunned by the suddenness of the sensation. Pieces fell into place. The events of the last four days sought to relate to each other in novel ways and with a fresh logic.

"Bloody hell."

He stood, reaching for his notebook before remembering that it was in his jacket pocket hung on the back of his office chair. Adrenaline flowing, he covered the mile back to the Constabulary at a pace that would have impressed a much younger man. He was exhilarated by the energizing power of raw, independent discovery. It was at times like these that he never felt more alive.

CHAPTER TWENTY-TWO

THE THREE POLICE officers stood in the lobby of Gorey Constabulary looking at one another in confusion. Banished from DI Graham's office while he made what seemed to be a series of phone calls, they were left wondering what on *earth* he might have stumbled upon during his afternoon walk.

"You don't think," Barnwell shared in a low tone, "that our new boss is a bit loopy, do you?"

Harding gave him a skeptical look. "No, Constable. I don't."

"I mean," Barnwell pressed on, "I like a breath of fresh air as much as the next man, but..."

Graham emerged from his office, swinging back the door so hard that it smacked into the wall. "Friends, Romans, Countrymen," he began, "lend me your car so I can get over to the *White House Inn* and put this sodding case to bed, once and for all."

"Breakthrough, boss?" Roach asked, excited.

Graham turned to him. "Maybe. I won't know for sure until we all do a bit of people-watching. I just called

Mrs. Taylor, and she's racing around right now, doing us a favor."

The drive over was purposeful and speedy, despite the wandering tourists on this sunny afternoon. They stopped at a pedestrian crossing to allow an elderly man to cross, but he changed his mind in the middle and headed back the way he'd come. "Dozy bugger," Harding muttered. "Does he think we're in a police car because we like the colors?"

"Should have put the siren on," Barnwell recommended from the back seat. "Give him a good scare."

"Thank you, Constable," Graham said, "but I'd rather deal with Dr. Norquist's murder than a random stranger's heart attack. And buckle your seat belt. You do know the law around here, don't you?"

Mrs. Taylor was as good as her word. "Good afternoon, Detective Inspector. I must say I was surprised to receive your call, but it's excellent news that this might all be over soon," she enthused.

"I make no promises, Mrs. Taylor," Graham reminded her. "But I've got a hunch. And sometimes that's enough."

The *White House Inn's* staff, including the bustling and efficient Marcella, had cleared the terrace except for one large table. Around it sat seven familiar figures. Per Graham's instructions, Carlos Alves was furthest from the door, followed by the Pilkingtons, Colonel Graves, and then Alice Swift. Mrs. Taylor and Marcella took the last two seats. Harding, Roach, and Barnwell positioned themselves around the terrace as Graham strode into the middle and addressed the group.

"Thank you all for being here this afternoon," he began. "I'm sure the past few days have been difficult for everyone. Sylvia was a popular and respected doctor, and she will be sorely missed by many, including some of you." Graham spoke his words carefully. He knew full well that not everyone on this terrace was devastated by this particular loss.

"You've all been very generous with your time and mostly," he emphasized, "entirely honest in your statements to the police." There was a flutter of concern throughout the group. Which of them was being accused of dishonesty was uncertain. "My team and I," Graham continued, motioning to the trio, "have exhausted every avenue of inquiry including the forensic angles, and we're here today for what amounts to...well, I suppose it's a final interview, conducted *en masse*. Does anyone have any objection to this rather unorthodox format?"

No one spoke. Roach was writing, just as Graham had instructed. He was keeping a log, not of what was *said*, but of what each person *did*. Before being reduced to surreptitious games of solitaire under the Constabulary's reception desk, Roach had been a decent poker player. He had even won a local championship. Reading people's reactions, he'd insisted to Graham on his first day in the job, was a specialty and one which the DI was keen to put to good use.

"I'll lay out the case as plainly as I can," Graham said. "Nothing is for certain in this game, but we're 99% sure that Dr. Norquist was murdered." The Pilkingtons both gasped slightly, but that was the only movement Roach could detect. "We are also 99% certain that someone poisoned her with an herbal concoction known as *tincture of aconite*, also known as *Wolfsbane*."

The Colonel looked thoroughly appalled. Perhaps it was guilt at the revelation of what he had done, Graham considered, or simply distaste at being told the very method by which his beloved was taken from him. Alice was frowning as though puzzling the matter over in her mind. On Graham's left, Alves was rolling an unlit cigar between his fingers, as though supremely indifferent to this entire business.

"*Aconite* or *Wolfsbane* is a deadly poison, but not an especially commonplace one. It has the virtue of being largely undetectable. It leaves no traces, save the symptoms of the poisoning itself: asphyxia caused as the result of a stopped heart."

The Colonel was having trouble gathering his emotions. For an instant, Graham wondered whether it was a mistake inviting the man here but reminded himself that for this conjurer's trick to be a success, every participant in the investigation had to be present.

"So, once we established those facts," he told the group, "our inquiry shifted its focus to potential motives. And here," he said, "we had an obvious place to begin." Graham turned to face Carlos Alves. "Sir, it is no secret that you harbored ill-will toward Dr. Norquist, correct?"

Alves said nothing, continuing to roll his cigar back and forth.

"She was responsible to an extent that varies depending on who you ask for the tragic death of your son." Alves raised his eyes now and nodded slightly. "There is no greater pain in human life than the loss of a child. But unfortunately, it made you our prime suspect."

"It would have been a pleasure," Alves said with studied malevolence, "to deny life to the woman who took my son from me."

Colonel Graves made to stand, but Barnwell responded quickest, a firm hand cautioning the incensed ex-officer to go no further.

"But I was not responsible for this crime," Alves said.

"No, you were not," Graham conceded. "You were on Guernsey at the time of the murder. Unless, of course," he added, "you paid someone to carry out this act."

Alves gave Graham a furious look. "*Paid?* I wouldn't pay to have such a thing done. I would have performed the deed myself!" He paused. "But I didn't."

"No, indeed," Graham asserted. "I believe you." Graham turned to look around at the group. "We were discussing *motive*," he reminded them. "Anne Pilkington. You had just such a motive, did you not?"

Anne's hand flew to her chest. "Me?" she gasped.

"You were concerned that your husband might be having an affair with Dr. Norquist. You are a jealous woman and suspected that, during your husband's cancer treatment, they had become close. Even intimate."

Nigel, for his part, looked thoroughly downcast and exhausted. Roach, writing notes, imagined that these repeated reminders of his life-and-death struggle with cancer must weigh on him. "I am not jealous and suspected nothing of the sort," Anne retorted. "Nigel and I are as close as we have ever been."

"But you were furious when you discovered they'd been spending time together," Graham reminded her. "Without your knowledge. Suspicions of an affair were where your thoughts immediately traveled when you found out."

Shaking her head firmly, Anne replied, "We made a pact after his diagnosis last year that we would be absolutely honest with each other. This was the first time Nigel had hidden anything from me since then."

"But it was for your own good, my love," Nigel offered sincerely. "I didn't want you to know the cancer was back.

This time...well, I couldn't put you through all that again." The Pilkington's sat, hand in hand. "I was going to walk out into the bay one night and never come back. I wanted, still want, to be done with it all." The couple embraced and then sat in intense, shared silence, seemingly no longer part of the drama unfolding around them.

Harding was close to tears, but Graham regained his focus quickly. "Which brings us to Colonel Graves." This was not, Graham could see, going to be an easy moment. "More often than you might believe," Graham said, "and far more often than any of us would wish for, it is those closest to their victims who are responsible for their deaths."

CHAPTER TWENTY-THREE

"**Y**OU CAN'T THINK..." Graves began, red-faced.

"I *have* to, Colonel. During investigations like this, we must ask the hardest questions and follow the most unlikely leads. You claimed to us that you were about to propose to Sylvia."

"I... I was," the Colonel replied.

"But we were forced to consider that you had already asked her to marry you, and had been refused. All of those carefully laid plans ruined," Graham speculated. "Your future happiness in tatters."

Graves was silently shaking his head.

"Or perhaps you asked Dr. Norquist for money to bail you out of your troubled investments in the States, and *this* was the refusal which cost Sylvia her life."

"I discussed that with you," Graves rasped, "in *confidence.*"

"And I apologize, but my business is catching a murderer, whatever misfortunes might have befallen yours."

"This is outrageous!" Graves roared. "You have *no right* to speak to me like this!"

"I have every right," Graham shot back, "to question those whom I believe may be complicit in a murder and to do so in any way I see fit."

Harding was becoming worried. Was Barnwell right, she wondered, and their new DI was a bit "loopy?" Were his methods, including this strange performance on the terrace, really sound? Were his conclusions, whatever they might be, truly to be trusted?

But before she could intervene, there was an angry voice from the table. "You leave him *alone!*" Alice insisted. "He did *nothing* wrong."

There was silence on the terrace for a long moment. Then Graham resumed where he had left off. "Miss Swift. I wonder if there's anything you'd like to tell us?"

Alice sat stubbornly, her arms folded.

"Perhaps you'd like to tell us why it was that you ordered *aconitum* flowers online?" Graham asked. "Perhaps why you chose to concoct a poison amid the dyes and inks in your room?"

Alice remained silent, staring straight ahead at the ocean.

"Perhaps why," Graham asked, approaching her now, "you added a fatal dose of *Wolfsbane* to Sylvia's wine while pretending to be her friend and sharing confidences?"

Carlos Alves stood, his cigar forgotten on the table, his face fixed with amazement.

"Perhaps why," Graham pressed, sensing the growing tumult among the others, "you stayed with her throughout the excruciating symptoms of *Wolfsbane* poisoning?"

Now the Colonel was up too. He stared at Alice.

Graham continued. "Why you kept her from calling for help? Took her phone? Told her that everything would be fine, even offered her more wine laced with poison which was even then causing her heart to flutter and gurgle in distress?"

"My *God...*" breathed Anne Pilkington.

"Did Sylvia know what was happening in those last moments?" Graham asked Alice. The group seemed to enclose around her as though preparing to tear her apart for her sins. "Did she realize you were responsible?"

"*Her?*" Marjorie Taylor exclaimed. "But *why?*"

"This is the only thing I don't understand," Graham confessed. "Why, Alice?"

Fists clenching, jaw firmly set, Alice Swift finally spoke. "She was a temptress." Alice's voice was a furious hiss. "A *Jezebel.* A consumer of men, heedless of others, and their emotions."

Alves said it for them all. "What in *God's* name is she talking about?"

The murderous woman addressed him now. "She seduced my George."

"*Your* George?" Harding said, almost unwittingly. "The Colonel, and *you...?*"

"That woman, the *doctor,*" Alice spat the word, "beguiled him, teased him. She dangled in front of him a life so comforting and saccharine and *dull,* he was going to *propose...*"

"Oh, God," Colonel Graves finally managed. "Oh, Alice, what have you *done?*"

"I *had to!*" Alice shrieked. "There was nothing else..."

Colonel Graves turned to Graham now, looking gaunt and ashen. "I'm sorry...I should have mentioned something about our dealings earlier...I just never, ever, in a *thousand years* would have thought..."

Without another word, Graham nodded to Sergeant Harding, who approached Alice from behind, handcuffs ready. "Alice Swift, I am arresting you on suspicion of the murder of Dr. Sylvia Norquist." As the cuffs clicked into place, Alice seemed to struggle with inner demons known to no one else, the boiling anger and resentment that had led her to commit calculated, cold-blooded murder causing her to twitch and shudder.

Harding finished reading Alice her rights and led the furious woman back from the tables toward the door where Constable Barnwell was waiting to escort the prisoner to their police car. As Harding guided her through the doorway, Alice turned viciously and yelled at them.

"I did it for you, George!" Her voice was a cold rasp. "I *killed* her for you!"

Graves dropped his head to his hands, inconsolable now. Alice was led away. "Oh, Sylvia," he said, again and again. Graham sat with the Colonel, relieved that his gamble had paid off and that he had successfully unmasked the murderer.

"It's alright, George. It's all over," he told the grieving Colonel.

"But how...?" The Colonel was plaintive.

"We now know that Miss Swift hatched a plan that involved ordering *aconitum* on the Internet and prepared the poison in her room before inviting Dr. Norquist out for dinner the night before her body was found," DI Graham explained. "They went to the *Bangkok Palace*. I saw a business card for the restaurant among Miss Swift's weaving supplies. When I questioned the restaurant staff about their dinner, I learned that Alice was overheard telling Dr. Norquist about your financial woes, possibly to discredit you in Sylvia's eyes so that she would be persuaded not to marry you. The two women argued. I believe that Alice, realizing Sylvia would not renounce you, laced her drink with the poison that she had brought with her."

The Colonel shook his head and exhaled. He looked up at the Detective Inspector, imploring him to go on.

"Instead of taking her back to the *White House Inn* when she became ill," Graham continued, increasingly feeling he was intruding on the elder man's grief but also respecting his need to understand what had happened to his love, "she drove to the steps above the beach, where she plied Sylvia with more poisoned wine, staying with her until she was dead. I think she planned to have the tide wash Sylvia's body out to sea, but having dragged her down the steps to the beach, Alice was too exhausted to carry her further and buried Sylvia in the sand instead.

"Returning to the *White House Inn*, Swift gave herself an alibi by making sure she was seen around the hotel the following morning. Using Dr. Norquist's key, Alice then let herself into Sylvia's room, ordered food, and pretended to talk on the telephone when lunch was delivered. Miss Swift most likely drunk the wine that came with lunch and took the glass with her, destroying it later so we would not be able to connect it to her.

"She created an alibi for herself and the impression that Sylvia was alive at a time when she had, in fact, been dead for several hours. With the time of death being so vague and using a barely detectable means of killing, Alice knew it would be extremely difficult to pin the murder on her. And she was right, hers was a canny plan that nearly worked. Alice is without a doubt a cold-blooded killer, Colonel. She was in love with you and sought to remove her rival. You had a lucky escape." Graham finished quietly, knowing his words were cold comfort to the bereaved man.

Graves looked at the detective ruefully. "I've lost the woman I loved, my life savings, my future. I wouldn't call that much of an escape."

Graham looked at the sad, broken man with great sympathy. He hesitated, weighing up the propriety of his action, then placed his hand on the man's shoulder. "I'm sorry, Colonel."

As Detective Inspector Graham completed his exposition, the tension drained from the room, its occupants left to quietly contemplate the impact of his words. The room became silent and still. After a few moments, DI Graham delicately withdrew and as he did so, another person in the room stirred.

Stepping away from the others, and hoping not to appear indelicate, Carlos Alves quietly lit his cigar and looked out once more onto the water. A slight smile played on his lips for the first time in months. As he drew deeply on his cigar, Alves closed his eyes momentarily and reflected on the events of the last few days. He exhaled with a small sigh, cigar smoke dissipating into the clear Jersey air. He had all but given up, but he'd been wrong. There was an ounce of justice in the world, after all.

SERGEANT JANICE HARDING shook her head firmly. "No way, Barnwell. You've finally lost it."

"No, I'm serious," Barnwell said. "I know she's not *exactly* the right age, but there's such a thing as 'artistic license.'"

Graham emerged from his office. He stretched and regarded the squabbling pair. "What's this all about?" he asked.

Barnwell explained. "We're figuring out," he said, not in the least embarrassed, "who should play all of us when the Norquist case gets made into a big Hollywood movie."

"Oh, great," Graham told them. "I'm glad it's hard-nosed police work that's keeping you so occupied."

"I thought," Barnwell continued regardless, "that Ben Affleck would make an excellent DI Graham."

"Did you, now?" Graham said, distractedly flicking lint from his suit trousers.

"And Jodie Foster could play the fiercely devoted Sergeant Harding," Barnwell said next. The *real* Sergeant

Harding couldn't have been less impressed and made a grotesque face at the grinning constable.

"And who's playing you, Barnwell?" Graham asked with a smirk.

"Cruise." Barnwell looked at them both. "I mean, *obviously*."

"Obviously," parroted Harding. She followed Graham back into his office.

Graham smiled at her. "Good to see Barnwell applying that razor-sharp investigative acumen of his," he quipped.

"I'd rather that than him showing up half-drunk," she said. "Don't think he's touched a drop since you arrived."

"Good," Graham nodded. "About time for lunch, isn't it, Sergeant?"

Harding checked the enormous wall clock. "I'd say so, sir."

"Well, I think it's my turn to buy. *Bangkok Palace?*" he recommended.

Harding grinned. "Sure. Sounds good."

Graham followed Harding out into the lobby where Roach was now fully involved in the Hollywood discussion. "Cruise, he says." Roach was laughing. "Can you imagine?"

"Not even a little bit," Harding said, pushing open the door. "Hold the fort, you two," she instructed.

"Will do, Sarge," they chorused.

"You know," Janice said, as she got in the car, "those two are in grave danger of becoming actual *police officers* one of these days." She chuckled, but not dismissively. Her respect for Roach and Barnwell was on the rise. Ever since their new boss had landed on Jersey, they had been punctual and diligent, keen to help the public, and willing to leave no stone unturned. "I barely recognize them. Still, just as well, Detective Inspector, a brilliant detective needs a brilliant support team."

Graham rolled his eyes. "Steady on, Sergeant." But with a self-contented smile, he put the car into gear and they headed off into Jersey's bright, afternoon sunshine.

EPILOGUE

DESPITE THE EFFORTS of counsel, the jury refused to accept a charge of manslaughter on the grounds of diminished responsibility in the case of Crown v. Swift. Alice was sentenced to serve twenty years for the murder of Dr. Sylvia Norquist. After two years at HMP Wainscott, Alice became involved in the prison's historic working farm and enjoys recreating various *tableaux vivant* for visiting members of the public. Her exhibition of Tudor tapestries has received high praise.

Colonel Graves left Jersey to join an affordable retirement community for military veterans on the British mainland. There, he has several ladyfriends but no one in particular. He has abandoned his Stateside investment plans, preferring to live a modest life that is within his means. He still quietly grieves for "my darling girl."

·   ·   ·

Anne and Nigel Pilkington quickly resolved never to speak of "the Jersey matter." They returned to Britain and never visited the island again. Nigel Pilkington is now under hospice care but bears his burden bravely to avoid upsetting his wife.

Carlos Alves sold his sailboat and returned to his native Ecuador where he reconciled with his wife. He has resolved to stay closer to home in the future.

Janice Harding, buoyed by the arrival of the new Detective Inspector, found herself looking forward to Mondays with unusual enthusiasm. Fancying herself a matchmaker and with some self-sacrifice, she has made a list of her friends for whom the DI might fit the bill.

Following the conclusion of the Alice Swift case, Jim Roach spent his next pay packet entirely on books purchased from the Jersey police force's online store. One Saturday at 2 a.m., his mother was surprised to find him reading *Policing Organized Crime: The Rise of the Military Cop.*

As far as locals could tell, the regime change at Gorey Constabulary had no effect on the burly Barry Barnwell save two notable exceptions. On his weekly visit to the supermarket, Barnwell was seen quietly abandoning a six-pack on an empty shelf just before joining the checkout line. He also seemed a little more cheery in the mornings.

. . .

Ever the ladies' man and a little bored by his current run-of-the-mill workload, Dr. Tomlinson embarked on a relationship with a feisty, glamorous widow from St. Helier. To Tomlinson's relief, she was not a fan of Asian food, and their favorite haunt turned out to be a tiny, but charming, hole-in-the-wall French restaurant in St. Brelade. After a few months, he ended the relationship when he realized that "hot and spicy" in any form was simply not for him.

DI Graham settled into the *White House Inn* and the staff got used to his quirks, finding him a humble, polite, and gracious guest. He was regularly seen alone, walking the beaches and the cliffs around Gorey. While Graham was a sociable, long-term guest, Mrs. Taylor would have preferred to see him mix with people closer to his own age. Graham was aware of Mrs. Taylor's preference and took great pains to thwart her efforts in this regard.

USA Today Bestselling Author

THE CASE OF THE
FALLEN
HERO

ALISON GOLDEN Grace Dagnall

THE CASE OF THE FALLEN HERO

BOOK THREE

Published by Mesa Verde Publishing
P.O. Box 1002
San Carlos, CA 94070

Edited by
Marjorie Kramer

PROLOGUE
ORGUEIL CASTLE, NEAR GOREY, JERSEY

Saturday, 3:30 p.m.

THE FOUR FRIENDS tumbled out of the minivan, thanked their driver, and stared agog at the imposing medieval castle that now towered over them.

"Bloody hell," Harry managed, wiping his glasses clean and staring at the immense walls. "It's *big*, isn't it?"

Emily retrieved her priceless violin from the van's back seat and joined him, looking up at the impenetrable, solid battlements that spoke of the castle's impressively deep history. "Going for your Masters in architecture, Harry?" she joked. "It's an eight hundred-year-old *fortress*. I don't think *big* does it justice."

Harry made sure his battered cello case had suffered no further indignities on the ferry ride over from Weymouth and hoisted its weight onto his shoulder with well-practiced ease. "Well, I wouldn't dream of upstaging our resident expert, you see."

Leo Turner-Price, an accomplished historian and

violinist, stared at the castle as though achieving a lifelong dream. "Emily is right about the structure being eight *hundred* years old. But there are records of substantial fortifications on this site that go back to the Bronze Age."

"Really?" Harry remarked. "Wow."

"All to keep out the beastly French," Marina observed. The youngest of the four members of the Spire String Quartet, Marina was a shy but—as Harry once described her in an unguarded moment—"insanely attractive" viola player who taught young children at two of London's most expensive schools. "Must have cost a fortune."

"Well, if that was their aim," Harry opined, keeping up his role as the "bluff Brit abroad," "it was money well spent."

Emily rolled her eyes. Fifteen years into her friendship with the wonderfully gruff plentifully bearded Harry Tringham, she found that he was still learning how to filter the thoughts that entered his overactive brain, far too many of which were given unwisely free passage direct to his equally active mouth. She spotted the visitors' entrance up some steps in front of them. "Shall we?"

Emily was the only member of the quartet to have visited Orgueil Castle before, or even to have performed on the island of Jersey. It was through her contact with the castle's highly professional events manager, Stephen Jeffries, that they had been booked for the evening's wedding festivities. Always in need of a dependable ensemble who could provide light background music one moment and a strident processional, the next, Jeffries kept Emily's name at the top of his hiring list. He had been heartily impressed when, during a wedding two years before, Emily had led a young string trio through various weather-related disasters, a collapsed marquee, and a bridal arrival so delayed that the groom was harboring the gravest of doubts. Having navigated these obstacles, Emily had still possessed the presence of mind to guide her fellow musicians through a beautifully polished *Prince of Denmark's March* as the sodden bride entered, still dripping, into the Great Hall.

"Emily, my *darling!*" Jeffries exclaimed as he walked out to greet them. "So lovely to see you! How's your teaching going? Didn't you just start at that exclusive little prep school?" he asked.

"Fine, fine," Emily told him. "It's going well. Some of the little blighters even practice before their lessons." The whole quartet was nodding. Finding students who were prepared to work hard was like finding gemstones in the desert. "It's nice to get a break, though, and a change of scenery."

"Better weather for this one, too, eh?" Jeffries said, hand aloft toward the bluest possible sky.

"Much better," Emily agreed. "And I want to thank you for this, Stephen. Gives us all a pleasant break from an unseasonably warm London. This is Marina Linton," she said as the tall blonde extended a graceful hand, "Harry Tringham, our cellist, and resident physicist," she added, "and the historian Leo Turner-Price."

"Delighted to be here," Leo enthused. "Remarkable building, really."

Jeffries led them into an open quadrangle, home in part to a beautifully kept maze, and then down some steps into the castle's administrative area. Here they would relax and tune-up until the wedding guests began to arrive at five o'clock. He moved paperwork and wedding paraphernalia off his biggest table to give them a safe, flat surface for their priceless instruments.

"Okay, did everyone's folders survive the journey?" Emily wanted to confirm. She received a trio of nods in reply. "Excellent," she said, quickly tying her curly, black hair into an unsophisticated ponytail. "So, we'll start with the little Baroque set..."

"Couperin," Harry said, finding the sheet music in his folder.

"And then the Purcell theater music?" Marina asked.

"That's right. Then *Eine Kleine*. Everyone loves that," Emily said.

"All four movements?" Leo asked.

Emily thought for a second. "Let's play it by ear. Depends on timings and such, but we can ax the repeats if we need to hurry things along."

"Righto," Leo said, slotting his sheet music in the correct order. "Which Processional did they choose in the end?"

Marina clasped both hands together, as if in prayer. "*Please* tell me it isn't Wagner again. I promised I'd quit weddings if I ever had to..."

"Nope," Emily reassured her. "*The Arrival of the Queen of Sheba.*"

All four sighed slightly. "It's a terrific piece," Leo allowed, "but too much of a gallop for a processional, surely?"

Emily found the music and finished organizing her folder. "She's the bride, Leo. And it's her..."

"*Special day!*" the three other members of the quartet chorused. They laughed together.

Jeffries watched this polished routine with unconcealed envy. "Honestly," he said as the four musicians finalized their folders, "I would simply *die* to make every aspect of these weddings as smooth as working with you guys."

"Aw, Stephen. You're an angel," Emily replied, kissing him on the cheek.

"I've already had a run-in with the mother of the bride," Jeffries admitted, his face relating just how ugly the encounter had been. "*Terrifying* woman. A foot wider than I am," he confessed, "and with a decidedly mean streak. These people get it into their heads that just because they've spent a fortune on getting their offspring hitched, they can treat people *however they like!*"

Jeffries was a stylish and experienced man, unused to brusque treatment. He allowed that the bridal party was under considerable pressure to ensure their lovely daughter's wedding day was as close to perfect as possible, but still, their discourtesy toward him seemed so unnecessary, especially when he was doing his level best to meet their every need.

"I'll leave you to it. Yell if you need anything," Stephen said with a companionable hand on Emily's forearm, and then, with a dramatic flourish, he left to supervise the preparation of the reception.

Emily's preference was to start playing even before the guests arrived, ostensibly to create the "right atmosphere," but more practically to check acoustics and intonation. The quartet seated themselves in one corner of the quadrangle where the marquee—the same one that had suffered the spectacular structural failure during Emily's last performance at the castle—was set up. Guests would shortly be wandering on the lawn of the quad, ducking inside to grab a drink or a canapé, and rubbing shoulders before the bridal party arrived.

As they waited, the group went through their plan. They talked quietly in the short gaps between movements of the tasteful Couperin suite Harry had arranged for them years before. Once it was confirmed that the bride was ready to go through with the ceremony (and in Emily's twenty-year experience of weddings, this was by no means an absolute certainty), the quartet would have only a few moments to quickly relocate to the Great Hall and prepare for the Processional.

Later, after the bride reached the altar, the musicians' time would be their own. Jeffries would hand them a generous check, and they'd enjoy the rest of the evening at the castle before retreating to a local hostel for the night. The castle would then play host to an extended party before the guests collapsed into bed. There was plentiful accommodation within the giant edifice so that, as Jeffries always thought of it, they wouldn't have to stagger far.

"Let's skip the minor-key Purcell movements," Marina said. "I don't feel like playing in D-minor under a sky as beautiful as this." The quartet unanimously agreed and launched into the joyously dotted rhythms of Purcell's more animated theater pieces. The eighty or so invitees were now arriving in a steady stream, and the quadrangle filled with music, the clink of wine glasses, and old friends catching up after too long apart.

Their intonation unimprovable and their balance as tightly controlled as ever, the quartet reveled in the freedom of simply playing for fun. After the second movement of *Eine Kleine Nachtmusik*, Harry leaned over to Marina and grinned. "Doesn't feel like work, does it?"

"Not even a little bit," she said, following Emily's lead for the beginning of the *Minuet*.

An excitable Stephen Jeffries scuttled over. "She's *here!*" he announced in a boisterous whisper. "Action stations!"

Emily used eye contact alone—as the best leaders can —to bring the Minuet to a quick but elegant halt, and the quartet made their way to the Great Hall slightly ahead of the politely ushered guests. Moments later, the ravishing Marie Joubert—soon to be Marie Ross—stepped steadily and confidently down the aisle in her white lace gown with its elaborate train, the filigree of Handel and the beaming smiles of her family her lasting accompaniment.

CHAPTER ONE

FTER A SUBSTANTIAL and satisfying breakfast, as only Mrs. Taylor's experienced kitchen staff could muster, Inspector David Graham inhaled the extremely promising cup of tea he'd just poured. He relaxed in his window seat. The view, all the way to France on a morning as clear as this, was a source of great tranquility to him. The crystal blue waters were dotted with little boats, and even through the hotel dining room's double-glazed windows, he could pick out the cry of seagulls, wheeling in the sky. Perhaps a hundred small vessels were moored in Gorey's ample marina, although some were already venturing out into the English Channel for what promised to be a memorable day of sailing. Graham savored the first sip of his Assam tea much like a wine connoisseur would appreciate a nicely aerated claret and watched the white canvas sails unfurl as a trio of small sailing craft made their way out of the harbor.

Graham had lost perhaps five pounds, he estimated,

since his arrival in Gorey, despite Mrs. Taylor's massive, traditional breakfasts and the occasional Thai curry night at the Bangkok Palace. He hadn't had a drink in over two months, not even on his thirty-sixth birthday, which had passed quietly three weeks earlier. Graham kept his fair hair a little shorter than before, both for ease of maintenance and because he thought it gave him a slightly more polished bearing. His blue eyes were rediscovering their old twinkle, especially after a good, strong pot of Assam and a mile or so walk around Gorey. He felt, in the main, that the worst of the past and its many challenges were now behind him. Jersey's sea air, the change of environment, and the much reduced workload were all doing him a world of good.

The home front was also nicely stable. Graham had come to a most reasonable arrangement with Mrs. Taylor following his recent investigative success. Amid the prospect of very unwelcome media attention, Graham had swiftly solved the brutal murder of a White House Inn guest whose body had been discovered on the beach below. Mrs. Taylor had chosen to express her gratitude by allowing Graham to stay on in a room with an even better view, at a heavily discounted rate. Originally, Graham had planned to find a cottage or apartment in Gorey or within driving distance of it, but he found that he liked the Inn enormously. The other guests were either long-termers, like himself, or were on vacation, and either way, it made for a relaxed atmosphere. The food was excellent, some of the best on the island, and the chef found marvelous uses for the varied local seafood.

Uppermost in Graham's decision-making, though, was Mrs. Taylor's admirable selection of teas. In the dark days prior to his long overdue departure from London, Graham had found himself leaning on tea – which he had found to be a surprising but effective crutch – during his painful journey staving off alcoholism. Tragedy had driven him to the brink of despair, and as his marriage had crumbled, Graham sought oblivion. Good friends, a superb physician, and the support of the Metropolitan Police had helped him pull through. However, once he'd cracked a murder case in his home village of Chiddlinghurst, just outside London, Graham found he could interest himself only in a quick and complete exit from the area and the painful memories it held for him.

Gorey, in welcome contrast, was proving idyllic, the single murder at the Inn, six weeks before, notwithstanding. Now Graham was finding gratification in both his professional and personal lives. Under his direction, the other three fulltime members of the Gorey Constabulary, the tiny policing outpost that was responsible for public safety in this part of the Bailiwick of Jersey, were fast becoming highly competent officers. Graham allowed that Constable Barnwell was still something of a well-meaning oaf, but he was showing promise and drinking a lot less himself these days. Young Constable Roach was committed to his own professional development and Graham couldn't ask for a more solid and dependable second-in-command than Sergeant Janice Harding. With her steady hand on the tiller, theirs was now a tightly run ship that was quickly gaining a reputation as a hard-working and effective outfit.

The community that resided at the White House Inn was also a genuine source of solace and enjoyment for Inspector Graham. A welcome break from his police work could be found in the dining room or on the spacious terrace where he had fallen easily into conversations and made fast friends with many of the long-term guests. Above all, he found time and time again, it was the tea that kept him happy, alert, and content with his lot. There was little more he would demand of the world, he noted to himself on this beautiful Sunday morning, than a good pot of Assam and this incredible view.

But Graham wasn't a man to sit around all day. He'd made a point of visiting a number of the historical sites in Jersey and its excellent zoo, and he was becoming something of an amateur historian of the area. The period of the German occupation was of particular interest. The old underground hospital with its built-in railway system, as well as the dozens of defensive positions and turrets that dotted the coast line – part of Hitler's Atlantic Wall – were fascinating to him.

And then there was Orgueil Castle – pronounced "Or-Goy" – the imposing medieval edifice that watched over the town like a sleeping stone giant. He'd visited it twice already, but he tended to find the place a little too crowded for his liking once the tour buses arrived. Visitors both from the British mainland and from France, which was actually far closer and had a comparable cultural influence on this little island, would swarm the castle at certain times of day. Because of that, Graham's plan this morning was to show up at opening time and see if he could have the place to himself, at least for a short while.

There was a shuttle bus that ran through the town, but it didn't run this early on a Sunday, so Graham decided to walk. Not even churchgoers were out and about yet, he noted as he glanced at his watch – only eight twenty-five. The castle opened its doors at eight-thirty during these last weeks of the tourist season, and he was glad to be their first customer. The imposing monument was a complex pile of thick stones, straddling the line between function and elegance. Striding up the steep approach road to the visitors' entrance, Graham could see signs of the repairs necessary to patch up the effects of many centuries of weathering, with some of the stone battlements a different, more recent color. As he reached the main gate, he marveled at the sheer immensity of the structure and the time and effort and expense it would have taken – all in pre-industrial times, he reminded himself – to hew and transport the rock. The *decades* of craftsmanship that were demanded by any truly solid fortification simply boggled the mind.

Graham's favorite parts of the castle, apart from the sweeping battlements and their commanding views of Gorey, the Channel, and France beyond, were the passageways beneath. Topped by thick, stone arches, these walkways burrowed within the castle itself. He never tired of strolling through them, imagining the heroics required to build precise arches in the days before calculators and computers, when an engineer was, by necessity of his profession, something of a genius. There was barely a straight wall in the castle, he noticed yet again, assuming that there was some military advantage to be had from constant turns and banks, rather than abrupt, ninety-degree corners. He admired the beautifully kept maze and then headed back under the castle, following a passageway that ran by a large bronze statue of a figure seated on horseback.

It was then that he heard it.

For an experienced police officer, there is something absolutely compelling about a woman's scream. This one was long, urgent, and panicked. Graham dashed at once in its direction knowing only one thing: something terrible had happened. When he came upon the source of the desperate, guttural cry, what he saw confirmed this finding and told him immediately that his plan for a relaxed Sunday was surely done for.

A woman was kneeling on the stone walkway that ran beneath one of the taller of the castle's battlements. As Graham approached, fairly sprinting out of the dark passageway and into the courtyard where she knelt, he could see she was cradling someone who was lying at a worryingly unnatural angle on the ground. From the size and shape of the body, he deduced that it was a man, and judging from the panicked wailing of the woman, kneeling by his head, Graham immediately feared the worst.

"Police, ma'am," he said, as he skidded to a halt by the body. "What happened?" The woman continued wailing, as though Graham were invisible, her hands under the stricken man's head. "I'm trained in first aid," Graham told her, following the received script. "Let me help him."

His condition, Graham could see, was extremely grave. Blood was rushing onto the stone from at least one serious head wound. Both ears were bleeding, which was never a good sign, and from the jagged position of his hips, Graham quickly diagnosed substantial fractures. "Did he fall?" Graham asked, but the woman stared at the sky and howled.

Graham gently moved her hands aside – they were covered in blood – and reached for a pulse. Finding nothing, he leaned in to listen for breathing and felt not even the slightest whisper in his ear. "We need to get him to hospital *immediately*," Graham told her, already certain in his own mind that medical help would prove futile. "Have you called for an ambulance?"

Receiving no answer, Graham stood, finding his own shirt bloodied now, and reached for his phone to dial 999. "This is Detective Inspector Graham of Gorey Constabulary," he told the operator. "I need an ambulance at Orgueil Castle immediately. A man appears to have fallen and has serious injuries." He listened while the operator confirmed the details and promised that an ambulance would be with him shortly. Turning back to ask the woman, once more, whether the gravely injured man was known to her, he was astonished to see her fleeing down the stone path, out of the castle grounds, and toward the village. "Wait!" he shouted. "*Attendez-vous!*" he tried next, but the woman either heard nothing or ignored his pleas.

"Well," he said, still slightly out of breath. "Well. Bugger." The man at his feet, now almost certainly a *victim* of some kind, remained resolutely inert. "What happened to you, eh?" A few early risers who, like Graham, had been strolling around the castle, were arriving now, attracted by the shouts. "Please stay back!" Graham ordered them. Then more quietly, almost as though the injured man might hear, "I don't think there's anything we can do. He's gone."

One of the first on the scene, his face etched with horror and panic, was Stephen Jeffries. He grabbed Graham, who was keeping people away from the body, imploring them not to take photos. "You're the police?" Jeffries asked, and then, stuttering over his own name, he explained who he was. "He was married... only yesterday," Jeffries told the detective. "Only *hours* ago..." Jeffries could barely speak. "Beautiful ceremony." Then it occurred to him. "Jesus... his *wife*! Did someone find her?"

It didn't take long to establish that the woman who had fled, wailing, into the village, was the grieving widow, Marie Ross. "I called after her, but she ignored me. Perhaps overcome with grief," Graham speculated, his phone to his ear.

"She ran?" Jeffries said, trying to piece together the scene. "Just *ran off*?"

"You'd be surprised what a sudden shock can do to a person," Graham told him. "I've seen people sprint off like an Olympic gold medalist seconds after getting the worst news of their lives." Finally, his call went through. "Sergeant Harding?"

A very sleepy voice confirmed what Graham had guessed; Janice was just waking up. "Boss?"

"I'm afraid so. Sorry to disturb your Sunday morning. Can you get over to the castle, right away?"

"Huh?" Harding managed.

Graham explained for a few moments while Jeffries wrung his hands. Two waiters from last night's wedding, who had volunteered to come in early to clean up, arrived to cover the body with a pristine, white tablecloth. It remained perfect for mere seconds before inevitably staining red.

"I'm..." He heard a strange clatter and deduced Harding must have dropped the phone in her haste. "*Bloody hell*, boss..." Harding muttered. "I'm on my way."

"Harding?"

"Eh? I mean, yes, boss?"

"Get Tomlinson on the horn and make sure he's up and about as well, would you? We're going to need the full works. You'll see for yourself how this looks, but if I've learned anything in this business, it's not to judge a book by its cover. You know what I mean?"

"I do, boss," Harding answered, struggling into her uniform blouse. "I'll call him next. Be there soon."

One of the saddest tasks relating to the death of a newly-deceased person, Graham found, was the necessity of establishing their identity. Beyond the bloodied remains now at his feet, he knew this young man had probably enjoyed a full life, was cherished by a circle of friends, and had a family who loved him. In this especially tragic case, he had a wife so new that the wedding guests had not yet dispersed following the festivities. He reached for and found the man's wallet in his trouser pocket.

"Mr. George Ross," Graham read from the man's local driver's license. "Thirty years old." Graham shook his head sadly. "Not nearly good enough, old chap." The remainder of the cards were the usual assortment of debit and credit cards, memberships to a couple of organizations, and store loyalty cards. There was the ubiquitous photo of his beloved, barely recognizable as the distraught woman who had wailed so inconsolably before vanishing into Gorey. Graham found some cash, in the form of the – still to him – rather unfamiliar Jersey banknotes and a room key marked "Bridal Suite."

"Not a lot to go on there," he admitted to himself. He

set the license aside to await an evidence bag. He found himself repeating, "Thirty years old." He imagined himself at that age, also newly married, a baby in the planning stages, documents drawn up for their first house, a future of togetherness and promise and possibility. "Poor sod."

CHAPTER TWO

HARRY TRINGHAM CLUTCHED his very welcome – if slightly gritty and questionable – take-out coffee as though it were the Elixir of Life itself, and ambled up the final few steps to the castle's visitors center. He was not used to early starts, especially on Sundays, and it showed.

"A little the worse for wear?" Emily asked brightly. She herself was looking energetic and ready for adventure in hiking boots, jeans, a bright red blouse, and a colorful silk scarf.

"You give musicians access to what is billed as an 'open bar,'" Harry retorted, "and you expect them not to make liberal use of it?"

Leo grinned sheepishly. He wasn't exactly feeling a hundred percent either, having helped put away some of the "spare" champagne from the previous evening's function with relish. "I tend to feel like one of those four-teenth-century troubadours," he related, "accepting the scraps from the table as part-payment for my musical services."

Emily finished organizing their tickets at the visitors' desk and pooled their contributions to pay the entry fee. "Here you go," she said, distributing the tickets. "Now, children, remember to hold hands, take only photos, and make sure you don't wander off without telling a teacher."

"Yes, Miss," the others chorused, and then giggled as they always did. Having performed in a good number of Europe's most fascinating cultural centers over the years, this was a cherished routine of theirs. Emily often thought that the Spire Quartet suited ancient spaces, chapels, museums, old libraries, and the like, having begun their days as a student ensemble amid the medieval splendor of Oxford University. Although hailing from four different colleges, the quartet had formed an instant bond, become a fixture on the local wedding and event circuit, and even produced a couple of CDs just after graduating. Then, "work intervened," as Harry put it, sending Emily and Marina to London, Harry to Cambridge, and Leo to the respected history department at the University of Warwick.

"Lead the way, Mister Historian," Marina told Leo.

Leo immediately assumed his role and led them down a passageway into the bowels of the castle. He launched into his spiel with gusto. "Let me know if I get boring," he added after a long explanation of medieval building techniques.

"Sure will," Harry muttered but then smiled. There was a genuine affection in the ensemble, which had survived the near-death experience of graduation from Oxford and their geographical dispersal, as well as more than one emotionally fraught "romantic complication," as Emily called them. None of the four were yet married, and only Leo had been in a long-term relationship. Even that had faltered after his girlfriend, a scholar of Italian literature, had received an offer she couldn't refuse from a university in Milan. In more ways than the four were comfortable to admit, they were already in a complex and rewarding relationship – with music, with each other, and with the euphoria of their very togetherness – perhaps sufficient in itself to ensure that none sought satisfaction elsewhere.

As they proceeded down the narrowing tunnels of the castle's well-lit interior, sounds of the surface receded entirely. "Three feet thick," Leo told them, patting the cool stone of the passageway's walls. "Designed to withstand *years* of siege."

"This morning, I feel as though I already *have*," Harry moaned. His hangover, the group's worst by some measure, was responding only sluggishly to the coffee and painkillers. "What is it about growing older that makes hangovers exponentially worse?"

Marina had the answer, and she lectured Harry briskly on liver chemistry as they continued through the passageways. Leo bid them halt at an exhibit on the castle's history as a prison. King slayers and traitors had been given accommodation here, some "as recently as" four hundred years ago, before the island's jail was moved to a "newer" facility at St. Helier.

"Jesus, imagine being stuck down here in the dark," Emily wondered morbidly. "They'd have gone out of their minds."

Leo peered into the gloomy mock-up of a sixteenth century jail cell. "I don't know. They were made of pretty stern stuff back then. It's remarkable how spending a lifetime sitting on wooden benches or horseback toughens you up."

"How the hell would you know?" Harry sputtered. "You're just another pampered toff like the rest of us. When was the last time *you* were on *horseback?*"

Leo's impulse was to bristle and complain, but he remembered to bear in mind Harry's fragile state. "Good point," he conceded, as the two women got a good laugh from the ham-fisted sparring of their men folk.

Marina felt a little sorrier for Harry than she otherwise would. Their fling, only eighteen months ago, had turned out to be rather more complicated than she'd hoped. There had been some acrimony, but she still felt a lingering affection for him which surfaced more as care and concern than any romantic desire. Certainly, their tryst – known to the others as was their policy – had not been the quartet-shattering cataclysm Leo had predicted. Besides, he'd made no such prophecy of doom, Marina noted, when he had asked her out a while earlier. Her refusal had sent Leo scuttling under a rock, and the quartet hadn't met for nearly four months, an unusually long hiatus.

"This was the magazine," Leo announced, gesturing to a vaulted space in the deepest part of the castle. The air was decidedly cool down here, a testament to their depth and the insulation provided by many feet of thick, ancient stone. "They stored gunpowder and other weapons here, for use in sieges or potential attacks against the French mainland."

"That's more like it!" Harry growled. "About time we got to the part about besting the horrid French."

"Those same horrid French who gave us a spectacularly successful recording contract?" Emily reminded him, hands on hips.

"Even though we were just out of Uni and hadn't the

foggiest clue what on earth we were doing?" Marina added. The French label, specializing in string repertoire and young quartets, had given them a tremendous boost and the opportunity to record some much-loved treasures.

"The very same," Harry continued. "Enemies of our blood, they are." He stood tall, like a Beefeater at the Tower of London, his dwindling coffee aloft in salute, bringing a good laugh from the others.

"That's the thing about you, Harry," Leo commented. "You know full well that you make absolutely no sense, and you just don't *care*."

"Nope," he replied. "I've got Union Jack underpants on. That's how I feel about the *French*."

Shaking their heads in unison, Emily and Marina moved on to the next exhibit, about one traitor who was locked up in the dungeons for a dozen years, despite a marked paucity of evidence against him. "Well, at least he wasn't sentenced to death," Emily observed.

Marina peered into the tiny cell and imagined for an uncomfortable second the life of someone incarcerated there year after year. "I don't know which I'd prefer," she admitted. "Might be better to get it over with quickly. Being stuck down here," she said, pausing to shiver slightly at the prospect, "would be my worst nightmare."

CHAPTER THREE

THE AMBULANCE CREW carried out their routine checks for signs of life. Finding none, they decided that given the extent of the poor man's injuries and the twenty-five minutes – at least, Graham estimated – since the discovery of the body, that no attempt would be made to revive him. "We'll only complicate things for the autopsy," the paramedic explained. "Tomlinson on his way, is he?"

The elderly pathologist arrived minutes later, partly winded after the long walk from the visitors' entrance. "Inspector," he wheezed in greeting, loosening the top button of his shirt. Then he saw the body, covered in stained white linen, with the small crowd of wedding guests and staff, curious and horrified by turns, keeping a respectful distance. "And I'd hoped you were joking. That it might have been an exercise or something."

"Afraid not, Marcus. Found him myself. The wife was here, kneeling over him, but she did a runner. I've got Barnwell and Roach looking for her."

"Ah, the dynamic duo?" Tomlinson asked. "We need

have no fear, then," he quipped. Graham let him have his little joke and escorted him to the body.

Tomlinson went through his initial routine, checking the state of the victim's pupils, taking notes on the skin tone and assessing the position of the body as well as its location. "Well, we can't rule out anything at this stage," Tomlinson began in his all-too-familiar way, "but these injuries are entirely consistent with a fall from a great height. Beyond that, I'll need to get in there and take a look."

Tomlinson's idiosyncratic style (Graham thought of the man as a little overly-familiar, even *cavalier* at times, if he were entirely honest) was merely a result, the detective knew, of his many decades of experience. Tomlinson was beyond shock and grief. He'd seen death in as many guises as anyone, whether arrived at through accident or misadventure, despair and suicide, or through violence.

Tomlinson made arrangements with the ambulance crew to have the body transported to the local hospital where he would carry out his post mortem in due course. "What's your gut telling you, Marcus?" Graham asked.

"I don't believe in speculating about something as serious as this," Tomlinson replied, a little haughtily. "But off the record, I wouldn't be surprised if something fishy went on here." He polished his glasses with his handkerchief and seemed unwilling to elaborate.

"Oh?" Graham prompted, ever hopeful that the elderly man might dispense more of his hard-earned wisdom.

"Well... How many men choose to end it all the day after getting married?" Tomlinson wondered aloud. "Most chaps wait eight or ten years." When Graham didn't respond to his trademark black humor, he continued. "And most suicides have empty pockets. Did you know that?"

"I think I did," Graham replied.

"This chap brought his driver's license with him. Very unusual in cases where there's no foul play."

They glanced up together at the looming battlements. "Hell of a fall," Graham commented. "He'd have needed to be *absolutely resolved*. You can imagine someone with suicidal thoughts getting all the way up there, distracted by this amazing view of the Channel, and then looking over the edge and thinking..."

"'Sod this, I'm going to go slit my wrists instead,'" Tomlinson said. "It takes real guts to throw yourself from a high place."

Graham rubbed his chin thoughtfully. "I do wish the wife hadn't done a runner."

"Now why would she do a thing like that?" Tomlinson asked. It was a rhetorical question.

Graham walked the pathologist to the two waiting medics who were ready to depart with the man's body. "Thanks, Marcus. Stay in touch, okay?"

"I have a feeling, old boy, that I'm going to *have* to."

Graham took a seat in the castle's reception area, just a row of chairs beneath the huge arch of the main gate and made a point of taking some deep breaths. Short of a cup of tea, something that he'd been without for far too long, a quiet moment to calm the senses and oxygenate the lungs was a surefire method of invigorating his deductive abilities. Frustratingly, though, his interviews with the staff and guests had so far revealed little more than he already knew. No one had seen a *thing*. Few were even awake at such an early hour, certainly not after the excesses of the evening before. The two witnesses who had come forward claimed to have heard the scream and only then come running.

Janice Harding arrived, looking slightly flustered but with her uniform characteristically neat. "Sorry, sir. Car wouldn't start, would it? On this, of all mornings!"

Graham smiled a little distractedly and bid her sit down. "Morning, Sergeant."

"You know, sir, I don't want to say the wrong thing or speak out of turn but..."

"There have been two mysterious deaths," Graham interjected, "within six weeks of each other," he added, "and both immediately following *my arrival* in Gorey."

Janice was a little red-faced to have it pointed out so bluntly. "Er, yes, sir."

"Am I a suspect, Sergeant?" he asked, turning to her with a weary look.

"No, sir!" she exclaimed. "I just meant..."

"Then let's leave coincidences and what-ifs to the conspiracy nuts and perhaps engage in some *police work*," he said, a little pointedly.

"Sorry, sir."

"It's okay, Janice. I was just looking forward to a peaceful Sunday under blue skies, and now I'm going to be interviewing distraught, teary relatives and listening to Tomlinson go on about compound hip fractures and intra-cranial hemorrhaging. Come on, let's go. I fancy taking in the view from the top."

They made their way up to the top of the castle via a narrow, stone, spiral staircase.

"I wouldn't fancy going up these in the shoes I was wearing last night, sir."

"This castle dates back to the thirteenth century. I don't think they envisaged Jimmy Choo's back then, Janice. Probably didn't figure in the architect's plans."

Janice couldn't decide whether to chuckle at Graham's dry humor or be astounded that he knew what Jimmy Choo's were.

"I can assure you, sir, that my wages don't stretch to buying such fine, luxury items, but if you're willing to rectify that, I'm willing to accept your generosity.... Ah, here we are. Phew."

It was still chilly, a welcome respite from the dustiness of the castle stairwell. They walked along the battlements and caught their breath.

"He fell," Graham said simply. "That's all we know."

"Falls," Harding explained, mostly to refresh her own memory, "tend to fall, if you'll pardon the pun, into three categories, according to the textbooks. There are accidents, for one."

"He wasn't all that drunk. The battlements are secure, with good footing, and it didn't rain last night," Graham intoned.

"You'd need to have the worst possible luck to end up pitching over these walls. They're nearly five feet high and two feet deep," Harding added. "Unless this was a category two fall, and the victim was *pushed* over one of these window-thingies."

Graham smiled. "They're called crenellations. The gaps were there for the soldiers to shoot through when defending against an attack."

They walked on some more, admiring the view despite themselves.

"We can't prove anyone else was up here. There are no surveillance cameras," Graham said, looking around, "and no witnesses report being here or hearing anything."

"Which leaves us with the third category: suicide."

"Hmm."

They walked back down to the castle's administrative area, just by the maze where the marquee had already been struck down, leaving the quadrangle fetchingly green and open. Stephen Jeffries was at his desk, staring out of the window at the quadrangle, and jumped slightly as Graham knocked at the door.

"You startled me," he admitted, and then collected himself. "Please, won't you sit down?"

"Mr. Jeffries, this is Sergeant Harding. She will be assisting me in this investigation."

Jeffries looked horrified. "*Investigation?*" he breathed. "So you think..."

Graham raised a cautioning hand. "Let's not jump to any conclusions," he said, grimacing inwardly at the unfortunate turn of phrase. "We are trained to observe the facts and then allow the prevailing circumstances to tell us what the body cannot."

At Harding's urging, Jeffries described in detail the events of the wedding, right down to the canapés and the music. "Everyone seemed happy. There were no arguments... except, well..."

"Except?" Harding prompted.

"I'm sure it was nothing, but the mother of the bride

did give one of my staff a chewing out about the tiniest thing: the arrangement of the wine glasses for the champagne. She wanted them in a particular pattern... you know how mothers of the brides can be."

Janice let her gaze fall on her empty ring finger. "Not really. Did she speak much with the groom?"

"No more or less than normal," Jeffries replied. "I've seen a hundred weddings, and it's surprisingly common for the two sides of the aisle to keep almost to themselves, certainly until the ceremony is over. It's later, when everyone's had enough booze, that the barriers tend to crumble. That's usually when the bridesmaids find themselves in an unfamiliar bed or the groomsmen decide that streaking through Gorey in the small hours is a simply *excellent* idea."

Graham made a note in his book: *booze.* They hadn't discounted a drunken mishap as the cause of George Ross' unfortunate demise. It would hardly be the first time a young man had drunk himself into a stupor and met with a grievous injury in the hours after his wedding.

"Well, Mr. Jeffries, we're keen not to disrupt things here at the castle, but we do need to interview a good number more of the guests," Graham explained.

"Background information, mostly," Janice clarified. "Building a picture of the relationships, the tensions, you know. A bit of history."

Jeffries shook his head. "Oh, there's not a lot going on today, and I've already done my best to preserve things as they were. We'll close the gates to visitors, of course. Someone should already have done that. The construction crews have Sunday off, and there are no other functions planned."

"Construction?" Harding asked.

"Yes, just some shoring up in the lower levels. This place needs constant maintenance, as you might imagine. I made sure they stopped drilling and hammering before the guests arrived yesterday, otherwise we wouldn't have been able to hear the 'I dos,'" he smiled.

Graham asked Jeffries to photocopy the guest list, annotated with room numbers. "And we'll need to speak with your night security guard, if he's still here."

"*She*," Jeffries pointed out, "is actually waiting in the Great Hall. I told her she might be needed, so she stayed on a little longer than usual."

Jeffries led Harding and Graham up to the Hall, a giant space with a dozen long, ancient tables, perfect for lavish feasting. They had only been partially cleared, Graham saw, with stacks of dishes and piles of cutlery still waiting to be carried away. Then he noticed the stocky blonde in a dark blue uniform who was obviously waiting for them. "Terrible, isn't it?" she said, shaking both their hands. "I'm Sam. Night security."

"It is, Sam. Absolutely tragic," Graham agreed. "Why don't you tell us what you saw?"

Sam shrugged. *Not a great sign*, Graham thought. "The wedding went off without a hitch. Lots of drinking, partying, dancing, the usual. People were filtering away by about midnight. The couple were already gone by then, you know," she said with a slight smile, which vanished as she remembered that half of that same happy couple was now on a mortuary slab. "There was one drunken woman, dancing by herself, until the DJ left at about two."

"Any disturbances?" Harding asked. "Fights? Arguments? Drunken brawls?"

"Oh, no," Sam reported. "Drunken brawls are my specialty, and there wasn't even a sniff of one."

Graham found himself smiling at the unswerving honesty of this tomboy character. "And what about this morning? At the time of George's fall?"

Another shrug. *Come on, Sam...*

Harding interjected. "I have to ask... There was a scream, the arrival of an ambulance, a crowd of people... Where were you during all of this?" she asked, trying to be delicate.

"Yes. I don't remember seeing you at all," Graham added.

Sam didn't shrug, this time. Instead, it was a resigned sigh. "Asleep," she admitted. "I'm on a new medication. You know. For my mood. Makes me sleepy sometimes."

"Where?" Graham asked, making a note in his ever-present notebook.

"I was crashed out on the couch in Mr. Jeffries' office." She gave them both a worried glance. "You won't *tell* him, will you?"

"Mum's the word," Harding promised before Graham could say anything. She knew a genuine soul when she saw one.

"Thanks," Sam said, her shyness rather affecting after the brawny bravado of earlier. "Wish I could help more."

So do I. You have no idea how much. "You've been very helpful. Maybe get yourself home for some rest," Graham suggested, snapping his notebook shut before indicating this rather fruitless interview was over by looking around him intently.

The Great Hall was among the rooms sealed off by Jeffries in his efficient zeal to preserve the record of the previous evening's events, lest they shed some light on the case. Jeffries returned now to check whether he'd done the right thing.

"Few would have been so thoughtful, Mr. Jeffries," Graham told him, hugely impressed for once. "You say that no one has been through here since the end of the dinner?"

"We have a policy," he said, "of letting our staff get themselves home at eleven. The bus service stops, and cabs are a nightmare in Gorey on a Saturday night, as you might imagine. Instead," he explained, gesturing to the piles of dishes and glassware, "we clean up during a 'blitz,' we call it, the next morning. Everyone comes in for three hours. We put on some music, I make big pots of coffee, and we get it all done."

"And this morning?' Graham asked, walking toward the top table.

"As soon as... Well, as soon as *it* happened, I called around and told them they weren't needed. If necessary, I'll clean up myself. Won't be the first time I've had these hands in hot water," he joked. "But I knew it'd be easier for you to work with fewer people here. Having twenty kitchen staff running about... Well, it didn't seem right under the circumstances."

Harding made notes. "You did the right thing, Mr. Jeffries. We're very grateful."

Graham was already at the top table, where the dishes seemed to have been left undisturbed since the previous evening. "This was George's place?" he asked. Jeffries nodded. "Would you be good enough to grab me a new box of zippered bags from the kitchen?" he added. "And a new pair of rubber gloves?"

Jeffries followed the request, and Graham began bagging up the dessert plate, the silverware, and both the water and wine glasses from George's plate setting.

Harding was by his shoulder. "Poison?" she asked quietly. "Not poison, *again*?" She had the image of George, crippled by stomach pain and wracked by confusion, tottering over the battlements to his death.

Their headline-making investigation, only six weeks earlier, had poison at its crux, but Graham was in no mood to infer anything before gathering all the facts. "Let's see. I'm hoping to hear from Tomlinson soon." Then, to the events manager, "Mr. Jeffries, could we bother you to show us the bridal suite?"

It was a room fit for a President or a King. Or, perhaps, a newlywed couple with deep pockets. Huge, and with a breathtaking view of the Channel and the French coast beyond, the bridal suite was beautifully appointed, complete with a four-poster canopy bed and all the finery a young couple in love could dream of.

"Not bad," Harding allowed. "What kind of, erm, cost are we talking, per night?" she asked, bracing herself for an answer bordering on the insane.

"About two thousand," Jeffries answered offhandedly, as if asked the question by virtually everyone who visited the suite, which, of course, he was. "Depends on the time of year."

Harding suppressed a whistle of amazement and began

taking in the details of the room. By her side, Inspector Graham was doing the same, but in that extraordinarily thorough way that he had made his own. She watched him absorbing the details, his eyes smoothly moving between each object, to the floor and across to the curtains, up to the ceiling and then down to the bed. Graham's ability to gather, store, and analyze visual data was a finely honed mechanism. It was something of a thrill for Harding to watch these remarkable skills being exploited at full tilt.

"Notice anything, Sergeant Harding?" Graham asked, pulling out his notebook to complete the habituated acts of observation and recording.

"Well..." She looked around more closely. "It appears to be a bridal suite, laid out very beautifully, awaiting the happy couple." Then she stopped. "But... They were supposed to have been here hours ago... Before midnight, Sam said."

"Precisely," Graham agreed.

"The bed is still perfectly made... I mean, what couple..."

"Even bothers to properly make their own bed at home, let alone in a hotel where you're paying a month's wages to stay for one night?" Graham discounted the notion. "They didn't sleep here, Harding. They didn't touch the Champagne," Graham said, gingerly lifting the bottle from amid a cold pool of melted ice in the bucket. "They didn't even nibble so much as a chocolate-covered strawberry, for heaven's sake."

"Weird," Harding almost whispered.

"I was married once," Graham said. "And immediately after the wedding breakfast, I had three things in mind." He ticked them off his fingers. "Food, because I'd barely eaten a thing amid all the socializing and well-wishing. A glass of something strong, because I'd been too scared to drink, in case I overdid it. And... well, bed."

Harding blushed at this uncharacteristic outpouring of personal information, something that Jeffries caught, responding with the faintest of smiles. "I think most married couples have those same priorities, sir."

"Although not always in the same order," Jeffries added. "But what does it tell you about the couple that they didn't even come back here?"

"Or open their luggage?" Harding said next, opening the walk-in closet to reveal two suitcases.

Graham once more shut his notebook. Even after weeks of teasing by his two constables, he had resolutely refused to begin using a tablet. He found the leather-bound volume reassuring, a bulwark against the tides of constant change. "I really don't know, Mr. Jeffries," Graham admitted. "But it tells us *something*. I guarantee you that."

CHAPTER FOUR

THE SIGN STATED, in terms not uncertain: EXHIBIT UNDER PREPARATION. NO ADMITTANCE. But, to Leo Turner-Price, this was like a red rag to the proverbial bull. "Seems like an invitation to me."

"What does?" Emily asked, eyeing the sign. "They're working on that part, Leo," she said, as though to an errant seven year old who just *had* to see *everything*. "Let's head back up. I want to see the Great Hall."

Leo was unmoved. "You don't want to see what exhibit they're 'preparing?'" he asked. "That doesn't pique your curiosity?"

"Nope," Emily replied.

"Mine's kinda piqued," Marina admitted.

"Why?" Harry asked. "I mean, it'll just be another preserved jail cell or something, right?" If the truth were told, he was enjoying the cool, dark surroundings, which were giving him welcome relief from the effects of last night's alcohol.

"Just a little look, and then we'll head up and see the Great Hall," Leo promised. "I want to see it too. I just want to see this first."

"Oh, for heaven's sake," Emily sighed, admitting defeat. She helped Leo shift the sign aside and slide the bolt back on the heavy wooden door, which opened with a spectacularly long, deeply ominous creak. "Okay, now even *I'm* kinda curious," she admitted.

The room was dark, but there was a light switch on the wall by the door, just sufficiently illuminated by the bulbs that lit the main passageway. Leo flicked the switch and a single bare ceiling bulb came on. "Looks like they're still working on the lighting too." Then he saw what the room contained. "Oh... No *way*..."

"Wait a minute, isn't that a..."

"Yep... I believe it is..."

A six-foot tall iron maiden, a human-sized metal cabinet offering perhaps the least comfortable method of incarceration, stood open by the wall, spikes protruding from every angle. Beside that was a worryingly authentic-looking rack, complete with a naked mannequin who seemed doomed to suffer painful stretching for all eternity. In the corner was a set of wooden shelves that held torture instruments of every description. "Oh man, they need to get this opened up *straight away*. The museum would be *way cooler* if this were all on display," Leo declared.

It warmed Emily's heart that such an esteemed and much-cited historian was reduced to childish glee at the sight of a few old torture methods, and it stirred in her the affection she'd felt for this complex, clever man since their undergraduate days. She'd been quietly furious with him for threatening the integrity of the quartet by disappearing like he did for four long months and was much relieved when he made contact once more. His reappearance had been tentative, much like a badger emerging from his sett, but the warm welcome he received from the group had been so joyous that the awkwardness of the situation was soon confined to the past.

Leo was examining a tapestry that adorned the far wall. It was perhaps sixteen feet square and very dusty, but he could make out a stylized battle scene of some sort, with horses in formation, their riders carrying pikes and swords. He lifted the material to examine it, and found that the tapestry had been placed to neatly cover a small, wooden door.

"Hey..." Leo began. "There's another doorway here." He held up the dusty tapestry to show the others.

"What's this one marked? *Verboten?*" Marina quipped.

"*Private,*" Leo replied. "I mean, *private* to whom?"

Harry took a look. "I don't know. Maybe the people who run this place?" he posed. "Come on, buddy. You've had your fun. Let's get out of here before we're deported from Jersey for trespass under some sixteenth-century law."

"Yeah," Emily joked, "they could imprison us down here or something. To discourage others."

Leo made a rude and dismissive noise, grinned at the other three, and opened the door with his shoulder. It took three firm shoves. "Gotcha!" he exclaimed.

"Er, Leo," Harry began, "you think, maybe, if the door's been closed for so long that it needs a shoulder barge to open it, then they might be serious about it being 'private?'"

Another rude noise and then Leo was gone, headed

down whatever passage he had discovered. A few seconds later, "Oh... This is *so cool!*"

The other three exchanged a worried glance, seemed to shrug together, and followed Leo through the small wooden door and into a tunnel barely broad enough for two people to stand side-by-side. "Wow, Leo, what the heck have you found, this time?" Marina asked.

"Must be a servant's tunnel or something," he guessed.

"Leading from the castle's torture chamber?" Harry responded. "'Hither, servant, and heed my will. All this stretching and maiming and removal of teeth with a spoon has left me parched. Pray thee fetch a flagon of ale to quench mine raging thirst.' That kind of servant?"

Their laughter echoed down the tunnel. There was just enough light from the torture chamber for them to see that the passage opened up into a larger room, but beyond that, they could not see.

"Anyone else think this could be a good point to turn back?" Emily asked the group.

"No fatalities yet," Leo objected. "I say we see if there's a light switch in the next room."

Marina was squeezed in beside him and gave him a friendly push forward. "I don't think they had light switches in the fifteen hundreds, genius."

Emily felt the skin on her neck begin to crawl unpleasantly. "You know, guys, I really don't think we should..."

A sharp sound behind them brought the group to an abrupt halt. It was the sound of stone on stone, a collision of some kind.

"Okay, you're right. Let's do an about-face," Leo

began, but there was another, more gradual sound, like stone sliding over something, and then a tumbling noise that became louder and louder, booming down the tunnel, bringing with it a cloud of dust and masonry and extinguishing all light.

CHAPTER FIVE

JEFFRIES DECIDED TO effectively hand over his offices in the administrative wing to the police. Not only was he determined to discover what happened and felt it his duty to assist however he could, he was also anxious that the castle not suffer unduly from this unfortunate incident. If it were a suicide, that would be something most people might accept without question, even that of a young man at the very outset of his married life. But something more suspicious, a *murder*...

He couldn't help thinking back to the mutterings and rumors he'd heard about poor Mrs. Taylor and the White House Inn after that terrible business with the dead woman on the beach. Mrs. Taylor seemed to have recovered now, and a quick chat in the street the other day had revealed that bookings were strong – they were "getting on with it," as the redoubtable lady put it – but Jeffries was horrified at the notion of Orgueil becoming some kind of sensationalized "murder castle." It was hard enough to market the place as a wedding venue, for all its virtues of facilities and location, when torture and illegal imprisonment had taken place in the castle's bowels. The delays to the opening of the torture exhibit were supposedly related to the construction work, but in reality some among the museum's board still found the whole idea rather distasteful and had repeatedly asked for more time to mull over its implications.

Jeffries was there when Detective Inspector Graham received the much-anticipated call from Marcus Tomlinson. "Hi, Marcus? Alright, lay it on me."

Graham listened for a long moment, took notes, and then asked, "You're quite sure?" He listened again, frowned at Harding, took more notes, thanked the pathologist, and ended the call.

"Damn," Graham muttered. "Not a lot to go on, I'm afraid." Harding looked crestfallen.

"Tox screen?"

"Alcohol, but nothing out of the ordinary, especially for a man who'd just got married. No drugs, no painkillers, none of the usual set of poisons. He even checked for that unusual one we ran into six weeks back: no dice."

"So what do you think, sir? Could it be suicide?"

Jeffries shook his head. "I can't understand why someone would do that," he muttered darkly. "Such a terrible crime against those you leave behind."

"Exactly," Graham commented. "If he chose to end his life, he did it while all his closest family and friends were right here. Surely, if he had dark thoughts, he would have reached out to someone. His family, his best man... his new *wife*, for heaven's sake."

"For me," Jeffries contributed, with the shyness of someone who felt they might be speaking out of turn, "it's a conundrum to consider that this man, who had just married Marie, a very beautiful young lady from a loving family and," he added with a hint of pride, "in a *stunning* location, with great music and food.... That such a man could consider this the very *low point* of his life? Such an act, for me, is simply *inconceivable*," he said very clearly.

Graham was nodding and making more notes. "Good points, Mr. Jeffries. Unless, of course, there are things we don't know. And there's nothing more certain than that." He turned to Harding. "Where do you think we should begin, Sergeant?"

Janice grabbed the list of wedding guests and scanned it quickly. "Mr. Jeffries, am I seeing this right? The bride's parents did not stay at the castle last night?"

He thought back for a second. "Oh, no. They didn't want to be among all the noise and partying after what I remember her calling 'a challenging day.' Honestly, I didn't care for the bride's mother at all. But, clients are clients, and we must..."

"Where?" Harding asked, without apologizing for the interruption, which affected Jeffries as though he'd been rapped on the knuckles.

"At the Inn, of course," the event manager replied. "The White House Inn."

Janice chose to make use of their unmarked police car for this visit. Poor Mrs. Taylor had seen more than enough uniformed men and women come and go during their investigation the previous month, and neither Harding nor Graham wanted to bring back bad memories. Not only had she been a stalwart help during the murder inquiry, she had extended Graham every courtesy since then. The least they could do was keep her lobby free of further intrigue and unpleasantness.

"Oh, Sergeant Harding!" the proprietor exclaimed happily, her necklace of giant beads bouncing. "Good to see you. Are you staying for lunch with the Detective Inspector?"

Graham quieted her with a serious look and cast a glance at the back office. They walked over to it and closed the door. "I want to do this discreetly, Mrs. Taylor," Graham said. "You're going to be hearing about a sudden and mysterious death at the castle."

Her hands flew to her mouth in shock. "Not again!" she gasped.

"The groom from that big wedding last night took a tumble from the battlements," Graham added, finding that his attempt to soften the tragedy had been a near miss at best.

"Oh no!" Mrs. Taylor cried.

"Steady, love, steady," Harding cooed, her hand on the older woman's shoulder. "Very quietly, we need to have a word with Mr. and Mrs. Joubert, parents of the bride. We understand they stayed with you last night."

Mrs. Taylor searched her memory, glad of the distraction. "Joubert? Yes... They might be at breakfast." A brief check and a glance at the dining room told them that this was true. A couple in their fifties were eating a leisurely breakfast by the window.

"Let's wait until they're finished, eh? Then knock on the door of their room a few minutes later," Graham said.

Graham and Harding tried to blend in with the guests filtering through the reception area. There were some new arrivals, others checking out, families heading out for the day, and couples wandering through, hand in hand. "Nice and normal," Harding observed. "Best this way."

"Hmm?" Graham asked.

"That we don't make a big splash, you know."

Graham spotted the Jouberts making their way up to their room and checked his watch. "You're learning one of the most important lessons of police work," he told her. "Never cause a big fuss if you don't have to."

A few minutes later, rather nervous but reassured to have the experienced Graham alongside her, Harding knocked on the door. "Breathe, Sergeant," he advised. "I can do the talking, if you'd prefer."

"I've got this," she told him, though she hardly felt that way. She had only done one other "notification of death," and that had been to the granddaughter of an old man who had been hit by a car. She'd taken it mercifully well, but Harding had to wonder if notifying the Jouberts of the death of their brand new son-in-law would be a tougher experience.

"Madame Mathilde Joubert and Monsieur Antoine Joubert?" Sergeant Harding asked in her best French accent. It wasn't simply politeness. Every notification required the identification of the family.

"*Oui*," Antoine replied, his expression puzzled.

"May we come in for a moment, please, sir?" Harding asked. All four of them stood in the spacious hotel room while Sergeant Harding delivered the terrible news.

Neither took it well. Monsieur Joubert was a tall, haughty, restaurateur, owner of a bistro in St. Malo, Graham later found out. Antoine was not unused to tragedy, but he was devoted to his family and horrified at the news. Mathilde, his short, stocky wife, was equally affected. When she heard the news, she went as pale as her bed linen.

"*Mais... C'est incroyable!*" she cried, for the third time. The Inspector prided himself on his ability to recognize genuine shock from the artificial, theatrical kind, and all the signs were there that this was the real thing. Unless he were quite wrong, the Jouberts had no knowledge of George's demise or of their daughter's strange and confusing disappearance.

"We have no reason to believe that George's death was anything other than an accident, but it is, as I'm sure you'll agree, especially ill timed."

"But it is hours..." Monsieur Joubert was stuttering, badly shaken, "only *hours* after their wedding. How can this have happened?" He helped his wife to the bed, where she sat in a daze. "How?" he repeated, tending to her.

"That's what we intend to find out," Harding told him. "Our first step is to interview anyone who might have seen the accident," she chose to call it, "or perhaps conversations or arguments between George and someone else."

Mathilde Joubert raised teary eyes to look at Harding. "Arguments? On his wedding day? *Impossible...*" she muttered, and then she began to cry with a long, moaning sob.

"What about Marie? Has she been told? Is she alright?" Antoine was anxious about his daughter.

"Marie ran off after her husband's fall. She left him lying on the ground."

This news exhibited another wail from Madame

Joubert.

"So," Graham insisted, "we must speak with everyone. I'm sorry to do this so soon after you've received the news. Can you tell us about the wedding?"

Mathilde stayed silent, so Antoine took over. "It was elegant, beautiful," he reported. "Everyone had a wonderful time." He was distant for a moment, Graham saw, perhaps thinking back to the day's highlights. "Wonderful," he repeated. "No arguments or bad feelings. Just a happy couple, two delighted families. Lots of dancing, drinking. You know."

"Of course," Graham said, making his usual notes. "How late did you stay at the festivities?"

Antoine thought for a second. "Perhaps eleven or a little after. We were both tired, my wife especially. We're not used to big parties at our age."

"And you returned directly to the Inn?" Harding confirmed.

"Yes. We were asleep within moments. It had been a very long day," Antoine replied.

Graham took the unusual measure of sitting on the edge of the bed, a couple of feet from the grieving couple. Harding watched him work, curious as ever, but confident that this experienced and brilliant detective could glean whatever evidence was required.

"Sir," Graham began, his voice deliberately low, "could you think of anywhere Marie might have run to at this terrible time? Perhaps somewhere on Jersey?"

His arm around his crying wife, Antoine shook his head. "They had plans for a honeymoon. I don't know where. They refused to tell us, you know... it was a couple's secret."

Graham nodded. His own, modest honeymoon, had

been a confidence mercifully well kept by both families. School friends of his were less fortunate. They had arrived at their secluded honeymooners' cottage to find six chickens in the kitchen and the phone disconnected. "Is there anywhere else she might have chosen to go?"

"St. Malo?" Mathilde suggested.

"*Non, chérie,*" Antoine said. "The boat does not leave for another hour or two. And the flights are always full. I can't see how she can have gone home." Then he added, "And I can't see *why* she would."

Harding asked the next question. "Where was the couple staying before the wedding? Someone talked about them driving separately to the castle. Marie in a Rolls Royce?"

Both of the French couple were nodding. "*C'est vrai,*" Mathilde confirmed.

"I arranged a little place just outside Gorey," Antoine told them, "on the hill overlooking the beach. A nice place for a bride to quietly prepare for her big day." Antoine reached into his wallet for the address, which Graham noted. "George had his own apartment. Marie would stay there with him but for the wedding, she went to her own place. So he not see her as is the custom."

"Is there anything more you can tell us? Any small detail?"

Antoine stood. "Sir... I hope this is not the conclusion you are forced to draw," he said severely, "but if... if this were *murder*... I want to know, *at once*, who was responsible."

Graham had encountered the understandable desire for revenge more than once. "Monsieur Joubert, it's important not to jump to any..."

"George was my family. He joined *la famille Joubert*

not once but twice. And my family are the dearest to me in the world."

Harding and Graham exchanged a confused glance. "Forgive me, Monsieur Joubert," Graham said. "Did you say, 'twice?'"

Mathilde reached out to her husband as if to stop him. "Antoine... S'il vous plait..."

The fifty-year-old patriarch petted her hand but pushed on. "My wife is not well," he explained. "This has been the most terrible shock." Then he addressed Harding. "I recognize it is a little unusual, but George has had the honor of marrying first one and then the other of my beautiful daughters."

Harding's face remained impassive, despite the overwhelming impulse to raise both eyebrows. She limited herself to a curious, "Is that so?"

"Oui," Antoine replied, clearly more accustomed than either Graham or Harding to the notion that a man might marry a woman, divorce her, and then marry her sister. "George and Juliette first. They had a baby, our granddaughter. She is in St. Malo with her stepfather, Juliette's new husband, this weekend. But our Juliette is... How can I say...?" He searched the room's walls for the word. "Flighty? N'est ce-pas?"

"I think I understand, sir," Graham replied, scribbling notes.

"Will she be able to help us, do you think?" Harding tried.

Antoine gave a short, hollow laugh. To Graham's ears, it was not the kind of noise any father should ever make in reference to his daughter, unless Juliette was, to the Joubert family, an apple that had fallen very far from the tree, indeed.

"She has problems," Mathilde said simply, beginning to gather herself. "Drinking. Smoking things she should not. You understand." It wasn't a question, but a request to move on.

Harding thanked the couple, and Graham made his final notes before they left together. "Rest assured, no stone shall remain unturned." Graham immediately doubted that the expression would translate and so added, "We'll do our very best."

They left the Jouberts to their indisputable grief, closing the door quietly. "Well, Sergeant," the Inspector asked as they crossed the lobby and waved courteously to Mrs. Taylor, "what did you make of *that*?"

They reached the car and Harding sat thoughtfully in the driver's seat. "I'd say, Detective Inspector, that if I ever married a fella, and then he left me and married my little sister, Sally," her fists coiled as though strangling a snake, "I'd spend the rest of *my* life making *his* a bloody misery."

The two police officers sat in their unmarked car by the side of the road leading away from Gorey. The bright Sunday midmorning sunshine was making it difficult to see the phone's screen. "The wonders of modern technology," Graham breathed. "When on earth did you do this?"

"Soon as I got to the scene," Harding explained, "and started bagging up his effects. Routine, these days," Harding replied. "At police college, I remember them telling us over and over, 'Pictures, or it never happened.'"

Graham raised the phone again and turned it to get a

better look at the picture of George Ross' driver's license. "I'd like to think that a notebook and pencil still count for something," Graham retorted.

"Only if you're a dinosaur. With respect, sir."

Graham shrugged off the remark. It was far from Harding's first at the expense of her boss and his stubborn refusal to be "upgraded," as she put it. "What works for me, works for me," he assured her.

"No arguing with that, sir," Harding allowed. "So, where should we start? Marie's rented cottage on the hill just there," she said, pointing over the next rise, "or George's bachelor pad?"

Before Graham could answer, his own phone rang. Resolute in his disregard for technology, the phone was a bulky, ancient, steam-powered model, barely capable of having its own address book. Harding stifled a fit of giggles as Graham took the call.

"Ah, yes... Thank you so much for calling back." He listened and took notes, the chunky phone trapped between ear and shoulder. "What's that you say?" he asked, his face concerned. "Well... that's something, isn't it?" He listened on for three or four minutes, but all Harding could hear was heavily-accented English of some kind. "Right... Well, look, I can't thank you enough. Would you do me a favor and keep me informed if anything else comes up?" he asked.

The call ended, and he completed another page of notes before turning to Harding. "That was my opposite number in St. Malo, erstwhile home of the Joubert clan. I put a call into them to do some delving into the family, see what they could tell us. And Poirot over there told me something rather interesting."

"Poirot was Belgian, sir,"

Graham pushed on. "He claims that there is something of a murky background to this story."

"Oh?"

"The Ross family owned a farmhouse outside of St. Malo."

Graham laid out the narrative just as his French counterpart had related it. "It seems there was an incident involving both of George's parents. A murder-suicide."

This brought Harding to a standstill. "Christ," she breathed.

Graham explained. "Although, it depends on whom you ask. Opinion is divided, even among the French police."

"So what happened?" Harding wanted to know.

"According to the officially filed report with the French cops, George's father shot his mother and then turned the gun on himself. George, who was thirteen at the time, and his sister Eleanor, eleven, were playing in a neighboring field and came back to find them."

"Bloody hell," Harding exclaimed. "Can you imagine the effect that must have had on him?"

"Only slightly," Graham conceded. "But other relatives, young George's paternal uncle and his maternal aunt, adamantly disputed that it was a murder-suicide. They claim that the family was entirely happy, loved being in France, and even planned on moving there permanently after George and his sister had grown and left for college."

"Hmm," Harding said, mulling this over. "Got to say, boss, it gives me a funny feeling."

Graham started the car. "Let us follow that funny feeling, Sergeant Harding. I suspect it might lead us in some very profitable directions."

CHAPTER SIX

T HEY CROUCHED TOGETHER amid the rubble. Surrounding them was that complete kind of darkness known only to those who explore the world's caves. Even in the hour since the tunnel's collapse, their eyes had not become adjusted because there was simply no light to see by. The air was thick with a cloying dust that had caused repeated coughing fits, but as it settled and the musicians resolved to stay still and wait for help, their breathing had become easier. There was, at the very least, fresh air coming from somewhere, though it was getting swelteringly hot.

"Okay," Emily said after a gap in the discussion, which was dominated by their prospects for survival. "We didn't bring any water, right?"

"I have this small bottle," Harry said, "I've drunk a third of it." It had been part of his anti-hangover plan.

"But basically, thank goodness, we're unhurt," Emily said next. "Basically."

"'Basically' is right," Marina moaned. She had taken some kind of sharp, rocky impact, which had left her shoulder and upper arm bruised and swollen. The others complained about the dust, but by some miracle, there were no serious injuries.

"Could have been a lot worse," Harry reminded them.

"It is what it is," Emily countered, quickly. "So, people, I want to get out of here immediately. Any thoughts?"

"Well," Leo observed, "I think you'll agree that yelling didn't work."

Within moments of discovering that they still could, the group had screamed themselves hoarse in a long, continuous canon of all four voices, but had heard absolutely nothing by way of a reply.

"Yeah. Walls are too thick. Or maybe there's nobody in this part of the castle," Harry assumed. "We might have to dig our way out."

This, too was a notion they'd visited before. "With what?" Marina asked. "We'd need shovels, picks, maybe even heavy lifting gear. We've only got four pairs of hands, and I don't know how much weight my shoulder will move."

Leo moved close to her – or, at least, where her voice was coming from – and she made no move to stop him as he gently put a comforting arm around her. "I'll be careful of your shoulder," he promised in a whisper.

"Better had, or we'll be dealing with the aftermath of a fatality, after all," she replied, only half-joking.

Emily held her cellphone aloft, something she'd done only sparingly since the crisis began, the better to spare its battery. "We've got four of these, right?"

Harry made a strangled, apologetic noise. "I left mine in my cello case."

"Three of these," Emily said, resolved to be accepting

of what they did and did not have at hand. "Anyone getting *any kind* of signal?"

In the dark, Leo shook his head. "Not a bloody thing. There's no cell towers, no internet, no local wireless."

Marina summed it up. "So, three really sophisticated mobile communications devices capable of speaking with outer space and almost every human on earth just became three really sophisticated flashlights?"

Emily sighed. "That's about the size of it. But at least we have them. Let's keep their batteries for as long as we can." The flashlight functions of all three, supremely bright and useful as they were, drained the batteries at an alarming rate.

"Give me a quick bit of illumination over here," Harry was saying. "I think I've found a gap in the rock fall. It's not big, but if we can enlarge it, we might see where it leads..."

"Don't touch *anything*," Emily ordered. "If we disturb things, the ceiling might come crashing down."

"Look," he said, shining Marina's phone in the corner of their apparently sealed-off chamber. "Check it out." The tunnel's collapse had obliterated the passage through which they had come. This end of their mini-chamber now culminated in a tall pile of jagged rock and masonry that seemed completely impassable. However, at the other end, where they'd seen, seconds before the collapse, that the tunnel opened up into a chamber of some kind, the pile of rocks was not quite as tall. "Looks more like a possibility," Harry declared, and reached to begin moving the debris.

"No!" Emily repeated more forcefully. "Don't touch the rocks."

"Look," Harry began. "I'll be really careful. If anyone

hears anything moving around like it's going to fall, I'll stop."

Emily was frowning glumly in the darkness. "I still don't like it."

Leo weighed in. "You're first violin, Emily," he said, "not our Health and Safety officer. Let Harry have a try. It might be our only way out."

There was a long pause as Emily considered this. Finally she acquiesced with audible reluctance. "Okay... Just go really, *really* slowly," Emily advised. "We have no idea what else is in store."

Harry moved very deliberately. "I'll take the advice," he said, taking a small rock from the pile, "of the first man ever to make a spacewalk."

Marina heard this and couldn't resist, "What, 'always hit the bathroom before you go?'"

No one actually laughed, but they all appreciated her attempt. "He said, 'Think five times,'" Harry related, taking a firm grip on a larger rock and sliding it out of the pile, "'before moving a finger, and *ten times* before moving a hand.'"

Within moments, he had begun to demonstrate that the rocks could be moved, apparently without disturbing anything above.

Marina held the phone and provided illumination while the other three carefully carried away rocks from the top of the blockage. They placed them at the opposite end of the mini-chamber in which they were trapped. The temperature began to fall as cooler air made its way through. "Doing better," Harry told them. He was closest to the jumble of rocks. "I can see how we might scramble over this stuff and into the next room."

"But what's in the next room?" Marina asked, half-rhetorically.

"It'll be better than in here. Not as hot, more air, more space. And maybe even another door, leading back to the main passageway," Emily speculated. "Wouldn't that be cool?" She'd taken on the role of morale booster and coach from the very outset. It would have been easy to simply give up and wait for help, but she was determined to keep the group positive and proactive in their search for a solution, even if she had had a slight wobble a few moments earlier. Even if the slightest mistake, she remained convinced, could bring the whole tunnel down on top of them.

CHAPTER SEVEN

INSPECTOR GRAHAM STOOD in front of a three-story, white building, which except for the local road and a small green on the edge of the cliff, looked directly onto the English Channel. Glancing over, Graham saw that the stretch of water was at its most spectacular, glittering blue in the midday sun.

He finished the rest of his soda in a long gulp and pushed the intercom button for the second-floor apartment. He was not, in all honesty, expecting any kind of reply. Unless George and his fiancée had invited guests to use their apartment for the weekend, there shouldn't be anyone inside. This expectation was shocked from him when a woman's voice called out.

"Yes, who is it?"

"Detective Inspector Graham of Gorey Police, ma'am. Could I ask you to open the door, please?" There was no camera that he could see, so he didn't bother holding up his identification.

"Police?" came the woman's voice, her tone obviously worried.

"Just a routine inquiry. Would you mind if we spoke inside?"

There was a long pause – far longer than Graham was comfortable with. One of his least favorite ways to waste time was being left to hang around "like a lemon," as his mother used to say. When others dallied or did something they considered more important than keeping him waiting, he became intensely irritated. There wasn't even a wisecrack from Harding to keep him occupied. She was shadowing the Joubert family and conducting more interviews with the staff at the castle. Finally, there was a buzz and the door opened.

Graham climbed the stairs and found his way to the second floor flat with a bright red door. He knocked.

"Just a second..."

"It's rather urgent, ma'am. Part of a police inquiry," he said, raising his voice to make sure he'd be heard over the noise of whatever the woman was doing. It sounded as though she were cleaning up the apartment.

"Hang on..."

Graham got that troubled, annoyed feeling that he was being played. "Would you open the door, please?" he said, rather more loudly than before. Ten seconds later, as he was about to knock very hard, the door popped open as far as the chain would allow.

"Yes?" It was a woman in her late twenties, Graham judged. In that first fraction of a second, when an investigative mind is at its most acute, he took in the details. There was a tiredness, a paleness, like that of someone whose last few hours had been difficult. Even harrowing.

"Good afternoon," Graham began. "We're investigating the..." Then, after another second, it struck him. It was definitely her. "Mrs. Ross?" he asked.

"Yes," she admitted sheepishly.

The Inspector's initial excitement was tempered by his training. "Is everything alright, ma'am?" he asked concernedly.

"*Must* you come in?" she asked. "Bad day. With everything."

Graham blinked a few times. "Well, ma'am, with respect, it's the 'everything' that I'm here to talk to you about. Would you mind?" he said, gesturing to the chain on the door.

"Come in, then," she said with unconcealed reluctance. She unhooked the chain and let him into the light, airy apartment.

Marie Ross placed herself on the couch and then sighed so deeply that Graham thought she might simply vanish down into the cushions, never to be seen again. "I'm sad," she said without preamble. "Confused." There was a pause. "He was wonderful," she said simply and turned to stare out the window.

"May I say how sorry we all are for the tragic events of this morning," Graham said. "Everyone I've spoken to assures me that George was very loved and much respected."

Marie was a beautiful woman, ephemeral almost. Her long, straight, dark hair hung loose and swished from side to side when she moved. Graham noticed her deep blue eyes were framed with long black lashes that gave her the look of an innocent child. He had to remind himself that she was possibly anything but.

He reached for his notebook, and though he hadn't been invited to, sat on the smaller couch opposite Marie. Observing her, he noticed just how tired she looked. Perhaps not surprising, given the circumstances, but he'd seen junkies with more life in their eyes. "Is there anything you'd like to tell me about what happened this morning?"

She peered back at him as though seeing him for the first time. "Maybe. I'm not sure. I don't remember much."

"Mrs. Ross, I was there within moments of your husband's fall. It was I who tried to help you both, just after it happened. Do you remember seeing me there? Asking you questions?"

She seemed to search a very fragmented memory, her eyes staring around, and then said, "No. Not even a little bit. I hadn't thought anyone else was there."

Making notes on her demeanor, as well as everything she said, Graham felt that he had to ask, "Mrs. Ross... You left the scene in a considerable hurry. Before, in fact, it was certain that George was beyond help. May I ask why you did that?"

She screwed up her face in a strangely child-like way and thought hard. "You know," she said in a dreamy voice, "the first thing I remember after all the screaming and blood... was being back here." She glanced around. "Yes. I think I must have run all the way."

Graham thought this through, imagining the journey in his mind. "That's well over a mile, Mrs. Ross. You must have been exhausted."

"I went... Yes, I think I went straight to sleep when I got back. Like a... a kind of self-protective coma or something," she said a little haltingly. "I think I knew what had happened, but there was no way I could bring myself to think about it. I'm surprised," she added, "that I'm able to think about it now. But I took some of the pills my doctor gave me, and I'm feeling a little better."

Graham scribbled. "May I see the bottle of pills, Mrs. Ross?"

Marie stood, obviously aching all over, and fetched the bottle from her nightstand. "Anti-anxiety," she explained, handing Graham the transparent, orange container. "I take others too. Anti-depressives. Anti-psychotics. I asked my doctor," she related with a funny smile, "whether he had antiperspirants I could take, so I wouldn't have to remember to use my roll-on each morning, but he said I was being silly."

Graham looked at her for a long moment before taking down the prescription information, which helpfully included the doctor's name and phone number. "What do you do for a living, ma'am?" he asked.

"Accounts firm," Marie said. "In St. Helier. Just for the last few months."

As he wrote the firm's name down, Graham privately questioned why *anyone* would be willing to entrust their financial matters to someone on so many drugs.

"Mrs. Ross, I have to ask... Do you know of anyone who might have wanted to hurt your husband?"

She blinked again. "You know, I haven't got used to calling him that yet. He was my fiancé and before that, my boyfriend. And before that," she paused slightly, "my brother-in-law." Again, she turned to look out the window.

Graham nodded. "I spoke with your parents a little while ago. Your father told me about the situation with Juliette, George, and yourself."

Now her expression was deeply puzzled, like a staggeringly drunk person trying to figure out why the pub vending machine had failed to dispense the cigarettes they'd paid for. "Parents?" she said, almost experimentally. "*My* parents?"

It was Graham's turn to blink. He referred back to his notes. "Mathilde and Antoine Joubert. Your mother and father." Graham paused, concerned that some ludicrous mistake had been perpetrated and instantly wondering who was responsible. "No?"

"No," Marie replied, puzzling over this information. "No, I don't know who they are."

Graham persisted. "Mrs. Ross, they assured me that Juliette and you are their daughters. They were very upset at the whole..."

"No, that's wrong," Marie said, more confidently. "I was raised in foster homes in France. From the age of five. I've never had a permanent home. Never knew who my parents were."

"Your name *is* Marie Joubert? Recently married to George Ross over at Orgueil Castle?" Graham was bewildered.

"Oh yes," she said, as if this information fit perfectly with what had come before.

Graham felt it best to stop there, and continue at the station. "Mrs. Ross, I'd like you to accompany me to our police headquarters," he said, aware that the almost embarrassingly modest constabulary building hardly fit such a grand introduction. "You're not under arrest, and you can refuse, but I think it'll be better for everyone that way."

Without a word, Marie gathered some things – her red leather purse, a light jacket, and the bottle of pills Graham had been holding – and followed him from the apartment. He ushered Marie into the car, and then, having closed the door, called Harding.

"Janice? Do me a favor and bring the Joubert parents down to the station, would you? Yes, right away, if you can. We'll meet you there." Then, he thought it best to prepare her. "Something *bloody funny* is going on."

The Jouberts stood stoically in the lobby of Gorey's tiny police station. Antoine was almost a foot taller than his wife, strong and wiry. They both walked toward the doors, ready to welcome their daughter, as Graham approached with Marie in tow.

"*Chérie*," they said in unison, but Marie simply stared at them. There were twin streams of French, incomprehensible to both Graham and Harding, who was watching this strange reunion from the door to her office.

Marie said nothing, but she then turned to Graham. "I don't know these people," she said. "I've never seen them before."

Horrified beyond measure, the Jouberts looked at each other, then back to Marie, then to Inspector Graham. They did not speak. Harding assumed that they *could* not.

"Monsieur Joubert, Madame Joubert, are you prepared to swear that this is your daughter? Beyond any doubt whatsoever?" Graham said, hoping the formality of the request would jog some sense into the errant Marie.

"*Bien sur!* Of course!" they answered together. Then Antoine rounded on Graham. "How could you suspect that we might not know *our own daughter*, Monsieur? What ridiculous parents we would be!"

Marie stood silently amid this confusion. She looked at one and then the other of this middle-aged French couple, without even the slightest recognition, as if they were two strangers, brought in from the street. Harding looked on, completely baffled.

"Okay," Graham said. "Let's all take a seat and sort this out." He sounded more optimistic than he felt. This was more than something *bloody funny*. The investigation had taken a turn for the truly bizarre. "Marie, I'd like you to go with Sergeant Harding. She'll get you some coffee and maybe chat a bit. Monsieur and Madame Joubert, I'd like you to sit with me for a few minutes. I'm sure we'll straighten this out."

Harding took Marie away to the furthest most interview room, while Graham took the one closest. As he was settling them in and trying to remember where the coffee was kept, the constabulary phone rang.

"Inspector Graham, Gorey police," he said, hardly thrilled at the interruption and praying that it might shed some light on the conundrums he faced.

"Afternoon, sir," the young police officer said at the other end, stuttering slightly. He was always a little on edge when addressing his boss. "It's Constable Roach. We're at the castle."

Graham grabbed a notepad. "What's the latest, Constable?" *And try to keep it brief, for heaven's sake.* Roach had the habit of both repeating himself and wandering off topic when relaying information. Graham was training him to provide "just the facts."

Roach hoped to sound competent and efficient. "Well, we've just now finished interviewing the staff, like you asked, and I'm afraid there isn't much to report. Nobody seems to have seen anything amiss. Typical wedding, all the usual stuff. No one saw the fall."

"Makes sense," Graham said, half to himself.

"There's something else, sir."

"Oh?" Graham said, pencil at the ready.

"The castle management asked us to stay around for a while, sir, and help with a separate matter."

Oh, hell's teeth. What now?

"Seems they managed to let in a group of visitors before the place was sealed off as a potential crime scene," Roach explained.

"So, have you escorted them out?" Graham asked pointedly, unsure as to why this trivial detail was suddenly important.

Roach cleared his throat. "They can't find them, sir. Looked everywhere."

Graham sighed. "People don't just vanish, Constable," he reminded his younger colleague. "How many are we talking?"

"A group of four. The receptionist says she recognized them as the musicians who played at the wedding yesterday. Came back for a look around the castle."

Graham silently shook his head. "Missing musicians. Just what we need. Look, get along and find them, will you? Let's just hope they've found the wine cellar and are having a fantastic time down there. And if they've buggered up my crime scene, we'll have words, Constable, you can be sure of that."

"Righto, sir. Over and out." The line clicked off and Graham took three slow, deliberate breaths before heading to the interview room.

Deeply upset, muttering together in French, the Jouberts held hands and wished away this mysterious calamity. "We cannot understand," Antoine said, again and again. "Our daughter doesn't even *recognize* us."

His wife continued, "She has not been well. She has many problems. But her doctor is the best, and he insisted that she was... 'ow do you say... *stable*. Not a danger. Getting better, maybe."

"Yes, getting better," Antoine assured Graham.

There was little to be gained, Graham could plainly see, from speculating upon how it was that Marie was suddenly a stranger to her own family. "I'd like to talk about George," Graham said. "Once my colleague, Sergeant Harding, has interviewed Marie, perhaps we'll learn more about her state of mind. But for now, tell me about the man who was your son-in-law." *Twice*, Graham didn't add.

The couple conferred for a moment in French. Graham didn't care for this one bit. He felt they might be colluding, or hiding something, or preparing to deliver some previously-concocted story. He cleared his throat.

Antoine took the lead. "He was... a very *limited* man," Antoine said. "Almost *simple*. Not sophisticated, not especially cultured in the ways of the world."

Graham made notes, including one that Antoine was entirely unafraid, it seemed, to speak ill of the dead, even less than half a day after George's demise.

"He was a teacher, you know. Not the best," Antoine said. "He was very quiet. Spent too much time with his nose in a book, eh?"

Mathilde shrank a little more at each new insult, but she remained silent.

"He didn't know how to have fun. Was too ... stiff, *n'est que ce pas?* Like you British often are." Antoine made a brief and absurd parody of some kind of wooden man, lumbering along a street. "No *joi de vivre*. No, not even a little. Just... *sad*," Antoine concluded.

Graham ignored the affront to his fellow countrymen and waited for more, but Antoine had run dry. "*C'est cas*," he concluded. *That's that*. "But my wife thinks very differently."

"Oh?" Graham said, turning to Mathilde. "Please..."

Tired, overwrought by the day's extraordinary events, and visibly unwilling to disagree with her husband but doing so anyway, Mathilde's delivery was halting, and not simply because she was struggling to express herself in a second language.

"George Ross was the best thing that ever happened to our family," she explained. "The *best*. He was kind and gentle. He read big books, *la littérature*, and he knew much about the world. He was a good husband to Juliette, but she rejected him. She preferred," Mathilde recalled, "the parties and the good times and... you know..." she screwed up her face in disgust and almost spat the word, "*drugs*."

Graham's pencil never stopped moving. "I see."

"When she tired of him, she left to marry a nobody who simply had enough money to support her... excesses... I looked after George. Made sure he was alright. He was broken-hearted by Juliette. Very ... how can I say...?"

"I think I understand," Graham offered.

"*Bien*. And so, Marie and I took care of him, helped him to find some work, new friends, places to go out. He was obsessed with the other man after Juliette's decision to leave him. You know, he couldn't stop thinking about it. We helped him focus on something else, something *good*."

Antoine chipped in, "This was when Marie and George became close." His fingertips drummed the table-top. "Too close, for my preference."

Mathilde had enough confidence to continue now. "George was not the perfect man. But, neither is my husband. Neither are you, *Monsieur L'Inspecteur*." Both men took the comment with good grace. Antoine gave a classically Gallic shrug. "He was *le héros*, too. We were proud of him." She looked pointedly at her husband, "But you know this already, of course."

Turning a page in his notebook, Graham confessed that he did not.

"Oh, it was in all the newspapers! It was a few years ago, his little moment of fame. When he was living in France with Juliette." Mathilde launched into the story while Antoine sat passively, apparently entirely unimpressed. "He taught the young kids, you know, at his school, but he also led some of those weekend *aventures*. When the children learn to camp and make fires and such. Yes?"

Graham nodded, writing constantly. "The Scouts?" he wondered aloud.

"Something like this. So, they were in the little boats... how do you say?" She mimed a paddling motion.

"Canoes?"

"*Ah, oui.* They were in the harbor, not far from the sea. Well, it should have been a safe place, but there was a sudden storm. Rain and wind and lightning. The children were all terrified. They were not experienced, you see."

"Sounds like a difficult situation," Graham said,

inscribing reams of what looked like hieroglyphs, but which comprised a highly efficient, personalized, note-taking system.

"Three of the... little boats? The *canoes*?" Mathilde said, finding the word again. "Yes, three of them went over," she said, miming throughout. "The children were in the water. George tied the others together and then jumped into the water to save them. Six young lives, *Monsieur L'Inspecteur*. They would have died without him, for sure."

"Extraordinary," Graham agreed.

"*Mais oui*. He was very quiet about it. Didn't give any interviews or make a big noise. George knew family *tragédie* too well. Perhaps this was what made him so certain to save all their lives. Even risking his own."

"Tragedy?" Graham prompted.

"Yes, of course! George's parents," Mathilde began. "They..."

"Mathilde, *ce ne pas important*," Antoine instructed his wife.

Graham's French was, by his own admission, quite terrible, but this snippet was one he could fully understand. "Monsieur Joubert, I'd be glad if you'd allow *me* to decide the importance of these details."

The surly restaurateur scowled briefly but made no argument.

"Carry on, please, Madame Joubert."

"George's parents died when he was thirteen. Maybe you know this," Mathilde said. "Terrible. The most *'orrible* accident."

Graham flicked back to his notes on the incident at the farmhouse. "I understand the police eventually ruled it to be a murder-suicide."

Antoine failed to, or chose not to, censor the thought before it reached his mouth. "Maybe suicide runs in the family. Who knows?"

Mathilde turned to him, indomitable now, and gave him a vicious blast of rapid, furious French. Then she turned back to Graham with as much color in her face as he'd seen all day. "I'm sorry, *Monsieur L'Inspecteur*," she offered. "My husband sometimes does not think before he speaks."

Mathilde completed her statement, mostly a reiteration of just how tragic the timing of this incident had been, and how George was a decent and loving man who would have made an excellent husband for Marie. Her own husband remained in stony silence, the occasional twitch of his mustache being the only sign of his vociferous objection.

"Where were you both when George fell to his death?"

"In bed, of course. It had been a long day and late night," Antoine replied.

"Very well. I think that will do for now."

As he stood to show them out, Graham thanked them both.

"*Ce n'est rien*," Mathilde assured him. "But I hope that you will also speak to George's sister. She was the one who understood George's... state of mind... from back then, no?"

"What about Marie?" Antoine inquired. "What will you do with her? I don't like leaving her here."

"Don't worry. We'll take good care of her. You go back to the White House Inn and we'll be in touch," Graham said. He was keen to see the back of these complicated people. He could only imagine the fiery bickering that would probably dominate the rest of the couple's day.

There were two phone messages; one from Marcus Tomlinson, the other from Constable Roach. He called the pathologist first.

"Marcus? What's new over there? We're having the strangest of days, I can tell you, and I'd love some nice, simple, concrete evidence."

Tomlinson made an apologetic noise. "Sorry, old boy. I've done an advanced tox screen and a few other tests at my own discretion. George wasn't drugged or poisoned. His hands hadn't been tied, and he wasn't gagged. No signs of struggle or a fight."

Graham closed his eyes and considered a more colorful oath before uttering simply, "Bugger."

"I don't make it up, I just report it," Tomlinson said apologetically.

"It's alright. Just need a break, in every sense of the word," Graham confessed. "Say, while we're talking, do you know of a local headshrinker named Bélanger?"

Tomlinson thought for two seconds. "Ah, yes. Has an office in St. Helier."

"You rate him?"

"I do. A good egg, by all accounts. Thorough. Completely bilingual. Why?"

"He's been prescribing Marie Ross the full works for a few months now." Graham read a list of six medications from his notebook.

"Right, well, you'll want to have a word. A patient

would have to be damned near cuckoo to require all that lot."

"You think so?" Graham pressed.

"Well... Doctors overprescribe these days. Lots of reasons why. But he must have thought there was good justification. I'd recommend having a discreet word. Mind, he'll be bound by doctor-patient confidentiality, so it's rather up to him how much he chooses to divulge."

"Well, let's hope he's feeling generous today, eh? Thanks, Marcus. "

Graham called Dr. Bélanger's emergency number and left a request for his immediate presence at the station. If anyone could shed some light on Marie's inexplicable behavior, it was her psychiatrist.

Graham used the radio for the next call. "Five-one-nine, come in?"

"Roach here, sir," the constable replied promptly.

"You called, young man?"

"Still at the castle, sir. Still looking for the musicians. Nobody's seen hide nor hair of them since they arrived. We've been down in the jail cells and everything, but there's nothing. We'll keep trying, sir."

"Good lad. Let me know if anything happens."

"Righto, sir. And... sir? Don't you think it's a bit odd?"

"What's that, Constable?" Graham asked casting a glance up at the ceiling momentarily. He would have physically mud-wrestled someone for a decent cup of tea.

"We get this odd incident with Mr. Ross, sir, and then four people go missing within hours of each other? Doesn't that feel a bit... well... *weird*? Sir?"

Graham took another set of deep breaths. "Son, this whole day has been bloody weird. And if you set off onto some paranormal train of thinking and decide the castle's got a *ghost* or some other ludicrous..."

"Oh, no, sir," Roach insisted. "Nothing like that. It's just a hell of a coincidence, that's all. And I thought we didn't believe in those."

Graham smiled. *He's learning. Ever so slowly, but still.* "Keep at it, constable. Let me know the minute you find any sign of them, alright?"

CHAPTER EIGHT

"**A**M I SEEING things?" Harry kept saying. "Shine it over there again. I swear I'm not seeing things."

"The battery's at twenty-five percent, Harry," Marina reminded him. "Make this your last one, okay?"

Their scramble over the mound of rubble and masonry that had blocked the tunnel had been difficult, but all four were now over the obstacle and into the much larger chamber beyond. There was no light from the single bulb in the ceiling. Using their phones, they discovered that the chamber, perhaps twelve feet by fifteen but less than eight feet in height, was itself badly damaged by whatever calamity had befallen the smaller tunnel behind them. One wall had crumbled, leaving a gap at its very top that was around two feet high.

"It doesn't make sense," Harry said, nodding to Marina to turn off the phone once more. "It looks as though the room's been divided into smaller chambers, but that those walls are just piles of bricks up to the ceiling and not connected to the ceiling itself."

"Maybe that's why they toppled during the 'earth-quake?'" Emily speculated.

"I guess so," Harry agreed.

"Looks like an opportunity to me," Leo offered. "If we can climb the wall, we should be able to get into the next chamber. Doesn't it seem lighter in there to you than it does in here?"

The four stood shoulder-to-shoulder in the gloom, peering at the new fissure in the far wall. "Can't tell," Harry admitted.

"Maybe," Marina said.

"It might just be that the room's got different contents or that the walls are a different color. Impossible to say."

They began making plans to build a "staircase," as Harry named their nascent structure. It would allow them to get a handhold on the cleft at the top of the wall and pull themselves over. Working almost entirely in the dark and by memory, they located the larger blocks that had been displaced by the "earthquake" and placed them around the foot of the wall.

It was exhausting work, hard on their hands and backs especially, and they desperately needed sustenance. They were running short of water. Harry's bottle was their only source. Leo had a small packet of toffees and was doling them out to the others carefully.

With Harry having forgotten his, and Emily insisting that they keep at least one as a backup source of illumina-tion in the event the batteries of the others gave out, they could only use two cellphones to shine light at once. Working as quickly as they could in the relatively tight space, the four found themselves bumping into each other in the gloom, and more than once, dropping rocks on each other's feet. After one testy exchange, Harry decided they should work in pairs, with one person resting, and the fourth organizing illumination. The phones couldn't be left on permanently, the batteries would drain far too quickly, so they rationed short blasts of light, far too bright in this almost complete darkness, to find their way.

The "staircase" took shape. They found they could move rocks from the tunnel without risking any further collapse. They began piling the larger ones in a layer about three feet wide. On top of these were slightly smaller rocks, and they agreed to find those with flat edges, suitable for a good foot-hold.

Leo and Marina found themselves sitting next to each other. Marina held the phone and guided Harry to and fro as he strained to bring across more rocks for their *ad hoc* solution, while Emily found smaller fragments to pack between the larger ones, creating a stable platform.

"Feels a bit like one of those adventure holidays, doesn't it?" Marina tried.

Leo marveled at the analogy in the circumstances, but played along. "Or those deathly dull team-building things where you all go out into the woods and solve problems together."

"Yeah. They always sounded awful," Marina commented. "I'd almost prefer to be stuck down here." She paused, her voice cracking a little. "Almost."

Leo put an arm around her. "It's going to be fine. You'll see."

"Sure," she said without real confidence.

"And it'll make a great story, right? Imagine telling your students about this?"

In the small chamber, Emily couldn't help but over-hear, and her earlier resolution to remain upbeat and posi-tive left her momentarily. "You mean, tell them how we got stuck under a castle like a bunch of idiots because one of our number," she said pointedly, "decided that curiosity *definitely wouldn't* kill his particular cat?"

Harry had his hand on her forearm in seconds. "Take it easy. We all agreed to come in here. And you have to admit," he said, resuming his work, "that this is *one hell* of a freak accident. I mean these walls have stood for centuries," he said, "and they choose *today* to crumble?"

"I'm honored," Marina quipped. She stood. "My shoulder's a bit better. I don't mind doing some of that leveling work, Emily."

Relieved, Emily took the seat by Leo. "You okay?" he whispered.

"Yeah," Emily replied. "This dust is playing merry hell with my allergies, though. Can hardly see straight, not that there's much to see. Don't suppose you've got any antihistamines lurking in your trouser pocket?"

"Sadly not," Leo confessed. "Hey, Harry? Want to take a break?"

They switched out regularly, and within half an hour, their hands sore and scratched, the quartet had built a three-foot-tall platform on which to stand.

"Right, then. Who's going first?" Marina wanted to know.

"I'll go," Leo said. "I'm tallest, anyway."

There were no objections. Leo was given all the light they had – three cellphones' worth – as he found reasonable footholds among the pile of larger rocks they'd assembled. As he reached the top, he stretched upward to see if he could get a grip on the ledge of the fissure. The bricks – thick, old-fashioned ones, each with a maker's mark – had come away from the wall in a pattern that left decent handholds, and Leo found the edge of a flat surface.

"The mortar must have been terrible," he observed, calling down to them. "The wall fell away in a nice, neat chunk." He experimentally pulled himself up, testing to see if the wall would hold his weight, then heaved himself hard up the face of it, aiming to get his elbows on the edge of the crevice.

"Just take it easy," Emily said.

As he pushed off, the rough-hewn platform beneath him gave way, and momentum was lost. Swearing, he struggled to get both hands on the fissure, but one slipped immediately and the other just couldn't get enough purchase. "I'm ... shoot... I'm going..." he wailed as he toppled back away from the wall and into the darkness below.

The quiet reception area of the police station was shaken by a piercing, harrowing scream. Seconds later, a door flew open, and Detective Inspector David Graham dashed to the interview room to see what on earth had happened.

"It's okay, boss..." he heard Harding say as he burst through the door. "Marie's just having a tough time."

"Bloody hell," he muttered. Marie was in the corner of the room, curled on the floor, hands over her ears. "What did you say to her?"

Harding was a little red-faced, though it hadn't really been her fault. "I mean.... She'd been talking about George in the past tense, and answering questions about him as if he were dead..." Harding began.

"But she hadn't truly accepted it. Not even after seeing his body this morning," Graham finished for her.

"Shock, sir," Harding said by way of explaining the scream. "Reckon it's sinking in now."

"Look..." Graham raced to form a plan which might help their investigation while protecting Marie from the worst of her demons. "Her doctor is on his way. Can you stay with her? Get her some water, maybe? Just keep her calm until he gets here."

Harding approached Marie and knelt beside her. "Would you like a glass of water, sweetie?"

The distraught woman said nothing. She was crying, hiding her face in her hands.

"How about a cup of tea?"

Marie lashed out suddenly, kicking at Harding like a cornered animal and bellowing in incomprehensible French.

"Steady..." Harding told Marie. "It's okay... We're here to help you, love."

Marie snarled again and tried to slap Harding's offered hand away.

"Not in the mood, sir."

Graham gave it a try. "Marie? Your doctor will be here in just a few minutes. Dr. Bélanger tells me that you've been getting much better lately," he fibbed – Graham had yet to speak to the psychiatrist – "and he's looking forward to..."

Marie yelled at him, inconsolable, desperate, and then lunged forward, trying to bite his hand.

"Right, that's it," Graham decided, stepping back. "Sergeant, I'm sorry to do this, but we're going to place her in a holding cell until her shrink gets here."

"Okay, sir."

"If you can do it without cuffing her, great. But if need be..."

"Understood, sir." It took cajoling and more force than Harding would have liked, given the circumstances, but they got Marie downstairs and into a cell within five minutes. By the time she was in the small, bare room, perhaps realizing what was happening, the fight had largely left her, and she was a little more docile. Still, Graham reasoned, he could take no risks with the safety of his officers.

Harding ensured that Marie had nothing with which she might harm herself, and she pushed a plastic beaker of cold water through the hatch. "Drink this, love, and breathe deep, okay?"

Graham watched with professional pride. "Well handled, Sergeant."

"It breaks my heart," Harding told him as they climbed the stairs together, "after the day she's had."

"It's not what we'd prefer," Graham agreed, "but it won't be for long."

The Detective Inspector's prediction was accurate. After only ten minutes in the cell, Marie seemed calm enough to talk to her psychiatrist, Dr. Bélanger. Graham and Harding escorted him downstairs, adding only a little detail to Graham's earlier phone message.

"She's becoming more aware of events, but only gradually," Graham told him. "The shock, I think, really knocked her sideways. We've tried our best, but neither Sergeant Harding nor I are experts at this kind of thing."

Bélanger was well over six feet tall, but he had a soothing, gentle manner. He straightened his navy blue tie and strode into the holding cells area. "On the left," Harding told him. "Second door."

Bélanger opened the hatch and spoke to Marie. "Madame Ross?"

She began crying again, but Bélanger motioned to the officers that he would be quite alright.

"I would climb mountains," Graham told Harding as they left Bélanger to it, "for a cup of tea. There just hasn't been a moment."

"I'll do the honors, sir."

"She is borderline in many ways," Bélanger told them half an hour later. "She is suffering from clinical depression as well as generalized anxiety. She's had a couple of psychotic episodes in the past that have required hospitalization, but with medication, support, and limited stress, she's able to function. Her husband's death, though, seems to have tipped her over the edge."

Harding listened carefully. Their little constabulary had brought in psychiatrists for a number of reasons during her tenure, and she always found what they had to say fascinating.

Bélanger appeared thorough, professional, and knowledgeable, even if he did spout a few too many buzzwords for her liking. "We really didn't want to put her in a cell, Doctor," Harding contributed.

"I don't think it exacerbated her condition," Bélanger assured them, "but I'm surprised by the sudden violence. It's not something I associate with Marie."

"Losing a loved one can turn a person into someone they themselves don't recognize...." Graham began, but then stopped. Harding and Bélanger waited, but Graham seemed lost in thought.

Bélanger recommended that they release Marie from the cell. He would ensure that she received her medication and would quickly move her to a psychiatric unit on the south coast of the island. As they were making the arrangements, the phone rang.

"Mrs. Taylor?" Graham was surprised. "Is everything alright?" He listened, flashed Harding a worried glance, and promised that they'd be right over.

"Trouble at the Inn?" Harding asked.

"Something of a 'commotion,' according to Mrs. Taylor," Graham related. "George Ross' sister has just awoken."

Stephen Jeffries sat in his office, wracking his brains. Across the simple, black desktop, Constables Roach and Barnwell observed the fretting figure, and as they were trained to do, wrote down everything of value. The problem for them both was that, especially when nervous, Jeffries spoke in a ceaseless, excited torrent.

"I really don't know how helpful I can be," he said, well into the fourth minute of a protracted, stream-of-consciousness monologue. "They played beautifully at the wedding, went back to their hostel afterward, and then apparently visited the castle this morning. I don't think I remember seeing them," he said, glancing around the room like a distracted squirrel. What he *could* provide, though, were cellphone pictures of the quartet playing at the wedding reception, which he promptly forwarded to Roach's email address.

Roach had done most of the talking – that which could be fit in edgewise between Jeffries nervous diatribes – and was committed to finding the missing foursome. However, Barnwell regarded this whole adventure as a waste of police time. "They're musicians, right?" he'd confirmed. "They'll be down the pub, getting hammered, spending whatever dosh they made last night at the wedding."

Roach, however, was a lot more concerned. Jeffries had left them in no doubt that, particularly for the curious with a disdain for closed doors and proscriptive signs, the castle could be an endless source of amusement. He had visions of the four string players locking themselves into some ancient basement or falling down some poorly lit spiral staircase, nursing broken limbs and calling for help. The thought chilled him.

"Well," Roach reminded Barnwell. "The lady on the front desk definitely saw them come in, but she did not see them leave."

"So she says, and I believe her," Jeffries agreed. He looked harassed, his hair ever so slightly out of place, This was most uncharacteristic and indicated that this had been the rarest of days, one on which Stephen Jeffries found himself genuinely flustered by one event after the other.

"We'll search the grounds again. Would you like to accompany us?" Roach offered. He didn't need to look over at Barnwell to understand the older man's utter contempt for what he saw as a senselessly wasteful plan.

"I wouldn't want to be in the way, but if I can be helpful," Jeffries replied, "I certainly will."

The grounds were immaculate. Not only was the castle host to a wedding, but the staff recognized the importance of neatness, "putting their best foot forward," and maintaining a dignified air at this historic landmark. Jeffries first led the two police officers around the quadrangles where the wedding had taken place. They were deserted now. Jeffries was glad to see that the remaining guests had resisted the temptation to simply mill uselessly about near the scene of the accident... or should that be *crime scene*.... No, he corrected himself. Let's not put the cart before the horse. *Scene of the accident* would do for now. Like Mrs. Taylor, he was intensely anxious that a mysterious, sudden death should not unduly color the public's opinion of this fine place.

"That's four times," Barnwell reminded Roach quietly when they had finished scouring the castle's exterior. "If you want to do a fifth tour of the grounds today, you'll do it alone."

"Right," Roach agreed, though he found Barnwell's habitual laziness particularly unhelpful today. "Let's head inside." He turned to Jeffries. "Where do the tourists normally go?"

Jeffries led them into the darker, cooler interior of the castle. The temperature dropped significantly, and all three men were glad of the respite from what had become an unseasonably warm day. "The old jail cells," Jeffries explained.

"Wonder if our missing quartet have managed to lock themselves in?" Barnwell offered.

Jeffries double-checked each cell, accompanied by Roach. "I'm afraid that's impossible. They can't be opened without one of the master keys." He led them down the narrow hallway, lit by wall-mounted electric lights that had taken the place of the torches that had for so long illuminated these ancient chambers.

"Is it worth calling their names?" Roach asked, mostly rhetorically.

Jeffries, for one, apparently felt it was worth a try. "Emily!" he called down the hallway, listening to the dull, stony echo. "Marina!" he tried next. All three men listened carefully for a response, but none came. Jeffries shrugged and led them onward.

They passed a closed-off room that Jeffries explained was earmarked as the home of their new torture exhibit. "Fantastic," Barnwell said. "Maybe they're torturing each other for fun."

The door was still closed, but Jeffries noticed that the sign barring people from entering had been moved. He slid it back into place. "Probably some kids. The room's not open yet. And what with today's accident, I'm not sure it ever will be."

"Pity," Barnwell said. "A little S&M never hurt anyone, right? Let's have a little look-see."

Roach rolled his eyes and opened the door to the exhibit. The three men went inside. The room was completely dark and smelled very dusty. "This is going to set me off," Roach complained, shielding his nose.

"Emily!" Jeffries yelled again.

"If it turns out," Constable Barnwell told his colleague, "that they're *actually* down the pub, you owe me dinner at the Bangkok Palace."

Roach had his hands on his hips. "Can we focus on the..."

"With drinks," Barnwell underlined. "Lots of them."

"I thought you were off the sauce?" Roach whispered back as Jeffries poked around the darkened room.

"Ow!" they heard him say.

Both officers were alert. "You alright, sir?" Roach asked, shining his flashlight in Jeffries' direction.

"Yes, yes," Jeffries said, a little embarrassed. "Just caught myself on this pike." Roach illuminated the seventeenth century weapon, a five-foot long wooden shaft topped with a truly nasty looking sharpened spike. "Oof. Wouldn't want to find myself on the wrong end of one of *those*."

"Shall we?" Barnwell, suddenly tired of his idea, urged the others toward the door and back into the relative comfort of the hallway.

Jeffries wrung his hands. "Where on *earth* have they got to?" he anxiously wondered aloud.

CHAPTER NINE

I T WAS IN David Graham's nature to try to bring compassion to every one of his encounters with the public, however challenging, but having to face his second hysterical person of the afternoon was not a challenge he relished.

"Okay, Mrs. Taylor. What's the story?" he asked a little wearily.

The proprietor was nearing her wit's end. "I can't *have* these disturbances, Inspector Graham. It's not *right*," she insisted, wringing her hands. "This is a *respected* hotel, and it's *Sunday*, for the love of all that is holy."

Graham made a conciliatory face. The White House Inn and its long-suffering owner had indeed been handed far more than their fair share of troubles in the past six weeks. Mrs. Taylor was all too aware that the impact of a negative buzz on social media could mean ruin. Gorey was hardly experiencing a "crime wave," but two mysterious deaths in as many months were two more than was reasonable for somewhere so idyllically quiet.

"Why don't you just tell me what happened?" Graham said, notebook at the ready.

"She woke up, well after lunch time."

"Who did?"

"Eleanor, Mr. Ross's sister," Mrs. Taylor said. "She knew nothing of the whole business, she was just sleeping off a hangover. I suppose she has a cellphone. Anyway, she woke up and suddenly finds out about her poor brother."

"Quite the shock," Graham imagined. "What happened?"

"She was *screaming the place down!*" Mrs. Taylor informed him. "Completely lost her mind. Tearing around the hallways, yelling for her brother, for her parents, kept saying, 'Not again, not again.' I really didn't know what to make of it. We got her back into her room, and one of the staff is sitting with her now."

With a heavy sigh, Graham made a note of the room number and headed upstairs. Harding joined him after checking the Inn's register.

"Once we've calmed Eleanor down," Harding told him as they climbed the stairs, "we've got Juliette, the victim's first wife, his new sister-in-law as it were, to deal with." She shook her head in wonderment.

"Oh," Graham said, simply. *Would this day ever end?*

Janice did the knocking. Eleanor's room was three doors down from the Jouberts' own suite, but apparently she had slept through alarms, nearby police visits, and the reports of tragedy on her phone. She had essentially received this avalanche of news and sympathy in the seconds after waking up with a ferocious hangover.

"Police?" Eleanor appeared to cling to the doorframe.

"May we come in, Ms. Ross?" Harding asked her

gently. Graham was relieved to see that the emotional maelstrom described by Mrs. Taylor had passed for the moment.

Eleanor opened the door wide to let them in. Polly, one of the breakfast waitresses, who had been sitting with Eleanor, now slipped quietly past her, looking greatly relieved.

"Inspector," she acknowledged as she passed into the hotel corridor.

"Polly," he responded with a nod.

When she had gone, Harding and Graham went into Eleanor's room and cast a better look at their victim's sister.

"I'm just... This is all just too much right now," she said, on the edge of tears. Eleanor Ross looked pretty awful, Graham saw, bleary-eyed and fair hair askew, the very picture of a hung over woman in her late twenties who didn't party very often and was suffering the consequences.

"It's a very difficult time, Ms. Ross. We don't want to make things any harder."

"Do you know what *happened* to him?" she said, slumping down onto the bed. She'd thrown on some jeans and a t-shirt, but she still looked thoroughly crumpled.

"He fell," Graham said, trying to find the gentlest explanation, "from one of the battlements at the castle. We really aren't certain yet as to the circumstances."

"Fell?" she repeated. "George?"

"I'm afraid so."

Eleanor pursed her lips, holding back her emotions rather better than she had an hour earlier. "Did he... Did he jump?"

Harding handled this. "There's no evidence of that."

"An accident, then?" she tried next. "Maybe he slipped and..."

"We really can't say that, either," Harding told her.

Now Eleanor looked at them both, fixing them with eyes that were dulled of all sparkle. "Pushed?" she brought herself to say. "Someone *pushed* George off the..."

"Again," Graham interrupted, his hands raised to stymie this train of thought before it could proceed, "we have no evidence. No one saw the incident occur. I was there but found him after he had fallen."

"You did?" Eleanor said, latching onto this fact. "Did he say anything?"

Graham shook his head. "I'm afraid not. His injuries were very serious."

"But he was alive?" It seemed particularly important that Eleanor understand these details, though Harding couldn't help finding her curiosity a little strange. Even slightly morbid. But Janice also knew that there is no guidebook for grief.

"He had no pulse," Graham related, "and he wasn't breathing. Like I say, he'd fallen from a considerable height and was badly injured. There was nothing anyone could have done," Graham assured her.

Eleanor sat on the edge of the bed, her shoulders slumped, pinching the bridge of her nose as if fighting both the grief of the moment and a savage headache. "Poor boy," she said, more than once, closing her eyes. "Poor, poor boy. He overcame so much... Did so well for himself. He practically raised his daughter alone, you know, with Juliette off doing her own thing," she said, her feelings about her sister-in-law immediately apparent.

"He was a hero too, you know. Saved some French kids from drowning."

Then the questions returned. It seemed that Eleanor simply had to understand this tragedy before she could begin to accept it. "What time did he fall?"

Graham checked his notebook, "It's difficult to say precisely." He felt it important to add, "But I found him shortly after eight-thirty this morning."

She considered this, looked at her watch. "I think I know what happened."

Harding and Graham exchanged a glance, both of them desperate for some movement in this fraught and awkward case. "Go on, Ms. Ross," Graham told her.

She sat up straight and took a deep breath. "You know that this was George's second marriage, right?"

"Yes," Harding acknowledged. "He was married to Marie's sister."

"And how do you think," Eleanor said testily, "that his druggy, ne'er-do-well ex-wife felt about *that*?"

Graham's eyebrow raised. "Well, you know her better than we do, Ms. Ross."

"She overreacts to things," Eleanor explained. "She can be as cool as a cucumber for ages, then she suddenly goes off the deep end for no reason. I mean, neither of the Joubert daughters are particularly stable, but Juliette was always someone about whom you wonder... you know, not *if* something bad is going to happen, but *when*. Constantly treading on eggshells, George was, both before and after their divorce."

Harding handled the question. "And you believe she might have had something to do with George's death?"

The word, *death*, incontrovertible and so shockingly

final, stabbed at Eleanor. She took a moment to collect her emotions once more. Harding reproached herself. Perhaps next time she'd choose a euphemism. *Demise* might have been better, she reasoned. Or even just *accident*.

"She certainly didn't like the idea of George marrying Marie. Even though it was her who left him. I'm not certain, of course, but if I were investigating, I'd want to have a serious word with her." Eleanor told them, some aggression now creeping into her tone.

"Ms. Ross," Graham said sternly, "I urge you not to make a bad situation worse."

"No, no." Eleanor said as she stood. "I understand. I'm not a violent person, mister, erm..."

"Detective Inspector Graham," he reminded her.

"Right. Juliette has nothing to fear from me." Then she added, "Perhaps from the law, but not from me."

Sergeant Harding didn't care for Eleanor's attitude, either. She tried to regard her kindly, but there was now an air of revenge about her, as if she had decided for herself what kind of disaster had befallen her brother and who had caused it.

Harding noticed that Eleanor's fists were balled tightly and touched Graham's shoulder to get his attention.

"If you'd rather," Graham said to the grieving sister, his tone even, "take a break, gather your thoughts, and get something to eat...

"You need my help," Eleanor insisted, "I know the people involved. Juliette, her meddling parents. Even that Marie. *None* of them are in their right minds, you know."

Graham could see that Eleanor was quickly cycling through the emotions of grief, jealousy, and anger. All were interspaced with moments of calm and lucidity, a common reaction to unbearable news.

"Is that so?"

"Juliette's nasty, spiteful. And Marie's *crazy!*" Eleanor said, suddenly rising and stomping around the room. "*Certifiable,*" she underlined. "She's depressed one day and on cloud *nine* the next. She treated George like a leper, then like a saint, then like someone she couldn't *stand*, then," she said, spittle flying as she raged, "like someone she couldn't live without."

"Please, Ms. Ross," Graham tried.

"You've got to listen. They all drove him to it. Or they did it themselves. That family is *poisonous*." Barely pausing for breath, Eleanor now seemed content to let her every thought tumble out, as though her brother's death had broken a dam and unleashed a torrent. Which, of course, it had....

"And it's not just this, the two weddings, the weird relationships with the sisters. It's the old stuff. With our parents. Back in France." Now she paused for a second, but neither police officer seemed to acknowledge her point. "You *must* have heard about that," she whined. "Didn't anyone tell you?"

Graham was caught between two competing needs. He had to try to keep Eleanor calm. At the same time, he was desperate for the effusive, unwittingly helpful Eleanor to simply *keep talking*.

"The accident at the farmhouse, you mean?" Graham said, motioning for Eleanor to sit back down on the bed. He'd have given anything to beam them all to the station, but this wasn't the time.

Eleanor ignored his gesture and paced the room. "That's one word for it," she said. "It's always been incredibly hard for me to believe that my father would have done something like that."

"And the Jouberts?" Harding prompted. With witnesses like this, the young sergeant was learning, it was often sufficient just to toss in the occasional encouraging prompt, rather than more direct questions that would only break up the flow of the testimony. She thought of it as adding a squirt of lubricant, so that the mechanisms would keep turning smoothly. So it was with Eleanor.

"*He's* a prig with a chip on his shoulder, despite his affectations," she told them. "And *she's* this weird, controlling, mother-hen figure," she added with a curious, distorted flapping-wings gesture.

Graham was noting this down with speed and precision. "But they never displayed any open hostility toward George?"

Another angry shrug. "Only on a daily basis," Eleanor grumbled. "You know how some parents are. 'Zer's not a man in ze world who's good enough for my leetle girl,' all of that nonsense. Him, especially. As though his daughters were the finest catches in all of France."

Eleanor sat now, palm to her forehead. Neither Harding nor Graham saw any theater in it. The woman was clearly suffering, and the pounding Champagne headache could not, they judged, have been helping her state of mind.

"I'll fetch you some water," Harding offered. "Maybe some painkillers."

Janice fished out a tablet from a stash in her bag and brought a glass of water from the hotel room bathroom to Eleanor who, with this kindness, seemed to drop down a couple of gears, her shoulders sagging. She was exhausted, Graham could see, and now she simply needed time, both to process this tragedy and to shake off the effects of the alcohol. "Yeah," she said, her tone low. "Thanks."

"We'll speak with Juliette and perhaps check in with you later," Graham said gently. "If there's anything you need...."

The two officers made to go, but Graham felt a hand on his arm. Eleanor looked up at him with the saddest eyes imaginable. "Look... I'm sorry. It's all too much."

"I do understand," Graham said with sincerity. "Believe me."

"Whatever happened, I know that George didn't kill himself," she said, face furrowed and eyes beginning to tear over. "He wouldn't. Not him. He knew what it would do to... you know... the people left behind."

Graham nodded. "We'll do everything we can." Eleanor returned to staring at the floor, holding her aching temples, while Graham and Harding took their leave, closing the door quietly behind them.

The two officers collected themselves outside Juliette's room. Graham readied a new page in his notebook, but they resisted the temptation to indulge in a discussion of the situation in such a public place.

"And now," he said with a funny smile, "for something completely different."

Harding remained deadpan.

"*Monty Python?*" Graham asked, incredulous. "Please don't tell me seventies comedy completely passed you by."

"Not my thing, sir," Harding replied.

Graham tutted quietly. "My dear sergeant. You

simply haven't lived." He wrote a few words in his notebook.

"Now for Juliette."

"Juliette, sir."

He raised his hand to knock, but his phone buzzed. "Hang on. This might be Tomlinson again."

But it was Graham's contact in the French police. Their conversation was a little longer this time, and Graham's face was a picture of intense curiosity. "Thank you, Monsieur," he said, "Most interesting."

Graham took Harding a few doors down the hallway and spoke quietly to her. "Remember the business with George's parents, over in France?"

Harding nodded. "Did 'Poirot' have something else for us?"

"No kidding," Graham replied. "Guess – I'm serious, just guess – who owned the farm *right next door* to the one where the Ross parents were found dead?"

Harding blinked. "No way."

"Way," Graham assured her.

"The *Jouberts*?" she asked. "How about that?"

"How, indeed," Graham replied. "That must be how George and the two sisters first met."

Harding brought out her tablet and with the information Graham gave her, produced a map of the farms. "Right next door. You'd actually have to walk or drive through their property," Harding noted, tracing the map with her fingertip, "to get to the main road. The two families must have been very close."

"Especially as the Ross clan were there most every summer, so Poirot said."

Harding chewed this over. "What did he say about the evidence?"

"That's where things get murky," Graham replied. "Ross senior's fingerprints were on the gun. Once the murder-suicide theory became the dominant idea, they didn't really look for any other explanation. Interviewed everyone in the area, apparently, then called it what they called it and closed the book."

"But your Poirot doesn't buy the theory?" Harding speculated.

"He's on the fence. Said it just didn't smell right. Bereaved families say this kind of thing as a matter of course, but it seems théy truly *were* a happy couple, adored George and his little sister Eleanor, loved the French countryside, were financially stable, all the rest of it."

"There was one more thing," Graham added. "The esteemed Monsieur Joubert has a checkered past."

"Oh?"

"He was involved in some kind of incident with a former business associate."

"Interesting."

"He was implicated but never charged in the stabbing of said business associate."

Harding made a note. "Sounds like Antoine has a temper. Hope it doesn't run in families, or this is going to be another bloody awkward interview."

Graham nodded, pulled himself up tall as he often did when approaching a potentially awkward situation, and knocked on the door. Harding was reminded of those animals that try to make themselves look large and fierce in the face of a predator.

In this case, their foe was Juliette Paquet, formerly Ross, née Joubert. She appeared at the door, an almost mirror image of her sister – the same long, dark, straight hair, the blue eyes. "Who are you?" she asked, none too politely, her accent very thick.

"Gorey Police, ma'am," Graham said, producing his ID. "We'd like to speak with you about the death of..."

"I was going for coffee," she said, and she made to push past them.

"Please wait," Graham said. "This won't take long."

"I need coffee," she repeated. She didn't meet their eyes. It was, Harding felt, like arguing with a truculent teenager, one who simply couldn't *believe* they were grounded again.

"May I suggest room service?" Harding tried.

Now Juliette stared at Harding as though meeting a new adversary for the first time. She turned on her heel and waved them in with little more than a grunt, taking a seat by the window, her posture sagging and her shoulders hunched. The curtains were closed. Graham saw that she had been working steadily through a pack of high-tar French cigarettes. The room had the visibility of a house whose kitchen was on fire, the smoke acrid and pungent.

"I wonder," Graham began, "if we might open a window."

Juliette gave them another noncommittal shrug, a gesture that Harding found intensely and unmistakably French. Graham popped open all the windows, though he stopped short of drawing back the curtains. A great welter of sunlight would have been entirely incongruous to Juliette's obviously jet-black mood and probably her entire existence.

Juliette's room was markedly smaller than both Graham's and the more comfortable suite Juliette's parents occupied. She sat in the only chair. The two officers stood. They found themselves being unselfconsciously ignored by Juliette, who merely lit up another cigarette and puffed on it disdainfully.

"We'd like to extend our condolences," Harding began. "This must be a very difficult day."

"What do you want to know?" Juliette interrupted rudely. "What do you think I can tell you?" She puffed out smoke as though from some hidden, internal source, the acrid fumes curling around her nose and ears.

Graham adopted a slightly sterner tone. "What time did you leave the wedding party last night?"

That shrug again. Graham analyzed it, absorbing the details.

"Late," she said. "Maybe three. There was music and champagne. Why would anyone want to leave?"

"And where were you," Graham asked next, "at around eight thirty this morning?"

Juliette blew out another great cloud of grey-purple smoke and slightly inclined her head toward the room's bed, which was unmade. "I was asleep."

Graham made a note. "How did you hear about the tragedy at the castle?" Graham asked.

This brought Juliette to a halt. She stubbed out the rest of her cigarette and turned to Graham. "Tragedy?" she asked, raising an eyebrow.

"Yes, the death of..."

"I know who died. And I know when. My mother told me."

"How?" Harding wanted to know.

There was another fed-up teenager gesture, rolled eyes and a pouting mouth. "She knocked on the door," Juliette said, as if explaining the situation to a child, "and said, 'Juliette, George has fallen off the castle. He is dead.' Then I went back to sleep."

Both officers were reading this young woman, her behavior, her accent, and her lack of any interest in helping them. Both were privately elevating her higher on their list of suspects.

"Do you believe it possible that George committed suicide?" Harding asked.

Another shrug. "People get sad. Maybe life with Marie wasn't so perfect."

Graham got straight to the point. "Were you jealous of your sister?" Juliette's eyes darted around to focus on him. "After all, he had been yours once."

There was a brief explosion of French. Harding recognized a couple of curses. Then Juliette said, "He was a *nobody!* Not even a real man."

Harding felt a new and genuine sympathy for George. She'd never imagined that the victim of a sudden and mysterious incident like this one should find himself so badly maligned by those who might be expected to mourn him. First Antoine and now Juliette. For a family into which he'd married not once but *twice*, at least two of the Jouberts appeared to have the lowest opinion of George Ross.

"But yet you attended their wedding. Traveled here, booked a hotel, took a full part in the celebrations," Graham reminded her.

Juliette was surrounded by thick smoke, as though she were a conjurer whose trick had gone wrong, but she made no attempt to wave it away, apparently inured to this poisonous atmosphere. "I knew there would be free champagne."

"But your sister?" Harding added.

"Is an idiot," Juliette spat. "I told her what she was

getting into, and she didn't listen. She *never* listens. We haven't had a proper conversation in years."

"What *was* she getting into, Ms. Paquet?"

Graham used the silence that followed to take stock. In the end, he boiled his thoughts down to a single question: "Juliette, can I ask what you think happened to George?"

One more shrug. Did it mean *I don't know*, or perhaps, *I don't care*? He felt it might be a mixture of the two. She'd shown no grief for George's loss, no sympathy for her sister, only a contempt for the emotions that always swirled around a sudden death. It was as if she'd been here a hundred times and was simply bored of it all.

"Maybe he was drunk and leaning over the side," Juliette pondered. "Or maybe he slipped. I have no idea. You're the detectives," she said, lighting up another cigarette. "You figure it out."

Graham paced around on the patio terrace of the White House Inn, waiting for Constable Roach to pick up his blessed phone. He gratefully filled his lungs with fresh afternoon air. It had been a long time since he'd been in so smoky an environment as Juliette's room, and he knew the smell would linger on his clothes and – much worse – his skin, until he could shower.

"Constable Roach, I'm going to listen for a brief moment while you tell me that your missing persons case is concluded."

"Ah," Roach began. "Erm."

"Oh, for the love of God, Roach," Graham muttered. "We need to interview twenty more wedding guests. I'm up to my ears in Gallic disinterest and sociopathic siblings. I need some good news. Lay it on me."

Roach explained the situation, none too proud of their having come up short, but unable to improve on the reality. "We've turned the place upside down, sir. No one's seen them, and they're not in any of the basement hallways."

Uncharacteristically, but in a moment that spoke of the stress and confusion of the day, Graham unleashed a brief, colorful torrent of vernacular.

"You alright, sir?" Roach asked.

Graham took six long breaths, so deep and determined that Roach heard every single one. Then the tired, frustrated DI said, "Constable Roach, I need several things in short order. I need a pot of tea so badly that I'd threaten Mrs. Taylor with a loaded gun if she told me that the kitchen had run out of Oolong. I need," he continued, "the witnesses to do a bit more bloody *witnessing* and the family to be a damned sight more *familial*." Roach knew venting when he heard it, and he stood quietly, phone to ear, letting his boss get things off his chest. "I need the esteemed Marcus Tomlinson to get back to me with something more concrete than, 'Sorry, DI Graham, this bloke's dead, and I don't know why.' And," he pushed on, "I need my crack team of missing persons experts to find some *bloody missing people!*"

"Roger that, sir," Roach could only say.

"Get on with it," Graham told him. "I hope there remains not an iota of confusion as to what I need from you, son."

"None, sir."

Click.

CHAPTER TEN

MARINA CRADLED LEO in her lap and made him as comfortable as she could. Harry's sweater – donned that morning in case the castle inner hallways were chilly – made a serviceable blanket, but they were very short of other ways to keep him warm.

"I'm telling you," Marina kept saying, "I heard something."

Harry alternated between kneeling, concerned about the stricken Leo, and trying to bolster the improvised staircase from which his friend had fallen. "All I heard," Harry said honestly, "was Leo yelling because he'd just fractured his arm."

Emily was never one to let sloppy summations slip by. "You're not a doctor, and we don't know what's happened to his arm." The stress of their predicament was getting to them all. Tempers were beginning to fray.

"Okay, okay, let's keep calm," Leo pained voice rose up out of the darkness. It was almost the first thing he'd managed to say since falling, twenty minutes earlier, except to repeatedly apologize for making their already bad situation markedly worse.

But Marina was adamant. "It sounded like someone shouting from out there," she said, nodding toward the pile of rocks that was all that remained of the tunnel through which they'd arrived.

Emily shrugged, unwilling to rule anything out. "Point is, we didn't reply."

"We were a little distracted," Harry said defensively, motioning to Leo's arm. It was lying across his chest in what had become the least painful position. "I thought he was out cold," he added. In the moments after Leo's fall and before light could be brought to where he had landed, it had indeed seemed that Leo was knocked unconscious. In the end, he was simply stunned. Leo had taken a long moment to realize what had happened, by which time Marina was already attending to his arm.

"Well, even if they are looking for us down here, I say we continue to try getting over into the next chamber," Harry said.

But Emily remained unconvinced. "There's no guarantee that the next chamber is any improvement on this one. Or that we could get Leo over the wall."

"We wouldn't have to," Marina told her, "if Harry could find a way out and get help."

There seemed no reason to debate any further. Emily, still full of misgivings, inspected Harry's "staircase," which was only a slightly more secure version of the rock pile Leo had climbed. "One foothold after another," she advised. "Super slow and careful."

"Yes, Mother," Harry quipped as he began his ascent. The augmented rock pile would take him a little higher than the point Leo had managed to reach, which should, he hoped, make the job of levering himself into the next chamber rather easier. What would happen on the other side, of course, no one could say. But Emily insisted that Harry agree to return if no safe way down into the chamber presented itself.

They waited as he steadily made his way up the pile of rocks, using carefully built footholds and finding it much easier to keep a grip than Leo had done. One of their three cellphones was now below twenty percent power, so Emily held it in reserve and used hers to light Harry's way. He had the other, and she hoped it would reveal some kind of good news.

"Okay, I've got a good grip on the top," he said, reaching the jagged gap where the wall of the chamber had crumbled, revealing the way into the neighboring room. "Here goes."

Harry hauled himself up so that the top of the wall, two bricks thick and noticeably shoddily made, was under his belly, and paused there. "Hey... You know what?"

"You okay?" Emily called up.

"There's a big pile," Harry called back, his voice constrained by his curious embrace of the wall, "of *boxes* in here."

Marina and Emily exchanged a glance. Leo had his eyes closed but was obviously listening. "What kind?" Emily shouted back.

"Wooden," came the reply. "Big, solid things."

"Is there a way out? How does the rest of the room look?" Marina was desperate to know.

"Like..." Harry began, and then pulled himself further over, so that he could reach down and brace himself against one of the boxes. "You remember... the end of that movie?"

"Which movie?"

"*Indiana Jones*," Harry replied, levering himself fully over the wall now and standing straight up on the uppermost wooden storage box. The pile must have been ten feet high, perhaps more. "You know, the huge room full of wooden boxes where they store the Ark of the Covenant? Bloody good movie."

Emily and Marina exchanged another glance. "Sure," Emily humored him.

"That's what it looks like in here," Harry said, shining his cellphone light around the chamber. "Dozens of them. In stacks, against the walls." He looked around, then down. "I think I can get down to the floor."

"Okay," Emily called through. Their voices were noticeably harder to discern through the wall of the chamber, and she found herself nearly screaming at him. "Just go slowly and watch your footing."

Harry didn't reply but was grateful to find the way down very easy. Within moments, he'd stepped down from the pile of boxes and was in the middle of the room. Above him, he noticed, was a single light bulb suspended from the ceiling. "There might even be a light in here. Hang on."

Miraculously, in perhaps the best news they'd had since the rock fall, hours earlier, the light still worked. "Eureka!" he cried. "I haven't seen a door yet, but this place is pretty interesting. Wonder what's in these boxes?"

"Markings," Leo said quietly.

"Any markings on them?" Marina related, grateful now for her voice coaching lessons. She'd taken them originally to help her with speaking to audiences during concerts, but now found they were excellent preparation for vocal projection in underground chambers. Who knew?

Harry put away the cellphone and took a close look at the nearest boxes. "This one says 'E.E.R.'", he said. "The font looks a bit familiar. I think I've seen that in a movie, too. Oh, wait..." There was a pause.

"Harry?" Marina yelled. The only response was a creaking sound, something like wood being broken. "Harry, I'm serious, if you release mustard gas or start a nuclear chain reaction in there, we'll have *words* later, I promise you."

The voice that came back was not at all jocular. "I think you need to come over here."

"Seriously?" Emily said.

"Yes," Harry confirmed. "All of you."

"But Leo..." Marina objected.

"Him too," Harry told them. "Find a way, and do it right now."

To the relief of the whole quartet, the journey into the next chamber was not nearly as awkward and painful as Leo had feared. First conquering his apprehension of once more ascending their improvised staircase, Leo then found a way to shuffle through the gap at the top of the wall, where Marina and Harry received him and made sure he suffered no further injury.

"Top man," Harry said. "Sorry to make you go through all that, but I believe you'll thank me in a moment."

The room was perhaps twenty feet wide and twenty-five feet long, larger than where they had come from, and well lit, for a change. Against all four walls were large stacks of wooden crates, each marked with the same three letters, E.E.R. Initial speculation about whether this might be connected to Queen Elizabeth was dampened by the font. It was as German as it could possibly have been, exactly the stereotypical Teutonic script.

"Jesus, Harry," Emily said, making her way down the final level of boxes and arriving on the floor with a short jump. "This could be a haul of secret weapons or poison or something..."

"No," Harry said. "It most certainly isn't poisonous. Or dangerous." He paused, enjoying the moment. "Unless, of course, it's the late nineteen thirties, and you're concerned about its potential influence on German culture."

"Eh?" Emily responded, but then turned to see the opened crate. Harry had unearthed its contents, removed the curtain-like packing material, and displayed the three unframed paintings, propping them up by the case in which they'd remained hidden for at least seventy years.

Marina said it. "What," she began slowly, "the heck..."

"Franz Lipp," Leo told them proudly. "Austrian, born around eighteen ninety, if memory serves." With his good arm, he ushered the others out of his light and took a close look. "Oh, yes," Leo grinned. "It's him, for certain. Look at these brush strokes. The confidence of an artist in his prime. And the colors," he pointed out, "vibrant, but serene." Undimmed by the years, the painting was a composite of arching, looping swathes, purple and green, invoking a pastoral scene, perhaps, with the whirl of a passing storm in the background. "He was Jewish, but before Hitler made his little power grab in nineteen thirty-three, Lipp's works found their way into some of

Europe's finest collections. Including," he added meaningfully, "that of the Rosenberg family."

There was silence as the others struggled to understand. "Leo," Emily said, transfixed by the painting. "What exactly is going on here?"

Leo continued, full of energy now. "These other two are probably his as well. Although this one," he said, pointing to the smallest canvas, "might be by a student. Or it could be Lipp's earlier work. See how it's a little more pedantic, more obvious; *here*'s a harbor and *here*'s a boat... While in his later works, his style became so much more fluid and amorphous."

"'Degenerate art,'" Marina breathed. "The kind of paintings that were unacceptable in the Third Reich. The modernists, Cubists, Surrealists... Can you imagine that Picasso was *illegal*?"

Emily was flabbergasted. "You've got to be kidding me." She looked around the spartan chamber, here in the deepest basement of a castle in the Channel Islands. "*Here*? Of *all places*?"

Harry shrugged. "Why not? The Germans knew that the British wouldn't bother invading, and that air raids or naval bombardment would only endanger the beleaguered public."

Her mind working at full speed, Marina said, "Wait, we never defended the island against the Germans? We just left the people here under *Nazi occupation*?"

Harry had read about the islands before leaving London and had a ready answer. "Couldn't be done. The Germans were pretty well dug in, and it would have been a horrendous job to boot them out. Besides," he added, "the strategic importance of the islands was pretty limited. The Germans occupied Jersey virtually unimpeded. So, this was as safe a place as any to store forbidden art works."

"Perhaps," Leo continued, "to sell after the war, or trade for more desirable works, as they so often did."

"Desirable?" Emily asked, taking a closer look at the paintings. "These are amazing."

"To us, sure," Leo said. "But to a Nazi, these symbolized the breakdown in traditional art forms, and everything that was wrong with twentieth-century society. Not to mention the fact that the artist was Jewish. I'm a little surprised, and very relieved, that they weren't simply burned, along with so many others."

"Remarkable," Harry intoned. Then he recognized the potential scope of their find. "Say, do you think *all* of these crates are full of confiscated art?"

Emily grinned, despite herself. Usually their level-headed leader, she was now as caught up in the moment as the others. "Dunno," she said. "But, I say we find out!"

CHAPTER ELEVEN

EVENTS BOTH LARGE and small had done much to undermine Detective Inspector David Graham's enduring belief in a benevolent God, but a well-timed and perfectly-brewed pot of Oolong did much to reaffirm it. How, he speculated as he poured his third cup with a steady hand, could such an extraordinary and healthful tonic be available to humanity, except through the guidance of a loving Creator?

Sergeant Janice Harding spotted his mood. "Thinking big thoughts?" she asked as she sat down. After a hectic day, she'd taken the time to grab her spare uniform back at the station, and was now at her resplendent best, her hair neatly tied back and eyes sparkling.

"Just putting some more fuel in the tank," Graham told her. "I suspect our day's work is far from finished."

Harding related something she had recently read. "The chances of an interviewee either forgetting something or embellishing the truth increase exponentially roughly twelve hours after the events in question."

Graham nodded.

"No eyewitness testimony can ever be regarded as one hundred percent accurate," Graham told her, "because we're relying on frail and fragile human beings."

"Makes you wish there were cameras everywhere," Harding offered. "It would cut crime in half."

Sipping his tea, Graham briefly thought this over, but having worked in London for so long, this topic was a well-trodden path. "At what cost?"

Harding replied, "They're not all that expensive, are they? And the information could cut down on investigative work and interviews, save us a ton of money..."

Graham raised a hand to bring her to a halt. "Police work is not," he said very seriously, "and never will be some kind of video game where you click a few buttons and suddenly you've got your suspect."

"Well, no, but..."

"And the notion that we might all have our every waking moment scrutinized by some looming, centralized authority is the pivotal script for every dystopian sci-fi novel ever written. That's how police states operate, Sergeant."

Chewing this over, Harding was forced to agree. "Yes, sir. The thing is, in cases like this, wouldn't it have been helpful if there were a drone hovering over Gorey, taking it all in? Or a bunch of cameras on the Orgueil battlements, filming everything that happens?"

The teapot was almost exhausted and Graham waved to the waiter for a refill. "You know," he said, sitting back and pinching his nose, "when I first joined the force, we had to jump through a dozen fiery hoops to get a wiretap. It was almost unheard of. And not only was the technology rather flimsy and the legal side full of problems, but there was an *ethical* side, too." Harding listened, doing her best to imagine an earlier, more innocent time, probably just a few years before. "After all, we were intercepting someone's personal correspondence. In doing so, we were breaching their privacy, and all because we *suspected* they were up to something. Convincing the judge each time was an absolute minefield."

"Really? It's a cinch these days, isn't it?" Harding remarked.

"Well, I can tell you, it took *ages* back then, and it wasn't that long ago, really. You had to stand there and swear up and down that the target was legitimate, that they'd definitely been involved in something or in touch with someone and then," he added, his fingers circling to evoke the endless nature of the process, "you had to sign documents detailing how you'd *treat* the information, who you could discuss it with, what you planned to do with it, the whole nine yards."

"Sounds like a giant pain in the bum," Harding said.

"Yes," Graham admitted. "But it was *police work*. It was genuine, and thought through, and we only spied on people when we absolutely had to."

Harding wasn't prepared to let this one go. "So, you want to return to a time when we fill in a stack of paperwork just to listen to one individual's phone conversations?"

Graham knew there was no easy answer. "I'd like the process to be more efficient, but the same standards have to apply. Not some broad-ranging, bulk collection system that just sucks up everything pretty much indiscriminately."

"But if it did," Harding persisted, "we'd know about crimes before they happened. We could prevent them."

"Maybe," Graham admitted cautiously. "But imagine

this. Two friends are talking on the phone. They get into a discussion about it how it might be nice to have a bit more money. One of them mentions that the corner shop has poor security, and the other one makes a snarky comment that the owner has been overcharging for years."

"Okay," Harding said, following intently.

"If the conversation stops at that point, and they *don't* rob the place, have they committed a crime simply by talking about it?"

"Not as the law currently stands," Harding had to admit.

"But we've made it our business to *listen* to them anyway," Graham said, tapping the table with a rigid index finger. "We acted as though they *were* committing a crime, *just in case they did.*"

Harding wasn't quite with him. "But if they *did* rob the shop, we'd have evidence pointing to them, and we'd able to arrest them."

"For *having a conversation?*" Graham asked, incredulous. "Imagine that the shop had no CCTV and that no one there was able to identify the burglars. We'd have no evidence to make an arrest, just an illegally gathered phone conversation."

"Yeah, but at least we'd have it," Harding countered.

"So," the DI wanted to clarify, "in your perfect universe, overhearing two people talking about committing a crime would be sufficient to arrest them for having committed that crime?"

Harding was loathe to risk the disapproval of her boss, and she was on uncertain ground. "I don't know, sir. But it certainly would be more efficient."

"More efficient than what?" Graham wanted to know as an elderly couple took their seats at the next table.

"All the interviews and forensics and what-have-you," she replied.

Graham found that they had reached his main point, and he made it with the certainty of many years' thought and experience. "All of that *what-have-you* is the very definition of police work, Sergeant. We find out *what actually happened*, not what was *planned to happen*. We interview witnesses, like the Jouberts and the people who work at the castle, to build up a picture of the suspects. We investigate the crime scene to see what it can tell us and investigate facts, such as George having his own place and that Marie stayed elsewhere before the wedding. All of that takes time and effort, and it's a royal pain in the arse, I don't mind admitting," he said. "But it's *authentic*, and it doesn't invade anyone's privacy."

"But what if you don't get a conviction, because you're not permitted to gather stuff like phone data?" Harding said.

"Then we don't," Graham said. "Simple as that. We're going to catch whoever murdered George, if that's truly what happened, using the same methods of deduction and the same examination of evidence that have served investigators since the beginning. But if the conviction can't be had through fair means, it doesn't mean we should indulge in foul ones."

It was Harding's turn to be incredulous. "But then, the murderer might just get away with it!"

Graham took a breath and chose to smile rather than continue down the road to anger, a journey he'd allowed himself to take far too often, and he never enjoyed where it led. "People have been getting away with crimes since our ancestors established the principles of right and wrong. No justice system can catch every crook, nor should they try to. A good part of what we do, for better or worse, is *deterrence*." Harding was nodding now. "Simply by being outstanding, professional investigators, we show the would-be criminals of the world that should they one day choose to be idiotic enough to commit a crime, we'll be all over them and won't rest until we've found what we need to get a conviction on them. In the process, we show that we will only do it by fair and authentic detection methods."

Harding reflected on this. Whenever she sat down with DI Graham, particularly when he was just finishing a big pot of tea, she always found that she learned something. Often something very significant that could change her world-view or explode a long-held myth. It was like having... she searched for the word... a *guru*.

"Hmm, I wonder, though," she cautioned, "if, in this particular case, someone thought they *could* get away with it. That we'd never find out."

The reminder of their present duties was unwelcome, but timely. "Indeed, Sergeant Harding, indeed. I wonder. Let's go and find out, shall we?"

They stood together.

"You know," he said, signing the check to bill the tea to his room, "I think I fancy another chat with the Joubert family. A longer chat. A one-to-one conversation with each of them, perhaps."

"Good idea, boss," Harding agreed.

"Because, and I've noted this before, as you'll recall, something is going on with this case."

"Agreed, sir," Harding said, following him to the lobby.

"And people don't just jump to their deaths for no reason. And they don't slip and fall from a walkway that has a two-foot thick medieval battlement all along its edge."

"They certainly don't, sir," Harding acknowledged as they ascended the stairs.

"And they definitely don't get pushed off, to their deaths, without someone *else* having a very good reason. In their minds, at least. Unless the castle had ghosts. And I don't believe in ghosts. Do you, Sergeant Harding?"

Janice found herself on an emotional pendulum, swinging between a renewed enthusiasm for cracking this *damned* case, and a growing respect – yes, an admiration – for the remarkable mind of this man, her boss. When he was in this kind of form, he was simply unstoppable, and it was exhilarating to watch.

"Ghosts? No, sir. I don't, sir."

"Good." He knocked animatedly on the Jouberts' door. "I'll kick this off, if you don't mind, Sergeant. I'm in a mood to be the one doing the talking."

Antoine and Mathilde Joubert were, Harding could clearly see, most surprised and put out to be receiving their third conversation of the day with members of the Gorey constabulary. Graham's polite request for a few moments of their time carried a tone of extra urgency, Janice noted, as though he had anticipated some degree of time-consuming, French bluster and wasn't going to have any of it.

"*Mais...*" Mathilde began, "you *still* do not know what happened?"

Graham remained on his feet while the others sat. The Jouberts were side by side on the bed, while Harding took the room's desk chair and sat opposite them. "We have several theories and suspects," Graham told her, watching the woman closely to judge her reaction, "but we are not yet – not *quite* – in a position to draw a conclusion or make an arrest." He paused rather dramatically, his pacing interrupted. "Or *arrests*."

Antoine did not care for this tone. "I believe, *Monsieur L'Inspecteur*, that we have already told you everything we know."

Graham brought out his notebook. Harding knew this as either the prelude to an incisive question or the precise logging of further details. It was the former. "Did you genuinely think it wise," Graham asked, "when describing your relationship with the late George Ross, to omit that your family owned a small farm that was directly adjacent to that of George's parents?"

Antoine appeared befuddled for a moment. "Farm?"

Harding chipped in with the name of the village.

"Well, yes," Antoine said, stiffly, "but we didn't see how that was important."

Graham blinked at him. "Really, sir? You didn't?"

Antoine was defensive now. Resolutely superior in temperament, he was not someone who was used to being interrogated or accused of errors. "What does this have to do with George's death?" he asked pointedly.

"Yes," Mathilde agreed. "What of it?"

The notebook flipped closed. "I really couldn't care less if you owned neighboring farms, Madame Joubert. What *does* interest me is that you were a few hundred yards away when George's parents died. And you omitted to say so."

Mathilde gave a curious tutting sound. "Very unfortunate," she said sadly.

"A terrible accident," Antoine agreed.

Graham turned to Harding, who recognized it was her moment. "Would you describe the events of that evening to us, please?" she asked.

The two officers bit down their frustration at receiving yet another Gallic shrug, this time from Mathilde. *What do those gestures mean?* Graham asked himself again. *There's a hearty dose of 'sod you, I don't care if your hair's on fire'* in each one. He found them intensely irritating.

"It's so long ago," Mathilde complained.

"And yet," Harding said next, doing her best to ask just what her boss might in this situation, "it must have been one of the most difficult and harrowing afternoons of your life. Comforting a young boy and his sister who had just discovered their parents' bodies following their sudden and violent deaths."

"Terrible," Antoine said, but apparently felt no need to say anything further.

"The children had all been out playing. George came screaming to our farmhouse," Mathilde reported. "He was covered in blood. It was *'orrible.*" There was a long pause, and Mathilde only continued when she noticed Harding on the verge of encouraging her to. "He was so young, so frightened. His sister was still with the parents, in shock."

Graham recalled that the two youngsters had been thirteen and eleven. A truly appalling experience for anyone, but doubly so for children so young.

"We went to the farmhouse and... Well, there was nothing anyone could do. The shotgun was lying on the floor next to the father. As though he had dropped it after firing for the last time."

"And what did you do?"

Antoine took over, "We had to keep the kids away from there. They took a bath at our place and we called the police. I mean, it was obvious what had happened."

"You are not, unless I am quite wrong, a forensic examiner?" Graham heard himself say. "Nor are you a medical professional. How can you possibly have adjudicated so finally in so complex a matter?" he demanded.

Affronted, Antoine stood. "I am also not an *idiot*, sir. The man shot his wife and then himself. A child could have known that."

With that, Antoine sat once more. "The police came to the same conclusion."

"That's not what I was told by one of the investigating officers."

"What?" Mathilde rasped.

"The children were told that their parents' deaths had been an accident," Graham continued.

"What would *you* tell two young children?" Antoine protested. "That their father had gone crazy and murdered their mother, before shooting himself? What kind of memories would that leave them with?" His fists were balled now. "You're not a father, I can tell."

Graham let this go. A common trick of those with things to hide, he knew too well, was to deliberately anger the investigator, so that his own problems and memories were front and center, rather than the case having his attention. It was an old trick, and Graham wasn't going to fall for it. "How do you explain it?" Graham asked. "A happy couple, a loving family on vacation together. Why would George's father have done something so terrible?"

Mathilde pressed her hands together. "*Monsieur*, we are no strangers to illnesses of the mind, as you know. Our two daughters have their difficulties, and both have expressed a wish, at different times and for different reasons, to end their lives. We know how the mind can be. Life is not easy, sir. And the darkest parts of ourselves can't always be explained."

Harding was struck by this rather sudden moment of unexpected eloquence from Madame Joubert who, until this point, had remained relatively quiet and stoical. "*C'est vrai*," her husband agreed, his brevity a marked contrast to that of his wife.

Graham found himself at an impasse. There was no way he could delve more fully into the tragedy at the farmhouse, and if he were to press any further, the Jouberts would almost certainly demand that they be provided legal representation, something Graham was keen to avoid. Instead, he tried to find a middle path.

"Sir, madam... This investigation is complex and ongoing. Today has been very challenging for us all. We will need to speak with you further, so please make arrangements to stay on in Jersey for at least another day. We'll also be speaking again with Juliette, Eleanor, and as much as is possible, with Marie."

"May we visit her?" Mathilde asked anxiously. "Is she... how do you say... *locked up*?"

Harding fielded this inquiry. "She's not under arrest, but her doctor believes that she needs to be detained for her own safety. He's recommended that she stay for a few days at a facility on the south coast of Jersey. You'll be able to visit her there, perhaps tomorrow afternoon?" Harding glanced at Graham, who nodded.

"Very well," Antoine said. "A difficult day, yes. Most difficult."

Graham made a point of shaking both of the Jouberts' hands and then ushered Harding out, following her into the hallway and closing the door behind them. He had his finger to his lips and took her down into the lobby, where they spoke quietly by one of the massive potted ferns with which Mrs. Taylor had chosen to decorate the place.

"Well?" he asked, as if Harding might have gleaned all of the answers by herself.

"It smells," she replied. "I don't believe the murder-suicide story for a second. I think Mathilde and Antoine know more about the deaths of George's parents than they're letting on."

"An astute observation, Sergeant Harding. So, we organize a wiretap and see if they call a lawyer, or anyone back in France, and incriminate themselves, right?"

Harding stared at him. "Huh?"

"Just kidding, Sergeant. Come on, we've got police work to do."

CHAPTER TWELVE

I T WAS REMARKABLE, Marina thought to herself, that a man with a badly broken arm could even form a coherent sentence, or stand up straight. The art discoveries, shocking and amazing by turns, had completely re-energized Leo, who gestured expansively with his good arm and gave them all a pretty thorough description of each work. Only two were entirely unknown to him, with neither the painting itself nor the artistic style clueing him in.

"I assume," he said, "that there are whole bodies of work which were simply destroyed without having been catalogued." Then, he added grimly, "Entire legacies lost."

"But so much has been saved," Harry remarked, picking up an unframed piece which he'd removed from its crate. "What's this, for example?"

Leo recognized it at once. "That," he announced gleefully, "is the portrait of Madame Margareta Knelling."

There was silence. "Who?" Harry and Emily said together.

"She was the wife of some industrialist or other. You wouldn't know her, except that her portrait was painted by George DuMarais, one of the most talented Belgian artists when it comes to representations of the human form."

"Kind of a shame, then," Emily said, "that Mrs. Knelling looks like a space alien."

The portrait was hardly a kind treatment of what was clearly an old and frail subject. Leo explained that DuMarais was known for hugely exaggerating the features of his sitters, almost in the manner of a caricature artist. "He took what she brought with her – wrinkles, dryness, extreme age, that haughty air she has – and made them the features of the painting."

"Maybe Mrs. Knelling hated the damned thing," Harry suggested, "and just gave it to the Nazis."

"Doubt it," Leo replied. "It was worth a fortune even then. Now it'd be worth perhaps six or seven million dollars at auction, – can I have some water? I'm unbearably thirsty."

"You need to take it easy," Emily advised him. "You've had a serious injury. I'd hate to think you'd make it worse and end up being unable to play for even longer."

"Yeah, yeah," Leo told her. "But this is a once-in-a-lifetime opportunity."

"These paintings will all see the light of day now," Emily replied. "We've achieved something remarkable down here."

"Yeah, right." Marina, who had been quiet through this exchange. "Great lot of good they'll do us if we're crushed to death *down here*."

"It's going to be dark outside soon," Harry said. "If they're searching for us, they might call it off."

"Okay, team." Emily said cheerily, clapping her hands. "We're still in a bit of a pickle, and we still need a way out of it. Anyone got any suggestions?"

They'd already thoroughly searched the room and found it entirely without doors or access points to anywhere else. It was sealed in from all angles. Beyond shouting for help, attempting to dig through the rocky mêlée of the entrance tunnel, or simply sitting and waiting to be rescued, they had none. The tunnel was a potential disaster, all agreed, with jagged rocks holding up the remainder of the structure. One wrong move, and the remainder of the tunnel could collapse, trapping them even further. Or worse, killing them all.

"I can't *believe* no one noticed that part of the basement just came crashing down," Marina complained. "I mean, the noise must have been something else." She was becoming increasingly agitated.

"Apparently not," Leo said caustically. "We're either too deep, or too far from civilization."

"And who's fault," Harry asked next, "is *that?*"

Emily quieted him with a gentle hand. "It doesn't matter. We're here, and we're going to deal with reality."

"Yeah, let's do that," Marina snapped. "Let's sit here and think about how *wonderful* it is that we're surrounded by priceless art, buried under a castle, with no one even trying to find us."

"Take it easy, sweetie," Emily put an arm around her, but Marina shrugged it off angrily.

"I'll take it *easy*," Marina growled, "when we have a plan for getting out of here. When we have enough water for more than the next hour. When I'm not bloody starving, Leo's arm can be properly seen to, and I feel confident that this whole lot isn't going to fall in on top of us."

"We're going to have to be patient," Harry told her. "It might even be best to go to sleep for a while. You know, save energy and pass the time."

"Sleep?" Marina shrieked. "How can you *possibly* think about sleep at a time like this?" She paced the chamber like a caged animal. "They don't even *know* we're down here. There's no way for them to get us food or water. We can't call them because there's no bloody signal. And all you can do is talk about ancient paintings nobody's cared about for donkey's years."

Leo spoke to her softly. "All true. And yelling about it won't change things."

"But we don't have a plan! We're just sitting here waiting for someone to rescue us! Waiting and waiting... We need to *do* something!" Marina protested.

"Why don't you try and get some rest, eh?" Emily tried again, and this time succeeded in wrapping a soothing arm around Marina's trembling shoulders. "Deep breaths, girl-friend. We'll be fine. You'll see." Then she said to the others, "I'm with Harry. Let's all see if we can get some sleep."

In the dark and quiet, it remained only to find a comfortable place. They put together crates, packing material and sweaters to make rudimentary cots, and within moments, half of the quartet was sound asleep, snoring even.

The other half was wondering whether they'd ever see daylight again.

Exactly sixty-four horizontal yards away from the sleeping musicians, but critically, eighteen yards *above*

them, Constable Barnwell was having trouble getting his boss on the phone.

"He's working that mysterious death, isn't he?" Roach reminded his older colleague. "Which is just a bit more important than this, I reckon. I mean, so far it's just been us two, rummaging around this castle like a pair of twits. Waste of bloody time."

Barnwell got a laugh out of this. "You've changed your tune, haven't you? What happened to our 'sacred duty to find the missing'? To 'bring home the lost'?"

"I'm tired," Roach confessed, "my feet hurt, and all I want is a takeout from the Bangkok Palace and a cold pint."

Barnwell did everything but lick his lips. "I'm right there with you. Let's just see what the gaffer says when I ask if we can call off the search for the night. " He did not, Roach thought, sound particularly hopeful.

Thirty seconds later, they had their answer.

"No, you bloody well *can't!*" Graham growled down the phone. "You're on a search, and unless they've changed the definitions of such things while I've been struggling with recalcitrant French witnesses, searches *continue* until they are *resolved*."

"Right, sir." Barnwell hesitated.

"Do you need something in writing, Barnwell?" Graham barked. "In triplicate? Witnessed by a Notary Public?"

"No, sir."

"Splendid. Then get back on it, and stick to it until you find them."

"Right, sir." There was little else he could say.

"Over and bloody well out," the DI said.

Barnwell slid the phone back into his jacket pocket and then let fly a particularly strong oath.

"Wow, Bazza," Roach said, stepping back to admire his colleague's colorful and flamboyant use of language. "I didn't even realize you *knew* that word."

"I know a few more than that," Barnwell warned him. "Okay, no *pad Thai* or cold beer until we've got this wrapped up. And if ever there was an incentive to find four missing prats..."

"Where do we begin?" Roach asked. It was the fourth time they'd been obliged to re-think their search.

Barnwell sighed heavily. "Okay, well first, let's see if that little Leprechaun guy is still around, and get him to call all the local cafés and bars to see if they are in any of them. It'd be a fine thing if that were the case and we were wandering around here looking for them."

"You mean Mr. Jeffries, the events manager?" Roach said. He never tired of giving Barnwell a hard time over his apparent inability to remember names.

"Yeah. Let's get him on the phone. Then we'll sweep the place from top to bottom. Again."

By now, Roach resented this assignment almost as much as his colleague, and the lack of any progress whatsoever had put him in a bleak and uninspired mood. He yearned for the opportunity to do proper police work, the kind of case-cracking, mystery-solving wizardry that Sergeant Harding was apparently being groomed for. What, he wondered in that sober, frustrated moment, did *she* have in her locker that *he* lacked? That it was because of her superior ability and greater experience never occurred to him.

They knocked on doors, beginning at the top of the castle where the more expensive guest rooms were. Most of the guests had left, released from the inquiry into George's mysterious demise, and only a handful of the large, comfortable rooms remained occupied. Nobody had seen a quartet of musicians; even Barnwell's unforgettably vivid characterization of the beautiful Marina failed to elicit any positive responses. The second floor, almost as empty, was similarly barren territory; the four had simply vanished into the stonework, it seemed.

Jeffries was found, and put to work in his office. He was, the two officers could see, extremely tired and put out. "I just want to be helpful," he muttered, the dark lines under his eyes testament not only to a stressful day of tragedy and confusion, but the taxing task of organizing the major wedding which had come immediately before. He called the first place on his list and received a negative response; Roach and Barnwell left him to it and headed into the basement for the fifth time that day.

"Even with the lights on," Barnwell admitted, "this place gives me the creeps."

"Afraid of ghosts, are you?" Roach asked, and then gave an appropriately long and eerie hoot which resounded down the basement passageways.

"Of course not, you idiot," Barnwell replied, with just a tinge of genuine frustration. He didn't enjoy being ribbed by the younger man, especially in these miserable circumstances. Apart from being a less experienced police officer, Roach, an island boy born and bred, could not claim to have lived through anything remotely like the tough and often downright frightening upbringing that Barnwell, a Londoner through and through, had faced. Roach was still a kid, wet behind the ears, really.

"I know what you mean, though," Roach allowed. "Some seriously grim stuff happened down here. Long-term imprisonment. Torture." They had both read the signage – several times, in fact, during their repeated searches – and were impressed by the depth of the castle's history. They were keenly aware of the stark unpleasantness of life down here for those who'd been unlucky enough to find themselves incarcerated, centuries before.

"You've got to be thankful," Barnwell observed, shining his flashlight into every dark corner, "for advances in the justice system."

"You mean," Roach replied, "that we no longer string people up and burn off their toenails because they won't give us a confession straight away?"

"Yeah, like that. I'm sure it got the job done, mind you."

"Cut down on paperwork, I'd imagine."

Roach headed down a passage, one he knew to be a dead end, just to make sure, and when he returned to the intersection, noticed that Barnwell was wiping his mouth with the back of his uniformed sleeve. As they walked together down the next passageway, the older man tried, but largely failed, to stifle a burp.

Roach stopped. Barnwell carried on for three paces, but then stopped too. Neither said anything, but then Roach extended his hand, palm up, his face stern and unyielding.

"What?" Barnwell asked.

"You know bloody well what," Roach told him. "Hand it over."

"It's nothing."

Roach moved toward him and Barnwell backed up a step. "Okay, take it easy," he relented. From his inner jacket pocket, Barnwell produced a small, silver flask. He looked at it for a long moment, almost as if contemplating tipping the contents of the container down his throat rather than surrendering it, but then sheepishly gave the flask to Roach.

"Christ, mate."

"I just..." Barnwell began.

But Roach wasn't angry. "You don't..." he began, glancing around rather unnecessarily to ensure they were alone. "You don't have to explain anything to me."

"But I do, mate. It's... You know, this job. I get so bored and down. Like it's all pointless. I don't feel like I'm going anywhere."

Roach gestured to a couple of chairs in a nook near a corner in the passageway, placed there for the docents who watched over the castle during tourist season. "You want to sit down for a minute? I need to get off my feet before they begin a rebellion."

The two men sat, and Barnwell took a long moment to compose what he was going to say. He was obviously embarrassed; both men knew that Barnwell's drinking had a long history, but that in recent months he'd been doing a lot better.

"I thought, with the new boss and what have you," Roach was saying, "that you were feeling, you know, a sense of forward motion, and all."

Barnwell shook his head. "It only stayed with me for a few weeks. After that murder at the White House Inn, you remember. I thought to myself, 'Good on you, mate, you actually helped solve a murder'. Felt like a proper cop."

"You *are* a proper cop, mate. You've just lost your way a little."

"No doubt."

"And bloody stupid errands like this," Roach said,

waving a dismissive hand at the great castle which loomed around them, "really don't help. Those four are probably in the pub, like you said."

Barnwell was silent for a moment. His shoulders were hunched over and he seemed thoughtful. "You know," he began, "I only chose Jersey because I figured nothing would ever happen." He looked up at Roach who, he knew, had chosen to stay in Gorey where he had grown up because it was small, the ideal place to show his talents and gain a quick promotion or two. "And now I'm here, after... Hell, is it really *seven* years? Now I'm here, I want to do something *more*."

"Like what?" Roach asked. His shoes were on the floor under his chair and he was massaging his aching soles.

"Become a detective. Spend time with Graham and Tomlinson, examine a few bodies, learn the tricks of the trade. Run an investigation."

"You will, one day," Roach said.

With a glum shrug and a derisive snort, Barnwell made his feelings known. "You're loopy, you are. The gaffer will have us chasing down bike thieves and the odd tax evader, arresting people for not having the right boating license or scuffling with their landlord over their annual rent increase. Nothing ever *happens* here," Barnwell complained.

"I beg to differ," Roach said, sliding his shoes back on. "Two mysterious deaths in the last few weeks. Crazy French people and nutty brides. I'd call those *happenings*. Granted it's not exactly *CSI Miami*, and I know we're not at the forefront of this one, but..."

"No, we're in the sodding basement again," Barnwell growled.

Roach stood. "Alright, I'll do you a deal. One more sweep of these haunted passages, and we'll report to DI Graham that we've thoroughly searched the place, and are about to become ineffective as law enforcement officers due to lack of sleep and sustenance. We'll recommend they bring in the big guns."

"Eh?"

"You know, heat seeking equipment, firefighters, land and sea rescue, if need be. Now that would be a happening."

Rising slowly, Barnwell smiled and gave his friend a nod. "Agreed." He straightened his uniform. "Just one more time."

CHAPTER THIRTEEN

I T WAS WELL into the evening before Graham
had a moment to consider just how odd it was that
these interviews were taking place within yards of
his *own* room. Mrs. Taylor had made sure to give him one
of her larger, more recently renovated suites, with a
terrific view of the bay and the English Channel beyond.
Now, he noted, it was directly above the room at which he
was now knocking for the second time that day. "Let's
hope it's a more productive meeting than our first visit,"
he whispered to Harding as they heard footsteps
approaching the door.

Juliette looked much more awake and had done
Graham the unwitting courtesy of keeping the windows
open, which aired out the lingering, blue fog of cigarette
smoke. The room still smelled awful, though, and
Graham wondered just how long it would be before Mrs.
Taylor was forced to make the entire hotel a non-smoking
one.

"Again?" was the first thing Juliette said.

"I'm afraid so," Graham answered. "May we come in?"

That Gallic shrug again. Graham took a deep breath and pulled up the same chair as before. Harding, following behind, found the room's third seat, and they began.

"I'm starting to think," Graham told her, relieved that the woman had not yet reached for the pack of cigarettes on the window sill, "that in order to understand what happened to George last night and this morning, I will also have to get to the bottom of events at the farm, back in France all those years ago."

Juliette was considerably brighter than before. "You mean, the accident with his parents?" she asked.

"It's becoming obvious that your two families are interconnected in some rather *special* ways," Graham said delicately.

"You think it strange?" Juliette asked, glancing at the cigarettes but failing to take one. "That a man would marry a woman, divorce her, and then marry her sister?"

Graham glanced at Harding. Their new rule was that, upon receiving such a signal, Harding was to ask the next question. It meant a much expanded role for the sergeant, and she was keen to make the most of the opportunity. "We're not here to judge anyone's marital choices," Harding said. "No laws were broken. But some serious questions remain concerning the death of George's parents."

Now Juliette reached for the smokes. *Bugger,* Graham muttered inwardly. She lit one quickly, with a well-prac-ticed and fluid gesture, and then emitted a thin plume of smoke as though she were a leaky industrial pipe. "He killed his wife," she said with a distinct lack of compassion. "Then killed himself. *Non?*"

"*Peut être,*" Graham tried.

"Everyone knows this!" Juliette complained. "They were unhappy, or in debt, or had some kind of problem in their relationship. The two children found them dead, and we helped them through it."

Harding decided to go for it. "What kind of relationship did you have with young George? He'd just lost his parents. How did you guide him through such a difficult time? You couldn't have been much older than him." Three years, Harding judged, no more than that.

Another blue-grey billow of smoke filled the room. "It is," Juliette announced solemnly, "a *man's* world." She let this cryptic aphorism hang in the air with the smell of burning tobacco. "Men run *everything*. Look at my father, and then at my mother. Who runs our family?" Neither police officer spoke. There was the sense that something meaningful was on its way, and Graham didn't want to stem this new flow of information, however characteristically cynical its presentation might have been. "My mother, oh, she might seem strong, but it is all an act," Juliette continued. "She is a little mouse, and my father is a strong, majestic lion. They had nothing in the beginning. He worked, and she cleaned. Eventually it happened for them, but it took *so* long. You think," she asked, "that I wanted to be like her? That I would spend thirty years waiting for my husband to make some *money*, to achieve something, to support me and his children?"

Harding spotted the magic word. "You mean to say... Did you have one eye on George's inheritance? Even at that age?"

Graham glared at her, very worried that she'd both

spoken out of turn and had risked grievously insulting someone who, though stubborn and decidedly odd around the edges, was well-placed to be extremely helpful.

Harding continued. "His family owned land and property in England and in France. They were successful. And everything they had would go to George and his sister."

Graham was stunned. *You've got,* Graham thought through the numbed haze of confusion, *to be kidding me.* "He was a boy... Hardly a teenager," Graham couldn't help pointing out. "And he'd just lost his parents in the most tragic way."

"But you saw an opportunity," Harding directed her statement to Juliette. It was a summary of the diabolical machinations of which she seemed more than capable.

"It was a way out," Juliette confessed. "He was good looking, a nice boy. I would have to wait for a few years but not too many. I was patient. We were friends already. It was just a matter of choosing the right moment to become *more* than friends."

DI David Graham had dealt with drug dealers, domestic abusers, tax fraudsters, and crooked businessmen, but this simply took the cake. It was breathtaking for its brazen, heedless, obsessive focus on Juliette's own well-being at the expense of another. George and his feelings existed solely to be manipulated for her benefit.

Graham and Harding exchanged another glance. "That's quite..." Harding began, but stopped.

"Calculating," Graham contributed.

"Yes," Harding said. "Quite so. Calculating. But you left him. What happened to your master plan?"

"I *mis*calculated," Juliette glared at them. "George did

not have ready cash, and he wasn't ambitious. He refused to sell his property. He said they were investments, and besides, they had sentimental value." The disdain dripped off her.

"Does your daughter stand to gain from her father's death?"

Juliette's expression brightened fleetingly but quickly settled back into a mask of disinterest. "I don't know. Maybe."

They were all quiet for a moment, deep in thought.

"So do you know who killed him?" Juliette said, interrupting the silence and stubbing out the cigarette. "Because if you don't, then you're only *playing* at being police," she said testily. "Just *pretending*."

In a sudden surge of anger, Graham wondered, just for a quarter of a second, whether he could arrest someone simply for smoking during a police interview. He was absolutely *dying* to put a set of handcuffs on this snide, horrid woman and drag her down to the station. But he couldn't, and his lack of a ready response to her pernicious evil gnawed at him.

"Thank you for your time," he said instead, and stood. Juliette merely turned to look out the window. She did not watch them leave.

Again, Graham escorted Harding quickly down the hallway before she could say anything that Juliette or other guests might hear. In the lobby, Graham stopped and then paced around briefly, gathering his thoughts. Or perhaps just letting his temper cool a little.

"What," Harding offered, "a piece of work."

"Grooming a grieving teenager for marriage," Graham summed up. "All so that she could get a piece of his dead parents' estate." He found himself staggered, yet again, by the seemingly diabolical, selfish, greedy behavior in members of his own species.

"But she didn't break any laws that I know of," Harding argued. "At least not *English* law."

"It'd be heartening to think," Graham replied, "that somewhere in some old, thick, French statute book there might be a Draconian edict that promises lethal punishment for being a complete *she-devil*."

Harding steered her boss into the quietest part of the lobby. "Don't let her get under your skin, sir."

"I don't know, Sergeant," Graham breathed. "These cases... with families hating each other, conspiring against each other... They get to me. I'm sorry," he said genuinely.

"Want to take a walk?" Harding offered.

Graham was about to agree, certain that the evening sea air would do him some good, especially after the intense pollution of Juliette's room, but a pair of figures caught his eye. They were moving rapidly through the lobby. *Scuttling* through it, in fact. The air of guilt around them and obvious desire for stealth were not lost on Graham, whose radar for such things was unerring.

"Monsieur and Madame Joubert," Graham said loudly, as if announcing their arrival – rather than their hurried, furtive departure – to the whole hotel. "What an unexpected surprise. I imagine you're heading out for dinner in Gorey?"

The two stopped in their tracks but did not turn to face Graham. At her reception desk, Mrs. Taylor appeared and stared at the retreating couple and then at DI Graham. Her face told the whole story: *please don't make a scene.*

"No, it seems not," the DI said, answering his own question with unconcealed relish. "In fact, it seems as though you're leaving Jersey." Neither of the Jouberts let go of the suitcases they were pulling behind them. "And doing so against the strict instructions of the Gorey Constabulary."

Mathilde finally turned and glowered at Graham. "And what is the problem? Why can we not come and go as we please? We are French citizens, under the protection of the European Union..."

"You cannot return to France because," Graham said, in that same annunciatory tone, "you are persons of interest assisting us with our inquiry."

There was complete silence in the lobby. People stopped chatting, put down their early evening drinks with a soft *ping* or a gentle *clunk,* and then simply gawked at this remarkable scene. "And as such, the only place you are free to return to is your room. Now, please leave your luggage behind and accompany Sergeant Harding and myself."

Mathilde gave Graham a look that could kill. "To where, exactly?" she asked defiantly. Antoine had kept silent, Harding noticed, clearly deeply ashamed to have been caught trying to skip town quite so publicly.

Graham took five paces toward the couple, his gaze fixed on them. "To where this all began. To where," Graham said, his fists balled, "I will find some *answers.*"

CHAPTER FOURTEEN

T HEY SAT IN the far corner of the strange storage room, leaning against a large crate which remained unopened. The quartet had been very keen to lever open each and every container, but Emily had put a stop to their "crowbar rampage," as Harry had styled it. She and Marina had dozed fitfully but were now awake. They had shuffled away a few feet so as not to disturb Harry and Leo who slept more soundly. Soft snoring echoed around the chamber.

"What about some kind of tie-in between the art," Marina was wondering aloud, distracting herself to avoid a repetition of her earlier panicked hissy fit, "and the string quartets of the time?"

"Hmm?" Emily asked.

"You know, performing quartets by Jewish composers who were forced to flee the Reich. Or maybe stuff by the Second Viennese School." The challenging music of the three greats of serialism – a concept in which all twelve notes of the octave carried equal weight and were freed from the conventions of major and minor keys – wasn't a standard part of the quartet's repertoire, but the idea did catch Emily's attention.

"I like the Berg *Lyric Suite*," she confessed. "Though it's been recorded to death."

"Sure, but never with the benefit," Marina pointed out, "of being associated with a host of recently discovered artwork. Found," she added with a raised finger, "by the quartet themselves."

Emily let her imagination run riot for a moment. "How about a coffee-table book about the art, with an accompanying CD of relevant works?"

"I love it," Marina enthused. "We could call it 'Exposure' or something else nice and modern."

"Great," Emily agreed. She shifted a little. The packing material they had assembled was reasonably comfortable, but she was still going numb. "Some wouldn't," she allowed, "but I, for one, kind of like how you're turning this into a commercial opportunity right from the outset. We could use a break."

"Right!" Marina replied brightly. "This could be *huge* for us. And that's before we get into finder's fees and all that."

The thought had occurred to Emily, but she'd put it aside.

"Whatever happens," Emily replied, "it should be equal between the four of us. I mean, Leo made the discovery by opening that door and later identifying the art. I didn't even know who Franz Lipp was, never mind his history and artistic style. But we were the ones who followed Leo in here and helped get him over that pile."

"We're also the ones stuck down here wondering if

we're ever going to get out," Marina grumbled before remembering her earlier resolution. "I can't wait to get out of here and tell the world about this place. It's going to be... Well, I have no idea what it's going to be like," she added more cheerily.

"Me neither," Emily said. "Like nothing we've ever experienced before."

Marina was thoughtful for a moment. Emily guessed she was imagining a bright future where she might not have to scrabble around for gigs and students, imagining instead the luxury of picking and choosing the projects she would be involved in. She was happy to let her have her daydreams. And join her in them. The alternative, trapped down there in the damp and the dark, was certainly not worth thinking about. Then Marina said, "You think one of us should check on Leo?"

Emily shifted again. She was losing the feeling in one foot. "Harry's over there with him. I think he'll be okay." Emily paused for a moment, "How're you getting along with Harry these days, Marina?" The fling between Harry and Marina had made things difficult for all of them for a while.

"We're fine," Marina replied. "Don't you think so? We're not affecting the group, are we?"

"No, I guess not." Emily murmured. They sat in silence for a while. "But you kind of are, really," she resumed, much more quietly. Something in Emily wouldn't let it go.

"What? How? I don't think so."

"But... It's just that..." Emily began. "You know, I've had... You know..."

"Feelings for him?"

Emily cringed but accepted the truth. "Yes. For years now. Almost since the beginning."

Marina thought it through. "Please don't tell me that's why you've never married," she replied. "That you were waiting around for him."

Emily blushed deeply in the dark.

"Good God, Emily, if you're in love with Harry, why don't you simply tell him?" Marina said this just a little too loudly. The echo sent her question reverberating around the chamber.

Grimacing and hoping like never before that both Leo and Harry were genuinely asleep, Emily let the echo peter out and then said, much more quietly, "Because I know that it's not me he wants."

Marina sighed. "He and I went down that road. It didn't work out."

"Yes you did, and no, it didn't. But I know that Harry would give anything to be with you. It was just a timing issue."

"Don't be silly."

"It's true! He's..."

"Maybe," came a voice, "Harry might like to decide for himself what he wants."

Oh, hell.

"I'm so sorry, Harry..." Emily started to apologize. "You weren't meant to hear that."

"I heard," he said, struggling up off the ground. He was stood ten feet away, arms folded. "I heard everything, and I want you both to know something."

Neither woman knew what to say. "What?" Marina tried.

"I've been in love with Emily since I was nineteen,"

Harry admitted for the first time. "That has never changed."

The silence was complete.

"But you know why I've never told you? Why I haven't even asked you out, all these years?"

Stumbling over the words, Emily said, "I don't know, Harry. I had no idea..."

"Because you were already in love," Harry said. "And so completely, so publicly. There was never even a hope for me."

She stared at him. "What do you mean? I've never so much as..."

"Schubert," he said, and then ticked the names off his fingers. "And Beethoven, and Mozart, and Haydn. You *idolize* them. There's hardly room in your life for a cat, or your students, let alone a big, bearded cellist like me. I'd have been competing with a room full of dead geniuses."

"But," Emily began and then stopped. There was no way to refute him. She lived and breathed music – especially the classical string quartets – so much so that she thought about little else. It was the sign of a dedicated professional, she would argue. But it was also the sign of an obsessive, a musician so enamored of her heroes that good romantic prospects and all of her life came and went without her even noticing. Perhaps too, it was a means of distracting herself from what, or who, she really wanted but believed she couldn't have.

Emily suddenly seemed fragile, uncertain, and painfully shy. It was not a side of her any of them had seen before. She hesitated, momentarily lost for words. "I didn't know. It's not fair to have kept that from me all this time."

"What would you have done if I hadn't?" Harry asked, still standing, arms folded.

Emily considered this for a brief moment, but it was a decision she'd taken years before. "I'd have said yes, you idiot. I'd have said yes in a heartbeat."

Marina sighed. "Oh, for God's sake."

A weak but jocular voice came from the other side of the room. "About bloody time, too," Leo contributed.

"Enough," Emily chided. Harry was by her side now, an arm around her as they sat together on the pile of old Nazi curtains and sheets.

Marina made herself scarce, "I think I'll open a crate to mark the occasion."

"That's a good idea!" Leo called. "Let me know what you find."

Marina went to him and saw that he was pale but conscious and seemingly in good spirits. "How you doing, champ?"

"Oh, just basking in the reflective, beatific light of someone else's new romance," he said. "I have to say I'm fractionally jealous, but it's been a long time coming."

"Jealous of whom?" Marina asked, wondering if some new admission of long-hidden, secret desire was on the horizon.

"Of anyone who can keep a steady relationship together," Leo admitted. "I'm bloody hopeless in that department."

"But not bad at all," Marina said, "when it comes to identifying stolen art."

"Sure," he chuckled. "And what a terrific bulwark against loneliness in my old age *that's* going to be."

Marina shone her phone around the room, looking for a suitably large crate to open, but scrupulously ignoring the corner where Harry and Emily were now alone in the dark. *Good luck to them,* Marina thought. She huffed and put the thought aside. Picking up the crowbar they'd found and weighing it in her hands, she selected her crate, a big one with that typically Nazi writing on the side. "Okay," she said to the room. "Cover me. I'm going in."

CHAPTER FIFTEEN

I N THE DAYLIGHT, the battlements of Gorey
castle afforded views of the island of Jersey and the
English Channel unachievable from anywhere else.
Its position, high atop the only major prominence on this
part of the island, was the very definition of "commanding." It would have taken a major armed force weeks to
successfully capture the place and certainly at incalcu-
lable cost. But now, in the dark of a clear night, Graham
looked out over the lights of Gorey and the boats in the
harbor and reminded himself that they were not here to
take in the sights or indulge in historical musings.

Large, powerful floodlights added drama as well as
illumination to the scene. Graham gathered his thoughts,
walking around the battlements for several minutes while
the actors in this particular piece of theater were brought
together by Sergeant Harding. Rounding them all up and
insisting that they accompany her to the crime scene had
taken time, presenting yet another point of confusion for
Harding on this extraordinary day. There was almost the

436 ALISON GOLDEN & GRACE DAGNALL

sense, she judged as she shepherded the Jouberts and Eleanor Ross *en masse* up the spiral staircase and through the narrow passageways to the battlements, that they didn't *want* the puzzle of George's death to be solved. Or perhaps one or more of them knew full well there was a murderer among their number and were fighting to keep it a secret.

Whatever the truth was, she knew DI Graham would get to the bottom of it. Or at least she hoped so. This case, only twelve hours old but relentless and intense, was already taking its toll on her, and she yearned for the comparatively quiet times they had enjoyed before George Ross' untimely fall.

Graham returned, looking surprisingly energetic as he paced quickly along the ancient stonework. "Good evening, everyone, and thank you for coming." Harding admired his confidence, his way of speaking to a group of people; not superior, or smug, and not like a lecturer or teacher. No, his was the style of a consummate investigator, someone dedicated to discovering the truth from those who would prefer that it remain hidden. As she knew from his performance on the terrace at the White House Inn six weeks earlier, he was a master in just this kind of situation. It was thrilling to watch.

The response to Graham's greeting was a collective rendition of that blasted Gallic shrug.

"Is this strictly legal?" Juliette asked.

"We made a request, and you kindly obliged," Graham told her. "None of you are under arrest." He couldn't resist adding, "Yet."

Antoine and Mathilde Joubert stood stoically while Juliette leaned on one hip insouciantly, her arms folded around her waist. Eleanor Ross brought up the rear. She found her way to the front to see what was going on and peered briefly over the battlements. "Whoa," she moaned nauseously. After a pause, she crumpled slightly, "Poor George."

"With any luck," Graham told her, "we shan't be here long. I felt that it would be instructive to stand at the actual spot from where we believe George fell and bring together what we know about his death."

"Know?" Antoine scoffed. "The man *threw himself* off. That's what we *know*."

Harding fielded this comment sounding more like a textbook than she'd have liked but responding correctly all the same. "We don't have any evidence to support such a theory and therefore can't proceed on that basis." Graham nodded at this neat summation.

"Then where is Marie?" Antoine wanted to know. "If we are required to be here, surely you brought her from her hospital to be with us, also?"

Graham had found it difficult to do so, but the situation demanded exactly that. Marie was, he knew, as much a suspect as any of them, maybe more so. With a family situation as complex and nebulous as the Jouberts, he needed everyone present, even if that meant requiring the patient and the helpful Dr. Bélanger to accompany her up to the battlements.

"She will be here shortly," Graham replied truthfully. Bélanger had called him moments earlier, assuring him that Marie was, in the doctor's words, '"calm enough *at the moment*" to take part in this – hopefully final – stage of the inquiry.

"So what do we do?" Mathilde asked, palms outstretched. "Some kind of stupid pantomime? A re-enactment of something that none of us saw?"

Graham addressed her with a steady gaze. "We establish the facts of the matter," Graham stated. "Beginning with your locations at the time of the... at the time of George's death," he said, trying to avoid calling it something it might truly not have been.

"I was asleep," Eleanor told him.

"*Et nous aussi,*" the Joubert parents added.

"And me," Juliette chimed in. "Too tired and drunk to be anything else."

Harding began taking notes on her tablet, while Graham was doing the same, using his traditional notepad and pencil. "And what time did you all leave the wedding?" he asked.

"Midnight," Eleanor said. "There wasn't much happening, and I was tired."

"Eleven or so," Antoine said. "We left together."

Graham turned to Juliette. "What about you, Miss?"

She pursed her lips. "I can't say for certain. I had a lot of champagne. I think I danced for a while. Maybe two o'clock?"

Harding made a note, finding at once that this detail triggered a memory. She swished her screen a few times and found reference in her notes from the interview with Sam, the castle's night security guard, to a lone, drunken dancer. *Was it only this morning that I spoke to the guard?* It felt like a month had passed, perhaps more. She showed the note to Graham, who nodded.

"So," Graham surmised, "you were perhaps the last to leave."

"I guess so," Juliette said. The others had the distinct impression that she'd been too drunk even to know where she had been, never mind how late it was. "But I was asleep by three or so."

There was an echoing, distant voice from the arch-ceilinged passageways that led to the battlements. "*Mon Dieu*, this is the place where..."

"Marie?" four people said at once.

The bereaved widow arrived, arm in arm with Dr. Bélanger, but it was hardly a romantic gesture. He had to make sure both that she safely navigated the spiral staircase and that she not bolt.

"This is where... he fell," Marie was saying, over and over. "George..." She had a dreamy, faraway look but was sufficiently engaged, both Bélanger and Graham judged, to become involved in this crucial fact-finding exercise.

"Fell, yes," Antoine said, taking Marie's arm from Bélanger and gesturing toward the edge of the battlements. "Through this gap, perhaps."

Harding stepped across, removed Antoine's arm with a deliberate, firm grip, and gave the grieving Marie a warm smile. "How are you doing, love?" She and Marie spoke for a few moments while Graham took Antoine aside for a stern talking-to.

"It will not help at all," he told him, "to put ideas in Marie's head. I'm interested in the *facts* and *only* the facts."

"She is *my* daughter," Antoine protested. "I may speak with her in any way I please."

"Not when you're all party to what is possibly a murder investigation," Graham hissed. "We should be conducting our interviews at the station, but, if you remember, the last time Marie was there, she became so upset we had to lock her up for her own safety."

He spoke to Marie now, leaving the furious Antoine to stew. "I'd like you to tell us where you were after the wedding dinner was over. Did you go to your bridal suite, here at the castle?" he asked.

Marie thought carefully, tracking through the day's events. "We were married. We had dinner with everyone, and there was dancing." Beyond this, she seemed unable to describe. "I... I really don't remember what happened next."

"Did you have a lot to drink?" Harding asked. This would, at the very least, offer some explanation for the strange gaps in her recollection of what should have been the most memorable day of her life.

"Not very much," Marie replied. "Two or three glasses, all evening."

"She wasn't drunk," Antoine reported for the record. "I remember her being very clear-headed at the dinner. And she danced beautifully."

"However," came the voice of Dr. Bélanger from the back of the little group, "it is possible for alcohol to interact with her medication in ways that might leave her vulnerable to episodes of amnesia, especially under stressful conditions."

It was now Marie's mother's turn to be furious. Mathilde skewered him with a furious stare. "Then *you* should not have prescribed them. Or you should have banned her from drinking."

"No drinking?" Eleanor asked, incredulous. "At a *wedding*?"

This made her Mathilde's next target. "If it was not safe, if it would make her worse even than before, then yes."

Graham quieted her. "That isn't important now. We have a gap in the record that we're trying to fill. There's no indication that George and Marie slept in the bridal suite."

There was no response from anyone to this awkward, if entirely truthful, statement.

"There is a gap of some eight or nine hours between Marie and George leaving the wedding party," Graham continued, "and their next appearance together at the foot of the battlements, just after eight-thirty in the morning. Marie, I ask again," Graham said, facing her, "is there anything you can tell us about that period of time?"

Mathilde butted in protectively. "She already told you that she does not remember a thing..."

"I asked your daughter, Madame Joubert. Kindly let her speak for herself," Graham spoke sharply.

But it was fruitless. Marie stared blankly at them. "I'm sorry. If I think back, I remember the wedding and the dinner and dancing. Even some of the music. But after that... nothing."

Antoine began to speak in French to his daughter, but Graham stopped him. "English only, please, from everyone."

"Not even..." Antoine translated awkwardly, "the memory of your first night together?"

Marie was shaking her head, staring around as if the battlements themselves might speak up and repair the fissures in her memory. "Nothing. There's just nothing there. I'm sorry. I know that's really not helpful. " Marie turned to her mother, "I'm scared, *Maman.* Did I kill George?"

"Shh, shh, *chérie*, it will be alright, keep calm."

To Graham, Marie appeared to have a genuine case of amnesia. It was also true, however, that claiming amnesia was an excellent way in which to deflect blame, avoid answering difficult questions, and deliberately leave the police with huge holes in their knowledge of events. Her mental condition was, Graham judged, either an elaborate plan to deceive or a genuine ailment with a hugely negative impact on her life – and his investigation. For the time being, he decided to err on the side of simply believing her, especially having witnessed her all-too-real struggles with her mental state back at the station in Gorey. But the fact remained, anything could have happened on those ramparts.

"Okay," he said, taking a step backward, both literally and figuratively. "Let's address something of the history of your families." Antoine stiffened slightly, Graham noticed. "I want to discuss the death of George and Eleanor's parents."

"This again?" Mathilde sighed, but then caught Eleanor's withering expression. "Whatever you want," she conceded with another shrug.

"Take me back to those events," he asked them all as Harding swiped to a new page in her notes. "And this time, tell me *everything*.

Leo was buzzing with excitement. "So?" he asked for the fourth time. "What have we got?"

"Hang on, Mr. Art Genius, I'm unwrapping the... wrapping," Marina explained. This painting was more heavily protected than the others, and with softer, more expensive material. "This one has been so carefully crated," she called over. "Perhaps it is the pride of the collection. Ah, I think I've got it." There were ten seconds of silence, which for Leo were an agony far greater than his broken arm.

"Well?" he almost shrieked.

"You need to come over here."

"Really?" he asked, beginning to stand.

"Please don't make him," Emily said from the dark corner she'd been sharing with Harry. "He's not well."

"I'm on my way," Leo said.

"Good. Because... well... you'll see," Marina said, her voice tinged with amazed wonder.

Leo held his aching arm to his chest, aided by a makeshift sling Emily had made earlier from her scarf, and tottered over to the crate where Marina was standing in front of her find. "Okay, my little detective, what have you...?" He stopped, stood, stared, and found himself utterly speechless.

The painting was in a large, highly ornate, golden frame. It was of a style entirely different from the modern pieces they'd been uncovering. This was the work of a Renaissance master. Even Marina could see that it was a particularly good one. It depicted a man dressed expensively, clearly a nobleman, but with a certain feminine air, as though he had allowed the artist to depict his inner self, and not simply the façade he presented to the conservative public. He was holding his left hand by his heart, and his hair was luxuriously dark and wavy. He had a certain pout to him and an undeniable allure that spanned the centuries. Marina thought him very attractive, certainly a seven or an eight; maybe a nine, if he changed his hair or grew some scruff.

She was about to relate this to Leo, but then she saw his face. He was ashen, as though stricken by some new ailment, and he trembled slightly as she watched him. "Jesus, Leo? Are you okay? Do you need to sit down?"

"Yes," he confessed. "But I'm not going to."

"Huh?"

Emily and Harry came over. "Another weird swirly thing from a guy I've never heard of?" Harry began. "Oh, no... Wait, this is... Well, a lot more conventional."

"That's one way to put it," Emily agreed. "Leo, what have we got?"

His voice was dreamy and uncertain, as though arriving from another room. "I don't believe it."

"It's very beautiful," Marina said. "Is it by someone famous, do you think?"

Leo turned to her. "Marina... Harry... Emily," he said, touching each of their arms in turn, as if to ensure he had their fullest attention. "We're standing in front of a miracle."

"We are?" Harry said, peering more closely at the portrait.

"This is..." Leo could barely say it. "I believe this to be *Portrait of a Young Man* by the artist known as Rafael."

"Whoa," Marina said, stunned. "You're kidding, right?"

"Jesus, Leo," Emily gasped.

"How can that be? This is a modern collection," Harry was saying. "This doesn't fit..."

"It doesn't, but it's real, and we've found it," Leo said, holding a trembling hand out toward the painting. "We've found it," he said again.

They watched him commune, transfixed, with Rafael's lost masterpiece for a long moment before Emily broached the inevitable question. "How much do you think it might be worth, Leo?"

He was lost in the details of the young man's face, the beautifully decorous accoutrements of wealth and class, the carefully depicted sable fur. But he managed to say, "Well over a hundred million dollars."

Then, with an abrupt folding of his knees and a strange, frightened moan, he collapsed under his own weight and hit the stone floor with a sickening impact.

CHAPTER SIXTEEN

HE TENSION THAT pervaded the
battlements could not have been less than that
of the castle's hardest-fought siege. Graham was
prowling around the group of five suspects, asking
increasingly terse questions and relentlessly demanding
more detail from each of them. Any pause or error was
seized upon. Harding had never seen him push witnesses
like this, but she took it as a sign that he was closing in on
his quarry. Or perhaps he was reaching the limits of his
patience. She couldn't help but wonder what he might do
when that happened.

"So, the shotgun was just lying on the floor by the
body of Mr. Ross, the elder." Graham confirmed. "There
were no signs of forced entry. And the nearest farm other
than yours was well over a mile away."

"*Oui*," Antoine said. Of the five gathered witnesses,
he'd spoken the most so far and had borne the brunt of
Graham's questioning.

"Did you check for signs of life?" Graham asked.

Mathilde answered this one, her head shaking. "You

must never have seen a shotgun victim, *monsieur*. There was no chance that either of them were alive."

Graham had, in fact, seen more than his share, but he kept that to himself. "And you're certain," he asked once again, "that this was a murder-suicide?"

"How many times?" Antoine protested. "We've told you what happened. We know what we saw."

"Let me try something else," Graham suggested. "Who might have had motive to murder a relatively wealthy couple?" He looked squarely at Juliette, who said nothing. "Someone who always had one eye on the future. Someone who was determined to move away from her provincial upbringing and see something of the world?"

Juliette spat furiously, "You're disgusting."

"Am I?" Graham asked. "Is it so disgusting to assume that your callous attitude toward human life could possibly extend to murder?"

"I have nothing to say," Juliette told him.

"You cannot think..." Mathilde began, but Graham cut her off.

"Madame Joubert, I've known people to kill for the most trivial of reasons. Over an old flame or the placement of a garden fence." It was, Graham thought given his own experience, remarkable that the public was so naïve to assume that murderers belonged in a special, unassailable category of people; that they were born, rather than self-created. He had learned over the years that *anyone* could be a murderer. And often, they became so for the most slender, even most absurd of reasons.

"So?" Graham said to Juliette. "Why should I rule you out?"

"You are quite insane."

Graham smoothly moved on to Eleanor. "What about

you?" he asked. "Were you perhaps awaiting a full share of the inheritance you were earlier forced to split with George?"

Aghast, Eleanor stuttered, "You think *I* did this?"

"You're not entirely without a motive," Graham pointed out.

"That's *outrageous*! He was my only surviving family. I would have died for him!"

Graham scribbled continuously in his notebook, but he knew that there was more than an element of theater in his doing so. Listening acutely, he was absorbing and memorizing every word and gesture, adding each detail to what he already knew, analyzing and critiquing and formulating his strategy as he went. The sure-footed mechanisms of his own mind, seldom at a loss and frequently surprising even to him, gave him the confidence to be knowingly brusque with these people. If he leaned on the right one in just the right way, he suspected, they might simply crack.

But Eleanor's reaction was genuine. She would not be the one in handcuffs at the end of the evening.

"Did you ever," Graham asked next, "have cause to disagree or argue with the Ross family, Monsieur Joubert?"

Antoine was pinching his nose, exhausted by the stress of this unbearable day. "They were our friends, our neighbors. We didn't argue."

"In fact," Mathilde added, "we were the same. Politics, religion, you know." She kept her voice mild, almost conversational in her attempt to defuse the rising, crippling tension.

Graham ignored her, pacing rapidly up and down the battlements. "And what about you, Marie?" he said.

"She was good friends with George and Eleanor both," Antoine replied.

"I suggest you let your daughter answer." Graham said. This was just the kind of juncture that was worrying Harding. Would Marie's last, tenuous hold on sanity finally slip under this barrage of questioning? It didn't seem fair to her, but there was no other way.

"We were friends," Marie recalled. "We played a lot together, both at their farm and ours. And along the river and in the fields." She remembered it as a happy time.

Graham stopped. "And did you have the same plan as your older sister, I wonder? A long game, where you inherited the Ross' money and land?"

Marie stared at him. "A game?" she said, very confused.

"Juliette already confessed to having planned her union with George from a very young age. And not *despite*, but *because of* the death of his parents. Did she concoct this plan with you?"

Marie was trembling now, her head shaking from side to side. "I don't..."

Graham looked at Juliette. "He marries the first sister," Graham said, playing out his grotesque version of their romantic lives, "and not to worry if things don't work out... We've got a spare!" he announced, still looking at Juliette but pointing at Marie. "All the wealth stays in the family. Very tidy. But there is a problem. You can't wait for him to die of natural causes. So you hatch a plan. Together."

Hands to her mouth, Marie shrieked in mental agony.

"You cannot speak to my patient in this way," Bélanger protested. "She is too ill for this kind of questioning."

"Maybe," Graham said, "but I'm finally getting to the real point of all this. Perhaps what we've actually got here," he explained to Harding, "is a neat, coordinated, sisterly conspiracy. First one, then the other."

For her part, Sergeant Harding was far from convinced. Not only did she not believe that a pair of human beings could be quite so devious as to plot for nearly twenty years to usurp a family's money, but she thought the two sisters too fragile to murder George to seal the deal. On the other hand, it did somehow make sense. It explained the twin marriages. It provided motive, if indeed George's death was murder, a fact they were still trying to determine, and the sisters' perceived mental frailty would help to deflect suspicion.

Could that really be it?

"I suggest that the two of you conspired to inherit George Ross' estate and then killed him when you felt you had waited long enough." Graham was warming to his theory.

Eleanor was breathing heavily in the background and started to snarl quietly. Marie whimpered. Juliette rolled her eyes. Antoine was boiling red with unexpressed rage.

"A conspiracy?" Juliette mocked. "We hardly even *speak* to each other anymore."

"The perfect cover!" Graham said, pushing forward with a zeal that for the first time gave Harding a flicker of concern. Was this a flash of brilliance or a detective so carried away by his own performance that he was in danger of appearing insane himself?

Janice was of two minds when Mathilde stepped forward. "You're wrong, *Monsieur L'Inspecteur*. Absolutely wrong."

Graham backed up and took a long look at her. "It seems you have something to say, Madame Joubert."

Mathilde shrugged off Antoine's restraining hand on her shoulder. "You will destroy us all unless I tell you."

"Tell me?" Graham prompted.

Mathilde drew herself up straight and stared ahead. "It was an accident, *Monsieur L'Inspecteur*. At the farmhouse. It wasn't Monsieur Ross who fired the gun. It was...," she said, looking at her daughter, "Marie."

All were stunned into silence except Marie, who was now wailing inconsolably.

"That day, she was over at the Ross' farm and found the gun. She did not know it was loaded. She was just a child, ten years old. She thought it was a game or a toy. *Mon Dieu*, it *was* an accident. "

"Really? But there were two shots, Madame. Why, if it was an accident, would she have fired the gun a second time? With one adult already lying dead in front of her?"

"I cannot tell you," Mathilde said. "I do not know. Perhaps the shock or perhaps her finger slipped."

Juliette moved closer to her father. Eleanor stood stock-still, transfixed.

Harding was speechless but managed to keep writing. Graham rubbed his face for a moment and then said, "And you got creative with the crime scene, making sure it appeared to be a murder-suicide. To protect her?"

Mathilde nodded. "I swore Marie to secrecy. I could see what this would do to her, her life, our family. It was *essentiel* that no one know what really happened, and for years, Marie and I have kept the secret. Everyone believed that Monsieur Ross shot his wife and then killed himself. I thought, the... *episode* was behind us."

"But?" Graham asked.

Mathilde took another step away from her husband now, perhaps to disassociate him from the horrors of the past or to ensure he could not move to quiet her. "Marie, my poor girl... Since that terrible day, she has not spoken of it. I think she forgot her memories, blocked them from her mind. To cope, you know," Mathilde looked over at Marie, sadly. "In time, she fell in love with George, after Juliette rejected him." She spat out these last words, casting a vicious glance at her elder daughter. "But she was becoming more and more anxious as the wedding approached." Mathilde added.

Marie was on her knees now, with Bélanger's arm around her. The physician was desperate to move her away from this chaos, but he knew that she had to witness its sad conclusion, whatever it might be.

"She began to have nightmares," Mathilde reported. "Very bad. Terrifying."

"And three nights before the wedding, with all the arrangements made and everyone arriving on the island, something happened." She continued over the sound of Marie sobbing into Bélanger's shoulder. "She was... how do you say... talking in her sleep. About the accident."

Graham put it together. "With George awake beside her."

"Until then George believed, as did everyone, that his father had become depressed and decided to end it all, killing his wife, then himself."

"George woke Marie and asked about what she had been saying, demanding to know if she'd been dreaming or was remembering a long-hidden truth." They all tried to picture such a uniquely horrible moment. "She called me, crying, saying that she thought she was losing her mind. That she'd said something that she could not take back."

Harding imagined George, struggling to deal with the unbearable knowledge that his bride-to-be had killed both of his parents. "Did you go to their apartment?" she asked.

"I did, and I heard them arguing from outside the door. George was screaming at her... It was very strange of him. But he was so angry, so confused. He kept asking, 'Why didn't you tell me?' I heard Marie explain how it was my idea to cover everything up, to avoid the scandal and punishment."

"And it worked," Harding noted. "Until now."

"*Oui*," Mathilde agreed. "George was a good man. Eventually he calmed down. They talked and talked, and he forgave her. They decided to work together, to trust one another. To go ahead with the wedding. But I worried that, like all men, he was imperfect and fragile. That he might, one day, expose Marie's accident to the police."

"In a way, I felt that they were finished, after her confession. He could destroy her life at any moment. I couldn't let him do that."

"And so, to protect your daughter and yourself," Graham added pointedly, "You killed him."

Mathilde sighed sadly. "I had to do it."

"*Maman?*" Marie wailed. "No... Don't..."

"*How* could you do it?" Juliette demanded. "How?"

"After the wedding, George was overcome. Anxiety, regret, I do not know. He left the wedding and went back to his own apartment. Marie followed him. On their wedding night, they did not sleep," she said, calmly. "Marie texted me early in the morning and told me that he was upset. Sometimes forgiving, other times angry. She didn't know what he was going to say next."

"They had gone for a walk and were here, arguing," Mathilde related. At this moment, Marie stared almost blindly at her mother, seeming to have no recollection of this part of the evening. Mathilde continued, "I left our room, Antoine was sleeping, and came to the castle. Oh, I don't know what I thought I would do, but I just had to be here, to make sure Marie was alright, that we would all be alright. I heard him again pleading with her for the full truth, to explain why she killed his parents. Marie just repeated that it was an accident, and that the gun went off without her doing anything."

"Except pulling the trigger," Eleanor added, her emotions only barely in check, her fists balled, seemingly ready for violence. "Twice."

"George said something, I didn't hear what," Mathilde continued, "and Marie ran off. He was leaning through a gap in the castle wall."

"The crenellations." Graham said.

"*Oui*. He was all alone, his back to me, looking out to sea. I saw my chance. It was so easy. He simply," she turned to look at Graham, "...disappeared."

There was silence for a moment as the stunning revelation sunk in. No one said a word. The only sound was the seagulls circling overhead, their cries providing a seemingly raucous commentary on what they thought of Mathilde's actions.

Suddenly, an angry flurry of arms and a burst of shouting broke the moment. Antoine was blocking a furious nails-first assault on his wife by Eleanor, whose velocity was threatening to push Mathilde herself over the edge of the battlements. Antoine grabbed her and held Eleanor in a bear-hug. He forced her to the ground.

"Sergeant Harding, if you would, please," Graham said.

Harding found her handcuffs and brought them out. Graham nodded to her. "Madame Joubert, are you prepared to sign a statement confessing to the murder of George Ross?" he said.

"I am," she said simply and held out her hands even as Juliette tried to stop her, to pull her back away from the officers. "And I am prepared," she announced more loudly, so that the whole group could hear, "to be punished for what I have done."

CHAPTER SEVENTEEN

R OACH AND BARNWELL found themselves, yet again, in the half-completed torture exhibit with the dusty tapestries on the walls. Over the course of the day, Roach had rebuked him so often for saying it that Barnwell had learned to stop protesting, "We've already been in there."

"The point is," Roach explained patiently, yet again, "the musicians remain unfound, and that means we keep looking *everywhere*."

"Even in dusty rooms marked with 'no entry' signs?" Barnwell shot back.

"Especially there." Roach had checked in with the harassed and exhausted Jeffries, whose spate of calls to local hotels, restaurants, and pubs had produced a couple of false alarms, but no string quartet. "I can't help the feeling," Roach shared, "that they're down here somewhere."

There was a tiny movement, and Barnwell's eyes were drawn immediately to it. "Hello, what's this?" he asked himself. A breeze was just slightly lifting the edge of a tapestry that depicted a battle scene. Barnwell pulled it back, curious. "There's a door here, mate. Still open."

Flashlights at the ready, the pair eased through the doorframe and illuminated the narrow tunnel beyond.

It was filled, from floor to ceiling, with fallen masonry and shattered rock.

The two officers looked at each other for a moment. "You're thinking," Barnwell said, "what I'm thinking, aren't you?"

Roach gulped slightly as his mind wrestled with this new information. "They're under that lot, aren't they?" he surmised glumly.

"We'll know soon enough," Barnwell said, taking off his uniform jacket and stepping forward to the edge of the rock pile. He began moving stones to the side with his hands. The pile seemed, at first glance, stable enough to begin the process of moving it, and with the musicians perhaps buried underneath, time was of the essence. Or of no import at all.

Roach called DI Graham, but it went to voicemail. He turned back to help Barnwell lift rocks out of the way, each encouraging the other to move slowly and carefully. Roach was almost sick at the thought of what their efforts might reveal.

"Can anyone hear me?" Barnwell shouted at the pile of rocks. "This is the Gorey police. If there's anyone there, make a sound." They both listened for ten seconds, hoping for a plaintive yell from beneath the rubble, but they heard nothing. "We're coming to help you," Barnwell shouted next.

Roach managed to get a call through to the local emergency dispatcher, who promptly sent a couple of fire service crews and a medical team. But there was still no reply from DI Graham or from Harding. "Honestly, he bothers us all day about this, and when we get a real lead..."

"Shut up, Roachie."

The rocks shifted from above, and new chunks of debris fell into the gap they were creating, missing their feet by inches. "This is bloody dangerous," Roach complained. "We're not trained for this, Bazza. We need to wait for the experts."

"There's no time," Barnwell told him urgently, and tried a new approach, removing rocks from one side of the tunnel and using them to shore up the weakening center of the pile.

"It doesn't look like they're under here. Look, there's a passage on the other side."

Roach reluctantly joined him and they worked together, carefully and steadily. Before long, they had created a slender passageway around much of the rock pile, but they were uncertain how long it would hold.

"Hello?!" Barnwell hollered down this new passage. "Gorey police!"

There was a pause, and then they heard it. "Hello! We're here!" It was a woman's voice, and seemingly some way off.

Finally! "Are you alright?" Barnwell yelled.

"Leo needs help," the voice came back. "He's in a bad way. He's breathing again now, but we need to get him out." Her tone was urgent but without panic.

Jesus. "Help is on its way," Barnwell promised. "Hang on. We'll be there as soon as we can."

The two constables stood silently for a moment, then

Barnwell suddenly started into life. He began the process of levering himself around the jumbled, dusty rock fall and into the chamber beyond.

"What're you doing?" Roach cried out.

"I'm going in," Barnwell replied. "I can't just stand here. They need help."

"But...but...." Roach stuttered, horrified that his fellow plod was willing to take such a risk and even more horrified that he might be expected to follow.

"You stay here. Tell the emergency crews where we are, okay?"

As he went through the gap in the rocks, Barnwell's shirt instantly changed color from its usual white to a desert yellow. He coughed and sneezed. There was a grating sound. Dust floated down. Roach jumped back. Barnwell froze.

"Careful, mate. I told you this whole lot could come down." Roach whispered, "Do you want to come back out? You don't have to do this, you know."

Barnwell looked at Roach, sucked in his stomach, and gently eased himself past the pile of rocks and into the chamber beyond.

Once through, he scrabbled over the jumble of rocks to the rudimentary steps the quartet had built, and scaled them until he could peer precariously over the ledge and into the next room. He shone the flashlight around, illuminating the exhausted, dusty trio who were kneeling in the center of the room, surrounding a figure who was lying down.

Putting his flashlight between his teeth, Barnwell, like the others had before him, levered his way carefully over the wall into the chamber on the other side.

"Gorey Police," he said, very nearly tumbling but

finding a handhold on one of the crates beneath. "This *is* quite a find, isn't it?" He jumped down to the floor. "Okay, chaps," he said, quickly dusting himself down. "Everything's going to be alright. How's the lad doing?"

Barnwell bent to give first aid to Leo, strapping his arm and putting him in the recovery position.

"Should we make our way out?" Emily asked.

"I wouldn't, love. It isn't safe. Castle's been here for over eight centuries, but it chose today as the day to show its age. Best wait for the fire service to shore up that opening before we make a move. Settle down and tell me what's been going on here. We might be a while."

Outside, Roach continued to try his boss on the radio. After a frustrating five minutes, DI Graham finally picked up. "Sir? We're in the basement of the castle."

"Have you found the musicians?" Graham cut in.

"Yes, sir. They were caught on the other side of a collapsed tunnel. Constable Barnwell is with them now, and the emergency services are on their way."

"Good job!" Graham said. "We're all done here."

Harding took the receiver and explained on for a moment. "You've got to hand it to him," she said once the story was told.

"He's done it again," Roach breathed.

He pictured the scene. "So he gets everyone together and hits them really hard with the truth until someone confesses?"

"A sworn and signed statement is being prepared as we speak," Harding assured him. "Are you two okay?"

Roach flicked a glance through the rock opening into

the distance where the illumination from Barnwell's flashlight lit up the tunnel. He grinned. "You know," he said, drawing himself up tall, despite his long, arduous day, "I think we are."

EPILOGUE

ATHILDE JOUBERT WAS summarily arrested and charged by Sergeant Janice Harding for the premeditated murder of George Ross. The case became something of a cause célèbre, fascinating audiences on both sides of the English Channel, and giving Jersey, and Orgueil Castle in particular, a certain notoriety. At the trial, her defense made much of Mathilde's desire to protect her daughter, who was portrayed as extremely fragile and in need of constant mental health supervision. The jury was not entirely without sympathy, but it was unanimous in its decision after a ninety-minute discussion. Mathilde Joubert was sentenced to twelve years in prison, a punishment that she received stoically. Upon release, if thought fit to stand trial, she will be immediately re-arrested and handed over to the French police, who have prepared a case against her for tampering with the Ross family crime scene and lying to investigators.

. . .

Antoine Joubert avoided prosecution, persuading the police that he had always believed his wife's explanation regarding the death of George's parents and was entirely unaware of her conspiracy to protect Marie. Exhausted and subject to intense media scrutiny, Antoine liquidated his retirement fund and bought a small plot of land on Tahiti, where he now lives.

Marie Joubert-Ross was committed to an institution on the south coast of Jersey known for its compassionate, modern methods of treating mental illness. She made good progress, and her conservators are currently negotiating the conditions of her release. The question as to whether Marie's shooting of her husband's parents was accidental or deliberate has not been resolved. Public opinion is divided on the matter. French police are still reviewing the case and have not yet determined whether she will face charges.

Juliette Paquet was badly shaken by the revelations surrounding George's death and has not spoken to her parents since. She returned to her second husband in France, but within weeks, the stress of the case and her husband's concerns that her family was, as he later wrote, 'a bunch of nutcases' brought an end to her second marriage. After brief but extremely bitter divorce proceedings, Juliette decided to make her home in the south of France, and now lives in Marseilles. Her daughter went to live with her aunt in England.

· · ·

Eleanor Ross inherited her brother's estate and adopted George's daughter. After founding a charity that provides support for bereaved children, she met her fiancé, but they have yet to set a wedding date. She is known to favor a very small ceremony close to home.

Emily and Harry married a little over a year after their visit to Jersey. Together, they manage the quartet's business operations and have secured several new recordings and a large number of media appearances, many in connection with the haul of art they discovered at Orgueil Castle. Their recording of the Berg *Lyric Suite* will be released in the spring.

Marina is dating a violinist who plays with the London Symphony Orchestra. She still performs regularly with the Spire Quartet as well as teaching in London. She also accepts speaking engagements on the subject of the art discovery on Jersey. She continues to harbor hopes of riches resulting from the find but has sworn never again to open doors marked "no entry."

Leo is semi-retired from music owing to his injury. He compiled "Dark Art," a seminal work in which he discusses the Nazi campaign to rid the world of "degenerate art." It also profiles the artists and the stories behind each of the paintings found in the castle. In the book, his contribution to the recovery of the artwork and the group's rescue from the castle basement features prominently. "Dark Art" received international acclaim with the New York Times calling it a *"splendid work of scholarship and one of the most important works of history of our time."*

Stephen Jeffries hasn't taken any wedding bookings for quite some time, but visitors to Orgueil Castle are fascinated by the murder. Alongside nighttime events that focus on the Ross-Joubert case, Jeffries also gives guided tours of the new "Metal on Skin" exhibit, which tells the gruesome story of those who were imprisoned and tortured at the castle. He is applying for other jobs in the events management industry.

The "Orgueil Art Haul" was removed from the castle and conserved over the course of the fall and winter. Many of the paintings were claimed by their rightful owners or sold by the castle to museums. Orgueil was permitted to borrow three of Franz Lipp's landscapes, which are displayed in the castle's hallways. The Rafael *Portrait of a Young Man* is currently undergoing evaluation and restoration work before appearing at auction. It is expected to fetch well over $150 million, with a large number of potential buyers expressing interest. The precise ownership of the painting is the subject of intense debate. Insurers, owners, and other interested parties are still negotiating the financial aspects of the find, including whether or not the Spire Quartet will receive a finder's fee. Industry insiders have speculated that 5% of the recovered value would be a reasonable figure. If agreed, it would set up all four musicians for life.

· · ·

Constable Barnwell entered a twelve-step program and now volunteers with the local Scouts. He is studying for the exams required for his promotion to sergeant and has lost over twenty pounds while training for a charity walk across Jersey.

Constable Roach met his new girlfriend Lily while investigating the case of a stolen lawnmower. He recently scored twice for the Jersey Police in the final of the local five-a-side soccer championship. He is still awaiting his investigative "big break."

Following the arrest of Mathilde Joubert and the rescue of the musicians, Detective Inspector David Graham, Sergeant Janice Harding, and Constables Roach and Barnwell ate a quiet, late dinner at the Bangkok Palace. The following morning, they were all back on duty at Gorey police station. They continue to police the Bailiwick of Jersey with a strong sense of duty, pride and professionalism.

THE CASE OF THE
BROKEN
DOLL

ALISON GOLDEN Grace Dagnall

THE CASE OF THE BROKEN DOLL

BOOK FOUR

Cover Illustration: Richard Eijkenbroek

Published by Mesa Verde Publishing
P.O. Box 1002
San Carlos, CA 94070

Edited by
Marjorie Kramer

CHAPTER ONE

IT WAS A Saturday morning, and it was not starting out well.

Graham awoke feeling groggy, tired, and uncomfortable. In his dream, someone had been knocking repeatedly on the roof of his police car, either demanding help or just trying to annoy him, he couldn't tell which. He remembered trying to open the driver's door, but it was stuck or locked, and so he struggled fruitlessly with it while the knocking became louder and *louder...*

"Bloody pipes again," he grumbled, swinging his tired frame out of bed. The White House Inn suffered from an antiquated heating system that struggled to warm the old building, and its pipes knocked and clanged throughout each night. As he started his morning routine, Graham remembered that the same knocking sound had afflicted his dreams for the past few nights, ultimately waking and leaving him in a state that was decidedly unrefreshed. He looked in the mirror, frowning at the dark lines under his eyes. "I look a lot older than thirty-six," he told his reflection. It showed no signs of disagreement.

He showered and shaved as he always did, but he knew that nothing whatsoever would lift his mood until he'd had his morning infusion of high-quality tea. In truth, Graham had never planned to stay at the White House Inn for ten weeks, but the daily pleasure of coming downstairs to the dining room and sitting at his own table by the window with a big pot of Assam or Darjeeling still felt wonderfully indulgent. Every day one of the waiters – Graham knew them all by name now – would bring him a steaming pot of utter perfection, and the day would begin in earnest. His eyes regained a little of their sparkle just thinking about it.

This Saturday morning, it was Polly, a bubbly redhead. "What'll it be, Detective Inspector?" Try as he might, Graham could not persuade the staff to call him simply "Mr. Graham." Even an informal "David" would have been alright, given how long he'd been staying there. But after success with two high-profile murder cases and the recent celebratory article about the Gorey Constabulary in the local paper, his title had become a firm fixture.

"I feel like having something from China today, Polly."

"Isn't that how you feel *every* day?" Polly replied, grinning cheekily and standing patiently with her notepad and pen.

"That," Graham admitted, "is probably a fair comment. Lapsang Souchong, please. And make sure to bring the..."

"Timer. Yes, Detective Inspector." Polly scurried away to place the order and handle Graham's unusual request. There was absolutely no point, Graham insisted, in serving some of the world's best teas if the customer had *no idea* how long the tea had been steeping when it arrived at the table. His solution was to have the waiter start a small digital timer as soon as the boiling water came into contact with the tea leaves. That way, Graham knew when his tea was at its absolute peak. Some would have called him fussy. But on matters of such importance, he knew he was merely being *correct*.

Polly also brought the morning paper. The front page was splashed with reports of the celebrations marking Guy Fawkes Night, the annual commemoration of November 5th, 1605, the day that King James I survived an assassination attempt by a group of English Catholics.

This year, two evenings earlier, the town had fired off its biggest ever fireworks display. An impressive sum had been collected for local charities, and better yet the district hospital was glad to report only three minor injuries, far fewer than in previous years. Graham made a note to give his team a solid "well done" for their "Safe Fifth" safety campaign. He especially wanted to single out Constable Roach, whose idea it had been.

On the "Announcements" page, there were the usual births, marriages, and deaths – none suspicious – but it was just this relative peace and quiet that was beginning to bother Graham just a little. His first few weeks in Gorey had seen a pair of thoroughly unpleasant murders, requiring the very best from himself and the Gorey Constabulary, but in the last few weeks, their investigative powers had been focused on more routine matters like stolen cars, shoplifters, and the odd break-in. There had been a spectacular case of vandalism at the high school, but even there, little challenge was to be found. The guilty party had obligingly signed his name, for heaven's sake, at the bottom of the colorfully defaced wall.

Revitalized by the tea, Graham set off on the day's

errand. He was determined to finish his Christmas shopping well in advance of the annual crush that he had been warned could make Gorey's small shops nearly intolerable. As usual, he assigned a single objective to this outing: a suitable present for his now ex-wife.

"What's she into?" asked the first shop assistant he spoke to. "You know, hobbies? Interests?"

The question stumped Graham. He could hardly confess that he was looking for the kind of gift that might cheer up a woman who had barely smiled in months. "I think she'd enjoy something a little... *different*." When this was no help, he tried, "Perhaps something with some history? With a story behind it?" Graham was met with a blank expression.

The second shop was hardly any better and was even more crowded. "You mean," the female assistant tried, "like something used by a sleb?"

"A what?"

"A sleb. You know, a celebrity, a famous person."

Graham tried again. "Something that is special because of where it has been or what it was used for, as much as for what it *is*."

The assistant frowned. "Nah, I don't think we have anything like that." Then she bustled off to address a question about Christmas lights, and Graham searched fruitlessly before making his exit.

Further along, he came upon an antique shop, and after some thought, he decided to give it a try. "How about this?" the storekeeper asked, presenting him with a highly polished, eighteenth-century pistol. "Belonged to a notorious pirate, that did," he said proudly.

"Anything a little more... *peaceful*?"

In the end, he found what he felt to be the perfect gift. It was a small and beautifully detailed painting of Gorey Harbor, based, he was told, on a sketch found in the notebook of a priest who had lived on Jersey some four hundred years before. It showed the castle, splendid and dominating on its hilltop, above a harbor busy with fishing vessels, the old wharf, and a bustling fish market. "Eighty-five pounds," the storekeeper said. "But for a member of our brave Constabulary, let's just call it eighty."

As he was leaving with the painting neatly wrapped in brown paper under his arm, Graham noticed something that he'd overlooked on the way in. In the front corner of the shop's window was a doll dressed in an ornate, eighteenth-century nightgown, with curly blond hair and blue eyes. Something about it stood out. Perhaps he'd considered one of these dolls for his daughter's birthday one year?

No, that wasn't it. He pondered the doll as he made his way back to the White House Inn, past the three other shops he'd tried. And there in the window of one was a nearly identical doll, dressed the same way, but with black hair in neat braids. It was displayed just as prominently, right by the door.

Moments later, he saw another one. This one seemed older, slightly more worn, and hardly in saleable condition, and yet it stood prominently in the center of the window. He spotted two more staring out at him before reaching The White House Inn, and as he made his way through the front doors, he saw yet another. On the reception desk sat a pale-skinned, beautifully made doll in a green bonnet.

"Mrs. Taylor?" he asked, his curiosity welling up.

The proprietor looked up from her tablet, which she had been studying with an unusual frown. "Oh, hello Detective Inspector," she said brightly. "Been doing your Christmas shopping?"

"Indeed so, Mrs. Taylor, but I have to ask... These *dolls*," he said. "I'm seeing them everywhere. They must be in half of all of the shop windows. Am I imagining things?"

She clicked off the tablet and sighed slightly. "No, sir, you are not. But I'm surprised no one's told you about her yet."

"*Her?*"

"Beth Ridley," she said sadly. "Poor thing."

Graham was embarrassed to admit the girl's name meant nothing to him, but obviously it carried real emotional weight for Mrs. Taylor. "I'm afraid I don't..."

"She disappeared, you see. Ten years ago today. Only fifteen, she was. The brightest, nicest girl you could ever meet. She was well known around Gorey. Everyone loved her. Absolutely tragic."

"What happened to her?" Graham asked.

Mrs. Taylor shook her head. "That's just it. She was walking to school one morning and simply vanished into thin air. No phone call, no sightings, *nothing*."

"But surely there was a search for her?"

"Oh, goodness me, yes!" Mrs. Taylor replied. "They searched the whole island. All the woods and the beaches. The Coast Guard patrolled out at sea, looking for her. But all to no avail."

"So what do people think happened to her?"

Mrs. Taylor frowned darkly. "Well, not long after she

disappeared, people started talking about her in the past tense, if you know what I mean, Inspector."

He nodded, his lips pursed. "Does her family still live on the island?"

"Oh, yes. Haven't you heard of Mrs. Leach?" The Inn's proprietor seemed to have extra time on her hands during this pre-Christmas lull. "The poor woman was beside herself, of course. Her only child, gone. Can you imagine?"

Graham didn't *have* to imagine, but he chose not to share that very private pain. He simply nodded again.

"So, the community rallied around her. Made sure she had everything she needed. Then some people at the Rotary Club, I think, set up a charitable foundation for her. People donated money so that she could keep the search going. She hired private detectives, forensic scientists, even sent experts over to Europe to look for her. None of it came cheap, of course, and I hear the private investigations have tapered off quite a lot lately, but her charity is quite well-known here, and a lot of people give what they can every month."

"Hmm, it's not uncommon for the parents of missing children to carry on the search and at least try to keep hope alive. Even when..."

Mrs. Taylor gave Graham a look that pulled him up short. "Hope springs eternal, Inspector. There are cases, you know, of kiddies going missing and then showing up in some basement years later..."

This, he had to concede. "It's rare, but it happens." But mostly, Graham thought morosely, there was a murderer who had thoroughly disposed of the evidence. Or had got lucky.

There were other possibilities, of course. A child

could be spirited away to live elsewhere. Or they might have simply run, never making contact with those they were running away from. All over the country, the filing cabinets of "cold cases," those with no practicable leads, grew in number while grieving families could be told nothing to ease their pain.

"Poor lamb," Mrs. Taylor said in summary.

"But why *dolls*?" Graham asked.

"Oh, yes, I quite forgot. She collected them, you see. Had quite a number. Her uncle in America sent them to her. She had one in her bag when she disappeared, as I remember. The theory goes," Mrs. Taylor confided, "that the doll was somehow damaged in whatever struggle took place. Nothing but its leg was ever found."

"Its leg?" Graham said, thoughtful. He reached for his notebook but found he'd left it in his room.

She caught him as he turned to go. "Are you going to...? You know... Look into it?"

Graham smiled thinly. "I really can't say, Mrs. Taylor. It's a very old case, and we're short-staffed at the station."

"People hereabouts," she said, leaning in close, "would think the world of you for even trying. Not that they don't already," she added quickly. "But, you know, it would give her family hope."

"I'll see what I can do, Mrs. Taylor. Would you be an angel and keep our conversation to yourself, just for now though, please?" he asked politely.

"Of course, Inspector. You can rely on me."

Graham returned to his room and set up his laptop. Mrs. Taylor had not exaggerated the case's high profile or the extent of public sympathy. There was a Wikipedia page, a dedicated website, and all manner of opportunities to contribute to the Beth Ridley Foundation. Graham began bookmarking sites and taking notes.

As his research deepened, he became engrossed in it, and he quickly found himself greatly enlivened on what would otherwise have been just another Saturday afternoon.

CHAPTER TWO

ON MONDAY MORNING, Graham arrived a few minutes early, as usual, and found Constable Roach at his desk, taking a phone call. Roach took notes as he listened, and Graham decided to hover briefly and find out what the call was about. But as he did so, he noticed that there was – of all things – what he now knew to be an "American Girl" doll on the edge of the desk, by the stack of public information leaflets. Next to the doll, in a small, silver frame, was a photo of a girl.

"Missing person, sir," Roach explained as he replaced the receiver. "Our old friend, Mr. Hodgson."

Graham sighed. "Oh, God, not *again.*"

"Seems that he did a runner in the middle of the night, according to his long-suffering mother. She found his bed empty and called us straight away."

Graham set down his briefcase and slid off his jacket. Gorey's weather had become markedly cooler, and he was finding the extra layer indispensable in the morning hours. "Well, Constable Roach, why don't you utilize your growing investigative acumen and have a guess as to what's going to happen next?"

They both stared at the phone for a second, and then it rang. Roach listened for a few moments, extended his thanks, and ended the call. "What do you know, sir? Mr. Hodgson has returned! Alive and well, yet again."

"What's that, four or five times, now? Where do you think he goes?" Graham asked.

"Sleepwalking?" Roach offered.

"Possibly. But consider this: how old is our Mr. Hodgson?"

"Seventeen, sir."

"And what does that tell us about the likely nature of his nocturnal adventures?"

"Well, if he's anything like I was at that age..." Roach began.

"I don't need to learn too much about your personal life, Constable," Graham warned quickly.

Roach blushed. "I'd just say, well, *girls*, sir."

"Wouldn't surprise me for a moment. Pity someone can't clue his mother in to the nature of seventeen-year-old boys and their nighttime habits. Save us all a bit of bother. And, speaking of missing persons, I've been noticing these dolls all around town." Graham picked up the doll and then the silver-framed photo. "Beth Ridley?"

Roach's face fell. "That's right, sir."

Two and two added up quickly. "You *knew* her?"

"We were classmates at Gorey Grammar, sir. Went to the same youth group, too, for a couple of years. We all called her 'Barbie.'" Roach saw that his boss missed the reference. "Because of her blond hair, sir," he explained.

Graham replaced the photo and sat the doll upright

on the reception desk. "I'm sorry, Roach. That must have been terrible."

"If I'm honest, it still affects me. Especially at this time of year. It was such a *shock*. But it's nothing compared to what her mother's been going through, all these years."

Graham regarded the younger man with sympathy. "Mrs. Taylor gave me the basics. Have there been any new leads recently, or..."

"Nothing," Roach said simply.

Graham wasn't, in all honesty, the greatest fan of cold cases. The act of re-opening old files always felt like a slight against the detectives originally charged with the case, as though by simply re-examining the evidence, Graham was accusing them of being unprofessional. But with such strong public interest, not to mention Roach's own emotional connection, it was a difficult case to resist.

"Constable, how would you feel about helping me take another glance at the case file?"

Roach gulped before answering. "*Beth's* case file?"

"She deserves a few hours of our time, wouldn't you say?" Graham said. "Do we have the file here?"

"No sir, it's lodged at the Jersey Police archive in St. Helier. I could ask Sergeant Harding to pick it up on her way in, if you like."

"Ah, yes," Graham remembered. "She'll only have come back from Manchester last night. Did you hear anything from her about the computer course?"

"Not yet, sir, but there was something on Facebook about how she was becoming a 'digital warrior,' whatever that means."

"Sounds impressive," Graham chuckled. "Anyway, she won't be long. Cup of tea in the meantime?"

Roach put the kettle on while Graham placed a call.

"Marcus?" he asked.

"Good morning, Detective Inspector!" came the cheery voice. Marcus Tomlinson had already finished his second cup of morning coffee and was in tip-top form. "What news from Gorey?"

"Marcus, I'm going to give you a name from the past, just to see if it shakes any old branches."

"Fire away, old boy."

"Beth Ridley."

Marcus was quiet for a moment. "Ah. Well."

"I'm listening, Marcus." Graham reached for his notepad. "I mean, I know it's a hell of a long time ago, but..."

"No, it's not that," Marcus began tentatively. "I remember the case, clear as day. But, you see, I'm a pathologist. There was never a body."

"Of course," Graham admitted. "Just looking for a bit of context, that's all."

Tomlinson cast his mind back. "Well, this was your illustrious predecessor, of course. He did a thorough job of interviewing everyone. People spent hours at the house with Mrs. Leach and her then-new husband, Beth's step-father... What was his name, now? Charles? Chris, maybe?"

"What happened to her father?" Graham asked.

"Oh, Bob Ridley? Haven't you heard of him?" Tomlinson replied.

Graham searched his memory, something that never took long. "Bloody hell, not the same Bob Ridley who's doing thirty-to-life in Wormwood Scrubs?"

"The very same," Tomlinson told him, impressed as usual with Graham's unfailing memory.

In one of Britain's most famous bungled robberies of recent years, Bob Ridley had shot a security guard to death before making off with cash and jewelry worth millions. When he was arrested after three weeks on the run, he claimed that he had fired the gun only to scare the guard away. Then he admitted that he'd "panicked," a word that proved catastrophic to his defense and dry persuasive to the jury.

"I'm going to guess," Graham said, "that their marriage did not long survive his incarceration?"

"Not by even a day," the pathologist confirmed.

"Got it. Go on, Marcus," Graham said, already filling a page with notes.

"Ann Leach was a nurse at the hospital in St. Helier. I knew her just slightly. I signed a card to congratulate her when she got married again. The second husband passed away a couple of years ago. Brain tumor or something similar. Nothing fishy about it. But as for Beth's disappearance, it was a strange thing. Frightening. One day, she was walking to school, and then suddenly, she was not."

Graham put down his pen. "People don't just vanish into thin air, Marcus. I know the world is a strange and mysterious place, but I'm still a big fan of cause-and-effect when it comes to explaining what people do and why."

"True, true. I know that some suspicion fell on an old, homeless chap who used to sleep in the bushes near the Ridley house."

"Okay," Graham said, noting this down.

"But nothing ever stuck. Couldn't say if she ran away, was taken, or what. Very frustrating for the police at the time."

It sounded to Graham, at first blush, as though it

would be equally frustrating for him. "Thanks, Marcus. I'll let you know if anything comes up."

"Tell you what, old boy," Tomlinson told him, "if you get some movement on this, even a little, it'll mean a great deal to the people around here."

"Yes," Graham agreed, "that's what I've been hearing."

"Dinner on me at the Bangkok Palace if you even develop a new lead. No expense spared," Marcus offered.

"I'll hold you to that," he promised. "Cheers for now."

Sergeant Harding knocked on Graham's door, case file in hand. "Morning, boss."

"Welcome back, Sergeant," Graham said warmly. "How was Manchester?"

She mimed a shiver. "Cold, but there were some very nice pubs."

Graham let her have her fun. "And did you *learn* anything?"

"Oh yeah," Harding assured him. "Tons. I'll be doing some review this week, and then I'll give you a rundown on all the new databases we're going to have access to."

"Splendid."

"In the meantime," she said, setting the Ridley case file on his table, "are we *really* going to be looking into this?"

Graham flipped open the file, disturbed to find it so slender. "How would you feel about that, Janice?"

She glanced back at the reception area and then spoke to Graham in a whisper. "Roach was very, very upset about Beth going missing. It damn near wrecked his teenage years, I heard. He's still cut up about it. And it's not just him. Frankly, the whole place would thank you if you took another look at it, even if it didn't come to anything."

Graham was put in mind of several cases back in London, where the entire community – even those who'd never even met the missing child or the family – came out to help, to comb through bushes and search woodlands or who brought meals or money. There was something of the "Blitz" spirit in those gestures, a determination to stick together and see it through. Even, as was so often true, when there was precious little hope of anything but a tragic outcome.

"I'm with you, Janice. Let's get everyone copies of this file and see what we can come up with."

Harding headed toward the copier in her own office. "Including Constable Roach?" she returned to ask.

"Yes, certainly," Graham replied. "He's going to play a very important role."

CHAPTER THREE

CONSTABLE BARNWELL GRUMBLED at being directed to man the reception desk while the others discussed the Ridley case in Graham's office. "I've got plenty to offer, you know," he told Roach.

"Sure." The younger man was memorizing Beth's case file, line by line. "Sure you do, mate."

"I'm destined for higher things than this," Barnwell insisted. "Answering the phone. I mean, seriously."

Roach didn't look up. "If no one answers the phone," he observed, "how do we know when a new crime has been committed? One that might demand just the type of skilled police work for which you'll one day be famous?"

Barnwell adjusted his tie. "Are you takin' the mick?"

Finally, Roach stood, clicked his pen closed, and headed to the meeting in Graham's office. "Only a little. Shout if you need help, alright?"

Roach found Graham deep in thought, filling up his notebook quickly. "Ah, Roach. You up to speed?"

"Yes, sir." Roach and Sergeant Harding took seats while Graham jotted down a final comment.

"Right," Graham said. "So, not exactly a mountain of information to go on, is there?"

Harding shook her head. "If nothing was seen, nothing was reported, and nothing was written down, we end up with..."

"Nothing?" Roach guessed.

"Nearly so," Graham said. "We've got reports of two interactions that Beth had on the morning in question, between eight o'clock and half past. It was a Monday." He thumbed through his notes. "First, we've obviously got her mother, who sent her off to school just after eight as normal."

Harding picked up the thread. "Then there's Godfrey Updike, a retired civil servant who was caravanning with his wife. He saw Beth walking down the road."

Roach finished off what they knew. "Finally, we have Susan Miller, a classmate of Beth's. And mine," he added. "They walked to school together every morning, and Susan waited for Beth as normal."

"But she never arrived," Harding added. "Susan waited for ten minutes but then went to school on her own, assuming that Beth was sick."

"I suppose," Graham tried, "that Beth might have decided to skip school. You know, left home and walked in the usual direction, but then decided to do something else for the day?"

Harding pointed out a sheet in the slender file folder. "The school secretary told your predecessor, sir, that Beth missed a grand total of four days' school in the four *years* before she went missing. So we know she was fantastically healthy, and there's just no evidence that she was ever truant."

Graham nodded, making yet another note. "Yes, I saw that, but there's a first time for everything." He changed tack. "Wouldn't it have been busy at that time of day? Surely someone would have seen something."

"Her route to school took her through a quiet, residential area before hitting main roads. The doll's leg was discovered in a street that would have been empty at that time of the morning. And people in their houses reported that they saw and heard nothing," Harding answered.

"Okay, what about a boyfriend?"

Roach was silent.

"There's nothing in the file," Harding said.

Graham turned to Roach. "Constable? Is there anything you can add?"

"No. She wasn't seeing anyone," he answered, his voice tight.

"Alright," Graham said. "So, like you say, this really isn't much to go on. I'm not proposing that we make this our top priority for the next week or anything, but I'd like to understand just why there's so very little in this file."

"Where do you want to start, sir?"

"Interviews," Graham said. "Let's talk to everyone again and see what shakes loose."

"Who should be first?" Roach asked.

"The mother. Ann Leach."

Harding was there first. "Happy to accompany you, sir," she said.

"Actually, Sergeant, I'd like you to take your new database skills out for a spin."

"Oh, right," Roach remembered, brightening up.

"How was that fancy computer course up in Manchester?"

"Actually, rather good," Harding said. She was a little surprised at Graham's decision not to take her with him to visit Beth's mother, but she was keen to demonstrate what she'd learned on her course. "What am I looking for, sir?"

"Would it be completely unhelpful if just for the moment," Graham asked, "I say *everything*?"

She shrugged and then gave him a smile. "I'll do my very best, sir."

"I'm sure you will."

Graham turned back to Roach, who had gathered himself once more. Graham could see this case would tax the young officer's emotions, but he was also in a unique position to be helpful, and Graham couldn't pass that up.

"Constable Roach, I want you to come with me to see Ann Leach. In fact, you can make the call and set it up. See if she's home, and tell her we're just doing a routine review."

"Right, sir."

"Careful, Roach. I don't want you getting her hopes up over nothing. I'm just not satisfied with a case file quite so slender, and I want to build it up, if we possibly can. With me?"

"Loud and clear, sir. I'll make the call now."

Roach returned to the reception area, where Barnwell was dealing with his boredom by reorganizing the community noticeboard. He dialed Ann Leach's number. In Graham's office, Harding wanted a quick, quiet word.

"You're certain that Roach is the right person for this, sir?"

Graham motioned for her to close the door. "I know, Sergeant. He's going to have to deal with some emotions,

THE CASE OF THE BROKEN DOLL   495

and that's going to be tough. But he *knew* Beth, and her classmates, *and* her teachers. He's lived on Jersey all his life. If you were me, wouldn't you want that kind of resource to hand?"

"I would, sir. I'd just tread lightly."

"Depend upon it, Sergeant," Graham told her.

"Very well, sir." Harding's fondness for their two constables was something that she'd share only with Graham, but it was genuine, and she didn't want to see either of them hurt unnecessarily.

"Besides, I want to season him a bit, give him more responsibility."

"Yes, sir," Harding said. "But..."

"You don't agree?" he asked mildly. Opinions from his colleagues were twice as valuable when they were open and honest.

"I think it's great to ask for more from him," she said. "I just wonder if this is the right case."

"Noted, Sergeant," Graham said. "If I see things getting away from him, I'll be sure to make a change."

Harding nodded and headed back to her office, across the hallway from Graham's. She turned on her computer and pulled out her notes from the Manchester course. Perhaps, there was some new clue to be found in the plethora of data that was just becoming available to provincial police forces like theirs.

The software started up, giving her access to the Police National Computer and its numerous related databases. She typed in, "RIDLEY, ELIZABETH" and began to read.

CHAPTER FOUR

GRAHAM RANG THE doorbell of Ann Leach's well-kept home in one of Jersey's more comfortable neighborhoods, a mile or so from the center of Gorey. He was very aware of the American Girl doll in the front window, alongside a banner that featured a photo of Beth, smiling as she cut into a birthday cake. There was also contact information for the Beth Ridley Foundation. The door opened and a short, dark-haired woman with thick glasses answered.

"Ah. You're the police who called?" she asked.

"We are, Mrs. Leach. I'm Detective Inspector David Graham, and this is..."

"Well, bless me!" Ann exclaimed. "Isn't that little Jimmy Roach?"

Roach grinned, suddenly red-faced. "I wondered if you'd recognize me, Mrs. Leach."

"Oh, for heaven's sake!" she said, waving them in. "You're even taller than I remember. Well," she chuckled, "I suppose nearly everyone's taller than me. Especially these days. I swear I've shrunk six inches in the last ten years."

She invited them into a spacious living room that was nothing less than a shrine to her missing daughter. From left to right, around the three walls not occupied by a bay window, were photos of Beth arranged in chronological order.

Graham took a moment to take in the display. It began with Beth's birth, a newborn wrapped in a pink blanket with her exhausted mother smiling down at her. It progressed to pictures of her early birthdays, her first bike, and to her first day at primary school where she stood neat and grinning in her blue and grey uniform.

"This isn't the house we were living in when Beth, um, went...disappeared. We moved. To get away from the memories."

"Must have been a wrench," Graham responded.

"It was, but it was for the best." Ann gestured around the room. "This is how I remember. This is how I keep her memory alive."

Photos from holidays in France, on a rollercoaster at a theme park, on horseback, standing in a field with mud up to her knees, on a trampoline, all told of a full and active life. There was a tender portrait of Beth smiling on a summer's day. Her blond hair shone in the sunlight, almost luminous, and her blue eyes sparkled. But then the sequence stopped abruptly.

"I keep one more space," Ann explained, motioning to a gap by the doorframe. "For the photo of her homecoming." She gestured to the tan couch and they all sat down.

"Mrs. Leach," Graham began. "First, I'd like to express once more the deepest sympathies of Gorey Constabulary. As a relative newcomer to Jersey, your daughter's memory is being kept alive by the community in a way that I find very moving."

Ann nodded in gratitude. She was very slight, and looked perhaps ten years older than she otherwise might. This wasn't surprising. Parents of missing or dead children often looked much older than their years. Stress, he knew only too well, can age a face shockingly.

"We made the decision, on this anniversary, to review Beth's case file. I have to say, with no disrespect to my predecessors, that I find the file rather thin for a case of its kind."

"I'm sure they did everything they could," Ann allowed. "But a mother always wants them to do more."

"Well," Graham said, "I'm hoping that by going over old ground once again, we might unearth a little more detail, and perhaps add a few pages to the file. I don't have any new leads, I'm afraid. I don't want to give you the wrong impression."

"Thing is, you see," Ann began, "it won't make any difference to me whether you find a scrap of new evidence or not. I *know*," she said, fist in her palm, "that my Beth is alive. I dream about her. I hear her voice in her room. I hear her footsteps on the stairs. She calls to me, but she's always gone by the time I turn around."

Graham gritted his teeth through a painful moment before he was able to speak again. "Mrs. Leach, I want you to know that I understand *exactly* what you mean." Roach looked at his boss in mute surprise. "And it's out of respect for just that certainty that we'd like to ask you again about the day she disappeared."

Ann checked the wall clock and with a guilty smile, said, "I know it's only lunchtime, but you won't mind if I have myself a little G&T, will you?"

"Not at all," Graham said.

"Join me?" she offered.

"No, thank you," Graham replied.

Inwardly, this simple interview was a tremendous battle for him. The greatest pain a human being could be asked to bear was the loss of a child, and the memories of his own were never far from the surface. Such pain made his whole system cry out for relief, and a bottle of good gin, the familiar sound of the tumble of ice cubes into a glass, and the fizz of the tonic, all called to him like the mythical siren on the riverbank. He swallowed hard, gripped his notepad and pen, took a deep breath and began asking questions.

"Tell us about that morning, Mrs. Leach. What time did Beth leave for school?"

Ann's eyes were sad and distant for a moment, and then she sighed and began to describe the day she'd lost her daughter. "I made her a packed lunch, as I had every school day for ten years," she said. "Her uniform looked clean, and she had washed her hair the night before. She was a bit tired, but a cup of tea and breakfast seemed to give her some energy. You know how teenagers can be in the mornings," she smiled brightly, her eyes filling with tears. "She wanted to drop her doll off at Mr. Greeley's on her way to school. The leg was a little wobbly and he would do doll repairs for her on the cheap."

"Did she say anything as she left?" Graham asked.

"Just, 'See you later, Mum,' as she always said. You know, I've wracked my brains about every moment, and about every day before that, and I cannot for the life of me think of any reason..." She stopped, and for a moment it was all too much. She pressed her hands to her face and breathed hard. Roach shuddered slightly.

"We can come back another time, Mrs. Leach..." Graham began.

"No," Ann said, gathering herself. "You'd get the same sad display. I've thought it through a thousand times, and I can't tell you anything to explain why she's not here with me, right now."

Graham glanced across at Roach, who seemed to take strength from Ann's fortitude. "Go ahead, Jim," he said quietly.

"Mrs. Leach, did Beth have anyone in her life who might have wished her harm?"

She shook her head.

"Please think about it for a moment, Mrs. Leach. Perhaps a former friend or a classmate she had a fight with?" The head-shaking continued. "Someone who claimed Beth had wronged them? Cheated them?"

"Everyone loved her," Ann said, her voice a thin wail.

"How well do you think she got along with her teachers?" he tried.

Ann thought for a few moments, drying her eyes with a handkerchief. "Her homeroom teacher was Mrs. Blunt," she said. "She was always very positive about Beth during parent-teacher evenings. Said she was a 'model student.'"

"Anyone else you can remember from her school?" Graham asked. Then he turned to Roach. "Who else taught your classes, back then, Jim?"

"Mrs. Wells," Roach said. "She was our math teacher. There was Mr. Knight, who taught geography and something else, I can't remember."

"And Mr. Lyon," Ann said, as if remembering after a struggle. "Her science teacher."

"Oh, yes," Roach confirmed. "He was a bit heavy on the homework."

Ann was nodding. "Yes, Mr. Lyon. I remember. He gave a lot of homework, and Beth used to go to the library after school to get it done. You know, they only had a handful of computers in the library back then, so two or three of the students used to share one and research the questions. Beth preferred books. She said she didn't have to wait for a modem to dial up, and she could just look things up in the back of a book."

Ann smiled a little at the memory.

As she was speaking, Graham noticed that in one of the more recent photos of Beth, there was a tall, heavy-set man with thinning, dark hair. "Could I ask about your late husband, Mrs. Leach?" Graham asked sensitively. "That's him, there, in the photo, isn't it?"

Ann didn't turn around. "Yes, that's Chris. He passed away two years ago last summer. Brain tumor. The doctors didn't see it until it was too late. Only twelve weeks, from diagnosis to funeral."

"I'm truly sorry," Graham said. "You must miss both of them terribly."

"More than I can say," Ann said.

"Did Beth get along well with her stepfather?" Graham watched carefully as Ann seemed to think this through at some length.

"Yes," she said. "He loved her very much. I know that she respected him and that she wanted us to be happy. To be together."

Graham made a note and in his own, personal hieroglyphics, inscribed the word "equivocation." Then he asked, "Do you have a room for Beth, Mrs. Leach?"

"Oh, yes. I've kept everything the same."

"I wonder if it wouldn't be too much of an imposition for us to see it."

Ann led them upstairs, apologizing for the mess in the other rooms. Ann's own bed was unmade, Graham saw to his surprise, and the upstairs part of the house could have used a lick of paint and a good airing out.

But Beth's room was immaculate. It wasn't so much a bedroom as a carefully arranged memorial. Every last object from Beth's original bedroom had been arranged just as it was in the Ridley's previous house.

"She collected dolls," Ann said. She showed them into the room, but she didn't follow. "She had nearly a hundred, but the American Girl dolls were her favorites. She was trying to collect the complete set," she recalled. "Lord knows how many there are in total." The dolls were arranged on Beth's bed in a neat display, their clothing pristine and positions neatly composed. "Her clothes, her books, everything is just how it was then."

While Ann waited outside, apparently unwilling to enter, the two officers looked around the room. Graham took his time, committing objects to memory – each book, each ornament, and the positions of the objects on her shelves. However, it was Roach who drew his boss' attention to an apparently innocuous green exercise book that sat with a pile of others on Beth's dresser. Rather than being entitled, "Geography 2004," or "French Vocabulary 2005," as others were, this book was simply inscribed, "SECRET."

"Her journal," Roach said quietly. "It was mentioned in the case file."

Graham thought back. "Didn't they dismiss it as... what was it? Plans for a cartoon, or something?"

"They thought they were notes for a children's book that Beth hoped to write one day," Roach replied. Graham opened the book and saw at once what his predecessors had meant. Over half of the book was filled with jottings that depicted the antics of various animals.

"You know what they say about a book and its cover, sir," Roach said. "I think we shouldn't judge this by how it appears. I'd like permission to have a closer look if Mrs. Leach doesn't mind."

"Go ahead and ask, Constable. If you've got a hunch about this, I say we should follow it."

Roach made the request as politely as he knew how, and Ann immediately responded that he could remove anything that might be helpful. "Just provided," she cautioned, "that you return it exactly as you found it. No damage or markings."

"I promise, Mrs. Leach," Roach said.

There seemed little more to add, and so Graham led Roach downstairs to make their exit. "We appreciate your time. Please, if you think of anything that might be helpful, let us know."

"I think," Ann said sadly, "of nothing else for most of each day."

She showed the two men out.

"Good work with that journal, Constable," Graham said as they made their way to the car. "I wouldn't have thought of that."

"Like you said, sir. It's just a hunch."

CHAPTER FIVE

J ANICE HAD RELUCTANTLY agreed to man the reception area while Barnwell responded to a call from the marina. She was continuing her investigation into the missing girl's case on her computer. Even a month earlier, it wouldn't have been possible, but with their police computers now networked, she could interrogate national – and even international – databases from any of the office machines or her own laptop through a secure connection.

"The marina? What's going on down there?" she had asked Barnwell.

"Theft reported, last night," Barnwell said, pulling on his uniform overcoat. "Shouldn't take long."

Barnwell was very glad of any excuse to escape. He found himself willing the phone to ring or for the door to swing open and present him with an exciting challenge. Anything to interrupt another dreary day. Graham and Roach had the car, so he laboriously cycled the mile and a half to the marina. He'd have given nearly anything, he mused as he locked up the bike, to hear the squeal of his pursuit car's tires as he chased down a fleeing bank robber. But for the moment, this rather less dramatic assignment would have to do.

He strolled over to a man who was washing his boat with a long-handled, soft-bristle boat brush.

"Morning, sir. Looking for Captain ...," he looked down at the note he'd made, "Drake," he finished.

"Aye, that's me." Drake was a weather-beaten sixty-seven year-old who had spent as much time at sea as any man alive. He was a professional fisherman who knew the seas surrounding the UK, from Iceland to the Baltic to the coast of Portugal, like he knew Gorey itself. Drake waved Barnwell aboard his boat, *Clementine*. "Mind your step, now."

Clementine was a dedicated fishing vessel. "Just back from the German Bight," Drake reported. "Bloody awful over there, even for November."

"Did you catch much?" Barnwell asked. For someone who had lived in Gorey for the last six years, Barnwell knew shockingly little about the town's primary industry.

"Damn near bugger all," Drake cursed. "But once the weather settles, we'll be out there again. And again, and again until we hit our quota."

Barnwell noticed how neat and orderly the boat was, until he saw one glaring exception. The glass window of the pilot house was smashed. "Tell me about this," he said. "When did you notice it?"

"I slept ashore last night," Drake said, "but when I came down at six this morning, I saw some filthy bugger had made off with my doobury!"

Barnwell took out his notebook but then paused. "Your what's-that-now?"

"My GPS!" Drake said. "That digital doobury that

used to sit up by the wheel." He pointed to a now empty spot on the boat's dashboard. "Good kit, it was. Had sonar and everything! Worth nearly one thousand pound."

"You're insured, I hope," Barnwell asked.

"Course I bloody well am," Drake replied. "You ask the others. This kind of thing happens all the time. I tell you, there's not a decent soul left in the world."

"So there's been more thefts? Like this, off the boats?"

"Aye, happens all the time."

"But why don't they get reported?"

"Dunno. They usually take smaller stuff. But they're getting cocky now. And I don't like being messed with."

The hair on Barnwell's scalp started to tingle. Was he finally getting something to sink his teeth into?

"Alright sir, let's take down your statement, and I'll look into it straightaway."

Barnwell completed his notes and wrote a detailed statement for Drake to sign. "Thank you for reporting this so quickly, sir. We'll be in touch if we need anything else."

Drake grumbled something about wasted fuel and wasted time, bid Barnwell a gruff farewell and went back to his scrubbing.

When Barnwell returned to the station, he found Janice deep in a search on the reception desk computer.

"Let me have a moment on there, Sergeant, as soon as you can," he requested, cheerfully.

"Please," he added quickly as Janice turned to give him an arch look. His first line of inquiry would be one unavailable to previous generations of investigators who were chasing down a potential fence. "I need to have a little look on eBay."

CHAPTER SIX

I T TOOK GRAHAM and Roach only a few
moments to track down Andrew Lyon, Beth's
former science teacher. They discovered that he'd
stayed in Jersey after leaving the teaching profession.

"Decided to make a career change, according to his
website," Roach said, reading from his phone as Graham
drove them to the address. "Sounds as though he's doing
his own thing these days. Freelancing."

Graham kept slightly under the speed limit as they
ascended the hill to the edge of the town and then turned
left into a secluded street lined with some of the oldest
trees on the island. "Nice spot to live," Graham observed
to himself. It would not be long before he'd be searching
for a place of his own. He couldn't stay at the White
House Inn forever.

"What kind of freelancing?"

Roach skimmed a couple of online articles that
carried Lyon's byline. "'Life in the Age of the Snooper's
Charter,'" Roach read. "Looks like a detailed piece for an

online cyber-security magazine about how to keep the government's nose out of your Internet business."

Graham raised an eyebrow. "Interesting." He pulled up outside Lyon's house and turned off the engine.

"And here's another," Roach read. "Oh, you're going to love this one, sir," he promised. "'Putting the 'Dark' in DarkNet: How to Browse Anonymously.'"

The DI took down a note as usual and then stepped out of the car. "Sounds as though our Mr. Lyon is someone who takes his privacy very seriously indeed."

"*Very* seriously, sir. You might say, to a professional level," Roach agreed.

"Well," Graham noted as they rang the doorbell, "let's see what he has to say."

The living room curtains twitched, and the door opened, "Yes?"

"Gorey Police, Mr. Lyon. Just a routine inquiry," Graham replied.

"Inquiry? What kind of inquiry?"

"It would be better to speak to you inside, sir," Graham told him, giving Roach a meaningful glance. "It's regarding the disappearance of Beth Ridley."

The reply was quick and rapid. "I don't know anything about that," the man said.

Andrew Lyon was in his late thirties, bespectacled but well-groomed, well dressed, and trim. Graham had been expecting someone pale and paunchy, a never-married white man with an indoor lifestyle and hobbies.

"I'm sure you don't, sir," Graham said, moving to his Plan B. "It's just that I'm new to the area, and with the anniversary of her disappearance this week, I'm trying to gain a little context from that period. Beth Ridley was your student. I just need a few moments of your time."

The man stared at them, then seemed to reconsider.

"Sorry," he said. "Please, come in."

As Lyon led them down the hallway, Graham glanced around, mentally cataloging what he saw. As he passed the living room, he noted white walls, polished hardwood floors, and two cream sofas facing one another. Chrome light fixtures were mounted on either side of the fireplace. Between them was a huge Dali print depicting melting clocks. The room was pristine. Graham revised his view of the man in front of him once more.

Lyon's office was dominated by his computer setup. It was also spotlessly tidy. Under the desk was a range of power strips, neatly labeled, their cables tied with green twine. In Graham's experience, computer cabling inevitably and without bidding took on a formation that made a plate of spaghetti look orderly.

"So," Lyon said easily, taking a seat in the office chair that faced his desk. He turned to contemplate the officers who were now seated on a couch, "how can I help you?"

He's like a Bond villain in his electronic lair, Graham thought as he began to speak. "Mr. Lyon, I'm sure you were as upset as anyone at the disappearance of Beth Ridley."

"I still am," he admitted. "She was smart. Engaged in her school work. Such a shock. There was nothing to suggest... It's something I've never really come to terms with. I donate to her foundation every month."

Graham turned to Roach who began to speak.

"Sir, I don't know if you remember, but I was a class-mate of Beth's, in your Year-10 Science class." When Lyon did little more than stare at him, the Constable added, "Jim Roach, sir."

"Ah, yes," Lyon said uncertainly. "How are you, Roach?"

"Well, as you can see, it's Constable Roach these days. I wonder if you could tell us what you remember about the day Beth disappeared."

Lyon puffed out his cheeks. "It's a long time ago. I mean, for me, it was a day like any other, right up until I got the call that evening."

"Call?" Roach asked.

"That Beth was missing, and that they were asking for volunteers to come forward and help with a search," Lyon explained.

"And did you volunteer?" Roach asked him.

"Oh, yes. Like everyone else. We walked all over the island, it seemed to me. That night, the next day, the weekend, and for several weeks after. I used to hike a lot before my knee went iffy on me," Lyon explained. "So I knew the countryside around Gorey as well as anyone."

Graham interjected, "What was the mood like, among those who were searching for Beth?"

Lyon sighed at length. "It was bleak. You know, Beth's mother is absolutely convinced to this day that she is alive. But when you're on a search like that, looking under piles of leaves, in burrows, and in ditches by the side of the road, you're not expecting to come across Beth looking all rosy and healthy. We were expecting to find a body. You know what I mean?"

"Yes, I think so," Roach said.

"But there was absolutely no sign of her. I mean, we found some old clothing in a couple of places, but there was no reason to suspect it was Beth's. I think that they even did DNA analysis or something, but she was wearing her school uniform when she went missing, and we never found anything like that."

Graham pressed on. "How well did you know her?"

The question was very deliberate. It was calculated to provoke a response that might be very subtle indeed. Like a camera programmed to take shots in bursts of six or twelve, Graham watched Lyon's reaction in slow motion. He took in every nuance of Lyon's facial expression, every movement of his hands. How his eyes darted one way, then another, then skyward. How he licked his lips, which suddenly seemed dry. Perhaps only high-level negotiators, successful poker players, and police detectives shared this special skill; that remarkable ability to read a person's reactions in the minutest detail.

"She was a student of mine for two years," Lyon said. "But they were big classes, twenty-five or thirty kids in each."

Roach waited and then said, "So, you wouldn't say you were particularly close?"

Lyon suddenly glared at him. "Close?" he repeated. "What do you mean, *close*?" Lyon glanced at Graham, then back to Roach, his expression stern and offended. "What are you trying to imply?"

Roach softened his tone. "Nothing at all, sir. Just trying to establish how well she knew her teachers. How she got along at school."

"And just because she was my student, you think..."

Graham jumped in. "No, he doesn't think anything of the sort, and neither do I. Please don't worry, Mr. Lyon. We have no reason to suspect anything improper of you."

"I should think not," Lyon replied tersely. "With all these new laws and students reporting every last thing, the situation has become ridiculous," he said. "Just completely *ridiculous*. It was one of the reasons I got out of teaching."

Graham made a note: *Complaints against Lyon?*

"I remember," Roach said, "that you assigned a lot of homework."

Lyon blinked at the abrupt shift of topic. "I mean, yes. We couldn't possibly cover everything in class time, and the school used to make a great deal about exam results each year. If they didn't improve, we got the Spanish Inquisition."

"And do you remember Beth as someone who did her homework on time?"

Lyon shook his head. "I couldn't say. Like I said, she was smart, and I know she wanted to go to college on the mainland somewhere, but that's really all I remember."

Graham's attention moved around the room. He took in the DVD titles on the shelves, and then began surveying the photos sitting on the desk. Lyon featured in almost all of the photos. There was one of him kneeling at the center of a group of exhausted hikers, shrouded in mist at the peak of some unknown hilltop. He'd done a parachute jump at some point; there was the obligatory photo of him falling to earth, grinning at the camera with two thumbs up. And there was a pub photo, a table full of adults, smiling and raising glasses to the camera. Graham noted something and decided to ask about it.

"Do you still smoke, Mr. Lyon?" The house didn't smell of it.

"Quit," Lyon told him. "Four years ago. One of the hardest things I ever did."

"Did you smoke a lot, back in the day?" Roach followed up.

"Oh yes," Lyon admitted. "Pack-and-a-half a day for

about ten years. Bloody filthy, I know, but it was just the best way to take a break in between classes. Helped when I was grading papers, too. Finally, I decided to clean up my act, and I feel all the better for it," he smiled.

They learned that Lyon had left the teaching profession after fifteen years and had begun freelancing as a journalist, writing for blogs and contributing chapters to those such-and-such for dummies books on computers, security, viruses, and the like.

"It pays the mortgage, just about," Lyon told them. "And I'm my own boss."

They found out nothing more, and eventually Graham thanked Lyon and drew the interview to a close. He led Roach to the outer hall. This time, Graham noticed a painting on the wall of the dining room. It was a classic Pre-Raphaelite scene of two young women by a riverbank. Both were naked, with alabaster skin and blond curls.

"Thank you for your time, Mr. Lyon," Roach was saying, "If you think of anything else, please be sure to get in touch." Lyon promised that he would and saw the two officers out.

On the drive back to the station, Graham and Roach silently considered the interview.

"What did you think, Roach?"

"I think he sounded a little too practiced, sir, but there was nothing concrete."

"Hmm."

"Do you think he's a person of interest?" Roach asked.

"Don't know yet, son," Graham said, "but we're going to find out."

Later that afternoon, with Barnwell and Graham gone for the day, Janice was still at the front desk. Twenty feet away, Roach was working on his own search, one for which a computer was of little help. Given the use of Janice's desk, he was hunched over Beth Ridley's journal, reading and re-reading the neat handwriting. He had photocopied it, transcribed it, and made endless notes on what the strangely elusive text might mean.

"Okay," he muttered to himself, as was his habit when engrossed in a task. "We've got six characters, all of them animals." He counted them again. "Bug, Mouse, Puppy, Canary, Cuckoo, and Cat." His pen tapped rhythmically on a legal pad. "An insect, three mammals and two birds. What does *that* tell me?"

It had been his most frequent question since first opening the journal. How could this seemingly innocent, rather childish collection of half-stories possibly connect to Beth's disappearance?

"There's no hero," he observed quietly to himself, "but there's at least one bad guy: *Cat*." He circled the idea in his notes. "Cat is devious and scheming, always trying to take something that doesn't belong to him. Definitely a villain."

The journal repeatedly referenced Cat as "smelly" or "stinky." Puppy, on the other hand, was well-meaning and loyal but rather naïve. "*I wish Puppy would grow up,*" Roach read from one of the last pages in the journal. And there, on the very last page, dated the day before Beth vanished: "*Puppy doesn't see the danger. She won't tell anyone, but I think I have to.*"

"*What* danger?" Roach asked himself.

Then, there was Canary, a flighty, unreliable character, and Cuckoo, who was selfish, taking things from others and calling them his own.

"Beth is never actually angry with Canary or Cuckoo," Roach concluded. "But she doesn't respect them at all."

Mouse, on the other hand, was even more naïve and lost than Puppy. "*Mouse gets eaten, but only because she chooses not to run away. Mouse is getting herself into trouble again. Cat loves it best when Mouse runs away, but only for a while. Then he chases, pounces, and Mouse is caught.*"

"Beth, dear girl," Roach whispered to the book, "what on *earth* are you talking about?"

The one element that did make sense was Beth's references to a character she called "Bug." "*Bug is kind and thoughtful,*" she wrote. "*Bug cares about me.*" And then, toward the end of the journal, "*Bug & Beth?*" The question was enclosed in a heart shape, shaded in with pink pencil.

It was the very strangest feeling to see his own nickname and his teenage self described in these pages. He sighed deeply, doing his best to stand back from the deep personal connection he had with the case. He and Beth had been closer than he'd felt able to admit to DI Graham, although their friendship had never had the chance to become anything more. Reading Beth's private thoughts made him feel deeply melancholy.

"Getting anywhere, Jim?" Harding asked from the doorway.

Roach snapped back to the present with a sudden jolt.

"Sorry. Didn't mean to scare you," Harding added, taking a seat opposite him.

"You need your desk back?" Roach asked, rubbing his eyes.

"It's six-thirty, Jim. I'm headed home. I'm surprised you're not on your way to practice by now."

"Oh!" Roach said, suddenly, noticing the clock. "Oh, shoot! Is it Monday?"

"It's been Monday all day."

Roach rose from the desk quickly and stumbled around, finding his soccer bag under the reception desk and apologizing before dashing out of the door. He was trying to secure a regular starting place in the Jersey Police five-a-side squad. They were defending the championship title, and the coach would make him do extra push-ups if he were late.

Once he was gone, Janice closed out her own workday by logging off and checking around the office. "Are you cracking the *Da Vinci Code* or something here, Detective Roach?" she observed dryly to herself as she perused the desk Roach had been working at. She tidied up Jim's notes and placed them in a manila folder. "Good for you, lad."

She turned out the station's lights and locked up. Barnwell would be on call tonight in case of emergencies. Janice tossed her bag into the back seat of her MG and started the car. She felt not a little lonely as she considered the evening ahead of her. "A girl like me," she reflected as she backed out of the station's small parking lot, "should be on her way to a hot date."

The car roared reassuringly as she found first gear and gave it some gas.

"Yeah, right. Dream on, Janice."

CHAPTER SEVEN

T HE ONLY CALLS Barnwell usually received in the middle of the night were dire emergencies, burglaries, or crank calls from bored people who couldn't sleep. At daybreak, though, he was often informed of crimes that had happened overnight and were only now becoming apparent. The call from Captain Smith was just such a report.

"Good morning," Barnwell said, locking up his bike.

"I wish it were a better one," Smith replied, stepping off his boat and approaching Barnwell. "And I wish I still had my searchlight, too."

The boat owner showed Barnwell bright, new scratch marks on the light's mounting, which was empty now but still bolted to the outside of the pilot house.

Barnwell started making notes. "You know, I was only down here yesterday. You're certain it was here last night?"

Smith stared at him as though Barnwell had suggested the experienced fisherman might have forgotten how many limbs he had or possibly the names of his children.

"Certain as Christmas," Smith replied. "Some bugger came along with a screwdriver and half-inched the damned thing. None too neatly, neither."

Des Smith was another weather-beaten old salt, even more leathery than the older Captain Drake. The two had been in a good-natured, decades-long competition, plying the unpredictable seas in a bid to consistently bring home a larger catch than the other. Smith's crew was a mix of younger men, including several sons of retired captains, and a couple of old-timers who had a few years left in them. As Barnwell approached him, he could see that Smith was dressed in a woolen sweater, fisherman's overalls, and was smoking a battered pipe, the very image of the Ancient Mariner.

"There's been a rash of these thefts," Barnwell told him. "Captain Drake's GPS yesterday, and now..."

"I *know* that, lad!" Smith exclaimed. "What I want to know is this, how can it happen here, night after night? This is why we need some kind of protection, dammit."

Security at the marina was a topic of contention. Gorey Police were woefully understaffed for such a task, while the consortium who owned the marina had imposed cutbacks after three straight years of financial losses. The first thing to go had been private security. They hardly saw the point in spending money to protect a dozen boats whose best days were long behind them. In response, the boat owners had withheld their dues and threatened legal action, leading to an unhelpful standoff.

Barnwell closed his notebook after taking Smith's statement. "We'll do what we can," Barnwell promised. "I can't be certain that these thefts are related, but it wouldn't surprise me."

This didn't impress the veteran fisherman. "We need

to bring back public pillory," Smith announced. "Stick 'em in the stocks in the middle of the market square and throw bad eggs at 'em. See what happens to the crime rate then!"

"I'll take that under advisement, Captain. In the meantime, you and the other boat owners might think about organizing a watch at night, just in case."

Just as Drake had done, Smith grumbled something profane and returned to his boat.

Barnwell jumped back on his bike and headed to the station, but as he cycled away, he was struck by a thought.

"Oh, hell." He turned the bike around and peddled straight back to the harbor.

"You caught him already, then?" Smith hollered as Barnwell approached.

"On second thought," Barnwell explained, "I'll stand watch tonight." The reception desk phone would be forwarded to him if he pressed the right buttons. "I'd like the thief arrested, not chopped into fish bait."

"Right y'are," Smith replied and smiled, revealing teeth Barnwell considered he wouldn't want in his own mouth. "Good luck with catching the bugger."

Back at the station, Sergeant Janice Harding was patrolling cyberspace on the hunt for Andrew Lyon. His employment history came up easily enough, largely due to the standard Criminal Records Bureau checks that were a requirement for teachers. She read through his credit history and found the dates of two property purchases. He lived in one home while leasing the other to a young family on the island. No complaints or incidents were on record for either, so she moved on.

The IP address relating to his home was listed on several Internet business databases, and it was straightforward enough to track down which websites he worked on. And that was when she began taking very detailed notes. Twenty minutes later, she called Graham.

"I'm on my way to the school, Sergeant," the DI explained. "What's new there?"

"Well, sir, I've been investigating Mr. Lyon, like you asked."

"Yes, good," Graham said, the noise of the car's engine rumbling in the background. "Anything interesting?"

Janice cleared her throat. "*Interesting* is one way of describing it, sir."

"Oh?"

"Well, put it this way. Once I'm finished with this, I'm going to take a long, hot shower."

"Ah," Graham said. "I did wonder if our Mr. Lyon might have a tendency toward the... how shall we say..."

"Prurient?" Janice tried.

"Well, you tell me," Graham replied.

"Not on the phone," Janice decided. "I'll give you as graphic a rundown as you can handle once you're back at the station."

"Understood, Sergeant."

Roach was doing the driving, and his curiosity was piqued. "So, Mr. Lyon's a pervert?"

Graham winced. "Picture a cart," he said patiently, "and now a horse. There is only one proper order for those two things, wouldn't you agree, Constable?"

"I would, sir. It's just that... well... I thought there was something not quite right about him."

Graham sighed. "It takes a lot more than a thought, Constable."

"Yes, but..."

"And, these days especially, it's a *hell* of an accusation to throw around. You know how many teachers have found their careers ruined because one of their students even *suggested* some kind of impropriety?"

"Too many," Roach agreed. "But how many students have been suffering in silence because they thought no one would believe them?"

"Difficult," Graham admitted.

They were reaching Gorey Grammar, the school Beth and Roach had attended. It was housed in a neat Edwardian building surrounded by well-kept playing fields. A game of field hockey was underway, and they could hear the coach's encouragement booming across the open space.

"Schools should be the safest environments we can make them," Graham was telling Roach as they got out of the car and crunched across the gravel toward the school's impressive entrance. "But it's misleading to call someone a 'pervert,' just as much as it is to call them a 'criminal.' You can't boil a complex human being down to a single word. Still less should that single word define your view of them or how they're treated by the law."

"Interesting point, sir," Roach conceded.

Jim had climbed the steps before him hundreds of times as a teen, and being at the school once again was making him feel nostalgic.

"Anyway, you're an alumnus, so you can do the talking," Graham offered.

"Thank you, sir. But I don't know how much they'll be able to tell us, this far removed."

They were greeted in the lobby by the head teacher, Liam Grant. He was almost impossibly tall, a thin bean-pole of a man, pleasant but reserved, with a broad Irish accent. He didn't appear overly thrilled to have police officers on the premises, especially when one of them was in uniform, but he was friendly enough.

After Roach had made the introductions, Graham asked Grant, "Were you head of the school when Beth was here?"

"Oh no, I was a wet-behind-the-ears English teacher back then. Straight out of teacher training. I had no contact with Beth."

Graham nodded.

"But I've asked Mrs. Wallace to talk to you. She's our school librarian and been here for nearly twenty years. The library is this way," Grant said, keen to escort the two investigators through the echoing hallways before the end of class.

"The place will be thick with students in a few moments, but they don't tend to spend their break at the library, so it will be quiet in there."

Roach was hit by a wave of memories as the three men walked down the corridors. They still had polished, wooden floors and rows of battered lockers opposite each classroom. He thought back to his old school friends, teasing each other, laughing about last night's TV, worrying together about exams.

They passed the classroom in which Jim had spent a whole year. He struggled to remember any more than five or six faces from that young crowd of twenty-five who had been as close to him as family back then. *Simon, Susan, Paula... What was the name of the little spindly kid? Ah, yes. Brian "Shady" Sycamore. Wonder whatever happened to him?*

Somewhere in those memories was Beth, but at that moment, all he could picture was the brightness of her blond hair with the sun behind her through the window.

Very little about the school seemed to have changed, until he saw the library.

"This used to be like the reading room of a monastery," Roach observed aloud. "And now it's more like the deck of the Starship Enterprise." Rows of computers occupied most of the library's old, wooden tables. But it still had that quiet, restrained air. The shelves of books stretching back into the depths of the spacious room felt very familiar. As they entered, two boys who had been poring over a large book at one of the tables seemed to take this as their cue to leave. They closed the book and left it on the table as they headed out.

"Funny you should say that, Constable," Mr. Grant noted as the two young men filed quietly past him. "This used to be the school's chapel, until the need for a library became sufficiently great. Now, the books are being usurped by computers and handheld devices, but it still retains that calm, other-worldly atmosphere, don't you think?

"Anyhow as I said, I'm really not sure how helpful we can be, but Mrs. Wallace was here when Beth went missing. As the librarian, she gets to know just about all the students. You're welcome to look around as much as you need to."

Grant left them in the company of the librarian whom Roach remembered from his time at the school.

"Things have changed, Mrs. Wallace," Roach said.

"Indeed they have." Mrs. Wallace turned to explain for Graham's benefit.

"Back in 2005, we only had two computers, and only one of those was connected to the Internet. The number of times I had to dash over to remind the groups to *share* the mouse..."

Roach chuckled at a memory. "Good times."

"Beth usually sat here," she said, indicating a table by the window. The view from there was over the largest of the playing fields and the woods beyond. "She didn't care for the computers. Worked from her class textbooks or others she took from the shelves."

"Did she come to the library alone, Mrs. Wallace?" Graham asked.

"It varied. Sometimes alone, sometimes with her friend, Susan Miller. They would sit side by side. Susan would usually leave before Beth, but Beth always stayed on until we closed."

"What time was that?"

"Five o'clock. Beth was always the last to leave."

"Did she talk to anyone while she was here?"

"No, I remember her as being very focused on her work."

"Were you involved in the search for her, Mrs. Wallace?" Graham asked.

"Oh, yes," she replied. "Terrible thing. Only time in my life I can remember when success would have meant disaster."

Roach was nodding. "Do you recall anything from that time that might help?"

Mrs. Wallace paused and cleaned the glasses that hung from a chain around her neck.

"You know," she said, "we all speculated about her.

Probably a terrible thing to do, but with no witnesses or evidence, we were bound to start guessing. I remember thinking to myself that she might have been keeping a secret. Something she couldn't tell anyone."

"What kind of secret might that have been?"

But Mrs. Wallace wouldn't be drawn out. "Speculation," she repeated. "Just trying to make sense of the incomprehensible."

"Please, Mrs. Wallace," Graham said. "We don't mind a little guesswork from time to time."

The old librarian leaned in close. "I think there was a *boy*, you see. Someone who wasn't at this school. And I've had it in my head ever since..." she said. "Oh, I know it's the silliest thing, but I just have the *feeling* that she'd got herself into trouble. You know, couldn't tell a soul. I think that they went away together, her and the boy, had the baby, and now are living out their lives, unable to return." She told her version of events in a rapid, hushed whisper.

Roach, who had stiffened at the librarian's hypothesis, thanked her. After confirming that this was all Mrs. Wallace could offer them, he escorted Graham out to the playing fields. "Interesting idea, but I wouldn't put it at the top of our list," Roach said.

"Agreed, Constable."

"It's a cliché, sir, I know, but..."

"She 'wasn't that type of girl?'" Graham guessed. Through the recollections of others, the family photos at the Ridley's house, and Beth's own belongings, he was building a picture of a girl who was seldom caught on the wrong side of the rules.

"Not even a little bit," Roach confirmed. "She really didn't have a reputation for being too friendly with the boys. In fact, we were all a little in awe of her."

"Smart, capable females are terrifying to teenage boys," Graham said. "Grown up boys, for that matter," he added. "I think you're right that Mrs. Wallace is being a little too creative. Been reading too many of those romance novels, I reckon."

They walked back into the school building. Classes had restarted, and they were surrounded by the all-too-familiar sounds of education: teachers calling names, chairs scraping hard floors, the clattering of students pulling books from their school bags.

"Amazing how little things change," Roach said.

They went outside and as they reached their unmarked police car, Graham brought out his notepad for a final update.

"So, what's next, sir?"

Graham spent a moment in thought, and then something seemed to click in his mind. "Hang on a minute. We've been idiots."

"Have we?" Roach asked, surprised.

"Come with me, lad. I can't believe this, but we've ignored the most priceless source of information at any school."

"What?"

"Not *what*. *Who*."

CHAPTER EIGHT

G RAHAM KNOCKED ON Mr. Grant's office door and soon discovered that his thought was correct. "Of course," Grant confirmed. "Couldn't run the place without Mrs. Gates. Her office is right next door, actually. This way."

Roach gave his boss a puzzled look. "Old Mrs. Gates is going to be our star witness?" he whispered.

"What makes you doubt that?" Graham asked as Grant knocked on the school secretary's door.

"Well, she was about two hundred years old when I was here, back in the day. I don't know if she'll even..."

"Constable, have you ever known a school that *didn't* have a long-serving school secretary who knew everything about the place?"

Mrs. Gates was closing in on retirement, an event that would clearly precipitate a giant upheaval for the school. Aged sixty-three, and possessed of an institutional knowledge that stretched back to the nineteen seventies, Mrs. Gates had an encyclopedic knowledge of staff and students. "Well, goodness, of course I remember Beth," she said. "Bright, full of energy and talent. The Lord only knows what happened to her."

"Well," Graham said as they took seats in her small but highly organized office, "that's why we're here. I'd like to find out as much as we can about Beth's time at the school."

Mrs. Gates nodded for a moment and then pushed back from the desk to unlock a filing cabinet in the corner. "Every year," she said, flicking through a drawer crammed with manila folders, "they inform me that these records are going to be put on the computer. And every year, we find another excellent reason to leave a perfectly good system well alone. Aha," she said, pulling out a slender folder.

"Another thin file," Graham muttered to Roach. "Just once, I'd like something the size of a phonebook."

"Elizabeth Victoria Ridley," Mrs. Gates announced. She handed over the folder.

"Good grades," Graham noted. "A after A, with the occasional A-minus."

"Damn near perfect attendance," Roach added. Then he lowered his voice. "Doesn't sound like the kind of girl who'd get herself 'in trouble,' does she?"

Graham was nodding, memorizing the file. "She had Mr. Lyon for two years in a row," Graham noted.

"Nothing unusual about that. The science courses are a full year long," Mrs. Gates told him.

"True," Roach recalled. "And a long year, it was too. And I still couldn't tell you why the moon has phases or why the sea is salty."

"That's because you were too obsessed with sport to pay proper attention," Mrs. Gates reminded him.

Roach blinked. "That was ten years ago!" he marveled. "How could you possibly..."

But Mrs. Gates simply tapped her temple and smiled.

"Told you, didn't I?" Graham muttered. "Mrs. Gates," he said, turning back to her, "I wonder if the school still has records of which teacher was on duty in the library after school? I'm assuming that was the practice?"

"Oh, yes," Mrs. Gates confirmed, making a beeline for another filing cabinet behind her desk. "Especially after we got the new computers. And there was that incident with the Year 11 boys."

"Incident?" Roach asked. Then, the memory suddenly came to him. "Oh *yes*, I know what you mean..."

"Terrible," was all Mrs. Gates would say.

Roach had a smirk on his face. "I only ever heard the rumors, sir, but it seems that a group of senior boys decided to have a poetry session at the very back of the library after school one day."

Graham raised an eyebrow. "A poetry session, Constable? Sounds a little unlikely."

"Well, this was *Jamaican* poetry, sir. With, erm, appropriate herbal accompaniment."

Graham stifled a laugh.

"Stank to high heaven!" Mrs. Gates complained. "Mrs. Wallace said it was like walking into a Rastafarian commune. Took us *days* to get the smell out."

She finally located another folder and handed it to Graham. "Here. Teachers still volunteer for library duty. It means that they're exempt from morning assembly or some other odious task. Back then, though, there was over-time allocated to it. If they needed a bit of extra money, teachers could sit in the library, overseeing the students while doing some grading or class prep."

Graham scanned the document quickly, unsurprised to see one name reappearing throughout 2004 and 2005. "Mr. Lyon seems to have done more than his fair share of library duty," Graham noted. "He was there at least once a week, sometimes twice."

"He was always angling for more money. His dream was to be his own boss. I don't want to tell tales, but I know he wasn't the greatest fan of our head at the time."

"Who was that?" Graham asked.

"Mr. Bellevue."

"Is he still around?"

"Only in the cemetery. He died of a heart attack the Christmas after Beth disappeared. I always liked him myself, but he and Mr. Lyon had professional differences. Mr. Bellevue expected a very special level of dedication from his teachers. Andrew was forever getting himself distracted by some plan to get rich. He liked to buy property and lease it."

Graham wrote all this down. "The original folders say there was no record of Beth being at school that day. Can you confirm that?"

"I can. She wasn't present for any of her classes." Mrs. Wallace, seemingly from memory, pulled out the attendance registers for each of the classes Beth had had that day. There was an "X" next to her name in each one.

"Well, thank you, Mrs. Gates. I think we have all we need for now, you've been very helpful," Graham brought the interview to a close.

Roach followed his boss back to the car. "So," he summarized as they got in and the car rolled slowly along the school's driveway, "there's no evidence that she made it to school on that morning. Everything points to the fact that she disappeared off the street on her way here."

"Yup, that is the logical conclusion," Graham agreed.

"But Lyon pulled a lot of extra library duty. To save up for a second house, do you think?"

"Or for some other reason, perhaps," Graham agreed.

"He did give a *heck* of a lot of homework," Roach pointed out.

"Knowing full well," Graham said, "that Beth and others would spend time in the library."

"Right where he would be." The thought was an uncomfortable one. "Is it a bit less presumptuous of me now," Roach asked, "to call Mr. Lyon just a little *creepy?*"

Graham drove them back at a slow, steady pace, deep in thought. Finally, he said, "I'm reluctant, Constable, really I am. He could have given a lot of homework precisely so he'd get the overtime to buy his second home or whatever his current scheme was. Or there could be no ulterior motive at all. We are speculating again. Where's the evidence?"

Roach looked at him, skepticism written all over his face.

"It's possible," Graham finally conceded. "But let's see what Sergeant Harding has got for us."

CHAPTER NINE

J ANICE WAS DRINKING a cup of tea when they got back. "Barnwell's at the marina again," she explained, "so I'm holding the fort."

She pulled a face.

"How's it going?" Graham asked, taking off his long coat and hanging it up behind his office door.

"Well, sir, put it this way. If things were different, and I worked for a company where the bosses check their employees' browser history, I'd be in big trouble right now."

Graham pinched the bridge of his nose.

"Okay," he said, "Roach, would you cover the desk? Sergeant Harding, let's use your laptop. I don't want these things in my browser history."

He waved her into his office. "Roach, check in with Barnwell and see that he hasn't fallen into the harbor or something."

Harding pulled up a chair and turned the screen so that it faced away from the door. "Okay. I hope you're ready for this."

Graham brought out his notebook. "Roach is certain there's something not quite on the up-and-up with Lyon," he reported.

"Well, sir, I tend to agree with him. I've turned up a whole lot of information about Mr. Lyon that would support his conclusion. The annoying thing about it, though," Harding told him, pulling up her research on the laptop, "is that it's all circumstantial. He's *definitely* creepy, no doubt whatsoever about that. But I can't prove that the filthy man has actually broken any *laws*."

"How do you mean?"

"Exhibit A," Janice said. She brought up a website. "The street address for this is in Denmark. Lyon has worked for these people for about three years. He designed their payment system, the front-end, and their shipping and tracking software."

"What do they do?" Graham asked, but as he clicked through the site, it became abundantly clear. "Oh, for heaven's sake."

"High-end, luxury bondage gear," Janice said, somehow managing to keep a straight face. "Whips, chains, you name it."

"I'd prefer not to dignify it with a name," Graham said. "Not my cup of tea, Janice, but I don't think it's against the law. What else have you got?"

"Well, there's this thoughtful group of contemporary artists," Janice said, clicking a bookmark that brought up a website dedicated to an "adult videographers' collective." I haven't downloaded anything, but the thumbnails might clue you in."

Graham peered a little closer and then wished he hadn't. "Legal?" he asked.

"Oh, yes," Janice replied. "All the required language is there at the bottom of every screen. Everyone's eighteen or over, pursuant to this section of that law, so on and so forth. As far as I can tell, the site is kosher, both in Denmark and in the UK. Which is a shame," she added, "because Lyon built almost all of it."

There were three other sites on similar themes, but nothing about them suggested that laws were being broken. "Immoral, arguably, but sadly not illegal," Janice concluded. "Mr. Lyon remains decidedly creepy, but we don't have a case against him."

"Not yet," Graham said ominously.

Janice frowned. "Sir, I've done a pretty thorough search here. Everything on the database is—"

"There's more," Graham interrupted. "I'm sure of it. But it won't be easy to get. When we do, I have a feeling it will be a great deal *more* than circumstantial."

He reached for the phone. "And I know just how we can get it."

Barnwell sighed heavily. He had come to detest riding around on the bike, however good for the environment or his own health it might be. There was something laughable about it, something weak and childish. He always felt overweight and uncoordinated on the damned thing, even after losing ten pounds in the last couple of months. He felt sure that one of these days, he'd crash into someone or tip himself into the harbor like an idiot.

As it was, the traditional modes of police transport – the horse, the patrol car and, most dynamic of all, the motorcycle – carried a note of authority. His bicycle simply announced the fact that Jersey police were underfunded and couldn't afford a second car for the Gorey force.

He locked up the bike, mopped his brow, and headed into a shop. Immediately adjacent to the harbor were a group of businesses that catered to professional fishermen and day anglers, as well as pleasure boat owners and scuba types.

"Afternoon," Barnwell said. "Is Mr. Foley in?"

For the last twenty-five years, Arthur Foley had made a living supplying Gorey's boating community with the myriad essentials of maritime life. There were huge tubs of bait, coils of rope, endless shelves of books, and big racks full of maps and charts. Furthermore, he sold every electronic gadget a mariner might ever need. Barnwell had been called out to investigate yet another theft. Immediately on spotting the glass case full of GPS devices and other expensive boat technology, Barnwell suspected that he knew what had been stolen.

But he was quite wrong.

"The blighters were away before I could even shout at 'em to stop," Foley explained. "They just strode in here, bold as brass, grabbed two cans of paint, and legged it."

"Paint?" Barnwell said.

"Aye. Not the kind of thing you'd decorate your kitchen with, either. Specialist paint for boats."

"Boats need special paint?" Barnwell asked, reminded yet again just how little he knew about the sea and those who plied their trade upon it.

"Gawd, yes," Foley explained. "Dutch company. Makes a range of paint that repels barnacles. Bloody magic, actually."

"What?" Barnwell quipped, "The barnacle takes one look and decides he wouldn't be seen dead on a boat with such a garish color scheme?"

Foley rolled his eyes but patiently explained. "It's chemistry. The barnacle can't stick to the paint."

"I thought every boat in the world had its fair share of limpets and such," Barnwell said. "Went with the territory."

"Aye, but it's bloody expensive," Foley told him. "You ask any of the old boys outside how much extra fuel they'd need because the streamlining of their hull was all shot, owing to barnacles. Slows them down by as much as a knot."

"Interesting." Barnwell said, "You know, I've learned a lot since I started investigating these thefts. Tell me about the shoplifters."

"Came in, looked around, found the paint, grabbed the cans, and buggered off like greased lightning," Foley repeated. "They were wearing those 'hoodie' things, so I couldn't see their faces."

"Do you have CCTV?" Barnwell asked, but Foley's facial expression gave him the answer.

"Costly," was all he said.

"Very well. I'll do my best, Mr. Foley. But it would help if you could take a stab at how old they were."

"It'd only be a guess," Foley told him. "Early twenties? I mean, they ran off at quite a pace."

"Height?"

About five foot eight, nine, I'd say. The other was taller, nearer six foot."

"Build?"

"Both slim."

"Anything else you can tell me?"

"Nope, can't say that I can."

"Well Mr. Foley, if you see or hear of them again, be sure to give us a call. I'll ask around and see what I can find out about these two, but I suspect they're the same ones who are nicking stuff off the boats at night."

"Yeah well, I hope you catch 'em soon."

Barnwell finished his notes and took his leave of the shop owner before clambering back on his bike and making his way to the station.

On his arrival, he found himself warmly welcomed by Janice.

"You're back! I thought you'd run away to sea," she exclaimed.

"Hilarious. I was called out to the marina again. They've had another theft down there. Paint, this time. That's two in one day. They're getting bold." Barnwell explained.

"Eh?"

"See, I've been thinking."

"Always dangerous," Janice interjected with a wry smile.

Barnwell ignored her. "I figure," he explained, "that there are three types of thief. The first type nicks things because he wants to sell them. Either to order or speculatively. Part of a plan or spontaneously."

Janice grinned as she typed another search into her laptop. "'Speculatively' and 'spontaneously,' eh? I think those are the longest words I've ever heard you use, Constable." Barnwell continued to ignore her, concerned only with expounding his theory.

"The second are those thieves who need the thing for themselves. In this category, I might include those who steal specialist boat-hull paint. It doesn't really make any sense otherwise."

"And the third?" Janice asked, reaching for her tea.

"Kleptomaniacs. Those who get a kick out of stealing. Wouldn't even matter what the goods were. It's all about the thrill."

Janice closed the laptop. It was about time to head home, and she'd done all the digging on Lyon and Beth Ridley's disappearance that she could for one day. "Couldn't kleptomania explain your paint thieves' behavior? They saw that security was poor and that they'd probably get away with it. Chose something portable to pinch."

"Sure," Barnwell allowed. "But there were a couple of them. Be unlikely to find two such weirdos in a small place like this. And why *paint*, of all things? I mean, there are plenty of other items in that store. Books, maps, fishing tackle boxes, boots, oars, you name it. But they chose something heavy and practically useless to anyone who isn't refurbishing a boat."

Janice packed her laptop into her satchel. "I think you're answering your own questions, Constable." She regarded him sympathetically. "Are you going to be at the marina tonight?"

"I told them I would," Barnwell sighed.

"Better you than me."

Barnwell nodded ruefully.

"Well, night, Bazza," Janice said. "Don't do anything I wouldn't do."

Barnwell took off his uniform cap and ran both hands through his short, brown hair. He glanced around the marina, where he'd spent the last three silent, freezing hours achieving absolutely nothing, and made sure he was alone.

"Bugger," he said with sincerity.

It had been a tedious night, one he was anxious not to repeat. There had been no signs of break-ins or likely thieves, only a drunken tourist who would probably have fallen into the harbor if Barnwell hadn't shocked him into sobriety with a flashlight and a judicious telling-off. The man staggered back to his hotel, full of apology and whiskey, once more leaving Barnwell to contemplate the deserted boats tied up at the wharf.

He'd already considered and roundly dismissed the notion that the fishermen were in cahoots with one another, pulling some kind of insurance scam. It just didn't fit with what he knew about them. They were fundamentally decent souls, wedded to their boats and the sea, far more willing than most to put themselves in danger in order to put bread on the table. He knew that the local fish stocks were depleted, but that didn't mean these old salts would descend to insurance fraud to make ends meet. He just couldn't see it.

No, this was targeted thievery by someone who knew what they were doing and what they wanted.

Aching and exhausted, Barnwell unlocked his bike and reluctantly hauled himself into the saddle.

As he was contemplating this disappointment, he spotted movement out of the corner of his eye. He turned to see two figures, both in dark clothes and wearing hoods. They were beating a hasty retreat from one of the boats at the far end of the wharf. Each of them held an oar.

"Oi!" Barnwell bellowed. "Stop right there!"

The two thieves bolted at an impressive speed. Barnwell cursed the confounded bicycle, turning it laboriously around and then peddling as quickly as he could along the pedestrian area that ran parallel to the boat slips. He gained speed quickly, his blood now singing in his veins.

"Gorey Police!" he shouted. But the two were swift, dodging between parked cars as they headed into the alleyways behind the shops that lined the street. They disappeared so quickly, he figured that they'd probably worked out an escape plan in advance.

Barnwell reached the shops and cycled around for a few minutes, hoping to catch the thieves breaking cover. There was no sign of them until he spotted two shapes in an alley opposite the Flask & Flagon, one of his favorite pubs.

He brought the bike to a squealing halt and leapt off as quickly as his bulky frame allowed, leaning the bike against the wall and proceeding down the alley.

"Gorey Police!" he shouted again. "Show yourselves!" He shone his flashlight down the alley and then winced at the sight.

"Oh, for heaven's sake," Barnwell growled. There was a sheepish smile from the woman and a terrified expression from the man.

"Get yourself home to the wife quick before I call this in." The man mumbled a quick thanks as he sidled past Barnwell and out of the alley. "And you should know better," he said to the woman. "Get going, and don't let me see you around here again unless you want to do another thirty days."

"I'm going, I'm going," she confirmed, before quickly leaving.

Barnwell returned to the bike and leaned against the wall. He was more exhausted than he should have been after a half-mile sprint on the bike and was furious that he had let the thieves get away. He checked left and right and saw that he was alone.

This time, he said it with real feeling. *"Bugger."*

CHAPTER TEN

I T TOOK NEARLY an hour after their arrival for Roach's stomach to settle down. A crossing from Jersey to the port of Weymouth, on England's south coast, made for a pleasant jaunt in summer, but in November, it could be hellish. The ferry had been tossed around, the sea sufficiently rough to have a good number of passengers reaching for sick bags. Roach was among them, embarrassed to be quite so stricken in front of his boss. One elderly passenger, seemingly immune to the rolling, pitching, heaving experience, commented dryly that a uniform and a badge did little to protect someone from the forces of nature.

"Reminds us that we're all equal before the Lord," the old man said. "Something to think about."

"I'm mostly thinking," Roach confessed as he breathed deep and hung onto a rail for dear life, "about trying to keep my breakfast where it should be."

Graham fared better, although deliberately over-dosing on seasickness medication had left him groggy.

They stopped at a café so that he could take on a pot of tea, after which he felt nearly human again.

"Did you get anywhere with Beth's journal?" Graham asked, just before requesting the check.

"I did," Roach said, showing more enthusiasm than he had thus far that morning. "I've identified at least two of the characters," he said. He chose his words carefully. He didn't want his closeness to Beth and appearance in her journal to jeopardize his place in the investigation.

"Good lad. Who are they?" Graham asked.

"'Canary' is her mother," he said with certainty. "She's attractive and bright, but not particularly deep or thoughtful."

Graham smirked a little at this. "I reckon a lot of teenagers would make similar criticisms of their parents."

"I certainly did," Roach admitted.

"Although canaries can signal a problem before anyone else realizes there is one. They can be pretty astute. Useful, too."

"And I'm pretty sure that 'Cuckoo' was her stepfather, Chris."

"Ah," Graham said. "The pretender who makes use of the nests of other birds. Very clever."

"As for the others, I think 'Puppy' might be a school friend who was especially immature, but I can't link the name to anyone. And 'Mouse' is another friend, someone who's making a lot of mistakes."

"Good work, Jim," Graham said, leaving cash in a saucer on the table. "Alright, Constable, let's have a quick word with Mr. and Mrs. Updike." They left the café, "And then I'm afraid it's back on the boat for us."

Roach took a look back at the port. It was enough to bring on a new wave of nausea. "Can't wait, sir. Really."

Godfrey Updike and his wife of fifty-one years, Petunia, lived in a row house about three miles from the port. Graham hailed a cab and re-read the pages from Beth Ridley's case file that described their original statements from ten years before.

"He saw Beth walking to school, and they had a short conversation," Graham summarized.

"Not much to go on," Roach said. The cab ride was bringing his nausea to the surface once more. He couldn't wait to sit on the Updikes' sofa or in fact, on anything that wasn't *moving*.

"I suppose we'll see. It's a bit of a long shot," Graham said. "You feeling alright?" he asked, concerned at the greenish tinge that was shading Roach's face.

"Will be, sir. Don't you worry."

Graham paid the taxi driver, and they found themselves standing in front of the Updikes' home. "Seeing as you're not feeling your best, I'm happy to do most of the talking," Graham offered.

"Righto."

As soon as Godfrey Updike opened the door, Graham realized that despite outward appearances, this was not an ordinary row house in Weymouth. "Good afternoon, there. Jersey Police I presume," Godfrey said, and then chuckled amiably. "Welcome to our little museum."

Shelves, alcoves, cabinets, and every other available surface were all crammed with ornaments and knick-knacks. Graham's encyclopedic mind went into immediate, involuntary overdrive, cataloging the vast array of objects. There was simply nowhere for the eye to rest.

"Come on through to the living room," Godfrey said after the introductions were handled. "Petunia's just working on something. Can I offer you some tea?"

"I'd never say no to that," Graham smiled.

Updike was now seventy-six, according to the file, but was sharp of mind, with clear blue eyes and a straight back. Godfrey gave the impression of a man given to rigor and order and Graham immediately suspected a military background, although that was at odds with the fussiness that surrounded him.

"Petunia, love, those two police officers from Jersey are here." His wife, a beaming woman with curly white hair, was sitting on the sofa, painstakingly assembling a three-inch tall scale model on a lap tray. "Can we tear you away from William and Catherine?" her husband asked.

"And little George!" Petunia pointed out. "Forgive me for not rising, gentlemen," she said. "But I'm waiting for William's glue to dry." Graham peered at the orderly assemblage of pieces and tools on the tray; the box for the mini-diorama showed Queen Elizabeth alongside the British monarch's grandson and his wife on the balcony of Buckingham Palace, exhibiting their new son George to the world.

"Coming along nicely!" Godfrey announced.

The Updikes' home was nothing short of an unofficial annex to a royal museum. Commemorative plates, mugs, tankards, paintings, models, books, photos, posters, and innumerable other objects showed that their enthusiasm for the British Royal Family had wandered toward the obsessive.

"We spoke briefly on the phone," Graham reminded the couple as Godfrey took a seat beside his wife.

"Yes," Godfrey remembered. "You're reopening the investigation into Beth Ridley."

Graham cautioned him politely. "I wouldn't go as far as that, sir. The anniversary of her disappearance is this week, and I was just a little disappointed to see such a paucity of information in the case file. We thought it was time for a review of the case."

Graham brought out his notepad. It was a reflex action, like a smoker reaching for his lighter. "For the moment, we're just trying to flesh out our understanding of what happened on that morning."

"Well," Godfrey recalled, looking down at the beige carpet, "Petunia and I took our caravan to Jersey every year for... What would it be, love? Ten years or so?"

Petunia explained, "We got a little bored of the Dordogne and fancied a change of scenery somewhere a little closer. Back then the South coast and Channel Islands were our stomping grounds. These days, we head over to the Brecon Beacons, sometimes the Cotswolds."

"We love the caravan, you see. Cost effective and we can do as we please," Godfrey added. "If we're not enjoying the scenery, we're following the Royals around," he added.

"Following them?" Graham asked. He glanced around the room, every wall reminding him of the Updikes' abiding fixation with the monarchy.

"You know, we follow their diaries and turn up to see them arrive at their official engagements. We like to wave to the Queen as she goes to church when she's staying at Balmoral in the summer or Sandringham at Christmas," Godfrey said with a smile. "That kind of thing. It's like a hobby."

"Once, she was gracious enough to wave back at us," Petunia added proudly.

Graham shifted in his seat, more than ready to move on from these anecdotes and return to the point of their visit.

"How long had you been on Jersey prior to the day that Beth went missing?"

"That was the Monday, wasn't it?" Godfrey said. "Our last day there. We were due to head back up on the afternoon ferry."

"And when did you see Beth?"

Godfrey's eyes narrowed as he recalled the details he could still remember. "I left the caravan at about ten past eight or so, after the news headlines had finished. I remember thinking that we needed a few things for the journey home, and that I'd pop into the newsagent. I was crossing the street when I saw her."

"What do you remember about her?" Graham asked, noting down Godfrey's recollections in a sequence of detailed hieroglyphs.

"Pretty," Godfrey said. He glanced at his wife but she said nothing. "Tall for her age, I'd say. She had a black rucksack over her shoulder, and just as I was crossing the road, she stopped and looked inside it."

"What happened then?" Graham prompted.

"She brought out a doll. It had brown hair and a green dress, I think," Godfrey narrowed his eyes as he remembered. "She seemed to check or confirm something, and then walked off with it in her hand."

"Did you speak to her?"

"I called out 'Good morning.' She turned and smiled at me. That was it."

"What time was that?" Graham asked.

"It was about a five minute walk to the newsagents so I'd say, what, 8:15? Naturally, once I came out again, she had gone."

"How long were you inside?" Roach asked.

"There was a line," Godfrey recalled. "People buying

their papers and such like. Probably ten minutes, all told."

Graham was nodding. "And that was the only time you saw her?"

"Yes, we left an hour later to catch the ferry."

"Godfrey likes to be there in plenty of time," Petunia explained. "He gets very agitated when the clock is ticking and he's afraid of being late. There was a time when we went to see the Duchess of Kent and—"

Her husband tapped his wife on the arm. "They don't need to know all my little foibles, dear." Then he said to the two officers, "I wish we could be more helpful. It's just terrible, the whole business."

"Any eyewitness report is potentially useful," Graham pointed out.

Godfrey rose with surprising agility for a man of his age. "I don't suppose you'd like a quick tour, before you leave?" he asked. "Seems a shame to head straight back so quickly after such a long journey."

Frankly, a tour of the house was the last thing the two officers wanted, but they acquiesced, and Godfrey showed them around the remarkable, crowded little museum that he and his wife had built over their fifty years together. Perhaps their proudest possession was a dinner plate from the wedding of Prince Charles and Lady Diana in 1982, signed by the head chef.

Downstairs were numerous photos of the Queen Mother the couple had taken, including a close-up of her during one of her last public engagements. Upstairs, there was a collection of figurines depicting the royal families of generations past, as far back as Queen Victoria.

Graham was frustrated. This interview had, thus far, only confirmed what they already knew. No new information had come to light. He was feeling antsy, and this guided tour around the Updike's home wasn't easing his mood.

He allowed his gaze to wander, taking in details but discarding most of them automatically. As collections of royal memorabilia went, it was superb, but it was hardly germane to the Beth Ridley case.

Then, quite when he least expected it, an object jumped out at him. It was in a box, on the bottom shelf of a battered, old corner unit. It was partially hidden by a host of other dolls and figures, apparently awaiting repair.

"Do you collect dolls, Mr. Updike?" Graham asked, leading the old man to the corner of the upstairs landing.

"Oh, those are some of Petunia's old projects. Been there for years. They're not part of our display. Now this," he said, lifting a ceremonial tankard from a shelf by their bedroom door, "was presented to us by the Prince of..."

"Would you mind terribly," Graham asked, "if I took a quick look at this box?"

Roach had already spotted the doll Graham was interested in and had his phone out, camera ready.

"Of course," Updike said. "Nothing very interesting, though."

Graham pulled out a doll, naked with brown hair. He noticed at once the manufacturer's mark on the back of the neck: *American Girl*. It was in less-than-perfect condition, but Graham could see it was the same type as the dolls he'd seen in the shop windows in Gorey, and among the huge collection on the bed in Beth's room.

Graham turned to Updike. "I'm afraid," he said slowly as Roach began to photograph, "that I can't agree." Graham turned the doll to ensure that Roach could photograph the most important detail of all.

One of its legs was missing.

"MR. AND MRS. Updike, I'm going to ask a simple question, and I'd like a simple answer."

"Of course," Petunia said. She had made the tea while Godfrey gave the officers their tour, and Graham found himself distracted by the aroma. "We're happy to help in any way we..."

"Is there anything more you'd like to tell me about the morning you saw Beth?"

The elderly couple looked at each other. "It happened just as I said," Godfrey replied. "Petunia, love, did I forget something? "

She was shaking her head. "You told him just what you told the police back then," she said. "Almost to the word."

Graham looked at the Updikes, sitting there with their perplexed expressions, surrounded by the countless collectibles that made up their earthly possessions. They were rather an *odd* couple. Eccentric. He'd known elderly couples who lived extremely private lives, indulging in whatever hobbies suited them best. But none of those couples had ever seemed remotely capable of a serious crime, let alone abduction or murder.

"I don't think there's any other way of putting it than this," Graham said. "The doll upstairs matches the description we were given of a doll Beth had in her bag on the day she disappeared."

"But..." Godfrey spluttered, "what can you mean?"

"And now, it seems, an identical doll is in your house," Graham pointed out. "Minus a leg. Did you know a doll's leg was found on the street from where we believe Beth went missing?"

Roach observed the couple closely. If they were faking their utter astonishment, then they were accomplished actors. He'd never seen people quite so stunned in all his life.

"They made *thousands* of those dolls," Petunia objected. "*Hundreds* of thousands! They were the most popular brand in the world for a *decade!*"

"Longer," Godfrey added. "How many of them are now missing a leg, eh? Hundreds upon hundreds. Cast aside, damaged, stolen by the family dog, torn apart in a childish fight over property."

"Where did you acquire the doll?" Graham asked. Roach glanced over at his boss' notebook and saw two words, in block capitals and underlined, among the dense, incomprehensible scribble: *BROKEN DOLL*.

Petunia blinked over and over, her hand covering her mouth, deep in thought. "Was it a flea market?" she asked herself. "A charity shop?"

"But why," Graham said, too impatient to wait for her answer, "did you purchase a doll with a missing leg?"

Godfrey smiled slightly. "Petunia enjoys her

projects," he said. "You know, fixing things up, finding replacement parts. Her specialty, for many years, was finding *just* the right replacement for a teddy bear's missing eye. Besides there's a market for these refurbished dolls. They're not cheap!"

Petunia was still deep in thought. "A collectors' fair, maybe? The one in Abbotsbury?"

Graham kept his frustrations to himself, but having made such an apparently vital discovery, the old couple's vacillating was a huge annoyance. After ten long years without progress, the case was finally bearing some fruit, and yet Mrs. Updike could only sit there, dithering and second-guessing herself as though she'd lost all her marbles at once. "Constable Roach and I are pressed for time," he explained. "We need some answers."

But nothing would come, however hard Petunia appeared to be trying. "I'm sorry," she muttered. "It was so many years ago, and I..."

"*How* many years ago?" Graham said, his frustration beginning to well up dangerously.

Roach glanced up at his boss with a flicker of worry. "I'm sorry, Mrs. Updike," he said, far more gently than his boss, "but it's important." He tried to catch Graham's eye, in a bid to calm the DI's mood, but Graham was fixed resolutely on the flustered elderly woman while he waited, his temper steadily rising.

"I... I really couldn't say," Petunia stammered. Then she looked at Graham pleadingly. "You can't possibly think that we had anything to do with... you know... that poor girl. Godfrey just saw her in the street that morning. That's all there is to it." Her face showed something close to panic at the thought of having become a suspect.

"Mr. and Mrs. Updike, we will need to remove the

doll for forensic examination. Taking your age into consideration," Graham said, "we won't be requesting that you accompany us to the station. But we advise you to stay in Weymouth. Please don't travel outside the area so that we can contact you, should we need to."

"What?" Godfrey said, aghast. "This is all just so unnecessary..."

"As the investigating officers," Graham said sternly, "*we* will decide what's necessary. You should know that this is the first concrete lead we've had in the last ten years."

"Lead? A lead?" Petunia was even more disturbed than her husband at this unexpected turn of events. "Godfrey, what must they think of us?" She looked at her husband imploringly and began to weep. Her husband put his arms around her.

Graham took a deep breath and softened his demeanor a little as they got ready to leave. "Look, the forensics tests will take a few days. I'm sure you understand, in a case of this nature, that we have to take any evidence very seriously."

Petunia was by now in a flood of tears that she was unable to stop. "It's just a doll!" she wailed. "A one-legged broken doll that no one wanted."

Ignoring her pleas, Graham left his contact details and reminded Godfrey not to arrange any travel until the tests were concluded. "We'll be in touch," Graham said as they were leaving.

Roach heard this as an ominous warning as no doubt did the elderly couple who were left badly shaken.

Graham said little on the cab ride back to the port, where they arrived just in time for the late afternoon ferry. "Don't forget your seasickness pills this time, Constable," Graham advised.

"Already took three," Roach told him.

"How many are you supposed to take?"

Roach glanced at the package. "Erm. One." Roach paused for a moment. "Sir?"

"Yes, Roach," Graham was staring out to sea, deep in thought.

"Were they telling the truth, sir?"

"Perhaps. We'll know more when we have forensics look at the doll." He glanced at Roach.

"It's just that, sir..."

"You think I was a little harsh on them?"

"Yes, sir."

"Hmm," Graham looked out to sea again. "Maybe I was, Constable."

Twenty minutes after boarding, Graham closed his notebook after much ferocious note taking. He turned to Roach to ask his opinion on the Updikes and their doll. It was an objective that went unmet.

The sea was much calmer on this return journey, but Roach had learned his lesson. There was no likelihood of an opinion from him on the Updikes or on anything. Graham's young colleague was completely, deeply asleep.

CHAPTER TWELVE

D I GRAHAM AND Sergeant Harding were
sitting together in his office when the call came
through.

Graham listened for a moment and then asked a few
questions. He made notes, checked his email for the file
he was expecting, and then clicked through to it quickly.
"Right, sir. Thank you."

Harding read the screen alongside him. "Wow," was
the first thing she said. "I knew they could do this kind of
thing, but I never thought we'd be able to..." She
continued reading. "Oh, *wow*."

The document was a list of every website visited by
Andrew Lyon in the previous eighteen months, and to a
criminal investigator, it made very interesting reading.
"The first thing to note," Harding said, making instant use
of her new skills, "is that he's a frequent user. You see all
these sites highlighted in red?"

"Yeah," Graham noted.

"Those are the ones the Home Office and the

Metropolitan Police have decided are basically... well... illegal websites, sir."

Some were just strings of letters and numbers, but others had names that left Graham in no doubt as to the kind of content one might find there. "Then there are the blue ones," she said. "They're not actually *illegal* as such, but they're close enough that they're banned in some countries."

Graham scanned the list. "He's on one of these, sometimes a whole string of them, pretty much every night."

"They're web forums, sir," Harding told him. "I can show you one that is relatively innocuous if you like."

"Is it going to appear in *my* browser history, Sergeant?" he asked.

"I'll show you on the laptop, sir." She opened her own machine and typed in the address. "See?"

It was one of the sites Lyon frequented the most.

"Has he broken the law?" Graham asked. He wanted to "see" as little as possible.

"It all depends on what evidence we're able to gather," Harding explained. "We've got records of him downloading files from the illegal sites," she said, opening a spreadsheet with hundreds of entries. The filenames alone were emphatically incriminating. "This data though, without other evidence, probably won't be enough for a jury. That said, at least he can't blame anyone else."

"How do you mean?" Graham asked.

"Lyon lives by himself, so he can't claim that someone else uses his Internet connection."

Graham frowned. "It's undoubtedly progress," he said, "but it's hardly 'game, set and match,' is it? All this tells us, really, is that he has some unusual proclivities."

He glanced back at the screen and then averted his eyes. "Can we close all this down for a moment?" he asked. "It's not helping me think this through."

Harding did as requested but sent the list of websites to the printer. "If nothing else, sir, we'll be able to scare the hell out of him. If this got out, it wouldn't do his reputation much good with the local community."

Graham looked at Janice sternly for a moment but said nothing. He brought out his notepad. "So, we've got a powerful method of putting pressure on Lyon."

"I'd say," Harding agreed.

"But you know as well as I do that we can't arrest someone simply for downloading a file."

Harding frowned. "I think that it's ridiculous, but yes."

"*Possession* counts, Sergeant. Anything else is just circumstantial evidence. A jury isn't going to convict him based on his browsing history. He would have to *own* copies of the images, and in this day and age, that means they have to be on his hard drive."

Harding didn't like this one bit. "But we *know* for a fact that he downloaded them. He wouldn't download the files and then not open them would he?"

"Probably not, but we have to *prove* it."

Janice sighed.

"He downloaded the files, but that's not enough for him to see the images," Graham continued. "I've worked on cases like this before, and the loopholes are enormous. We'd have to prove that he unpacked the files and stored them on his hard drive or on a removable disc. That's the only evidence a jury would find compelling enough to convict on."

"That's crazy," Harding concluded.

Graham rubbed his eyes. "I don't disagree, Sergeant, but we're constrained by the laws as they currently stand. Juries tend to see records like *these*," he gestured at the screen, "as second-hand evidence, a *report* of an event, rather than direct evidence of the event itself."

Janice puffed out her cheeks. "I mean," she sighed, "do they *want* us to catch these creeps, or not?"

"The person I want to catch," he reminded her, "is the person who caused Beth Ridley to go missing. I don't know if Lyon's adventures on the Internet relate to that in any way, but it does point to an unfortunate interest in young women and girls, and that's the line I think we should take with him. Let's lose this battle," he gestured at the screen again, "in order to win the war, eh?"

"Might it be a good idea to have another chat with him? Ask for an explanation? Even just to shake him up a bit?"

A small kitchen timer trilled on Graham's desk, and he stood to walk the few paces to the corner cabinet where a teapot stood ready. He poured a cup and savored the aroma before turning to Harding. "With all that you've shown me, we could probably get a warrant to seize and search his hard drive," Graham said. "But he's not our only suspect."

Harding thought for a second. "Don't tell me that you've got something on that old couple in Weymouth?" Harding asked.

"They had a doll, as near as I could tell *identical* to the one Beth was taking for repair on the day she vanished. It was also missing a leg."

"Wow," Harding breathed.

The station's front door opened and Roach appeared. "Morning," he called.

"Morning, Constable," Graham turned to Janice. "Roach has been tracking down a homeless man who was sleeping in the bushes near Beth's home around the time she disappeared. We need to chase that lead down, too, *before* we take any action on Lyon. And we still haven't spoken to the friend who walked to school with Beth every day. This has a long way to go, yet."

Roach came to Graham's office door. "So, I've found him," he announced with a certain pride. "His name's Joe Melton, and he lives on Guernsey. With your permission sir, I'd like to head over there this afternoon and see what he has to say for himself."

"Granted," the DI said, "as long as the water's calm. Don't want you out for the count again."

"Got anything more on Lyon?" Roach asked.

"Not half," Janice answered.

"Don't tell me, let me guess. He's a complete pervert."

This time, Graham made no move to disagree. "Creepy," he confirmed. "Uncommon interests."

"Hmph," was all Roach said.

"But," Graham said, a finger aloft to caution against speculation, "he's not the only suspect, and we still have other leads to chase down. Right, Constable?"

"Yes, sir," he said. "Guess I'm off to Guernsey, then."

"You are indeed," Graham replied, "and while you're doing that, Sergeant Harding and I will speak with Susan Miller."

CHAPTER THIRTEEN

T HEY CLIMBED THE stairs together, making their way to the third and highest floor. The stairwell was painted forest green with orange baseboards and steps so that it looked more like the back stairs of a chain restaurant than an apartment building.

"Do you ever find this to be a bit of a chore?" Harding asked.

"Hmm?"

"Traveling to interview people, I mean."

Graham glanced around and found that they still had one more floor to go. "Would you prefer that we had the power to summon people to the station?"

Harding gave an equivocating tilt of her head. "It'd be more efficient for us," she said.

"Sounds a bit too much like something that might happen in a police state to me," Graham countered. "Ordering people around, when they're not even under suspicion."

Harding thought this through. "I guess it gives us a

chance to see where people live," she said. "Their context."

"Precisely," Graham said. "For example, here we are in a modest apartment building in Gorey. What have we already learned before even meeting Miss Miller?"

They were on their way to visit Beth's best friend.

Harding thought, glancing back down the stairs. "We know that she lives in a studio apartment, so it's unlikely that she has a family. The place isn't close enough to the harbor to have a view of the water, and I doubt there'll be a view of the castle either, so the rent will be fairly low."

"Anything else?" Graham asked.

"Parking isn't easy around here, and the building doesn't have its own spaces, so we can guess she doesn't own a car. There's a bus stop outside, though, so she might have chosen the building because she works somewhere beyond Gorey, perhaps St. Helier."

"All reasonable assumptions. Of course," Graham said, "that's all they can be, until we know more." They finally arrived at the right landing and found the door marked 7B. "What kind of job do you think she does?"

Harding puffed out her cheeks. "Could be almost anything."

"Well, there's at least one piece of evidence on that score," Graham reminded her. When Harding's expression remained blank, he tapped his watch theatrically. "Her job allows her to meet with police officers in the middle of a weekday afternoon."

Harding pursed her lips and nodded while Graham knocked on the door.

"You're the detective?" A woman answered.

"Detective Inspector Graham, ma'am. And this is Sergeant Harding."

"Hi, I'm Susan Miller." She extended a hand. "Come on in."

She was exceptionally attractive, Graham noticed, tall and elegant, with long, auburn hair and a figure that suggested many diligent hours in the gym. "Thank you, Miss Miller. As I said on the phone, we're investigating..."

"Beth, yes," Susan said. "I think it's great that you're trying again. Who knows what might come up?"

"That was our thought, too," Graham said, taking the seat offered around her kitchen table. The apartment was small, with a bedroom partitioned from the remainder of the space by curtains printed with an Asian motif. A calming Buddha watched over the room from a large print hanging on the wall as Graham began taking notes. "I wonder what you can tell me about that morning."

Susan poured them all a glass of water, but as she sat down opposite Graham and began to drink, she paused and set hers down. Tears came so quickly. "I waited for her," Susan said, "until I risked being late. I had to run to school in the end. I just couldn't imagine what had happened. It was so unlike her."

Harding used her most consoling tone. "You did nothing wrong, Susan. We're just here to learn more in the hope that we can finally figure out what happened to Beth."

"I just don't know *anything*," she reiterated. "She didn't call or leave me a message on my locker door the day before like she sometimes did. There was nothing. She just didn't show up."

Graham made a note while Harding produced a map of Gorey and asked Susan to point out where she had lived back then. She did so without hesitation.

"You see, that was her house, and here's mine. My

house is closer to school. Beth would walk to the corner of my street and wait for me, or I would wait for her."

"How long did it take to get there from her house?" Graham asked her.

"About fifteen minutes," Susan responded, shakily, "we always met at twenty past eight."

"Had she ever been late before?"

"Never," Susan said, drying her eyes. Graham kept up a professional front, but part of him couldn't help regretting that such a beautiful face should be marred by distress. "She was one of the most punctual people I've ever known. We walked together every day for years. And then, she just disappeared into thin air."

"Did anyone pass you as you waited?"

"Of course. Our meeting place was on a main road. I saw lots of people – people going to work, kids like us going to school, even saw a couple of teachers making their way in."

Graham asked Susan the same questions he'd posed Beth's mother. Did Beth have any enemies? Who did she hang out with? Did she have trouble with any of her teachers?

Susan latched onto this last question. "Well, not trouble in the academic sense. She was an excellent student, you know, always on top of her work. Would probably have scored A's across the board if she'd taken her exams." Susan let her emotions resurface for a moment before biting them down again. "But she really didn't like one teacher."

"Who?" Graham asked. But he already knew the answer.

"Mr. Lyon, the science teacher," Susan told him, her

voice tight. "He was always assigning her extra work, but..."

She paused, staring down at the tabletop.

"It's okay, Susan. We're speaking in strict confidence today," Harding assured her.

It took a long moment for Susan to gather herself and summon the courage to say what came next. "He and I... we had a relationship," she said almost in a whisper.

Janice waited a moment to see if anything else was forthcoming, then asked, "When was that, love?"

"In the summer before Beth disappeared, before Year 10."

Graham was like a volcano ready to explode. It was all he could do to stay seated. After a pause, he went to make tea in the kitchen, giving the two women time to talk.

"Go on, love," Harding said. "I'm listening."

Susan closed her eyes briefly and took a deep breath. "I managed to convince myself that he was in love with me. I was in love with him."

Susan took another deep breath.

"I would go over to his house during the day and then after school when we went back in September."

It began as a friendship, she told Janice, one that seemed harmless at first. "He was good-looking, much older than me, of course, but nice to me, kind. I was having problems at home, and he seemed genuinely concerned. It was a relief to talk to someone and I felt kind of privileged. I was flattered by his attention, I suppose."

Janice was full of questions, but she knew to let Susan tell the story in her own way.

"And it kind of went on from there. I didn't say no, but

I never really said yes, either," she recalled. "He treated me like a girlfriend even though we were never seen together outside his home. I didn't have the heart to refuse him, though I suppose I must have known, deep down, that what we were doing was wrong." She sniffed for a moment, avoiding the officer's gaze, tears in her eyes. "Now I know differently. I can see how naïve I was, how manipulated. I should never have even gone to his house, let alone..." She broke down and needed a long moment to collect herself.

"Did you ever suspect," Graham handed Susan her tea after she had dried her eyes once more, "that there was anything more to his relationship with Beth?"

She sniffed. "I know he was interested in her. I mean, of course he was, she was so pretty, and he paid her a lot of attention. He singled her out, gave her the odd smile. But she never told me about it, if there was."

"And did Beth know about Lyon and you?" Graham asked.

Susan shook her head. "I kept it a secret. He told me it would get him sacked if it ever came out." She burst into tears again. Harding rose to comfort her, and an arm around her shoulders seemed to calm Susan.

"When did your relationship with Lyon end?"

"Erm," Susan dabbed at her eyes, "before Christmas. After Beth disappeared."

Graham and Harding exchanged glances.

Graham completed his notes. "Susan, I understand why you wanted this kept quiet at the time, but ten years have gone by. I wonder if, with the new investigation, you'd like to proceed differently."

"I don't want to do anything," she said definitively. "I don't want to be the victim in all the newspapers and on TV. You *have* to keep me out if it," she insisted.

Harding spoke to her softly. "Susan, this man is a menace. If we can bring one case against him, he might tell us about others. Maybe even," she hazarded, "about Beth."

"You think," Susan said, "that he had something to do with her disappearance?"

"We can't know until we have something solid," Graham told her. "We have uncovered some new leads, but until whoever was responsible tells us what he did with Beth, or we find..."

Susan was shaking her head now. "You're wrong."

"About what, love?" asked Harding.

"There's no way he could have been involved. He wasn't like that." Susan was certain. "It must have been someone else."

Later, emotionally drained and tired, Harding walked slowly down the stairs of the apartment building with Graham.

"That was a lot more intense than I expected," she admitted. "Poor girl. She just couldn't tell anyone what was going on."

"Hmm, it sounds like she thought it all so normal at the time. The one great love."

"More like naïveté, hormones, lack of a stable home life, and the ability to keep a secret. Sir, do you think there's a connection between Beth's disappearance and the ending of their relationship? "

"I don't know," Graham replied grimly, "but now that Susan's told us her secret, we're going to make that count for something. Come on, Sergeant, we've got work to do."

CHAPTER FOURTEEN

I T WAS VERY quiet in the Sanctuary when Roach entered, hoping that the big, heavy, wooden door wouldn't squeak or bang loudly in this silent, echoing place as he closed it behind him. St. Michael's wasn't the smallest church he'd been in, but it had that cozy intimacy familiar to rural houses of worship, especially those with considerable history. The smell that he remembered from his childhood – dust, old books, stonework, and something else that was hard to define assailed him with a wave of memories.

The stone altar was covered with a brilliant, white cloth and adorned only by a gold, bejeweled cross that shone fetchingly in the late-afternoon light through the stained glass windows behind. Two people prayed silently in the front pews. Roach discreetly began to look around for the man he'd been told would be there.

Joe Melton was sweeping the vestry, a small room just off the Sanctuary to the left. His movements were very slow and deliberate. He was of average height but very thin, bearded and gaunt, dressed in old jeans and a check-ered shirt.

"Mr. Melton? I'm sorry to disturb you at work."

Joe looked up to see the young police officer in his uniform. "Trouble?" he asked, but carried on with his slow and steady sweeping.

Roach closed the vestry door so that their conversa-tion would remain private. "Just a routine investigation, sir. We're looking into the disappearance of Beth Ridley."

Joe stopped mid-sweep and straightened his back. "Ridley?" he asked.

"Fifteen years old," Roach said, producing a photo of Beth on his phone. "She disappeared ten years ago this week, and we're asking around to see if any new informa-tion comes to light."

Melton peered at the digital photo for a long moment. "She was Ann's daughter."

"That's right," Roach answered. "Do you know Mrs. Leach?"

Melton sat down on a hard, wooden chair, wincing at some pain in his back or knees, Roach couldn't tell. "She was kind to me," he said, gazing at the vestry's stone floor. "Good."

Melton was a known transient. An alcoholic, but not a drug user. No convictions or arrests. There weren't even any reports of suspicious activities, something almost unheard of among the homeless community.

"This was when you were sleeping rough, back on Jersey?"

"Aye. Hard times."

"Go on."

"Ann talked to me. Gave me food. Kept me going. I've got demons, you see," he said finally looking up.

Roach took the only other seat in the room, next to the bookshelf. "How do you mean, sir?"

"Drink," Melton answered.

"You seem to be doing well now," Roach offered. It was a half-truth at best. Melton had the face, and in particular the eyes of a man who had been through a great deal. His bent body had clearly weathered storms, and Roach suspected he was suffering from a long-term illness of some kind.

"Passable," Melton qualified. "Haven't had a sip in eight years. Not one."

"Good for you," Roach said genuinely.

"This is the best place for me."

Roach glanced around. "Are you a volunteer here?"

"I live here," Melton said. "Made a deal with the pastor and the church commission. Take care of the place, morning and night. Make sure the kids aren't getting drunk in the churchyard. That kind of thing."

Roach made notes on his tablet. "And what do you remember about Ann's daughter, Beth?"

Melton shrugged. "Saw her walking to school a few times. Wasn't stupid enough to speak to her. Kept my head down. Best to keep a low profile," he added.

"So you wouldn't remember seeing her on her way to school that morning?"

Melton relaxed in his seat. "Ten years ago?" He cracked a smile. "Couldn't have told you what month it was back then. Lived day to day, bottle to bottle. Was all that mattered."

"She used to walk right past the spot where you slept at night," Roach said.

"You think," Melton said, the smile fading, "I spirited her away?"

"We're just trying to trace her movements on that morning."

"Would have been easy enough," Melton said next, raising his chin and scratching his neck thoughtfully as if considering it.

"Easy?"

Melton ignored the question. "Did they find a body?"

"No, sir."

"Pity," was all Melton said.

"How so?" Roach asked.

"Ann will forever think she's alive somewhere," Melton said. He trailed off and seemed to lose interest in their discussion, casting his eyes around the room before standing and resuming his sweeping.

"Do you have any knowledge of what happened to Beth?"

Melton shook his head.

"Where were you, sir, on the morning of Monday November 7th, 2005?" Roach said, suddenly.

"No idea. I told you. Probably sleeping rough somewhere. Probably near Ann's house, like you said."

"Can anyone vouch for that?"

"Course not." Melton hadn't stopped his sweeping.

"Is there anything else you can tell me?"

"Nope."

Feeling defeated after his sudden burst of forthrightness, Roach fought not to telegraph his dejection through his body language. He held out his Gorey Police card.

"I see. Well, that will be all for now, sir," Roach said, his voice tight. "We'll be in touch if we have further questions. And if you remember anything—"

Melton didn't look at Roach. His eyes were fixed on the floor as his brush went back and forth, back and forth.

Roach left the proffered card on the table and departed the vestry without another word.

CHAPTER FIFTEEN

JANICE HARDING WAS tapping her teeth with a pen, thinking hard. "How about a wild-card search?" she asked. "Add an asterisk to the search term and see what we find?"

"Good plan. Give it a try."

Harding was working with Jack Wentworth, a computer engineer who provided support to the Jersey Police when they faced technological challenges. He had already proved his worth in assisting Janice with the reams of data returned by Andrew Lyon's Internet Service Provider, and now she was engaging him on another issue.

"I'm not sure the online records go back far enough," Jack said. "We're looking for cash transfers or payments to Lyon from about ten years ago, right?"

"Surely they were electronic back then?" Janice asked.

"Some were, but a lot were still manually typed in by a bank teller. Those records are either in an archive somewhere or lost, I'm afraid."

The work was fascinating, if at times a little frustrating. Janice was tasked with tracking down financial transactions between Lyon and the owners of the websites for which he'd done work. It had become part of her personal mission to build a case against the science teacher, and she secretly hoped to uncover evidence of his involvement in Beth Ridley's disappearance.

Working with Wentworth was a bonus. He was an expert in "digital criminality," as he called it, a computer forensics expert. He had had remarkable success in tracking down wrongdoing by those who'd been careless when conducting illicit transactions online. It also didn't hurt from Janice's point of view that he was about her age, good-looking, and single.

"Here," Wentworth pointed out. "There are monthly payments going back at least to 2007 and continuing until the present day."

Janice scrutinized the columns on the spreadsheet in front of her. "Decent amounts, too. They are all a few hundred pounds, at least."

"As payment for what, though?" Wentworth asked rhetorically. "He set up their website years ago. The basic format hasn't changed, just the content, which they can plug into a set of boxes on a traditional web form themselves. Wouldn't even need him to approve it, let alone do new work on it."

The website they were looking at was in the same category as many of the others built by Lyon down the years: technically legal, but morally questionable. It purported to be a "dating exchange," but in reality it had all the hallmarks of an escort service.

"I just can't believe," Harding commented, "that there isn't an actual *crime* in here anywhere."

Wentworth had been impressed from the very beginning with Harding's zeal for her work. He hadn't seen this level of conscientiousness in other police officers he'd worked with. She was absolutely determined to find a way of putting pressure on Lyon. A *lever*, she called it, something she could use to force new information from a man who had been involved with at least one underage girl.

"Writing HTML code isn't a criminal offense," Jack told her. "He did decent work for people who weren't breaking the law. They paid him. The end."

"But there are regular payments to him for no apparent reason."

"Yes, there's that. But so far there's nothing to take to a judge.

"Ah, yes," Harding said. "I wanted to talk to you about that."

Wentworth wondered what was coming next. There seemed no limit to the effort Harding was prepared to put in to bringing Lyon to account.

"Yeah, after our conversation with Susan Miller, we pulled in a few favors. Well, the DI pulled in the favors, and I did the legwork. As a result, I am delighted to be able to give you," she said, reaching into her desk drawer, "*this.*"

"Don't tell me," he smiled. "Andrew Lyon's hard drive."

"The very same," Harding said. "The data from his ISP was reason enough to carry out a search and seizure. You should have seen the look on his face when we showed up with the warrant."

Wentworth immediately went to work cataloguing what he had in front of him, then took out an adapter cable he kept in his work satchel.

"Thing is, I doubt there's a smoking gun in there," Harding said. "I mean, unless he's the most complete kind of idiot, he'll have deleted anything to do with Beth."

"If," Wentworth cautioned, "he had anything to do with her disappearance at all."

"Of course."

Janice's initial certainty that Lyon stood at the center of this mystery had been tempered by Susan Miller's strong insistence that Lyon had nothing to do with the case. The thought nagged at her. "People do strange and inexplicable things all the time," she said, mostly to herself.

Wentworth clicked the cable home. "Sounds as though you're familiar with the Jersey dating scene, Sergeant," he quipped. "Alright, the drive is functioning and... Hey, presto!"

Wentworth's laptop screen immediately showed a window listing the drive's contents. "I know you said that he's unlikely to be idiotic enough to leave evidence hanging around for us to find, but I have to tell you, that's often just how it works."

"Really?" Harding asked, shoulder to shoulder with the young man as she read the screen in front of her.

"I helped the St. Helier police nick a guy who had illegally bugged his wife's laptop," Wentworth explained. "He installed spyware, which might sound like nothing, but it breaks the law."

"Sure does," Harding confirmed.

"He was trying to find out if she was having an affair, but when a security scan caught the spyware, and she saw the install date, she called the police on him. They grabbed his hard drive, just like you've done with Mr.

Lyon here," Wentworth said, "and do you know what the incriminating folder was called?"

"Enlighten me," Harding smiled.

"'Spying,'" Wentworth said, rolling his eyes. "With subfolders called 'Gina's Skype Chats' and 'Gina's Emails.' I mean, honestly."

"Honestly," Harding echoed.

"So, some people are not as smart as you think they..." Wentworth's explication of the idiocy of common criminal habits came to a gradual stop as he found something that demanded his attention. "There are over a hundred files in this folder," he said.

"What's the folder called?" Harding asked, peering over Wentworth's shoulder. Then she saw it.

"Beth Ridley."

CHAPTER SIXTEEN

G RAHAM ARRIVED AT the station half an hour early, pulling into his parking space a few minutes before eight. He knew that Janice would not have requested this early meeting unless something of real significance had emerged from her work with Wentworth. The air of excitement around them as they prepared to begin the presentation of their findings was palpable.

"Hang on, you two," Graham said. "I'm a morning man, but only when I've had my second mug of tea." Janice smoothed the process by boiling the kettle while Wentworth double-checked the presentation on the laptop. "Are you going to sell me a timeshare, or is this something about Beth Ridley?" Graham asked.

"Very much the latter, sir," Wentworth assured him.

Once her boss was seated behind his desk, sipping on Earl Grey, Janice launched into her prepared spiel. "Sir, I want to thank you for your help in securing the warrant to seize Lyon's hard drive," she began. "Without it, we'd never have found all of this."

She began to click through a set of slides showing newspaper articles on Beth's disappearance, pages from her school essays, and scans of her school photos, including some that Graham remembered seeing on Ann Leach's living room wall. "We found all of this, unencrypted, on Lyon's hard drive. Right there in a folder labeled with Beth's name."

She continued to show slide after slide of evidence that demonstrated Lyon's obsession with the case.

Graham sipped again. "Go on, Sergeant."

"He kept records of every local and national newspaper report on her disappearance, coverage of events surrounding each anniversary, and even TV news clips relating to the case." Janice clicked to an example, which showed a newsreader recounting the details of Beth's strange vanishing. "He's been studying and archiving the case, sir."

Another sip. "And?"

Janice stared at him. "Well, sir, it's very suspicious. This isn't normal behavior. Why would he be so meticulous about recording a case like this?"

"I'm meticulous about tea, Sergeant," Graham retorted. "And although I often tell you I could murder a cup, it doesn't make me a criminal."

"But, sir," Harding began.

"Say that someone keeps a detailed file on every aspect of the Kennedy assassination. That doesn't tell us that he was the man on the grassy knoll, now does it?" Graham continued.

"Sir, I see what you mean, but don't you find it very suspicious that Lyon would have a collection like this, especially given that he was Beth's teacher... I mean, his collection is *comprehensive*, sir."

"He's still bothered by her disappearance," Graham said. "It occupies his mind. He might even be fixated on it."

"Because he *did* it?" Janice tried. She was still clicking through slides.

Graham stood, walked around his desk and closed the laptop, ending their presentation. "Sergeant Harding, you're a fine police officer. One of the most zealous and committed I've ever worked with."

"Thank you, sir," she said, blushing slightly. She glanced at Wentworth.

"But you're culpable of putting two and two together and getting seven. Fascination doesn't equate to criminality. Obsession doesn't connote murder. And his preoccupation with Beth Ridley shouldn't lead us to assume guilt. What you have here is evidence of "suspicious activity," perhaps a good working definition of "circumstantial evidence," but without something more concrete..."

Janice's face fell. "But think about the ISP results, sir. All those websites, you know, the ones I showed you..."

Graham raised his hands. "He's strange. I don't doubt that for one second. He's got tastes in digital entertainment that are going to get him into trouble. But the reason we don't yet have him under arrest is that we can't charge him. And we can't charge him because we have nothing to charge him *with*."

"I think we could, sir," Harding protested. "The Crown Prosecution Service would probably find the case pretty reasonable and..."

"I simply don't agree, Sergeant. Having questionable predilections doesn't make him a murderer. In the absence of any hard evidence, which this folder unfortunately is *not*, we'd have to hear the words directly *from his own mouth.* It would have to be a full and willing confession."

"Then let's go over there and get one," Harding said, more directly and a good deal more loudly than she'd ever spoken to the DI before. "Let's show him this folder and the ISP records and pressure him into making a statement. Force him to admit what he did."

Graham sighed and returned to his seat. "I could equally go back to Weymouth and arrest the Updikes," he said.

Janice reeled for a second. "But they're just a doddery, old couple."

"According to the criteria you've applied to Lyon, the one-legged doll would more than satisfy the requirements for bringing a criminal case against them," Graham said pointedly. Then he stopped and pulled out his notebook. "That reminds me. Would you two give me a moment, please?"

Harding and Wentworth exchanged a glance and left. Janice closed the door behind them with a decisive click. Graham dialed a number and waited for Dr. Miranda Weiss to pick up.

Dr. Weiss was head of the forensic science lab in Southampton that Jersey Police cases were referred to. She was a tall, sturdy woman in her early fifties, with salt and pepper hair that curled over her shoulders and a penchant for hats that spanned the range from wide-brimmed, formal feather confections to wooly beanies.

An adjunct professor in criminology at the University of Southampton, Miranda Weiss could be stern, but was nevertheless revered by her colleagues and beloved by her students. After thirty years in the profession, her reputation for careful, diligent work that had sent many a criminal to jail was spotless.

"Good morning, Dr. Weiss," he said brightly. "I wonder if you have any news on the doll we submitted to you."

Miranda Weiss was an unabashed coffee addict and was still in that foggy part of the morning between receiving her first cup of caffeine and actually drinking it. "Yes, indeed I do, Detective Inspector" she began. "But I hope you know how much of a longshot this is."

"I know, Dr. Weiss, but your thoughts would be most helpful," Graham admitted. "A lot of water has gone under the bridge in the last ten years."

"You can say that again," she replied, "So many people must have come into contact with this doll."

Graham sighed. "But we know what we're looking for, don't we?"

Dr. Weiss did not have good news. "Well, not exactly. The hair and fiber samples from Beth Ridley's room were imperfectly stored, I'm afraid, and there's been some deterioration."

Graham swore silently.

"Even if we got a solid hit from DNA on the doll, I don't know if a jury would be convinced. It's been so long. I just wouldn't be able to prove that it was hers, not beyond reasonable doubt."

Dr. Weiss paused to take a sip of her coffee.

"We've got fingerprints from three individuals. You can try running a match, but they're faded and partial. Probably inadmissible. There's also DNA from two females, but that's the most I'll ever be able to tell you about them."

Making notes as usual, Graham asked, "Two females? Definitely no males?"

"You're assuming her abductor was male?" Miranda Weiss asked.

It was both a practical question and something of a challenge to the preconceived notions with which most investigators began missing schoolgirl cases.

"I suppose I was," Graham said, "There's little hard evidence either way." He dropped his pen resignedly. "Is there any good news, Dr. Weiss?"

"Only for the Updikes," she said. "Reconditioned and fully restored, a doll like this could fetch a pretty penny."

Graham drummed his fingers on his desk.

"I know it isn't what you wanted to hear, Detective Inspector," Miranda said, her voice a little more brisk and confident now that the day's first caffeine was beginning to race around her system, "but the technology only *reveals* the evidence. The information has to *exist* first. We can't invent it. It has to come to us through luck, good judgment, or most often, just painstaking, excellent police work."

It was a timely reminder. "You are right, of course. Thank you, Doctor. I'll run the fingerprints through our database and go from there."

"Any time. Let me know if anything else comes up."

Graham sat at his desk, alone and in silence, for another twenty minutes. Even if the Updikes, with their quirks and strange habits, were actually responsible for Beth's disappearance, the chances of proving it had just shrunk dramatically. But Dr. Weiss was right, the evidence had to be the master of their suppositions. Everything flowed from that.

He strode into Janice's office where she and Jack sat at their computers.

"We can't arrest someone because we *feel* they are suspicious," he said, abruptly picking up the conversation where he'd left off. "Our legal system is the envy of the world, exactly because we presume innocence until guilt is firmly proven."

"Right sir, but..." Harding stopped and frowned, feeling embarrassed. In that moment, made worse by Wentworth's silent presence, she knew that she was being taught another valuable lesson.

"I mean, say that we asked the CPS to read Roach's transcript of his meeting with the homeless man, Joe Melton," Graham continued. "Constable Roach brought up the abduction, and the guy didn't deny it. Said it would have been 'easy' to abduct a girl like Beth. Should we get the Guernsey police to pick him up?"

Staring at her shoes, Janice sighed deeply. "Sorry, sir. Guess I got a bit carried away."

"For all the right reasons," Graham added. "You're focused and passionate, I'll give you that. And you want to nail whoever did this, just like the rest of us. But you're *angry* with Lyon."

"Bloody right I am," Janice growled.

"We know what he did to Susan Miller. We know he works on dodgy websites and has socially unacceptable tastes. We know he's *not a pleasant man*."

Harding nodded. "But that's all we know, sir."

"Yes." He took a deep breath. "Unfortunately, that's all we know."

"Sorry again, sir." She brushed down her uniform and straightened her jacket. "I let him get to me."

Jack Wentworth who had been sitting stock still, his

592 ALISON GOLDEN & GRACE DAGNALL

eyes flicking between the two throughout this tense exchange, cleared his throat. "Sir, we did find something else rather interesting," he said.

Graham ushered them both back into his office and took the opportunity to regard the computer engineer. Wentworth was perhaps five or six years Graham's junior and reminded him of a Hollywood actor whose name he couldn't quite remember. He noted the younger man used gel in his hair. It was spiked up at the front. This was all he needed to underscore their dissimilarity. "You're a civilian, Jack. You get to call me David."

Janice gave her boss a look as though he'd suggested streaking naked through the middle of Gorey.

"David it is then," Jack continued. "Thing is, there are repeated payments to Lyon from at least one Danish website from 2007 right up to the present," he reported. "The website has hardly changed at all during that time, as far as we can tell. Certainly not enough to warrant bringing in a web design professional. If that's not too charitable a description for Mr. Lyon."

"So, what were the payments for?" Graham asked.

"That's what we're trying to find out," Wentworth said. "He must still be providing them with something valuable."

Graham considered this for a moment. "Maybe they're paying him for his silence," Graham wondered aloud. "Maybe the website's really a front for some illegal activity and Lyon demanded regular payoffs to keep quiet about it."

"We'll keep digging," Wentworth promised, and nodded for Janice to lead them both out. "Thanks for your time. I'm sorry this wasn't more of a slam-dunk."

"Oh, they never are," Graham chuckled as Janice and

Wentworth turned to leave. "Building a case is more like achieving a maximum break in snooker. You just keep chipping away and chipping away until you get there."

Janice was nodding as she left. Her disappointment was visible, but she knew her boss was right. And, painful though it was, this setback would do absolutely nothing to slow down her pursuit of Andrew Lyon.

CHAPTER SEVENTEEN

C APTAIN SMITH TAPPED out his pipe on a black-painted stanchion by the marina's railing. "You mean," he said, his gray, bushy eyebrows askew, "like some kind of Special Forces types? Like the ruddy SAS or something?"

Captain Drake, for whom a crackpot theory was always worthy of at least a little enjoyable speculation, set his old friend straight. "All I said was they use *stealth*," he reminded him. "You know. Creeping around at night, and what have you. Dark clothes. Silent movements. That kind of thing."

Barnwell pretended to continue making notes, mainly to mollify these two furious mariners. They could now count five occasions on which their boats had been "boarded and burgled," as Drake put it. There had also been another instance of brazen daylight shoplifting from the nearby store.

"Sorry, Captain Drake, what was that?" Barnwell asked.

"*Stealth*," he said once again. "They sneak around, low and quick, like bloody commandos. That's my theory."

"It's a theory, I'll grant you" Smith commented, "but not a particularly good one."

"Oh yeah?" the other man said, pointing his finger accusingly at Smith. At sixty-seven, Drake thought of the other man as the junior captain, despite both of them having logged an unlikely number of sea miles, many of them in foul conditions. "Let's hear *your* theory, then."

Smith straightened his back. "Common criminals, they are," he said. "But they know just when to strike. It's not *stealth*, it's *intelligence*."

Barnwell narrowly stopped himself from rolling his eyes. "Captains, if we were truly dealing with the gifted master criminals you're imagining, I hardly think they'd spend their evenings raiding Gorey Marina for bits and bobs of nautical equipment."

"Some of it's worth a pretty penny," Drake objected, "if you're selling to the right market."

"He means," Smith pointed out to his friend, "that if they were like the crooks from that film... *Ocean's Eleven*, that's it, they'd be stealing the sodding Crown Jewels or some such, not ruddy bits of rope and nautical charts."

"Hang the bloomin' Crown Jewels," Drake growled. "What are you going to *do* about all of this?" He pointed at Barnwell, his temper was up.

"Well, that's what I'm here to talk to you about," Barnwell told them.

He explained for a few moments, hoping that his news would come across as the well-considered plan it truly was. Barnwell had been working hard. He had dragooned two extra officers from St. Helier to help patrol the marina at night and had consulted with an expert at the Metropolitan Police in London who had arranged to loan Gorey a set of sophisticated detection devices.

"Motion sensors?" Drake asked, examining the small, black, rectangular box with its three protruding antennae.

"*Anything* that moves down here," Barnwell explained, gesturing across the marina, "right down to the size of a house cat, this baby will pick it up."

"Then what?" Smith said, rather nonplussed.

"It triggers a high-definition camera system that we're going to mount on the sea wall and on three of the boats. They'll all be connected, and they'll all go off at once, taking a set of pictures that will give us a complete view of the Marina."

Drake handled the camera as though it might explode. "Fancy," he announced. "But what about *below* the waterline?"

Smith exploded in a gale of laughter. "Christ alive, what now?" he guffawed. "You think these thieves are gonna approach by submarine like Seal Team Six?"

"I'm just saying..." Drake tried, but Smith waved him down, crumpling with laughter.

Barnwell hid a smirk and pressed on. "I've also asked the boating supplies shop to re-task its brand new CCTV cameras to scan the marina at night. With two lines for potential photographic evidence, we should have a good shot at identifying the thieves."

Smith recovered sufficiently to give Barnwell a clap on the back. "Well, fella, you've thought this through, I can tell. I just hope you get some results."

Barnwell left the pair and began setting up the

camera system. He was proud of his plan and hopeful it would bear fruit. With luck, he'd soon have stand-up-in-court photos of the perpetrators. With a little more, he'd personally catch them red-handed.

CHAPTER EIGHTEEN

F ROM HER SMALL office at the station, Janice
was distracted from her work as she listened to
Constable Roach making another phone call in
the reception area. She sat up straight and made a
conscious effort to focus on her screen. Jack was due in a
few moments, and they had more work to do. She wanted
to be prepared so they could hit the ground running as
soon as he arrived.

Their topic of research was a new one. With Lyon's
illicit past laid bare, but without any hard evidence, and
with DI Graham still apparently chewing on how best to
proceed, Harding had suggested that she and Wentworth
investigate a different area: The Beth Ridley Foundation.
She wanted to do some digging and see what, or who, they
turned up.

"Okay, Sergeant," Graham had said when she'd
suggested it, "a little due diligence would be in order. You
might look at all the people connected with it – organiz-
ers, supporters, donors, even the investigators they've

hired. It's possible that Beth's abductor is hanging around among that lot."

"Surely not, sir."

"You'd be surprised. Wouldn't be the first criminal to stick around and get his jollies from witnessing the chaos he created," the DI had warned.

All of this, happily enough for Janice, kept Jack around for at least one more day. She enjoyed working with him and was happy to give up her Saturday if it meant gaining the benefit of his expertise.

"Damn."

Janice pulled herself away from her computer once again and popped her head around the office door. "Everything alright, Jim?"

He was still holding the phone receiver. "I really thought I had something there," Roach said, almost to himself. "Damn it all."

Janice put things together quickly. "Joe Melton?"

"The very same," Roach said. He was still staring at the phone, perhaps in the hopes it would ring and he'd hear a different kind of news.

"Still a potential suspect?" Janice asked.

"Nope."

"Ah."

"Owing to the remarkably good recordkeeping of our local hospital, we are now able to say categorically that Joe Melton was not responsible for the abduction of Beth Ridley. He was admitted with 'chest pains,'" Roach explained, "and eventually treated for mild hypothermia and dehydration. He had a night in a comfortable bed, and then returned to wandering around Gorey, sleeping in the bushes, and drinking himself stupid. He was discharged the same day Beth disappeared, but not until the middle of the afternoon."

"So, he's off our list," Janice summed up. "Bugger, indeed."

Roach looked at her. "You know, there was something about him. I *wanted* it to be him. I *wanted* that possibility, so I could track it down, prove it, and make everyone see that he wasn't some reformed drunk, but rather a monster."

Roach had a pleading look in his eyes now, which was soon met with a fluster of self-doubt. "That's not a great way to think about a criminal case, is it?"

Janice took a seat in the otherwise empty reception area. "It's not, Jim, but I understand it."

Roach was crestfallen. His only solid contribution to the case had evaporated. Beth's journal continued to make only partial sense, and it hurt him, almost physically, that Beth's abductor, whether it was Lyon or someone else, remained free.

"But, you know," Janice continued, "our job is all about the *truth*. Uncovering it, describing it, and proving it. We can *want* a certain outcome as much and as deeply as we like, but in the end, only the truth matters."

Roach propped both elbows on the reception desk. "You want it to be Lyon, don't you?"

Janice nodded. "I'm *aching* for him to stand there in front of a judge and be handed some long sentence. I've found myself daydreaming about it."

"Understandable," Roach commented.

"Sure, but it's still *wrong*," Janice cautioned. "We've both been fixated on the *person* and not on the *evidence*."

It was Roach's turn to nod. "You're getting wiser by the day, Sergeant Harding, if I may say so."

"You may. Reckon it's down to that brainbox who runs this place," she smiled, heading back to her office again. Then she paused and approached the desk, speaking in hushed tones. "Do you know what our illustrious leader did the other day?"

"What?" Roach said, happy to distract himself with a little office gossip.

"I showed him a list of websites... I don't know, maybe thirty or forty of them, all different and all with pretty complicated names. Some were just a string of numbers and letters. Made no sense to me at all."

"Yeah?" Roach said.

"He *memorized* that list, Jim. All forty addresses. I couldn't have shown it to him for more than a minute. He remembered the whole lot."

Roach nodded, smiling. "Impressive. Probably really handy in the field, too.

"I shouldn't wonder. I mean, he's a bit of a marvel, isn't he?" Janice said.

"And how are you getting on with Jack?" Roach tried to keep a teasing tone out of his voice.

"Great! He's been so helpful. He's going to do a complete forensic investigation on Lyon's hard disk. Do you know they can find proof of files existing even after they've been deleted? He's a bit of a marvel, too."

From right behind her came a familiar voice. "Well, I don't know about that, but I'm willing to agree with you if you force me to."

Roach greeted the new arrival brightly. "Morning, Jack! Welcome to a sunny Saturday at the Gorey Constabulary."

"I'm missing the big game right now, you know.

Fourth round cup tie," Jack said. "But I guess Saturday pays time-and-a-half, so there's that."

Janice, who had been shuffling papers on a desk finally turned, gave him a smile, and gestured to her office. "Morning. Shall we get started?" As she shepherded Jack to her door, she shot Roach a glance. He shrugged, grinned at her, and returned to a stack of filing he'd been putting off for days.

"So," Jack said, setting down his satchel and taking his usual seat behind her desk. "I've actually made a start already," he explained. "Did a bit of digging through the electronic records last night."

Janice couldn't resist. "Didn't you have anything better to do on a Friday night, Jack?"

He didn't take the bait. "Oh, I love a bit of sleuthing. Makes me feel like I've wandered into a crime novel."

Roach appeared at the door. "Sorry, Sergeant, but could I bother you for a copy of that list you were talking about?"

"The websites?" she asked, with a glance at Wentworth. "There's some pretty hot stuff in there, Jim. You sure you can handle it?"

"I'll manage," he said, hands on hips.

"Go ahead and print it off the Jersey Police mainframe," she said. "It's in the Ridley investigation directory. Lyon folder."

"Well," Janice said, returning her attention to Wentworth, "what did you find?"

Jack opened his laptop and showed her a summary, just under a page long. "The Beth Ridley Foundation," he said simply, "is an open-and-shut case of fraud."

"Bloody hell." Graham re-read Wentworth's printout of the document for the third time. "How come no one knew about this?"

"There's been a crackdown on charities, sir," Jack said.

Jack had been struggling to heed Graham's request to use his first name. Like everyone else, he couldn't shake the automatic deference Graham's presence elicited.

"But they've been focusing on ones likely to be laundering money for terrorists or drug cartels, that kind of thing. Foundations of this size tend to slip under the radar. Besides, it couldn't help but look insensitive. Ann Leach is on the foundation's committee. Their mission is to help find her missing daughter, after all."

"Yes, indeed," Graham said, handing him back the document, "but that's *not* what they've been doing, is it?"

Janice shook her head. "So far, I've found at least three different ways in which Beth's mother has rerouted funds from the charity to a small network of shell companies that she directly owns."

"Amazing," Graham allowed. "Just goes to show, doesn't it? She plays the grieving mother like an Oscar-winner, and not the brightest bulb at that, but all the time, she's been conniving and fiddling the books with the best of them."

Wentworth glanced at his notes again. "Not *all* the time, sir. The fraud seems to have begun about three years after Beth went missing. Before that, the private investigations, lab tests, all the rest of it, they were genuine. But after that point, an increasing number of the expenditures were bogus. Now, nearly all of them are."

Graham poured himself yet another cup of tea. It was more out of habit than any urgent need for caffeine. Jack and Janice had called him away from a pleasant afternoon at the library reading up on Jersey's local history, but under the circumstances, he didn't mind a bit.

His initial surprise at Ann's deceit was giving way to a determination that they must build the best possible case. "It won't do for us to charge the mother of a missing girl and then have it dismissed on some technicality. This has to be absolutely watertight."

"Right, sir," Janice agreed.

Graham paused for a moment, thinking. "Any sniff of a suspect behind this smoke and mirrors act?"

"Doesn't look like it, sir."

"Hmm, okay then. I want you to bring this in for a landing. Build the case, interview people, get whatever help you need within reason. Jack here, for instance. He's been very helpful, wouldn't you say?"

Janice gave Graham an especially careful nod. "Yes, sir. He's an expert in this stuff."

"You're too kind," Jack said with a smile.

"Great. Work on it together, and then liaise with the CPS to make sure all our ducks are in a row before we make the arrest. I'd love a couple of co-conspirators as well, if you can manage it. Look into siblings, accountants, and those who gave large amounts to the charity."

Janice made quick and detailed notes. "You're thinking that they took the tax breaks for charitable donations, but then got a nice kickback from Ann?"

Graham shrugged. "It's what I'd do, if I were giving to a charity I knew was crooked. Look into it, and keep me posted."

CHAPTER NINETEEN

J IM ROACH MADE a second pot of coffee and
then returned to his screen. He'd been up since
five and at the station since six, unable to settle
into his normal Sunday routine of fitness training,
lunch down the pub, and maybe an old movie on BBC2.
The case was bothering him on many levels, not least his
own inability to meaningfully contribute to it.

He was poring over Beth's journals once more,
desperate to make meaning of her teenage musings. As he
carefully turned the page, the pencil in his hand skim-
ming the edge of the paper, he suddenly paused. He
backed up and read over the looped, girlish handwriting
on the previous page. As his thoughts swirled, he looked
around, tapping his pencil.

He turned back to the journal again and flipped a few
pages ahead. Backward and forward he turned the leaves
of the book, making notes on a yellow legal pad as he
checked details. His excitement was mounting. Finally,
he reached for the phone.

"DI Graham? Yes, I know it's Sunday, sir... Well,

thanks. Erm, is there any way you could come to the station, sir?"

DI Graham burst through the doors of the small police station like an explosion.

"This better be good, Constable. This is the second day and the second weekend in a row I've been called in. I was in the middle of one of Mrs. Taylor's overwhelming but utterly delicious breakfasts."

"I'm really sorry about that, sir. But I think this is important."

"Oh?"

"I saw something in Beth's journal that went *click* in my brain."

"Show me," Graham said.

Roach pointed to his own notes from their interview with Andrew Lyon.

"He said he was a heavy smoker. And it connects with something Beth wrote about Cat in her journal. That he stank."

Graham took seconds to make the connection. "So, you think Lyon is this Cat person, and the smell she referred to was cigarette smoke?"

"Yes, sir. She talks about him all the way through the journal. Always in rather childish language, as you can see," Roach said, flipping through some pages he'd book-marked with yellow tabs, "but it's beyond dispute who she's talking about. And, you know, '*Lyon*', sir," He emphasized the name.

DI Graham raised his eyebrows, and turned his head very slightly to look at Roach.

"As in 'king of the jungle,' sir."

"Ah."

Graham went into his office and sat alone, reading the journal carefully over the next ten minutes. He reappeared looking determined. Angry, even. "Right, that's it. I know we're waiting to have a cast iron case against Lyon for doing *something* to Beth Ridley, but we can needle him on the Internet stuff, and if Susan Miller will agree to contribute anonymously to the trial, nail him on at least one set of underage abuse charges."

Roach nodded, "Okay, sir. So, what now?"

"We bring him in," Graham's jaw jutted out. "We stop mucking around. I want him in an interview room, under arrest, so we can sweat him for forty-eight hours. Come on. Let's go nab him before he sees the writing on the wall and spends his ill-gotten porn money on a flight to a non-extradition country!"

Graham sat opposite Andrew Lyon and his lawyer, Mr. Sutton, in the station's small interview room.

"Do you understand these charges as they have been read to you?" Graham asked Lyon after reading the sheet out loud.

Harding had produced a long list of offenses, but Graham knew that without further evidence, he'd be hard-pressed to make most of them stick.

The pale, now rather crumpled ex-teacher nodded. For the most part, he'd been staring at the green tiled floor or the freshly-painted white walls. Anywhere but at Graham.

"For the tape, I can verify that Mr. Lyon nodded his

assent." This wasn't the first time in the hours-long interview that Graham had been obliged to report Lyon's responses for the record. Sutton was making sure he said as little as possible.

Graham knew the lawyer to be seasoned; one who worked hard for his clients, and someone with experience defending others on similar serious charges in the past.

"I remind you once more that my client has the right to remain silent," Sutton said. He had a haughty, reedy voice, like a private school tutor from a hundred years ago. "We'll be filing a request that the charges are dismissed on technical and procedural grounds."

Graham had been expecting something of this nature.

"We believe that your seizure of Mr. Lyon's personal possessions are in contradiction of legal directives regarding the privacy of information," Sutton announced, officiously.

"Such a filing is your prerogative," Graham said.

"Is there anything more you would like to say, Mr. Lyon?"

There wasn't. Graham stood to leave.

"Mr. Sutton, it would be in your client's interests to begin cooperating with us. I have a strong suspicion that the list of charges against him is only set to grow." With that, he left Sutton to advise Lyon further and went in search of tea in the reception area.

CHAPTER TWENTY

"FRESH POT BREWING, sir," Roach told him.

"Top man, Constable." Graham leaned against the desk with a sigh. He looked tired; interviews during which the suspect said absolutely nothing were wearing.

"How's it going in there, sir?" the young officer asked.

"Sutton's making sure that the little bugger is staying as silent as a monk. But we'll get to him, don't you worry."

"Right, sir," Roach said.

Sergeant Harding appeared in reception, shaking out her umbrella. "Just started pouring down!" she told them, and then she set a plastic bag full of takeout on the reception desk. "Chicken jalfrezi with extra chilies, lamb curry, poppadums, and naan bread. That'll be seven pounds each, please." Roach and Graham fumbled for change in their pockets while Harding peered through the peephole of the interview room door. "That blasted lawyer's still here? Has Lyon said anything?"

"Silent as a church mouse," Roach told her as he

opened the takeout box of outrageously spicy Indian food. "And looking to stay that way."

Graham ignored his meal for the moment. He paced the lobby, walking past the notice board with its posters about community events, firework safety, and the best ways to deter burglars.

"Constable Roach, Sergeant Harding... Would you step into my office? Bring your food."

"Everything alright, sir?" Roach asked.

"We need to mull this whole thing over in peace. We'll leave the door open in case anyone comes in to reception."

Janice and Roach followed their boss and took seats in Graham's office.

"Okay, so we've been looking at three suspects, basically," Graham began. He went to the small whiteboard on the far wall. "The Updikes, Joe Melton, and Andrew Lyon," he said, writing the three names alongside each other.

"Melton's not our guy," Roach reported. "Like I said, the hospital records..."

"Yeah," Graham said, crossing out the name. "The timing doesn't fit. Then there's the old couple."

"They had the broken doll in their possession," Janice said.

Graham wagged the pen at her. "They had *a* broken doll in their possession, Sergeant, and sadly, but not unexpectedly, we did not get a match for Beth's DNA or fingerprints from it. Two and two make four, and no more than that."

"But we matched the manufacturer," Roach argued. "It was the same type as the doll Beth was carrying on the morning she vanished. It *could* be the exact same one."

Graham put a large question mark next to the Updikes' name. "It *could* be, but it's certainly not going to work in court as it stands. We'd need firm evidence..."

"Of which there is precisely sod all," Janice noted with frustration.

"...Or a cast iron witness," Graham added.

"Of which there are none," Roach concluded.

"So, the Updikes are out, too?" Janice asked. The smell of curry was making her distinctly hungry, and she began to wish she'd ordered something for herself.

"There's just no motive," Graham said, "no reason for a quiet, old couple to grab a teenager off the street and make her vanish. I mean, they're a bit odd..."

"A *bit*?" Roach interjected. "Their most prized possession in all the world was a plate signed by a chef from a royal wedding thirty odd years ago."

"Being a bit quirky," Graham retorted, "doesn't make one a murderer. I mean, we've all got our vices, but that's all they are. For the most part."

"Alright," Janice said, her stomach growling. "So, speaking of vices and whether or not they're harmless, we're back to our old friend, Mr. Lyon. Can we really pin this on him?"

"Susan Miller says no," Graham said. "She insisted that Lyon isn't the type."

Roach scoffed at this. "I'm sure she'd have sworn blind that he wasn't the type to mess around with school-girls until he started doing exactly that," he said. "Neither was he the type to work for a Danish porn site, until..."

"Point is," Graham interrupted, "we still don't have any concrete evidence linking him to an abduction or even Internet wrongdoing, if we're honest."

"Well," Janice said, still frustrated, "she didn't abduct herself."

"No," Graham agreed. "Unless, I mean..."

Roach spotted the line of thought. "She did a runner?"

"On her own?" Janice said, picking up the thread. "Without money, or a passport, or credit cards?"

Roach frowned. "You have to admit, sir, it's the least likely explanation. What about her mother?"

"Ah," Graham said, readily moving on, "Yes."

The case against Ann Leach had been developing steadily, and Graham was now certain they could justify bringing her in for questioning. "We're police officers, not politicians," Graham said, "but we have to be aware of the gigantic fuss we'll create in this community if we arrest Ann Leach."

Janice nodded. "She's received a lot of sympathy and accepted so many donations over a long period of time. I've no idea what the public will make of an arrest."

"Or what they'll do," Roach added. "They might turn on her."

"Or us," Janice added.

"It's a risk, certainly" Graham said. "But do you think she had anything to do with Beth's disappearance?"

"Maybe Beth didn't get along too well with Ann's second husband," Janice suggested. "You know how teenagers are... Big changes tend to bring heightened emotions, with lots of yelling and crying. Don't forget that Beth's biological father was sent down for murder."

Janice visualized the scene.

"Her father gets sent to jail on the mainland, her mother immediately divorces him, and then there's some new guy in the picture. Must have been traumatic, especially for a young girl. She's stuck in the background, seething with resentment and hostility."

Graham drew a spidery set of lines on the board, connecting these different points. Seeing it laid out like this was often a help to him, but so far, nothing was falling into place.

"We can only imagine how Beth responded, how difficult she might have made things for Ann," Janice added.

Graham looked at her oddly. "So, Ann decides one morning to abduct her own daughter, just so she can have a nice, quiet life with her new man?"

Janice shrugged. "We're throwing theories around, and that's a theory," she said. "Perhaps they were in cahoots together. Beth wanted out, Ann enabled her disappearance, and spun the story as a way to commit fraud."

Graham looked her doubtfully. "Okay, maybe not, but I'll say this, sir," she continued, "I've been doing this job long enough to know that, well, people are *weird*. They do *weird* things that defy explanation. I'm just saying."

Graham opened his takeout and began eating. "They do, Sergeant. For sure."

While Graham and Harding were back in the interview room, attempting to wring information from Lyon, Roach made sure that no one entered the station while his back was turned. Given the nature of his research, he was most grateful that his workstation wasn't visible from the station's lobby. A desperate member of the public staggering in for help and finding the desk constable surfing through dozens of Danish websites, many of them questionable, would not be a good PR or a wise career move.

Some of the websites he was surfing were found in the colorful and rather incriminating browser history of Andrew Lyon. Others were owned by companies for which Lyon had done web design work. Most of them featured women in various stages of undress.

There were redheads and brunettes, even a smattering of Asian and African women, but the majority were blonds, mostly with clearly eastern European backgrounds. He lost count of the number of women named "Anna" or "Katya," though some went by professional names – "Jewel," "Sunshine," and "Glitter" among them. They were bright, upbeat names for those involved, whether entirely willingly or not, in a decidedly dark and seedy business.

He browsed through portrait shots of dozens upon dozens of women, briefly reading what he guessed were their largely fictional biographies. Every half hour or so, when his eyes began to blur and ache from the constant stream of images, he stood and stretched before reading another section of the Beth Ridley case file. Every interview and lead was chronicled there, and he'd built a comprehensive picture of what his colleagues had already investigated.

When Roach had directly exhausted the list of sites for which Lyon had done work, he began rather aimlessly clicking links to their affiliates. He brought up a gaudy affair with a host of flashing banners and looping animations on fast repeat.

The site boasted that it had over two hundred of the "hottest girls in Europe." He shivered slightly and then moved onto another site. This time the presentation and tone were quite different. Whether legitimate or not, the website design was tasteful and restrained. None of the women advertising here were overtly offering libidinous experiences. Some specialized in massage or other forms of therapy.

"Yeah, right," Roach muttered to himself. "I bet, in real life, they don't look anything like their..."

He stopped and doubled back.

"Wait a minute."

Roach peered at the screen and then clicked on the photo to enlarge it.

"Wait a cotton pickin' minute."

He downloaded the picture, zoomed in, and printed it out in three different resolutions. A visitor to the station would now have found him staring at three identical pictures of the same woman, laid out on the reception desk.

He toyed with the idea of knocking on the interview room door when it abruptly opened and the DI appeared.

"Sir? You need to see this. I think I've got something."

CHAPTER TWENTY-ONE

"**B**ETTINA," GRAHAM ANNOUNCED, reading the woman's one-paragraph biography.

"Might not be her real name," Roach advised.

Graham nodded. "Hardly ever is, right?" He returned to the description. "This twenty-five year old is an educated blond who specializes in...'" He read on for a moment. "*Blah-blah-blah*, this and that, services and therapies... All euphemisms, I'd imagine. But this one's clearly captured your attention, Constable. Want to tell me why?"

Roach stood up straight. This was his moment, and although his theory was certain to be controversial, perhaps even instantly rubbished by his colleagues, he was going to state it and then stand by it. He'd never felt more certain in his life.

"That's Beth Ridley, sir."

Graham looked at Roach with something approaching shock, then back at the picture, and then back to Roach. "Son, that's one hell of a... Are you sure?"

"Yes, sir."

Graham stared at the pictures again. He leaned over the desk, picked up the case file that Roach had been looking through, and took out Beth's school photo. He put it next to the ones taken from the website, his eyes flicking rapidly between them.

"I know it's a shock, sir... But hear me out," Roach pressed.

Graham stopped him. "Get Sergeant Harding. Have her pick up Susan Miller. We need more eyes on this."

"Should we bring in her mother?"

"No. Not yet."

"Righto, sir." Roach went to pull Janice out of the interview room. Within moments, she was on her way.

"And, Constable?" Graham said, still looking at the photographs.

"Sir?"

"If it turns out you're right about this, I'm going to make sure the whole world of British policing knows that it came from you."

Once again, Graham felt it prudent to shift the discussion about the photographs into his own office. He was very keen not to let the cat out of the bag. Part of him was, in fact, still rather uncertain as to whether the metaphorical bag genuinely contained the requisite cat.

"She's the right age," Roach reminded him as they waited for Sergeant Harding to return to the station with Susan Miller. "Twenty-five, give or take, right?"

Graham decided that it was best to play Devil's Advocate. He wanted to guard against jumping to conclusions.

Susan would confirm Roach's suspicions if they were well-placed.

"Half the girls on that website are in the right age range, Constable. Probably more than that."

"Okay," Roach admitted. "But her eyes, sir. They're quite distinctive." Roach showed him a copy of the last portrait from Ann Leach's living room wall, and Graham was reminded just how amazingly blue Beth's eyes were, like a pair of sapphires, gleaming out from the photo as she smiled for the camera.

"But not unique," Graham cautioned.

Roach sighed and walked back to the reception desk. It seemed that his boss was determined to rain on his parade, and just when he had finally begun to harbor some hope.

The front doors opened and Janice arrived with a rather worried-looking Susan Miller in tow. They made their way to Graham's office, passing Roach on the way. He caught Susan's eye and nodded awkwardly, mindful of their mutual past and her recently revealed secret. From his work on Beth's journal, he suspected Susan Miller was "Mouse."

Graham extended a hand. "Very good of you to come in, Miss Miller. Especially on a Sunday and at short notice."

Susan seemed on edge. Janice looked at her carefully. She understood the truth behind those worried looks. She knew Susan wanted to help find Beth but was desperate to avoid any public revelations about her past. Janice showed the younger woman to Graham's office and had her sit down. She brought her a glass of water.

"We're working on an image of Beth as she might appear now," Graham said to Susan. Janice looked on as her boss worked through the narrative he'd composed earlier. It was aimed at ensuring secrecy. "It's so difficult to extrapolate facial features over a period of ten years," he explained, "so we're asking people who knew her well whether or not they'd find the image convincing."

Roach had carefully cropped the photo so that only Beth's face and hair were visible. Graham showed it to Susan and asked, "How do you think we did?"

Susan picked up the image, her lips pursed. She scrutinized it closely, clearly searching for particular details. "It's..." she began, then glanced at Graham and Janice in turn before returning to the picture. "It's *uncanny*."

"Really?" Graham said, feigning pride to conceal the immense rush of adrenalin he suddenly felt. "You're not just being kind?"

"Absolutely uncanny," Susan repeated. "Her eyes... The shape of her nose... You've captured her perfectly."

"Well, that's great news," Graham told Susan. "You've made my day, I'll be honest. Thank you."

Graham raised his eyes to Harding.

Get her home. We've got work to do.

CHAPTER TWENTY-TWO

ROB AND CHARLIE waited until sunset to make their final preparations. Rob quietly brought out a stash of equipment from the lean-to they'd roughly constructed from an old door and a couple of sturdy planks. Charlie set about stowing them onboard. They worked on the boat in silence, following a careful plan agreed upon long before.

Charlie was particularly proud of the boat itself. The *Sea Witch* was a sturdy fishing vessel, probably sixty years old. The original idea to restore it had been Rob's, and together they drew up plans to patch the leaky hull, install new equipment, and work to make the old girl seaworthy again. If only for this one vital expedition.

The *Witch* sat on a makeshift boat ramp at the bottom of the garden. Charlie's family home backed on to the beach, and the carefully tended lawn close to the house gave way to coarse, reed-like grass and then sand. At high tide, they could launch the boat directly into the water.

Most of the boat's hull was obscured from the house, certainly from anyone looking out of the kitchen windows, but much of it was visible from the house's upstairs bedrooms. This didn't bother Rob or Charlie too much. Those in the house knew they were reconditioning the boat and had seen the change in its color as the two applied new coats of paint. It was all fine just as long as those in the house never found out the real mission behind their restoration project.

Rob brought out the third box of equipment. The two would-be sailors began finalizing stowage and proper mountings for the gear. There was a powerful lamp that Charlie screwed to an existing metal mounting outside the pilot house. Rob then attached the GPS to the battered wood of the console.

"Jesus," Charlie observed as he came back into the boat's pilot house. "Couldn't you have managed to put the bloody thing on straight? It's as crooked as a mafia lawyer, man."

Rob pushed annoying strands of ginger hair from his eyes and offered Charlie the screwdriver. "Have a go yourself, then. This wood has been warping for longer than we've been alive. I'm amazed it didn't splinter into pieces when I drove the screw in."

"Alright," Charlie conceded. "Just provided we're all stowed and ready to go in four hours."

"Ready or not," Rob reminded him, "that's when we go. No more waiting around. It's high tide, and it's high time."

Charlie agreed. "Dunno why we waited this long, honestly. Come and help me with the last lot, alright?"

These were the heaviest items yet; a pair of storage boxes that weighed enough to have them both heaving and complaining as they were shoved aboard and stowed under some tarpaulin.

Once they were secure, Charlie flexed his tired shoulders and then turned to his friend thoughtfully. "You nervous?"

"About tonight?" Rob asked.

"Our first time out in her," Charlie reminded him. "Might be dangerous."

Rob took his friend by both shoulders. "It'll be worth it. Imagine the upside, eh?"

"Right," Charlie agreed. "I just wanna be sure we're doing the right thing."

Rob gave a short laugh. "Course we are, mate. This time tomorrow, all our problems will be over." He gave Charlie a wink. "Trust me. Tonight at ten, alright? We'll aim for the deep water and put some miles between us and trouble. It'll all go fine."

"Sure it will," Charlie agreed. "This time tomorrow, eh?"

Graham approached Roach at the reception desk.

"Well, sir?" Roach asked anxiously. "What did Susan say?"

Graham wanted to clap the young man on the back and buy him a slap-up dinner at the Bangkok Palace. But he knew that there were still hurdles to overcome and that they carried the burden of proof.

"You might be onto something," he said simply.

"Bloody hell," Roach breathed.

Graham turned to head back into his office but stopped and approached the reception desk. "I meant to commend you for sleuthing out the nicknames in Beth's journal," he said quietly. "But I couldn't help noticing that 'Bug' remains unidentified."

"Yes, sir," Roach said. "It's been difficult to piece together the—"

"Constable?" Graham said, yet more quietly.

"Sir?"

"You do know that I sniff out lies, cover-ups, and deception for a living, right?" Graham put to him.

"Lies, sir?" Roach said, his heart thumping. "I don't think I..."

"It can't have been easy, seeing your own nickname in her journal after all these years and in these circumstances," Graham added delicately. "I can only imagine the turmoil you've been going through."

Roach swallowed and then closed his eyes for a moment. "I didn't want you taking me off the case, sir. You know, for loss of objectivity, or because you couldn't trust my judgment."

"Jim, you're becoming a very able officer, and I'd have wanted you as part of this case, no matter what," Graham said. "You knew her. You've been the only one to make sense of her journal. And now your diligence and persistence have given us a hot new lead. I can't think of a more valuable resource than you right now."

"Thank you, sir. I'd do anything to help get to the bottom of this," Roach said. Harding waited patiently at a distance for Graham to finish this rather mysterious, private conversation with his subordinate.

"But mark this, Constable Roach. If you've got evidence, I want to see it. I don't care if it's inconvenient, troubling, or emotionally draining. In fact," Graham continued with a slight smile, "I don't care if it shows that my old Granny Graham was a ninja assassin. Don't hide things from me, son. We'll always be able to work it out. I want you to trust that. Alright?"

Roach met the DI's gaze. He was grateful beyond words, but he was going through a curious mix of sensations: relief, embarrassment, regret, admiration for his boss, and an ongoing determination not to let *anything* get in the way of this investigation.

"Alright, sir. Thank you. Honestly."

"'Honestly' is the only way I want it, son. Keep doing what you're doing. And in the meantime, Constable Roach," Graham said much more loudly, for Harding's benefit, "you'd better see about organizing some plane tickets for the two of us. Leaving early tomorrow, if you can," he added.

"To where, sir?" Roach asked, suddenly much more excited.

"Denmark, of course."

Later that evening with Janice off home and Barnwell out pounding the beat in and around the streets of Gorey, Roach knocked on Graham's office door. The DI waved him in. Their flights were booked and plans for the trip to Copenhagen had been laid.

Roach sniffed the air. "It smells like a curry house in here, sir."

"Occupational hazard, Constable. What can I do you for?"

Roach raised an eyebrow. "Constable Barnwell's on the phone, sir. There's been a sighting of an unregistered boat acting suspiciously just offshore."

"Unregistered?" Graham asked through a mouthful of leftover naan bread. "How common is that around here?"

"Not in the slightest, sir. The local sailors and fishermen all know to have their paperwork in order. He reckons something sketchy is going on. The lifeboat's been called out but he wants permission to get the Coast Guard helicopter from the mainland."

Graham rose. "Put him through. I'll talk to him. I don't doubt his judgment, but I'd like a few more details before we do something expensive. It'll take an hour to get a chopper here, anyway." He thought for a second. "What's the boat's name?"

Roach reached for his notepad once more. "The *Sea Witch*, sir."

CHAPTER TWENTY-THREE

C HARLIE GRINNED CONSTANTLY as the boat made steady progress across surprisingly calm waters. Illuminated by the boat's two powerful lamps and the light of a waxing moon, the English Channel looked inviting and easily navigable, absent the foamy, terrifying swells that would have made this journey impossible. Their luck, so far at least, was definitely in.

"Twelve knots," Charlie observed as Rob clunked the heavy door of the pilot house closed, returning from a quick look outside. It was only half a dozen degrees above freezing tonight, but the pilot house was warm, thanks to a small space heater that ran off the old boat's creaking power system.

"How many knots did you say?" Rob asked him.

"Twelve!" Charlie repeated proudly.

"Christ, I never thought the old girl would have it in her. How much cruising time, do you think?"

Charlie checked their GPS and a nautical chart they'd brought as backup. Neither of them was prepared to say how long the electrical system might hold up. "Should be there in about two or three hours," Charlie announced. "Two AM or a little after, unless we hit trouble."

"We'll be fine," Rob assured him. He patted the wood of the pilot house interior. "She's got more miles left in her than anyone would guess."

The *Sea Witch* had something of a checkered history. Almost broken up for scrap in the early 1970s, the twenty-four foot vessel had come into the possession of Charlie's grandfather, who had done a creditable repair job and put the *Witch* to sea as a day-fishing boat. He'd spent most weekends for a few years puttering around the coast of Jersey, but he became notorious locally for his inability to ever actually catch anything.

This notoriety peaked, when on returning home one dark evening, he'd steered the small boat onto submerged rocks. The *Witch* limped home, its sole crewman required to constantly bail out a worrying amount of seawater. He'd made a decent job of repairing the boat, but within weeks of lowering its patched-up hull back into the water, Charlie's grandfather had been diagnosed with lung cancer and was gone within the year.

After his death, the boat was hauled onto a ramp and effectively forgotten about, becoming a strange, light-blue relic fossilizing at the bottom of the family garden until Charlie and Rob, propelled by their plan, made it an evening restoration project. They had worked often well into the night, sometimes through the night, but no one ever suspected that the boat might actually float, let alone achieve a princely twelve knots. Now, the *Witch* was on her most daring adventure. One that had to remain absolutely secret.

"Say that again, would you, Constable? It's ruddy noisy where you are."

Barnwell stepped away from the roar of the Caterpillar diesel engine that was warming up. "Sorry, sir. They're saying it's an old boat that was registered years ago but not since. Reckoned it had sunk or was scuppered somewhere."

Graham thought quickly. "So, what's the idea? That someone is using an unregistered boat to commit a crime?"

Barnwell stepped further away as the lifeboat's second diesel lit up. He raised his voice further.

"I'm not sure, sir. But I'll tell you my first thought, if you'll allow some speculation."

"Go for it," Graham told him, reaching for a pen.

"Is there any reason we can think of," Barnwell said, "why someone might be moving an object from land to sea, at this particular moment in time?"

Graham was silent for a moment. "What are you thinking, son?"

"That case, sir. The one you've all been talking about in the office. Beth Ridley. I mean, sir," Barnwell continued, the noise behind him becoming fierce, "that if time were of the essence, perhaps because of an ongoing police investigation, then it might be a rather neat way to dispose of *evidence*, sir."

Finally, it dawned on Graham what Barnwell was suggesting, and he grinned at the new-found investigative prowess of his constable. "Is this where our two investigations find a meeting point, Barnwell?"

"Like I say, sir, it's just speculation. But if I knew the

location of evidence relating to the Beth Ridley case, and knew that my fingerprints or DNA were all over them, I'd certainly consider asking a friend to dump them in the Channel for me."

"Interesting conjecture, Constable. Whether you're right or not, get the lifeboat out there, and tell them not to spare the horses. Or, whatever you say when you need a boat to get a serious move on."

"Yes, sir." *Click.*

Graham put the phone down, looked from Harding to Roach and back again. Then he marched straight to the interview room and flung open the door.

"Detective Inspector..." Sutton began, rising in complaint.

"Lyon, I'm going to ask you this straight. If you answer me in a comprehensive fashion, I might try to persuade the judge from handing down the most horrific of jail sentences."

Sutton blustered, "My client has already asserted his right to remain..."

"Lyon, listen to me," Graham said, staring hard at the pale, terrified man. "Do you have friends who are at sea tonight?"

Lyon blinked a few times, then shook his head.

"The *Sea Witch*. A knackered, old fishing boat. They're out there, right now. Did *you* hire them?" Graham demanded.

Lyon looked at Graham for almost the first time since his arrest. "I have no idea what you're talking about," he said quietly.

"Think carefully now, Mr. Lyon," Graham continued. "Because if we intercept that boat and find something incriminating, you'll spend the rest of your life in the darkest, most horrible hole in the entire United Kingdom, I personally guarantee you of that."

"Andrew, I must remind you," Sutton began once more, "that everything you say in here is part of the record..."

"I have nothing to say," Lyon said, finally.

The image presented itself to Graham of Lyon's bruised, battered face, a horrified Sutton screaming at Graham to stop, and Janice Harding dashing into the room to pull her boss off the whimpering, bleeding Andrew Lyon.

Calm down, Graham warned himself.

Janice appeared at the doorway. "Could you come to the phone, sir?" she asked gingerly.

Graham took a long moment to pull himself away from the table. Part of him still wanted to make Lyon bleed. At length, he straightened up, turned away, and headed to the phone, barely in control of his emotions. Another image flashed into his mind: that of his two year-old daughter sitting in her high chair as he blew soapy bubbles over her head, laughing as she tried to catch them, squinting as they burst on her nose. He pushed the image away.

"Graham," he said distractedly into the receiver.

"Sir, it's Barnwell again." The background noise was different now, a rhythmic sloshing as the *George Sullivan* made its way across the nighttime waves.

"Yes, Constable?" the DI replied, his mind still very much elsewhere.

"I've got something on that boat. You remember I put in a report about some shoplifting from the store by the marina?"

Graham's mind swam slowly back to the present moment. "Shoplifting?" he asked.

"Paint, sir. That special stuff they use on boats, to stop the hulls from..."

"Yes, I remember," he said. "A few days ago. What of it?"

His boss sounded stressed, so Barnwell cut to the chase. "The description of the boat we're chasing. The *color* of the paint, sir. It's the same color as that on the hull of the *Sea Witch*.

"I'm not *following* you, son," Graham said tersely.

"Sir, the two men who did the shoplifting that day... The men I chased from the marina... This boat. I think they are connected."

"What?" Graham said.

"The marina thieves, sir," Barnwell said. "*They're* the crew of the *Sea Witch*. They've been nicking gear for weeks. Radar, GPS, maps, paint, all the things you'd need to re-fit an old boat and then navigate to a point only they know where."

"Navigate?" Graham said, the cogs of his mind only just beginning to revolve usefully again. "Navigate *where*? And *why*?"

"I don't know, sir, but we're on their tail. We'll find out."

CHAPTER TWENTY-FOUR

T HE SOUND ARRIVED unexpectedly, and it
was as dreadful as it was worrying.

"Jesus, Mary, and Joseph," Charlie spluttered. The steady droning of the engine, which had been
a reassuring bass line throughout their journey, was interrupted by a horrendous, metallic clanging, as though an
elementary school percussion ensemble had taken
delivery of a large bag of hammers.

"Shut it off!" Rob yelled. Charlie's hands were
already at the engine controls, throttling back the ancient
diesel and allowing it to stall. "What the hell, man?"

A plume of black smoke arose from the diesel engines,
illuminated now by two powerful lamps that Charlie
turned toward the stern. He swore colorfully.

"Okay, okay. We can fix it, right? We've got the tool
box, haven't we?"

They did indeed, but in the dark and with the engine
still scorching hot, it would not be an easy task.

Fifteen minutes later, sweating, angry, and in pain

from the scorch marks he'd picked up from brushing against hot metal, Rob stood up.

"Try her again," he cried to Charlie, who was at the controls. Charlie turned the engine over. Nothing. Rob threw down his screwdriver, "Godammit!"

Charlie came outside, and the pair stared at the motor as though demanding that it explain itself. Rob walked to the bow of the small fishing boat. "Let's face it, Charlie," he finally said. "It's over. Time to call for help."

Charlie stared at Rob, then lurched forward grabbing his friend by the collar of his waterproofs. "Are you serious? What are we going to do? We have too much riding on this to give up now! How the bloody hell are we going to explain what we are doing out here, eh?"

Rob shrugged. "We tell them the truth."

Charlie snorted. "Oh, great! Terrific! That's just *vintage* Robbie, that is. Absolutely classic. Let's call up the Coast Guard and tell them everything. Maybe ask them to bring the police, too! Make a *real* party of it!" Charlie gestured wildly at the dark sky. "Maybe just ask them to take us straight to jail and be done with it. Why bother messing around with a trial? Do not pass 'Go,' do not collect two hundred pounds, just end up banged up for theft and God knows what else..."

Rob stared impassively in the face of Charlie's tantrum. "We have no choice unless we want to die out here."

Charlie took another breath, ready to continue, but the look on his friend's face stopped him. The breath left him in a long sigh of resignation. "Sorry, Rob, lad. I didn't mean all that, mate. I'm just, you know, with the...We'll get *crucified*."

"I know. But it's over, Charlie." Rob sighed. "Let's

radio for help." As he turned there was a sloshing sound at his feet. The two youths looked down and then at each other in alarm.

The boat was taking on water.

Sergeant Janice Harding remained determined to project an air of professionalism throughout this trying night, but she couldn't help enjoying the *Schadenfreude* that came from locking a cell door on Andrew Lyon.

"Now, you just keep quiet like a good boy," she chided, "and once DI Graham is free again, I'm sure he'll have you brought up for further questioning." She had already deprived Lyon of his belt, and their recently-installed CCTV system would free her to observe Lyon's incarceration from the reception area.

She returned there to join Roach, who was helping liaise with the lifeboat dispatcher at St. Helier. The Coast Guard helicopter from Lee-On-Solent was on standby in case of trouble, and the dispatcher told them that there was even a Royal Navy warship that could be there in ninety minutes, complete with a helicopter full of heavily armed Royal Marines, if necessary. Janice didn't anticipate they would be required, but it was clear that whoever was piloting the *Sea Witch* for whatever reason, was in for a very rough night.

The phone rang. Janice listened for a few seconds and started taking notes.

"Right, ma'am. I'll send someone out to you as soon as we can...Yes, ma'am...We will...Thank you... Yes."

As soon as she put the phone down, she turned to Roach.

"Guess what? Report of a stolen boat." She ripped off a page from her notebook and handed it to Roach. "Get yourself down there, lad. Might be the one Barnwell is chasing. Let us know what you find out."

"But, Sarge, I was just about to go home, I've got to be on a plane in a few hours."

"Sorry, Roachie, but this is what real policing's all about. All hands on deck and that." She smiled at her own little witticism as Roach slapped on his police cap and made his way outside.

With Janice manning the phones and radio and Constable Roach dispatched to check out the missing boat report, Graham found himself with little more to do than speculate on what on earth might happen next.

"What if it's Ann Leach making a run for it?" Janice put forth. "You know, she got wind that we're about to pull the plug on her charity and decided to do a runner with the rest of the money."

Graham regarded her with a mix of skepticism and obvious amusement. "Sergeant, if you ever tire of police work, you might try your hand at writing mystery novels."

"You're too kind, sir."

"Besides," Graham added, "how could she know that we've discovered so much about her financial situation?" When Janice shrugged, Graham raised a finger, his eyes wide. "Aha! Jack Wentworth! He's secretly playing for both sides!"

Janice blushed a little. "Leave Jack out of it, sir. He's doing no such thing."

Graham's serious demeanor gradually returned. "I mean, it could be a lot more innocent. Just two idiots taking a boat out for a joyride."

"At night?" Janice pointed out.

"Sure," Graham replied. "Nice and quiet, a bit of fresh air..."

"In winter?" she said next.

It was Graham's turn to shrug. "Alright. People traffickers, how about that? You know, those gangs who bring in migrants for exorbitant fees. They've got a boat load of refugees, and they're trying to make it to the mainland."

"Via Jersey?" Harding said.

Graham thought quickly. "Just for a refueling stop."

"What about drug-running?" Harding asked.

"Oh, good one," Graham said. Then he paused for a moment. "Has there been much of that around here?"

Before Janice could answer, the phone went again. Graham picked it up, glad for something to do.

"Roach." Graham listened for a moment. "You're where? Shelton Avenue?" And then he groaned. "Hodgson."

Janice recognized the name. "The lad who's always wandering off at night? Is he missing again?" she asked.

Graham listened for another minute, thanked the Constable, and replaced the receiver. "Well, I'll be a monkey's uncle. Charlie Hodgson and his mate, Rob Boyle are missing, along with their boat."

"My father used to swear he'd put a lock on the *outside* of my bedroom door if I..." Janice began, but noticed that her boss was deep in thought. "Sir?"

He looked up at her. "There's bad news, and there's bad news."

"Bad news first, please," Janice said.

"Our theory about intercepting the imminent disposal of the remaining Beth Ridley evidence and wrapping the case up beyond a shadow of a doubt appears to have fallen apart," he said. "There's no way that these two are involved in something like that. They're seventeen and barely have a functioning brain cell between them."

Janice breathed a loud and sincere sigh of disappointment.

"And the other bad news?"

"They have about as much seafaring experience as I have."

"How much is that, sir?"

"None."

CHAPTER TWENTY-FIVE

"RIGHTO, SIR, I'LL tell them," Barnwell said into the radio. He had earlier ruefully considered that after all his high tech efforts down at the marina, it was a simple sighting by a fisherman setting up for an early start the next day that had set them on the trail of the rogue boat. Now his hopes of solving the Beth Ridley case had come to naught, too. It just didn't seem fair.

The lifeboat crew consisted of volunteer, well-trained mariners with the Royal National Lifeboat Institute, whose mission was to help those in distress around the British coastline. They had been called out by the Jersey Coast Guard. It was too dark and windy for the spotter plane to be of any use, and the mainland helicopter was too far away.

"Understood," Will Ryan, the captain of the lifeboat said after Barnwell explained what he'd learned from Graham about the identities of the two they were chasing. "I'm not a gambling man," Ryan explained, "but I'd wager a bottle of scotch that the *Sea Witch* is not having a good time. From your description, it sounds like she should have stayed on her boat ramp. I just hope we get there in time."

Ryan imagined their troubles while scratching a bushy, brown beard that his wife had once described as "enthusiastic."

The *George Sullivan*, named after the lifeboat's designer, ploughed handily through the waves, keeping up a brisk but not yet nausea-inducing twenty-six knots. She was a capable, 53-foot vessel, in the unmistakable orange of the RNLI, with two powerful diesel engines. The crew were seasoned, dedicated volunteers, all holding down jobs on the mainland that allowed them to be called out at any time of the day or night to rescue those who got into trouble out in the cold, coastal water.

The *George Sullivan*'s radar scanned the horizon ahead while a crewman broadcast a repeated message over the emergency channels, requesting the *Sea Witch* respond and cut its engines. So far, there had been no reply.

Barnwell answered his radio once more and then relayed another message to the captain. "One of the young men on the *Sea Witch* has a very irate mother. She'd prefer that we pick him up and bring him home, but 'only if it's not too much trouble,'" Barnwell reported.

"Someone's in for an earful," a crewman observed.

"If he's not drowned himself by now," Barnwell pointed out.

There came a loud, clear call from the lookout positioned on the lifeboat's railing. "*Light ho!*"

Captain Ryan followed the lookout's pointing arm, and saw a tiny glimmer on the horizon. "Good eye, man! Hang on, everyone." The lifeboat lurched as Ryan demanded full power from her twin diesel engines. With a surge of noise and power, the *George Sullivan* rocketed over the waves toward the light, while her radar confirmed that this was a small, seafaring craft and not one of the big container vessels that routinely passed through the channel.

"*Sea Witch*, *Sea Witch*, this is the *George Sullivan*, are you receiving me, over?"

The only reply was static.

"*Sea Witch*, approaching from your northeast. Please cut your engine and signal with a flare."

"I wouldn't be too hopeful," Ryan said. "If they're daft enough to put to sea in a rusted wreck..."

"Actually," Barnwell felt it fair to say, "they nicked a box of flares the other week. And life jackets, for that matter."

The lifeboat's captain gave him a very strange look. "Just what kind of people are these?" he asked, mystified.

"Teenagers," Barnwell replied simply.

"Ah."

"*Sea Witch*, *Sea Witch*, this is the *George Sullivan*. We are to your northeast, five hundred yards and closing. Please signal."

Moments later, as the lifeboat's powerful main light found the cobalt blue vessel, the reason for the lack of reply became obvious. "Oh, hell," Ryan muttered. "She's down at the bow."

Barnwell struggled to view the scene through the front windows. The lifeboat's spotlight caused extraordinary glare, and he could barely make out anything amid the choppy waves. "What does that mean?" he asked, blinking at the sudden brightness.

"She's bloody well sinking," Ryan reported, "just like

I warned you. She won't be above water for much longer. Pete, get on the loudhailer. The crew, for want of a better word, must be around here somewhere. Names?"

"Uh... Barnwell thought for a moment, "Charlie and Rob."

Pete grabbed the ship's bullhorn and headed outside to the railing. Barnwell heard the call, which would have been audible a mile away. "Charlie? Rob? This is the RNLI. Shout if you can hear me!" Pete's day job as a Phys Ed teacher at the high school in St. Helier gave his raised voice an insistent clarity that was impossible to ignore.

Barnwell's radio crackled. "Constable?" He cursed under his breath. Barnwell had promised Graham updates every ten minutes, and he was long overdue.

"Yes, sir. Sorry. We've arrived at the location of the *Sea Witch*, but she's taken on a lot of water. There's no sign of the boys."

Barnwell heard the DI swearing on the radio. "I wish we could do more to help you, son," Graham finally said. "Is there no sign of them at all?"

"Not at the moment, sir, but we're on it. I'll give you an update shortly."

Captain Ryan ordered the boat's engines to be cut, the better to hear faint yells across the water. "Start a search pattern with the light," he ordered. "Focus to the landward of the wreck."

"Why is that?" Barnwell asked. His best recourse, he knew, was to simply stay out of the way, but he also hoped to be helpful.

"Because, nine times out of ten, people moving away from a sinking ship will head in the direction of land, even if it's miles away." Ryan was as anxious for news as he was angry at the two young idiots who had risked their lives in a hopeless vessel. "Why the hell didn't they get a distress call out?"

"Maybe their radio broke," Barnwell offered.

"Well, I'll be very glad to be wrong, Constable, but at the moment it looks as though you and I are going to be delivering some bad news later tonight," Ryan said, thudding the console with a curled fist. "And I bloody well *hate* it, when we lose people out here. And for no reason at all! It's not as though we're trying to get a convoy past the U-boats or navigating through a sodding hurricane. I mean, we're six miles off *Jersey*."

The island was off to their right, little more than a long, thin band of distant lights now.

Pete kept calling as the whole crew silently waited for a response, scanning the seas around them for a sighting of the lads. "Come on, you silly buggers," Barnwell muttered to himself. "Come *on*..."

The light swept back and forth, searching the area north of the sinking boat. "There!" Pete shouted.

Barnwell was at the rail before he knew it. "Where?"

Pete was gesturing with a straight arm. "Three points off port."

That meant little to Barnwell until he saw movement within the cone of light thrown by the big lamp.

"Jesus," he breathed. "Charlie? Rob? Can you hear us!" he called out, as loud as he could.

"Here!" they heard. It was a faint, tense, panicked sound. "Over here!"

The spotlight had picked up Rob, his head and shoulders bobbing above water buoyed by his stolen life jacket.

"Can you see the other one?" Ryan demanded, now ordering the lifeboat's engines to minimal power and steering her toward the flailing teenager.

"Rudder amidships and prepare to cut engines."

As they approached, the *Sea Witch* began her final dive, her silent engines briefly facing the sky as the boat nosedived to the bottom.

"Okay, cut it now." The lifeboat's diesel engine died once more, and Pete tossed a rope to Rob, who immediately grabbed for it. "Good lad! We're pulling you in."

Ryan was becoming more and more agitated. "Where's the *other one*?" he growled. "Get that searchlight moving again!"

It was Barnwell who saw Charlie Hodgson first. "There!" he shouted. "Christ, he's drifted away. Get the..." But before Barnwell could even find the right nautical words, he found himself taking off his shoes and jacket.

"Oi, wait, we've got a..." he heard Pete saying behind him. But Barnwell slung a leg over the railing, took a deep breath, and jumped feet first into the English Channel.

The water was shockingly, unbearably cold. Barnwell surfaced hurriedly and roared out an oath worthy of a seasoned sailor and then swam hard in Charlie's direction. The ship's light had found the boy now, an incongruous, linear shape in this world of watery curves. He was resting high in the water, his orange life vest inflated, but he was facing away from Barnwell. And he wasn't moving.

Barnwell heard splashes to his left as a rope was tossed into the water. He reached for Charlie's life vest and spun the boy around.

Charlie lolled in the water, unconscious. His eyes were half-closed, only the whites visible. He was ghostly pale. "It's okay, lad. I've got you." Barnwell slid the rope around Charlie's chest, and locked it in place. He signaled to the boat that had come in as close as it could.

Swiftly, the immobile teenager was dragged through the freezing water and pulled to safety. One member of the lifeboat crew immediately began chest compressions while the other prepared to winch Barnwell in.

Another rope was thrown to Barnwell. He grabbed it with frozen hands and locked it around his chest but as he turned and began to swim, he felt a strong tug as his line went taut before it slackened as the locking mechanism gave way. The rope was gone, splashing uselessly across the surface ahead of him.

"Bugger!" He tried to grab it, but he was losing the feeling in his arms. The cold was now seeping deep into him. Barnwell grasped at the surface, trying to push the water down and away, but it always rose again, shoving icy water in his face, chilling him down to the bone.

Dazed, he saw a hazy, fading figure at the rail of the lifeboat. Something flew into the air, but he hadn't the strength to follow it. His legs felt unbearably heavy, his soaked clothes acting as anchors and dragging him down. He found that he was all but motionless, hovering above a chasm of freezing darkness that was pulling at him, insisting, demanding, tugging harder and harder...

Slap.

It was sudden, rude, and harsh.

"Again," came a voice.

Slap.

"Oi!" Barnwell grumbled indistinctly. "Wossat all about, then?"

Slap.

"Stop!" he finally roared, his eyes blinking open as he raised himself up, only to find his progress impeded by four strong hands.

"Take it easy, Constable." It was Pete and another crewman whose name he hadn't learned. "You're going to be fine."

"Where am..." But he heard the sounds at once; the noise of the diesel motors, the waves sliding under the hull and lapping at the sides of the *George Sullivan*. Then came warm applause from the lifeboat crew.

"Welcome back, son," Will Ryan said, handing Barnwell a big mug of steaming hot coffee. "Drink this. Slowly," he warned.

Barnwell sat up on the comfortably padded stretcher that he had been laid on. Next to him were Rob and Charlie, pale and silent but conscious. Lifeboatman Pete helped to keep the thermal blanket wrapped around his chest and shoulders as the wet, chilled Constable reached out to take the mug. Though his features felt like they were chiseled from a block of ice, he managed a grin of gratitude. "Thanks, Captain."

The older man chuckled. "I hope you're not a teetotaler or anything, 'cos there's an enormous tot of navy rum in there."

Barnwell noticed the aroma immediately, and it seemed to warm his whole being. "Just this once," he said, taking a cautious sip and finding the coffee to be sweet, strong, and excellent, "I think we'll be alright."

CHAPTER TWENTY-SIX

THEY WERE STANDING in front of the converted industrial buildings that were now home to many of Christiania's inhabitants, a four-story, weather-beaten place with plenty of greenery planted outside. A couple of dogs were asleep in its shade.

"Can't say I've ever been anywhere quite like this before," Roach admitted.

"Can't say I have, either," Graham said. "Probably because this place is unique in all the world."

Christiania, they'd found out via the Internet the evening before, was a self-administered commune, right in the center of Denmark's capital city. Its independence was protected by the state, and the commune enjoyed the freedom to decide some of its own laws. This, as the two officers had instantly noticed upon arriving, included the legal and public consumption of marijuana.

"Can we, you know," Roach asked a little awkwardly, "get a bit high from just being here?"

"Why do you ask, Constable?" Graham replied with a

slight smile. He checked his phone once more. "Are we completely sure this is the right building?"

"I'm pretty sure this time," said Roach.

Graham had instructed Roach not to wear a uniform or any insignia today, leaving him feeling odd and slightly naked. They were well outside of their jurisdiction, and Graham was keen to carry out this most delicate part of the investigation without unnecessary fuss. In this part of the city more than any other, uniforms would attract unwelcome attention and suspicion.

After working all through Sunday and into the early hours of Monday morning confirming that Constable Barnwell and the two teens were safe, Graham and Roach boarded a plane to London and from there another to Copenhagen. Both of them dozed off on each leg of the trip.

They awoke for the final time as the second aircraft landed smoothly in what was a considerably wet and dreary Copenhagen. Feeling as dreadful as the weather, they caught a taxi into the city center and immediately decamped to a local café. There they found the buttery, sweet pastries and steaming, strong coffee overcame their fatigue as they strategized the next part of their mission.

Roach had been in favor of informing their Danish counterparts of their visits and told Graham so during the previous evening. Graham had overruled him, and by the time they landed, he had persuaded Roach of the virtues of a more clandestine approach.

"If it really is Beth," Graham had reminded the younger officer, "we've got no idea what her status is in Denmark. She might be staying here illegally, or with people who are wanted by the police, or she may even be wanted herself for all we know. If we show up with uniformed Danish cops, she might run, and then we'll never find her again."

Graham rang the intercom button for apartment 452, and only then realized that he had no idea what he was going to say if anyone replied. He blinked for a moment, thinking rapidly.

"*Hvem der?*"

Graham cleared his throat. "Er, yes. I'm here to visit Bettina," Graham said. "Erm. We're, erm..." *Get it together, Dave, for heaven's sake.* "I called this morning?"

He'd called an automated service organized through her website, which let him leave a voicemail message. She had responded with a short email.

"The Englishman?" the voice asked. Bettina spoke without a distinctive Danish accent.

"Yes, that's right. I made an appointment."

The silence that followed grew so long that it became agonizing. Graham glanced at Roach, who was hopping nervously from foot to foot. In the café, Roach suggested that he might simply reveal himself to be her old classmate, but Graham had scotched that idea, too. His objection wasn't specific. They just couldn't predict even slightly how she might react to being identified after so long. Instead, Graham had pretended to be a potential client. Bettina had advertised herself as an aromatherapist and reiki healer.

Graham reached for the intercom button again. Then, "Come in." *Buzz.*

Graham made a sudden decision, "Constable, I'm going in alone. If you hear nothing from me in thirty minutes, ring the doorbell. If no one answers, call the local police. It's 114 on your phone. Then call Harding. Got it?"

"Got it," Roach replied. He watched his boss enter the building and walk up the first flight of stairs and around a corner.

The place needed a lick of paint, but Graham had been inside the bolt-holes of runaway teenagers and other dislocated types plenty of times, and they'd been far worse than this. The apartment block had a neglected, slightly foreboding feel. He didn't pass a soul.

Short hallways branched off each landing, leading to groups of four apartments on each side. A black cat glared at him as he rounded the corner onto the third-floor landing. The cat shot down the hallway as if to warn someone. Graham shivered and wished once more that it had been possible to bring some kind of weapon, even a can of pepper spray. He also wondered how anyone could run much of a business from a place such as this.

There it was, apartment 452. He knocked softly and waited.

The door opened, its chain still in place. "I'm sorry, I thought the appointment was for later. I'm not quite ready." she said through the gap. Bettina was a tall, attractive woman. Graham guessed she was in her mid-twenties. The right age. Ocean blue eyes. Her hair, though, was an audacious experiment, a kaleidoscope of purple-blue-green-red that formed a psychedelic spiral around her face.

"I can come in and wait." Graham had wondered whether a casual or a formal tone would sound better, and ended up lapsing into his usual, deferential politeness.

"Alright," she said resignedly, and the chain slid back. "But, like I said, nothing's ready."

"That's really not a problem."

The apartment was neat, airy, and well-kept. Plants

adorned every shelf in the kitchen, where there were dozens of cookbooks and a surrealist sculpture of the Eiffel tower, swollen and deranged but oddly transfixing. Off the kitchen was a bedroom, its door mostly closed. Opposite the small kitchen island sat a thoroughly beaten-up leather sofa and some bean bags. If he didn't know better, he'd have taken it for a shared student apartment.

"Sit here for a moment while I set up my therapy room." The woman looked over toward another door, completely closed this time, to the right of the bedroom.

"Erm, no, please," Graham demurred, "Could we just talk for a moment?"

"I'll just—"

"No, really."

She looked at Graham quizzically, considering him, then walked to a tall barstool at the kitchen island and gestured for him to sit on a second one. She reached for a half-consumed joint that lay in a thick, glass ashtray.

"So?" she asked, "What do you want to talk to me about?" She lit up and now regarded Graham with a genuine curiosity. He didn't look like a regular customer. He was too straight-laced, too "establishment." If anything came across in those first moments with this tall British visitor, it was *loneliness*. "You know, most of the people who come here are pregnant women and their boyfriends," she said.

"They are?" Graham asked, wondering how he was going to begin.

"Yeah, you know. People who are looking for a different way to relax. I use aromatherapy and the power of touch, sometimes crystals, to restore balance and sweep away stress in the body."

Graham smiled slightly. "We could all use a little of that, I suppose."

"Were you looking for something in particular?" she asked. Her deep, blue eyes were pleasant and welcoming, the kind he normally associated with peace-loving hippies and mind-blown festival-goers. There was nothing in them that spoke of trauma or loss. He cringed inwardly at the thought that he might still, after all of this, be speaking to entirely the wrong woman.

"I've actually just come from Jersey," he began.

Bettina puffed out a cloud of smoke. "Oh, yeah?"

Graham watched for any signs of recognition, but she was either hiding her reaction or had never given the Bailiwick any thought. He plowed on.

"I've been there for a few months, and recently I was asked to investigate something that happened there a few years ago."

Now she paused. He was certain he saw it. A little hiatus in the way she lifted the joint to her lips. "Investigate?" she asked.

"Yes, there was an anniversary, recently," Graham explained, "of the day a local girl went missing. A school-girl, only fifteen years old."

Bettina took another puff but said nothing. Her eyes left Graham and roamed the room. She had begun to look just a little on edge.

"No one had any idea what happened to her," Graham continued. "Her mother has been searching, all these years," he added, very aware of the risk in bringing Ann up so early in this complex interview and choosing not to use her name. "And other people too, her friends and family, everyone's just desperate to know what happened to her."

The woman stubbed out the joint carefully. "And have you found out?" she asked as she watched the smoke rise in a final grey curl.

"I think I'm beginning to understand what happened, yes," Graham said. "But I was wondering if you might be able to help me."

She was breathing faster now.

"Help you?" she asked. "In what way? How has any of that to do with me?"

Graham took a breath. He was too far in to back out now.

"Because I believe you to be Elizabeth Ridley, formerly of Gorey, Jersey who disappeared on Monday November 7th, 2005."

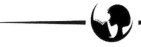

S HE LOOKED AT him squarely. "Don't be ridiculous. I am Bettina Nisted. I grew up in Aarhus. I moved to Copenhagen three years ago."

"I don't believe that's true," Graham replied. She was cool, he'd give her that.

"Of course, it is."

Graham raised an eyebrow but said nothing for a moment.

"Miss Nisted, facial recognition software and age progression imaging techniques, as well as testing on various biometrics such as fingerprints, your ears, or the irises of your eyes, will prove beyond a doubt whether you are Beth or Bettina," Graham said, his gaze level, watching her reactions closely. "But they are expensive techniques, and they take time. Besides, I suspect your mother would know you at a glance. It would be better if you'd simply tell me the truth." He paused, but seeing no reaction from the woman in front of him, he continued, "Perhaps you can tell me why you came here."

She stood suddenly, the stool skidding away from

under her with a metallic shriek. "*Came* here?" she said loudly. "You think I *chose* to come here of my own free will?"

Graham was caught in a whirlwind of emotion, but as the furious woman stood there before him, red-faced now with anger, the sensation he felt most keenly was one of the very sweetest relief.

He stood then, both palms face down as he sought to calm her, "Beth, I know you didn't choose to come here."

"Don't call me that," she spat.

"I'm sorry. Bettina. I've been investigating what happened to you."

"You shouldn't have come here." She reached into her pocket for her phone. "You're going to get me into trouble."

"Andrew Lyon is at my police station in a holding cell," he said.

Everything stopped. Her hands were still. She couldn't take her eyes off Graham now. "A *cell?*" she asked. She was silent for a moment, and Graham wondered if she was picturing the scene. "You're the police?"

Graham brought out his wallet and showed her his ID. "Detective Inspector David Graham of the Gorey Constabulary," he said.

"Gorey," she said, as if finding the word in her mind for the first time in many years. "You're from Gorey?"

"I head the local police unit there," Graham explained.

"And... You've arrested him? Cat?"

"Yes," Graham confirmed. "We have him, and we're not going to let him go. We just didn't understand what had happened to you and... well, with no evidence, we feared the very worst."

Her expression changed yet again. "Well, I'm alive. But nobody can know I'm here," she said resolutely. "You *mustn't* tell *anyone*." The final words came out in a hiss.

Graham held up his hands. "Absolutely. It's your right, and I'll abide by whatever you say."

She stared for a moment assessing him, then sat back down, and took a deep breath. "Does my mother know?"

"No," Graham said quickly. "You can tell her if you want to. But she doesn't know we're here or even that we're following a lead that you might still be alive."

The young woman pursed her lips and wrapped her arms around her waist.

Graham felt as though he were treading on deep wounds that were covered with shards of glass, any slight misstep threatening to not only re-open old injuries, but also to cut them deeper. "Your mother gave us access to your old journal. She thought it might be helpful."

"My journal?" she said, as though she hadn't thought about it in years.

"Beth, we've been carrying out two investigations. One was into Andrew Lyon's past and his use of the Internet. He's in a lot of trouble."

This time, she didn't react to his use of her name.

"He should die for what he did to Susan," she said simply. She saw Graham's look of surprise.

"Oh, she thought I didn't know, but I did. You should help him hang himself or something."

Graham moved swiftly on. "And then, I'm afraid, we've had to take a closer look at the charity your mother has been running."

"I saw something about it. All those investigators and

researchers. I was afraid they might find me." She paused. "She's been stealing, hasn't she?"

He blinked for a second before telling her, "Yes, it looks very much as though she has."

"Typical."

"How so?" Graham asked.

Beth snorted derisively. "Because she's a liar and a cheat, and she never thinks about anyone except herself. I knew that Gorey, my mother, and Lyon weren't going to just vanish. But I wish they would."

B ETH STARED OUT of the window. The view beyond was horizontally dissected by the faux wood blinds. "I did hope Lyon might die before I ever heard his name again," she said.

She didn't sound malicious. It was more as though she were convinced that the universe, in its own sweet time, would discover and punish Andrew Lyon for all he had done.

"An investigation is ongoing," Graham told her, "but try as we might, Lyon hasn't been persuaded to tell us anything about you. Or about his relationship with Susan Miller."

There was another dismissive, unimpressed snort. "*Relationship*? Oh, please. It wasn't roses and candles, you know. He didn't wine and dine her. He groomed her, made her trust him. I guess she told you the rest."

"Yes, but she won't testify against him," Graham pointed out.

"I'm not surprised. The media, everyone in Gorey, the

whole of Jersey would be all over her, and it's the last thing she deserves.

"I need to ask you something, but please take your time," Graham began.

"How did I come to be in Denmark?"

"Yes."

Graham brought out his notebook, his mind filled with equal measures of curiosity and dread.

"One minute, I was on my way to school, trying to decide if I had time to drop my doll off for repair. The next, I was blindfolded and in the back of a van being driven somewhere."

Graham's gut knotted. "What then?"

"A day or so later, I'm not sure, the door opened, and I was pulled out into a muddy field. There was a conversation in a language I didn't understand, and then I was shoved in another car and driven to a house in the countryside. Training, they called it, at first. Then "work." she said simply. "Lots of threats, lots of men, lots of foreign languages. They never hit me, but they used drugs and coercion, and they told me lie after lie. I didn't know which way was up."

She sighed.

"I can't remember a lot of it. Blocked it, I suppose. I prefer to focus on my future."

Graham leaned forward, his elbow leaning on the island, his hands clasped. "I appreciate you telling me this," he said quietly.

"Oh, I've been through it all before," she said, matter-of-factly.

Graham blinked.

"With the Danish police. Seven years ago, now. I told

them everything, right down to the names I heard, the addresses I thought I'd been taken to, everything."

Graham could barely believe what he was hearing. "But they never contacted the British authorities," he said. "There wasn't a *word* about you."

"Good! I made them promise not to."

"But *why*?" Graham asked. It came out as a desperate plea. "Why would you want to stay here and not go home to your family and friends? Or even let them know you're alive?"

She made him wait for an answer, looking out of the window again. "They've got this special unit, for informants or witnesses, whatever you'd call me, and they cut me a deal."

"A *deal*?" Graham asked. The very thought that Beth had been free but unwilling to let her family and friends know, bothered him intensely. *Not every daughter gets the chance to come back and make her parents' lives whole again.*

"I asked for a passport, a new identity, the lease on this place," she said, glancing at the kitchen, "and some money."

"And in return?" Graham asked.

"I helped them take down a bunch of sickos. They're all in jail now," she said, simply.

"A trafficking ring." Graham said gravely. "You took a huge risk, testifying against them."

"I guess. But it was a good deal, and I knew I had to take it. There's no way I could go home, not after all this."

"But why not? Gorcy is full of people who love and miss you."

She shook her head. "They *did*. But what would they

say to me now? What looks would I get in the street? What would they mutter to each other down at the pub?"

Graham said nothing. He wanted to think the best of the community, but he had to concede that Beth would have had the most difficult time. The story of her abduction would follow her everywhere, through college, and into job interviews and the workplace.

"It would have taken time, but they'd have got over it," he said. But in his heart, he knew how ambitious that was.

"No, no they wouldn't. They are small town people. I would have had years of strange encounters with old friends, people who could barely look me in the eye. There would be rumors. Terrible, awful, lurid rumors. And then I'd have left anyway and started somewhere new. At least I know that I like it here. The people are kind. It's cold and dark in the winter, but I'm used to that, now."

After a long moment's thought, Graham admitted, "Perhaps you're right. There's bravery and standing up for the truth, and then there's having to live your life, knowing every day what people are secretly thinking about you. I wouldn't wish such a life on anyone."

He closed his notebook. "But what about your mother?"

Another shake of the head. Graham saw that this was an issue long since decided in Beth's mind. For him, her mother was real and present, someone they'd spoken to and investigated. But for this brave young woman, Ann was the distant past, to be set aside and forgotten. "You know, I did look her up. I saw that she'd moved and had a larger house. Probably three times what our old family home was worth. Her and Chris could never have afforded one like that. So, I had a look on that 'street view' thing on the Internet. And I saw those posters in the window. About the foundation."

Graham nodded. "They're still there, in her window."

"That's not a foundation or a charity," Beth said, her voice bitter now, "or anything to do with finding me. That's an *advertisement* for attention on behalf of a lonely, scared old woman who never learned how to make her own way."

Graham was silent, letting Beth's pent-up anger flow.

"My mother was always so insecure, always presenting this image of herself as the perfect parent, hostess, and backbone of the local community. But cross her, and she'd turn into witch. Most people wouldn't believe the things she said to me when I didn't do or say or look as she wanted. If I didn't support this image of her that she so badly needed to uphold, I was nothing to her. She needed a husband for that image, too, but the first got himself sent down, and the second was a no-hoper. And then he died, didn't he?"

"Yes, two years ago," Graham told her.

Beth showed no grief whatsoever at this piece of news. "All the more reason for her to lean on people, to guilt them into helping her. Did you know the foundation's website reckons they've got 'active investigations' going on?"

"Yes, we saw that," Graham said.

"Well, here I am!" she exclaimed. "You found me after a bit of good police work. *Ten years later*, my mum's 'investigators' haven't been within a hundred miles of me. There's been no one asking questions or trying to get me to come home or anything. You should arrest her."

"You *want* us to arrest your own mother?"

"She's spent ten years dining out on the worst thing

that ever happened to me. I'd say she deserves what's coming to her."

Graham conceded the point. "Beth, we're ready to take action against your mother, but what do you want us to tell her about you?"

She shrugged. "As little as possible." She had calmed down now. She fidgeted for a moment. "Tell her I'm alive. That I'm happy. And that I'm never coming home."

Graham's first instinct was to try to help put the family back together, to act as a mediator between an angry daughter and a deeply flawed mother, but he knew utter conviction when he saw it, and he let the thought pass without comment.

"I have someone else with me. He is waiting outside."

"Who is he?" Beth asked. "Another cop?"

Graham nodded. "We both spent time with your mother, investigating what might have happened to you, and... The other officer is a friend of yours. The young man I believe you used to call 'Bug.'"

Beth was stunned far beyond words.

"Would you like me to call him? I know he'd love to see you again."

She managed, at length, to nod slightly. Graham saw a flicker of guileless innocence cross her face. He pressed a button to send the text he'd prepared earlier.

"Beth... or Bettina, if you'd prefer?"

"Beth..." she cleared her throat, "Call me Beth."

The intercom buzzed. Beth rose to walk across the room and press the button on a wall panel by the door. She looked at the small grey box, hesitating for a moment before glancing up at the ceiling, her hand in mid-air as though considering the wisdom of what she was about to do. Then she covered the button with her finger, giving it a long, definitive press. She said nothing as she returned to her stool.

"It's been ten years," she said, "and I look a sight."

"Please don't worry. He'll just be so glad to see that you're alright."

She was at the door before the knock came, and then it was open, and she was beaming shyly at him. "Hey, Bug."

Roach's eyes shone. "Hey, Barbie."

Graham averted his eyes during the very long hug that followed. His eyes lighted on the joint languishing forgotten in the ashtray. His hand gave a tiny twitch.

"I can't believe it." Roach pulled back to look at her. "You're even prettier than you used to be."

"Oh, stop it," Beth said, waving him away. "You're *tall*," she marveled. "I'd never have thought it."

"Give a man ten years, and he'll grow a bit," Roach said, before dropping his voice, his expression serious. "We've all been so worried about you. Out of our minds."

Beth made to speak, but Roach shushed her, looking at her carefully. "You don't have to say anything now, if you don't want to."

She waved him over to the much-abused leather couch, and there they sat, catching up on old times and old friends. Tactfully, Graham made his way outside for a breath of fresh air, although if he were honest, he'd much have preferred a cup of tea.

An hour later, Graham knocked on the apartment door.

"We have to make a move. We have a plane to catch."

"Yes, of course," Beth replied, and Roach made a

move for the door. "You say you've got Lyon under arrest?"

"Yes," Graham said. "We think we can get him between six and eight years in jail for his Internet crimes, especially if we get the right jury and a judge who takes a sufficiently dim view of that sort of thing. We could get more, if you would..."

Beth ignored him but reached for Roach and pulled him into a hug. "Thanks for coming. It was so good to see you."

"You too." Jim whispered. He blinked rapidly, his lips trembling. "Take care, Barbie."

"One last thing, Inspector," Beth turned to Graham. "You're wrong about one thing. It wasn't Mr. Lyon who kidnapped me."

Graham stared at her, time standing still.

"Then who did?"

"Mr. Grant. He's the headmaster now, I believe."

CHAPTER TWENTY-NINE

ONCE AGAIN, GRAHAM, Roach, and Harding worked through the night. They called in Jack, and he sat alongside them in a t-shirt and sweatpants, having been brought from his bed.

Before they left Copenhagen, Beth had told Graham what happened.

"He did his student teacher training at our school the previous year. He had digs with Mrs. Devizes, two streets down from ours and would sometimes walk home with me if I'd stayed late to do my homework in the library. When he joined the school as a teacher the following year, I didn't have classes with him, but that morning, I recognized his voice. It was definitely him. Irish."

After a consultation with the Chief Constable, a pre-dawn raid was swiftly executed at the home of the head-master of Gorey Grammar.

Graham and Harding led the charge, backed up by three constables drafted in at short notice from St. Helier. They found Grant asleep in bed. He put up no resistance and was driven away quietly from his home without disturbing the neighbors.

Now, Graham looked at him from across the table in the interview room. Next to Graham sat Janice Harding. The headmaster looked bleary-eyed and was blinking rapidly, the early morning light catching the gray in his stubble. His hands, placed one on top of the other, were on the table, relaxed.

"So, Mr. Grant, tell me about your association with Beth Ridley."

"There is none. I told you before, I never taught her."

"But you lived near to her, did you not?"

"Gorey is a small place. Everyone lives close to one another here."

"You are obfuscating. Why would you do that, Mr. Grant?"

"Oh, I'm sorry. I don't mean to. Must be the early hour. I'm happy to help however I can, but I fear that isn't much."

"So you keep saying. You have nothing to do with Beth Ridley's disappearance, then?"

"Of course not. Absolutely none."

Graham turned over a page that was in a folder in front of him. He wanted to keep this interview moving. Grant had had a long time to perfect his story.

"Tell me about your movements on the morning of her disappearance."

The headmaster let out a deep breath. He started to explain. "It was just an ordinary day. I got up. I was renting a room on Bryony Road. Had my usual breakfast of cereal and a mug of tea, then I left for work. I was an English teacher back then. It was my first year."

"What time did you leave the house?"

"I always got up at seven and liked to be at school by eight to prepare my classroom before school started. It was about a twenty minute walk so I'd always leave at seven forty, or thereabouts."

Graham got out his phone and looked on a map, tracing the route from Bryony Road to the school.

"The majority of your route was the same as Beth's, including the spot at which she disappeared."

"So? I repeat, I had nothing to do with her disappearance. I didn't even see her."

"You didn't see her." Graham repeated. "Did you see the leg?"

"The leg?"

"Yes, the leg of the doll that was left in the street. The only trace of Beth that was left behind."

"No," Grant replied. "I had already been and gone from that spot by the time she went missing."

"So you didn't see Beth at all?"

"No."

"Okay, tell me about your phone records."

With Jack's help, they had gathered Grant's phone records from ten years ago. It had been a feat of almost superhuman endurance taking nearly the whole night, but he'd eventually cracked it, to Janice's delight and Graham's eternal gratitude.

"They show you made a phone call at 8:16 on that morning. What was that about?"

"I forget. It was a long time ago. Nothing important."

"But a student from your school disappearing isn't a common occurrence. Surely you remember what happened that morning."

"No, sorry. Not that."

Graham rapidly switched tack again.

"Your bank records, Mr. Grant."

"Yes, what about them?"

"You were badly in debt, weren't you? Why was that?"

"Oh, you know, I was young. Living beyond my means, student debt, that kind of thing. That's all an unpleasant memory, now."

Graham looked hard at the man across the table. Grant was wearing a pair of jeans and a red t-shirt that advertised a local hardware store across his chest. On his feet were flip-flops. His hair was short, and he looked a little disheveled after his rude awakening, but otherwise he seemed unruffled. He didn't show any signs of anxiety or concern. Certainly nothing that Graham would like to see. Some sign of guilt.

"Brand new teacher to headmaster in ten years, Mr. Grant. That's some ambition you've got there."

"Not really. Not if you work hard and get some lucky breaks. I've been very fortunate."

"What drives you, Mr. Grant? What are your ambitions?"

"Oh, you know, same as most other people, I expect. A nice house, car, professional respect. I like to see the kids get a good education."

Grant said this all with a straight face, looking directly at Graham.

"Okay, Mr. Grant. We'll leave it there for a while. Let's take a break. I'll come back for a chat later."

Graham switched the tape off and left the room. As he walked into his office, he fought the impulse to punch the filing cabinet.

"He's not giving us an inch, sir. What's the next step?" Harding said.

"Give me a timeline, Sergeant."

"Well sir, we know that Beth left the house just after eight o'clock. Updike saw her at 8:15. Susan normally met her at 8:20 but she didn't show up. Everything points to her going missing in the intervening five minute period between being seen by Updike and not arriving at her meeting point. The location of the doll's leg confirms it, sir."

"What about Grant?"

"Sir?"

"His timeline. What do we know about that?"

"He left the house at 7:40. Got into school at eight."

"He made the phone call at—?"

"Sixteen minutes past eight, sir."

Graham stood at the window of his office and tapped the wooden frame furiously with his pen. Harding wisely waited.

Then, without a word, Graham took off. Harding watched as he grabbed his jacket and walked out into the reception area.

"Roach?" he barked.

"Yes, sir!" Roach stood to attention at the sound of the DI's voice as he strode across the room.

"Keys!"

Roach spun around, taking the keys to the police vehicle from their hook and throwing them smartly across the room. He watched with satisfaction as his boss caught them equally smartly with one hand and strode out of the station without stopping.

CHAPTER THIRTY

GRAHAM DROVE SWIFTLY, and as he passed through the gates of Gorey Grammar, he looked around for the visitor parking spaces. He jumped out of the car and quickly trotted up the steps to the school.

Inside, he made his way to the school secretary's office and rapped on the door. Mrs. Gates looked up from her computer screen.

"DI Graham! Good to see you again. Can I help you with anything?"

"I certainly hope so, Mrs. Gates.

"You didn't see Mr. Grant outside, did you? School has started, and there's no sign of him. No message either. Most unlike him. I'm getting worried."

Graham sidestepped her question, not wanting to impart that he knew exactly where her employer was.

"Mrs. Gates, what time does Mr. Grant typically make it in?"

"Oh, he's normally here at eight. We get in around the same time. We're both creatures of habit.

"Who opens up the school?"

"The caretaker unlocks the school and classrooms, but Mr. Grant and I have keys to our own offices. Whichever of us gets in first opens them both. I've worked with my heads of school like that for years."

"I wonder if I can ask you to cast your mind back, Mrs. Gates. To the day Beth Ridley disappeared. What happened that morning?"

"Well, let's see. Most of the teachers pass by my office and say good morning." Mrs. Gates tapped her chin with her forefinger. "It was a long time ago, but of course, I've gone over the day in my mind many times."

Graham let her think in silence, even though he was desperate to hurry her up.

"Mr. Bellevue was off sick. With hindsight, it was an early sign of his heart problem, but we didn't know that then. Oh, it was so embarrassing. You see, I'd forgotten my key! Most unusual! I couldn't open our offices. I had to go home for it. When I got back to school, there were parents and students waiting for me in the corridor outside my office."

"So you missed seeing the teachers come in to work?"

"Yes, most of them."

Graham sighed. He felt the energy drain out of him.

"Except for Mr. Grant."

"Oh?"

"I remember because he walked up the steps with me."

Graham pounced. "And what time was that?"

"8:32 precisely."

"Are you quite sure?" Graham felt blood rush to his face.

"I'm positive. I pride myself on my punctuality and

when I saw those parents waiting for me, I looked up at the clock to see how late I was. I had to apologize to them profusely. I've only been late three times in twenty years, so I remember exactly how late I was. Thirty-two minutes."

DI Graham stormed back into the police station.

"Harding! We're going back in."

"Yes, sir!"

Back in the room, Grant jumped as the door to the interview room opened.

"Mr. Grant, you told me earlier that you arrived at school at eight o'clock as usual. Fifteen minutes before the final sighting of Beth Ridley."

"Yes, that's right."

"But you didn't, did you?"

"Didn't what?"

"We have a witness who says you were late that day. She says you didn't arrive until after half past eight. She's prepared to testify to that. What do you say?"

Grant didn't say a thing.

"Mr. Grant, it is in your best interests to tell us exactly what happened that morning."

Still nothing. Grant merely blinked back at him.

Graham tried again, "Mr. Grant, I believe that you were deeply in debt and were looking for a way out. We can place you at the spot where Beth disappeared. You have no alibi. You did, however, make a phone call just after the last sighting of Beth. Were you paid to abduct a girl, Mr. Grant?

"Of course not. What is this?" Grant appealed first to

Janice, then to Graham. Beads of sweat began to appear on his upper lip.

Graham looked squarely into Grant's brown eyes. "We also have Beth's own account of her abduction. She recognized your voice, Mr. Grant. Your accent."

At this, Grant twitched violently.

"She's alive?"

Grant stared at the two police officers in front of him, his eyes switching between them for several moments. His head sunk into his hands. When he looked up again, his face was red, his expression desperate.

Janice and Graham stared back at him, still playing their parts in this game of poker face. Grant turned his face to the wall and closed his eyes before turning back and opening them again. He looked directly at Graham. He still said nothing. Later Graham estimated they faced off for a full thirty seconds.

He began quietly.

"I was using. I started in college. But now I couldn't pay. They needed a girl. A blond girl. They said if I could get one for them, they'd wipe out what I owed. And if I didn't... Well, they didn't specify exactly but you know..." He trailed off. "I thought of Beth. I knew her routine. So I set it up."

"What was the plan?" Graham asked his question quietly.

"They would have a car waiting and I was to call them to initiate the pickup."

"Who were these people?" This time, it was Janice who spoke.

"I don't know, exactly. Contacts of my drug dealer. Cocaine," he added, answering their unspoken question. "On that morning, I left my digs as usual and waited for her. I followed her and made the call when the coast was clear. A car pulled up and I pushed her inside," Grant shrugged.

Janice and Graham waited.

"There was no struggle, but the doll got caught in the car door. The leg must have come off. I didn't notice. They drove away. That was it."

"What did you do then?"

"I carried on walking to school."

Grant glanced across at Harding, who was looking at him impassively, apparently unmoved by his admission. This seemed to light a fire under Grant. He slammed the table with his palms.

"I was in a bad place, okay? I owed them money. A lot of money. God knows what they would have done to me!" Grant was shouting now. "I didn't have a choice!"

He stopped and lay his head on the table in front of him. The room was silent except for the faint sound of seagulls screeching overhead.

Graham considered for a moment the contrast between the freewheeling, seaside bird and the shaking, terrified wretch before him, but unable to feel any sympathy, he clicked off the tape and left the room.

CHAPTER THIRTY-ONE

AN ELDERLY COUPLE waited patiently in the reception area, trying to ignore the inconsolable wailing coming from the interview room a few yards away.

"I'm sorry to keep you waiting," Constable Roach told them, doing his best to bring some brightness to the room amid the sound of the woman's distress. "I'm hoping for a call back from the pound in a moment, and they'll confirm with you that the dog is yours."

"He's never run off before," the old man said. "Always been a good dog."

"We'll have him back to you in a couple of hours," Roach assured him. The phone was ringing yet again. It had been, by any standards, an extremely busy morning.

The wailing showed no signs of stopping. "Oh, for Pete's sake," Roach muttered under his breath. "Calm down, will you?"

Ann Leach was going through the unimaginable. Just after breakfast, she'd found herself arrested for fraud. An hour later, she'd been shown a picture of her daughter, smiling and confident with sparkling blue eyes and multi-colored hair. From the fragments of speech that Sergeant Harding had managed to understand, what had most upset Mrs. Leach was this second cruel loss of her daughter; that she was alive but refused to see her mother.

Harding left the interview room, unable to bear another moment. It had been a lengthy and genuine outpouring of emotion from Ann Leach.

Initially, Janice had managed some sympathy for her, but after an hour's solid wailing, even her patience was wearing thin.

"I don't mean to be unkind," Roach began.

"But she needs to get a grip?" Janice said. "You're telling me. Who've we got in reception?"

"Couple whose dog wandered off and was growling at school kids at the bus stop. The animal unit from Bouley Bay picked it up. They'll be reunited shortly."

Janice gave him a smile. "Pretty mundane after all this, isn't it?" she said, nodding toward the interview room.

DI Graham emerged from his office and stretched. He looked tired. After picking up Grant, they'd moved on Ann, and by ten o'clock that morning, she was in custody.

Ann had found herself, all in the same hour, charged with fraud, informed that her daughter was alive, and told that Beth would not be visiting. Not today. Not ever.

Graham paused at the desk. "Everything alright?"

Another wail of grief and sadness erupted from the interview room.

Graham winced. "Yeah," he said simply, answering his own question. "What's the name of the psychologist chap we called in after that death at the castle?"

"I'll call him," Janice said.

"Any more news about Lyon?" Roach asked his boss.

"Well, his transfer to the mainland went off without a hitch, and the CPS thinks we've got a winner. They reckon they can put together enough to get him eight years, maybe ten, for the Internet stuff."

While Roach and Graham had been in Denmark, Jack Wentworth had completed a forensic examination of Lyon's hard drive. On it, he'd recovered deleted files that proved conclusively that Lyon had received, downloaded, and viewed illegal images.

"Serves him bloody well right," Roach said.

"I have to tell you though, his face was a picture when I told him he was no longer a murder suspect," Graham said. "Sutton looked so relieved that you'd have thought he'd been facing jail time himself."

"Maybe he should," Janice opined, the phone to her ear as she waited for the psychologist's office to pick up.

"He was just doing his job," Graham reminded her.

Roach noticed a vehicle pulling up outside. "Third transfer van of the day. You don't see that very often around here."

Together, the three of them ushered Ann Leach to the waiting vehicle. They eschewed handcuffs. She was visibly too weak and distressed to do anything other than what she was told. As Graham made to close the doors, she said, "I'm sorry. Really. I know I've done wrong. But you've got to let me see my daughter!"

Graham closed the first of the two doors. "Not our decision to make, Mrs. Leach." He closed the second door and knocked on the van's chassis to let the driver know he could head out.

Graham went inside and spent half an hour simply

sitting at his desk. With the dog emergency resolved, he, Roach and Harding found themselves with little to do.

"Have we heard from Grace Darling this morning?" Graham asked. Janice caught the reference, but Roach had to quickly Google it.

"He's taken the day off," Janice reported. "Said he'd never been so cold in all his life. The lifeboat captain said he nearly drowned, sir."

Roach scratched his chin. "I can't believe I'm suggesting this, sir, but do you think it'd be entirely out of line for... well, you know..."

"An official commendation?" Graham finished arching an eyebrow. "Seems appropriate to me. What do you think, Janice?"

She gave Roach's shoulder a squeeze. "A couple of those are in order, if you ask me," she smiled. "Just don't let it go to your head, Roachie."

"And in the meantime, dinner?" Graham asked. "Seven o'clock? Bangkok Palace?"

"As long as you're buying," Janice said.

"I'm in," Roach added.

"Great. Now, go and find some police work to do. I've got to make a phone call."

Graham thought for a long moment before dialing the number. In every investigation, there were red herrings and missteps, but he felt the need to apologize.

"Mrs. Updike? I'm so sorry to bother you again. This is DI Graham from Gorey Constabulary, down in Jersey... Yes, that's right... No, please don't worry. Is your husband there? I'd like you both to hear this, you see... No, there's no trouble at all, I assure you. Quite the opposite, actually. I have some very good news for you both."

The waiter gave Graham a worried look. "Sir, please. The chef uses Thai chilies. Extremely hot." The waiter was new.

Graham folded up the menu and handed it back. "Yes, I understand."

"He adds a small *pile* of them to the pan, sir. Not just one or two."

"And I'm saying that I'd like it just the way he'd make it for himself," Graham specified once more.

The waiter dithered but couldn't leave the table without dispensing another warning. "Sir... Management can't be held responsible for any—"

"Don't worry, son, honestly. I won't sue if I explode."

The waiter made a note on his pad. He trotted back to the kitchen, muttering to himself in his native language.

Janice stared at him. "This isn't some weird, macho competition, is it?"

"Huh?"

"I mean, Constable Barnwell nearly loses his life saving a drowning teenager, so you feel the need to prove your manhood by eating fatal levels of Thai spice."

"Don't be ridiculous," Graham said. "I just like a bit of zing in my Asian food, that's all."

Marcus Tomlinson shared their concern, but he'd at least watched Graham handle what the chef called the "five-chili special" variant of his chicken with holy basil, and that unforgettable red curry, which a stunned reviewer from the *Gorey Herald* later memorably described as "part traditional curry, part nuclear treaty violation."

Graham raised his glass. "I have some people to

thank," he said. "First, Constable Barnwell, the hero of the hour..."

The whole table – Harding, Roach, Tomlinson, Jack Wentworth, and the RNLI lifeboat captain, Will Ryan – warmly applauded the slightly red-faced constable.

"... for his devotion to duty, selflessness in the face of danger, and successful rescue of a very reckless, very..."

"Stupid," Ryan chipped in, good-naturedly.

"... lucky," Graham continued, "young man. I'd also like to thank the perceptive and persistent Constable Roach..."

More applause and table-thumping were his reward.

"... for his remarkably keen eye, especially when it comes to young women long since thought lost to us." Everyone got a kick out of that, but for Roach, it was bittersweet.

"And, not to be outdone, the potent new team of Harding and Wentworth for their sterling work in tracking down a dangerous predator and then uncovering a decade of fraud. I thank you all, most sincerely. It's a privilege to work with such able and dedicated profes-sionals."

Dishes arrived with steaming platters of fried rice. Graham found himself in a debate with Wentworth about the "Snooper's Charter," while Barnwell was forced yet again to recount the story of his remarkable journey on the *George Sullivan*, complete with Captain Ryan's deroga-tory remarks about the erstwhile crew of the *Sea Witch*.

"What in the seven hells were they doing in that old wreck of a boat, anyway?" Ryan wanted to know. "They'd have both died in that cold water if we'd taken much longer to get there."

Barnwell had heard the boys' story from Charlie as they'd sat under warm blankets in the ambulance that had picked them up upon their return to dry land. "They were skipping their exams," he explained, "and planned to sail to the French coast. There they'd ditch the boat and hitchhike their way to the South of France and on to Spain. They thought they'd get work in bars down in one of the resorts."

Ryan guffawed at this. "Silly buggers. They'd have been recruited as drug mules as soon as they got short of money. Are they going to pay for all those thefts, then?"

Barnwell swallowed his massaman curry before answering. "I'm thinking of recommending to the magistrate that they be given community service down at the marina," he reported. "Helping paint the older boats, clean up after the seagulls, that kind of thing." Ryan seemed content with this.

"You know," Roach said, "it's impossible to ignore how important computers were in this whole business. But I think I really learned something about police work, too."

"Oh?" Graham asked. The red curry had brought him to the point of sweating but not yet to the acute discomfort he secretly feared.

"Well, I wouldn't have spotted Beth if I hadn't been prepared to put the time in," he noted. "No software could have found her. Just someone who was looking for the right things."

Janice nodded. "And while we *used* the Internet a lot, we had to know what we were looking for. That required a human brain."

"So," Graham summed up, dabbing his mouth with

his napkin, "I need not worry, quite yet, that police officers are about to be replaced with heartless robots?"

"Not *quite* yet," Harding agreed. "A good pair of eyes and a thoughtful mind can do an awful lot, still."

"Doesn't hurt to have a decent mentor, either," Roach observed.

Graham just smiled. The arrests were his reward, along with the knowledge that they'd done the right thing in a case that had been too long ignored. He felt pride, too. In his officers and in his methods. And there was no harm, he decided, in letting that show just a little.

Later after they'd all finished their food, chattered, and laughed themselves hoarse, the events of the last forty-eight hours began to take their toll.

"Right, then," Graham said, finishing his drink and rising. "I'm going to head off before things get out of hand here. Marcus? Can I give you a lift?" He signaled for the check. When it arrived, the waiter inquired three separate times about Graham's health. "Really, I'm fine. I think the chef went easy on me."

"Please, sir. Call us tomorrow, and let us know you're okay."

Barnwell left next, offering Captain Ryan a ride to his coastal cottage, and Roach headed for his bicycle, chained to the railing outside the restaurant. Janice and Jack were left alone at the table.

"Last pair standing," Jack observed. "Would you like anything else? Maybe we could share some dessert?"

Janice felt herself blush a little and glanced away for a moment. Then she smiled at Wentworth, and realized just how much she was beginning to enjoy his honesty and that friendly, expressive face of his. "Sure," she said finally, her eyes meeting his. "That sounds nice."

EPILOGUE

A FTER HER DEFENSE successfully cited Ann Leach's emotional distress as a factor in her crimes, she was convicted of fraud but received a suspended prison sentence. Leach was also ordered never to attempt to travel to Denmark, where she was blacklisted by the immigration authorities. She had no contact with her daughter. After her trial Ann moved away from Gorey and to Wiltshire, where she took work in a small hotel.

The members of the Gorey community were shocked, saddened, and in some cases angered by the revelations resulting from the police investigation into the Beth Ridley Foundation. A committee was set up by a local council member to discover whether any of the funds could be recovered, but after ten months of rancor and no progress, the matter was quietly dropped.

· · ·

Andrew Lyon was sentenced to seven years and three months for possessing, distributing, and financially benefiting from the distribution of indecent images of minors. His time in prison has been marked by a campaign of intimidation and violence toward him by other inmates. His repeated requests to be moved to a different prison have been ignored. He is on constant suicide watch. On his release, he will be placed on the Violent and Sex Offenders Register (ViSOR) and never allowed to work with children again.

Despite a confession, the Crown Prosecution Service felt the evidence to support a conviction in the case against Liam Grant for the kidnapping and trafficking of Beth Ridley was not conclusive. The case was never brought to trial. Grant resigned from his post at Gorey Grammar and moved back to his native Ireland. He died in a car crash six months later.

Mr. and Mrs. Updike received a Royal Mail Special Delivery three weeks after Andrew Lyon's arrest. It was a rare and much sought-after invitation card from 1868, sent to a noted politician of the day, requesting the pleasure of his company for a late supper with Queen Victoria. The invitation immediately took pride of place in the Updikes' collection. The card accompanying the gift said simply, "Best regards, DG."

Constable Barnwell was presented with the Queen's Gallantry Medal for his sea rescue of Charlie Hodgson.

He remains friends with the teen's parents, for whom he has become something of a mentor. Since his experience on the *George Sullivan*, Barnwell has signed up for life-saving lessons.

Charlie Hodgson and Rob Boyle were arrested upon their return to Gorey in the *George Sullivan*. The jury heard an honest recounting of the boys' plans to skip three "terrifying" school exams scheduled for the following week and instead sail to the French coast and from there head to Spain. They were found guilty of eight offenses and sentenced to sixty hours of Community Service at the Gorey Marina. Having impressed Captain Smith with his attention to detail and punctuality, Rob was offered an apprenticeship on Smith's fishing trawler and spent three weeks in the mid-Atlantic. Charlie returned to school and was later accepted onto a vocational college course to learn boat restoration.

For his work on the Ridley case, Mrs. Taylor decided to give DI Graham a generous discount on the next month's rent of his room at the White House Inn. She also continued, with a quiet determination, to have his path somehow cross with that of an eligible young woman.

Jim Roach received a police commendation for diligence and persistence in the Beth Ridley case. His framed certificate sits on the mantelpiece above the fireplace in his mother's home. He now regularly starts for the Jersey

Police five-a-side squad. There are high hopes that the team will win the league this year.

Bettina Nisted got married in the summer. She and her husband Johann are expecting their first child early next year.

Janice and Jack shared a leisurely dessert and sat talking for well over an hour after the last diners had departed the *Bangkok Palace*. They were seen strolling slowly down the road, hand in hand, talking together as though neither wanted the evening to end. As he locked up and cleared their table, the headwaiter was delighted to find a generous tip. As he pocketed it, he reflected on the fact that unlike their older dining companion, he would not need to consider the young couple's wellbeing when he woke the following morning.

To get free books, updates about new releases, promotions, and other Insider exclusives, please sign up for Alison's mailing list at:

https://www.alisongolden.com/graham

INSPECTOR DAVID GRAHAM WILL RETURN...

WHAT HAPPENS NEXT for our intrepid team in the Bailiwick of Jersey? Find out in the next book in the Inspector Graham mystery series, *The Case of the Missing Letter*. You'll find an excerpt on the following pages.

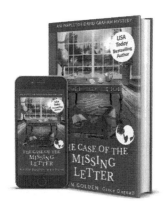

THE CASE OF THE MISSING LETTER
CHAPTER ONE

DAVID GRAHAM TROTTED downstairs. The dining room was becoming busier by the week, but at least his favorite table by the window was still available on this bright Saturday morning. The White House Inn staff were busier than they had been since Christmas, welcoming and looking after new arrivals who had chosen to exchange the snow of Scotland or the dreary rain of Manchester for a few sunny days in Jersey. He took his seat and opened the morning paper, part of a reassuring and established routine he had enjoyably been following for the last six months.

As he settled into life on Jersey, Graham had followed the changing of the seasons as the island's surprisingly mild winter gave way to an even warmer and quite invigorating early spring. By mid-March, the island was once again beginning to look its splendid and colorful best. The spring blooms were out. Swathes of bright yellow daffodils and the unmistakable, bell-shaped blue hyacinth dotted the island. Economically, Jersey had also started to blossom. Most of Gorey's small fishing fleet had completed a month of refit and repair. Shortly, they would be heading out among the Channel Islands to catch lobster and oysters, or further into the Atlantic for cod.

"Good morning, Detective Inspector," Polly offered carefully. Before his first cup of tea, Graham could be sleepy and even uncharacteristically sour. Guesthouse owner, the redoubtable Mrs. Taylor, occasionally reminded staff not to engage him in anything beyond perfunctory morning pleasantries before he was at least partially caffeinated. "What will it be today? Or are you going to make me guess again?"

Graham peered over his newspaper at the freckled twenty-something redhead who had become perhaps his favorite of the staff. "I have to say, Polly," Graham told her, folding the paper and setting it on the table, "that you're becoming something of a psychic. What is it now, four correct guesses in a row?"

"Five," Polly said proudly. "But on three of those days, it was that new Assam you were so excited about."

"True, true," Graham noted. "And I hope you'll agree it was worth getting excited over."

Polly shrugged. "I'm not really a tea drinker," she confessed. "But today I'm going to guess you're in... what do you call it sometimes... a 'traditional mood'?"

"I might be," Graham grinned. "Or I might be feeling spontaneous."

"Lady Grey," Polly guessed. "Large pot, two bags, sugar to be decided on a cup-by-cup basis."

Impressed, Graham raised his eyebrows and gave her a warm smile. "Precisely. I don't know how you do it."

Polly tapped her forehead cryptically and sashayed off to the kitchen to place Graham's order. Since arriving at the White House Inn, and with the enthusiastic support of the staff and Mrs. Taylor, Graham had taken sole "curatorial control" over the dining room's tea selection. He took this role exceptionally seriously. The kitchen's shelves were now stocked with an impressive array of Asian teas, from the sweet and fruity to the fragranced and flowery, with much else in between.

Lady Grey, though, was becoming Graham's favorite "first pot." It was often given the responsibility of awakening the Detective Inspector's mental faculties first thing in the morning. It was in the moments after the first life-giving infusion of caffeine, antioxidants, and other herbal empowerments that Graham's mind came alive.

One useful byproduct of his daily tea ritual was the ability to memorize almost everything he read. His knowledge of local events was becoming peerless. With the aid of the local newspaper, Graham stored away the information that Easter was two weekends away, and the town's churches were inviting volunteers to bake, sing, decorate the church, and organize the Easter egg hunts.

Also stashed away for future retrieval was the nugget that Gorey Castle's much anticipated "Treason and Torture" exhibit was about to open. The gruesome displays were only part of the attraction, however. Two recently opened chambers had, until their inadvertent discovery a few months earlier, contained an unlikely and entirely unsuspected trove of artistic treasures. The discovered paintings had mostly been returned to their owners or loaned to museums that were better equipped to display pieces of such importance. But, interest in the find was still high, and ticket sales had been, to quote the Castle's events director, the ever-upbeat Stephen Jeffries, "brisk beyond belief."

"Lady Grey," Polly announced, delivering the tray with Graham's customary digital timer which was just passing the three-minute mark.

"First class, Polly. And it'll be bacon, two eggs, and toast today, please."

"Right, you are," she nodded.

Graham put the paper aside and focused on this most pleasing of ceremonies. First came the tea, promisingly dark and full-bodied, tumbling into the china cup. Then came the enchanting aroma, an endless complexity from such a surprisingly simple source. Next would come the careful decision-making process regarding the addition of milk; too much would bring down the temperature, and as Graham liked to think of it, risked muddling what the tea was attempting to express.

Finally, he would add just the right amount of sugar. Graham had taken pains to instruct the wait staff to ensure that it was available in loose, as well as cubed form, so that he might more carefully adjudicate its addition. He tipped an eighth of a teaspoonful into the cup and stirred nine times, counter-clockwise. Some things, as he was so fond of reminding his fellow police officers, are worth doing well. He chose to ignore their barely suppressed eye-rolls.

He took a sip and cherished the added bergamot that complemented the traditional Earl Grey flavor. But then, contrary to his usual practice, Graham set down the cup. An article on page six of the newspaper was demanding his attention. The headline was *Our Cops are Tops*, and he read on with a quiet flush of pride.

After their successes in recent months, it goes without saying that Gorey has the most capable police officers on the island. Led by the indefatigable Detective Inspector

Graham, the Gorey Constabulary has successfully raised the rate at which it solves reported crimes from twenty-six percent, one year ago, to forty-nine percent, today.

"For once," Graham muttered contentedly into his paper, "the media have got their numbers spot-on." It meant, he had observed proudly to his team the previous day, that anyone planning a crime in their small field of jurisdiction would know that they had a one in two chance of getting caught. "Splendid."

Moreover, the actual crime rate has dropped by sixteen percent in the last twelve months. This is surely cause to congratulate DI Graham and his team, but Sergeant Janice Harding was modest when asked for a comment. "The Gorey public have been enormously supportive," she pointed out. "We rely on their vigilance and common sense, and they've stood by us through some complex and challenging cases." The popular sergeant, who has lived on Jersey for nearly seven years, was referring to the conviction of former teacher Andrew Lyon, who began a seven-year sentence at Wormwood Scrubs in January. Gorey Constabulary also met with success after murder investigations at the Castle and the White House Inn. It seems our "top cops" are equal to any challenge. Gorey is fortunate to have such a dedicated and dependable crime-fighting team.

"'Top cops.' Sounds like one of those ghastly TV reality shows," Graham grumbled. "But I'll take it."

To get your copy of The Case of the Missing Letter *visit the link below:*
https://www.alisongolden.com/missing-letter

BOOKS BY ALISON GOLDEN

FEATURING REVEREND ANNABELLE DIXON

Death at the Café

Murder at the Mansion

Body in the Woods

Grave in the Garage

Horror in the Highlands

Killer at the Cult

FEATURING ROXY REINHARDT

Mardi Gras Madness

New Orleans Nightmare

Louisiana Lies

As A. J. Golden

FEATURING DIANA HUNTER

Hunted (Prequel)

Snatched

Stolen

Chopped

Exposed

ABOUT THE AUTHOR

Alison Golden is the *USA Today* bestselling author of the Inspector David Graham mysteries, a traditional British detective series, and two cozy mystery series featuring main characters Reverend Annabelle Dixon and Roxy Reinhardt. As A. J. Golden, she writes the Diana Hunter thriller series.

Alison was raised in Bedfordshire, England. Her aim is to write stories that are designed to entertain, amuse, and calm. Her approach is to combine creative ideas with excellent writing and edit, edit, edit. Alison's mission is simple: To write excellent books that have readers clamoring for more.

Alison is based in the San Francisco Bay Area with her husband and twin sons. She splits her time between London and San Francisco.

For up-to-date promotions and release dates of upcoming books, sign up for the latest news here: https://www.alisongolden.com/graham.

For more information:
www.alisongolden.com
alison@alisongolden.com

facebook.com/alisongolden.books

twitter.com/alisonjgolden

instagram.com/alisonjgolden

THANK YOU

Thank you for taking the time to read the first four books in the Inspector Graham series. If you enjoyed them, please consider telling your friends or posting a short review. Word of mouth is an author's best friend and very much appreciated.

Thank you,

Made in the USA
Middletown, DE
03 February 2021

32946082R00430